RED GLOVES VOLUME 1: DEVILRY
The London Horrors

To celebrate his 25th year of writing award-winning horror stories, Christopher Fowler has created two new collections totaling 25 tales.

This first volume contains stories set in London, where deceptively ordinary events like an evening in a pub or a night on the town have terrifying consequences. Here you'll find hauntings, revenges, murders, monstrosities, redemptions, and the dark hands of the urban night reaching out to seize the unwary. And to top it off, there's a short story featuring disreputable detectives Bryant & May.

What fresh devilry is this? Step into a city of darkness, derangement and deadpan laughter and find out with the nation's most sinister storyteller.

"Fowler's collections are laced with unease. He turns to the fantastical to realize a system of karmic retribution. There is a note of innocence in his stories; though they deal with nastiness, they bear out the author's hope for justice."

—*Time Out*

Christopher Fowler was born in Greenwich, London. He is the award-winning author of thirty novels and a dozen short story collections, and creator of the popular Bryant & May mysteries. He worked in film, creating movie posters, trailers and documentaries, fulfilling several pathetic schoolboy fantasies, releasing a terrible Christmas pop single, becoming a male model, posing as the villain in a Batman graphic novel, running a night club, appearing in the *Pan Books of Horror* and standing in for James Bond.

He has written comedy and drama for the BBC, has a weekly column in the *Independent* on Sunday, is the crime reviewer for the *FT* and has written for *The Times, Telegraph, Guardian, Daily Mail, Time Out, Black Static, Smoke, Big Issue* and many others. After living in France and the USA he is now lives in King's Cross, London. He recently wrote the *War Of The Worlds* videogame for Paramount, starring Patrick Stewart. His books for 2011 are the supernatural thriller *Hell Train*, and a Bryant & May book, *The Memory Of Blood*.

In the past year he has been nominated for eight national book awards. He is the winner of the Edge Hill prize 2008 for *Old Devil Moon*, and the Last Laugh prize 2009 for *The Victoria Vanishes*.

RED GLOVES

VOLUME 1

RED GLOVES

VOLUME 1

THE LONDON HORRORS

Christopher Fowler

2011

Published in October 2011 by PS Publishing Ltd. by arrangement with the author. All rights reserved by the author.

FIRST EDITION

ISBN
978-1-848631-98-4
978-1-848631-99-1 (Signed Edition)

Story credits appear at the end of the book.

Design and layout by Alligator Tree Graphics.

Printed in England by the MPG Books Group.

PS Publishing Ltd
Grosvenor House
1 New Road
Hornsea, HU18 1PG
England

e-mail: editor@pspublishing.co.uk • *Internet:* http://www.pspublishing.co.uk

CONTENTS

Zygomaticus 5

The Rulebook 13

Dead Ground Zero 25

Locked 53

Lantern Jack 69

An Injustice 75

The Adventure Of Lucifer's Footprints 89

Down 103

The Stretch 116

The Deceivers 131

Killing the Cook 145

Oh I Do Like To Be Beside the Seaside 153

Enjoy 167

Bryant & May In The Soup 187

RED GLOVES

VOLUME 1

For Sue Gibson, our gal in Oz.

*'If Death Was Something Money Could Buy,
The Rich Would Live, The Poor Would Die.'*

I'VE ALWAYS HAD TROUBLE WITH TITLES. MY LAST COLLECTION, 'OLD DEVIL MOON', borrowed the title of a beautiful but forgotten song from a peculiarly whimsical sixties musical about racism, socialism, drugs and, er, leprechauns, called 'Finian's Rainbow'. Originally I was going to call this volume 'The Horrors', a phrase often associated with wartime and panic, a sudden overwhelming sense of the weight of the world. Put another way, a rush of awareness. My mother still speaks of having 'an attack of the horrors'. But I realized that the title would prove misleading to anyone expecting the frisson of revulsion you get from exposure to blood and guts—these are tales that step into areas of unease rather than the abbatoir.

'Red Gloves' suggests to me that no-one is innocent, and carries all sorts of interesting connotations, from Macbeth to Giallo. The hand stained with blood is a mark of lost innocence.

At the start of each collection, I outline some of the press reports that have provoked me during the writing of the stories, and use them as a sort of timeline running beside the production of the book. The remit of journalism is to make the important interesting, but there are often times when it does the reverse; press releases are now routinely recycled as substitutes for real news. The absurdities of life we all face have a way of turning a genuine smile into a forced one, hence the title of this foreword. *Zygomaticus* refers to the muscle that makes the difference between two types of smile.

As I came to write the stories, I realized they were falling into two distinct groups—ones that were primarily set in London, and ones set in the rest of the world. I love to travel and I love my home town, so it seemed a good idea to create two volumes for this, my twenty fifth year of writing such tales. The stories in this volume all take place in London—I count Sherlock Holmes because he's a Londoner, and there's a seaside tale because it's a London day trip that's familiar to everyone who lives in the city.

And so to the writing of the stories themselves, and the press items I was reading that often seemed to me more outrageous than anything I could devise from my imagination.

As I started the second volume's New Orleans-set tale 'Piano Man', a devastating cyclone killed thousands in Burma and left many more without shelter, food, water or electricity, facing the ravages of disease. The Burmese militia responded to this by banning emergency aid imports and handing out DVD players to homeless villagers who had no food or power.

During the writing of the next story, the fifth most read item on the internet was the crash of world stocks. But the most-read story was someone getting voted off the reality TV show 'Big Brother' for spitting. As the credit crisis deepened, columns about collapsing banks finally took the lead over tales of exploding hamsters or supermodel Naomi Campbell's latest screaming fit.

Meanwhile, it was revealed that Sarah Palin, the gun-toting cartoon-brought-to-life former running mate of Senator John McCain, once asked her librarian how to go about getting books banned, as there were some she didn't like. Oil-worshipping Sarah was Alaska's biggest polluter, but promised to give everyone in her state a $2,000 cheque in return for destroying it.

Before he went, George Bush reneged on his few climate change promises and bade farewell to a disastrous G8 summit meeting with the words 'Goodbye from the world's biggest polluter'. He then punched the air and grinned as the French and British prime ministers looked on in shock. The scene is still on the internet—a total jaw-dropper.

On the subject of the environment, ministers announced that 'Plan A' (carbon reduction) had failed and that 'Plan B' (invent something fast) was now the only remaining solution. But planet management never gets easier.

On the island of Macquarie, between Australia and Antarctica, cats left by ships got rid of the mice but preyed on rare flightless birds, so conservationists culled them, only to watch horrified as the rabbit population exploded and stripped the island of its vegetation, causing a landslip that wiped out a rare penguin colony. The chain of events is an example of 'trophic cascade' leading to 'ecosystem meltdown'.

In the last week before he quit the white house, George Bush declared his intention to exploit the vast oil and mineral wealth hidden below the Arctic Circle by extending America's sovereign rights over the seabed. As he bowed out, I was reminded of his quote about books. 'One of the great things about books is sometimes there are some fantastic pictures'. In the broadsheets, as is traditional during times of regime change, his apologists began his immediate rehabilitation.

Three months after I wrote a story called 'The Conspirators', the fiction found a peculiar parallel in real life when a millionaire hotel owner was charged with the murder of a Middle Eastern pop star in Dubai. The emerging details were, once again, stranger than anything I had created.

Meanwhile, the Czech artist David Cerny was paid £350,000 to commission artworks forming a huge sculpture of 27 nations for the atrium of the European Council, but admitted hoaxing the EU by knocking it up with his pals. Officials began to smell a rat when they noticed that Romania was represented by a Dracula theme park and Bulgaria by a Turkish lavatory, but in a typical state of indecision they went ahead with the opening anyway. Britain was represented on the sculpture as a blank space.

Mexico's long border with the US, the world's main drugs consumer, became the site of more killings than Iraq. The chances of kidnap became so high that we heard about microchip tracking devices being implanted into the arms of wealthy schoolchildren.

On a lighter note, Adam Deeley, 34, a mature British student, choked to death in an impromptu challenge to see who could eat the most fairy cakes at the Monkey Cafe, Swansea. He managed five at once. Or rather, he didn't. Paging Mr Darwin.

In Britain 1 in 10 children now lives in a mixed-race family, with mixed-race relationships so common that traditionally distinct ethnic groups have started to disappear. Not in the royal family, however, after Prince Harry was rebuked for using the term 'Paki' and Prince Charles admitted to calling an Asian friend 'Sooty'. Hating to miss out on any publicity, Margaret Thatcher's daughter Carol publicly called the handsome and talented French-Congolese tennis champion Jo-Wilfried Tsonga a 'golliwog'.

In Washington, a Christian group called *Pray at the Pump* started gathering around petrol pumps and praying to the Lord to lower prices. 'If we keep this up,' says its leader Rocky Twyman, 'we can bring down prices to less than $2 a gallon.'

Thanks to rising oil and food prices, the production of a new food staple was stepped up in Haiti as mud cakes soared in popularity; the baked grey discs of dirt apparently taste like—well, dirt with margarine in, but stop stomachs from feeling empty. If the starving weren't prevented from leaving by US coastguard patrols, they could have gone to stare through shop windows at the Hermes 'Birkin' handbag, which went on sale in New York for $37,000. At the time of the stock market crash, it was still selling well. And in case that's not enough, Louis Vuiton started selling custom-made travel caviar sets, for all your urgent caviar-on-the-go needs. And spa treatment centres started including a 'caviar face pack' for old vultures with too much time and money on their claw-like hands.

As the credit crunch hit home, an article appeared in The Observer about hot new fashion scents; Wode, which sprays the wearer blue (sadly the effect quickly wears off), and 'the very first internet perfume', called 'Violence', a scent based on old photographs of skinheads hitting each other. The makers say it smells of 'sweat, boot polish, Indian food and warm bricks', although if it's based on old photos it should surely smell of developing fluid. Harvey Nichols announced their own best-selling scent, *Molecule*, which according to their advertising smells vaguely of something, and then of nothing. I guess it makes a change from most scents, which smell of either roses or lemons.

Advertising got even more slippery. The film *Sex and the City* had—unsurprisingly—95 brands cunningly dotted through its running time. Shane Meadows' neo-realist film 'Somers Town' went one better and had the entire film sponsored by Eurostar trains. But it was in black and white and he's an auteur, so that's all right.

The *Big Brother* show finally faded to the faintest of radar blips and was binned, but not before its producers burrowed below the ground zero of bad taste. In a twist of Jacobean grotesquery, they informed reality TV star Jade Goody that she had cervical cancer in the Big Brother house, India, so that her tearful reaction could be captured live. Goody undermined the media leeches feeding on her by inviting camera crews in to film her wedding to a convicted felon, then remained in the spotlight as the press gloatingly ticked down the days to her death. Goody, from a deprived, abusive working class background, ultimately attained grace by confounding the critics who harped on about her intelligence; she behaved intelligently.

As Channel 4 and other inept, failing TV networks scrabbled around for viewers, channel director Michael Grade announced that televised fiction was dead because we all prefer talent shows and documentaries about fat people.

Arnold Schwarzenegger championed gay marriage in California. This is largely the same legislation we have in the UK, undermined in the US by fears that appropriation of the word 'marriage' would somehow diminish its mythical strength. Mormon-backed Proposition 8 promptly banned it again, leaving the 18,000 couples who got hitched in the four and a half month period when it was legal stranded and exposed to the proposers' next attempt—to retroactively annul the marriages. The California Supreme Court upheld the proposition but invoked a grandfather clause allowing the existing marriages to stand.

It transpired that Tanzanian albinos were living in fear of their lives because people were seeking their body parts for witchcraft. There are over 200,000 albinos in the country, and with over 30 murders in 10 months, many were frightened they would be skinned alive and partially dismembered. Meanwhile, Southern Australia held a 'Sorry Ranga' day to celebrate its ginger-haired population, Ranga being short for Orang-utans.

Channel 4 aired a 'child reality show' in which 20 primary school children were left without adult supervision for a fortnight. Unsurprisingly, this led to cries of abuse and an outcry from psychologists, as the parents used their own children as leverage for fame. The show flopped.

As economists announced the financial end of the world and climatologists paced up their doomsday scenarios, a social networking site provided the world with the conversational equivalent of polystyrene when Twitter's bitter chatter spread to celebrities. Exchanges between singer Lily Allen and tagalong webfan Perez Hilton descended—not that it had anywhere to descend to—into hurled abuse, reminding us yet again how far the Hilton brand has fallen since the 1950s.

The Jade Goody (1981-2009) Official Tribute Issue of OK! Magazine appeared, featuring her final words and bearing the banner 'In Loving Memory'. There was only one problem; Ms Goody was still technically alive at the time. Magazine lead-times were apparently to blame.

Google street-mapping arrived in the UK. Across the country, a million cries went up: 'Why did they have to film our street while the scaffolding was up at number 57?'

A German couple abandoned their three children in an Italian pizzeria because they had run out of money on holiday. They thought the authorities would probably figure out where they lived and send them home. Luckily, money is just something poor people have to worry about. On the same day, a Thai jewellery designer displayed a $4.2 million dog tiara at a canine fashion show.

The massive expenses scandal engulfed MPs from both sides of Parliament, as Tory MP Douglas Hogg revealed he spent £2,000 of taxpayers' money getting his moat cleaned. Another was caught having a duck-house built from public cash, and complained that the ducks had never really enjoyed using it anyway. Best of all was Tory MP Anthony Steen, who shoved the inspection of five hundred trees on expenses and had this to say about being caught out.; "I think I have behaved impeccably. You know what it's about? Jealousy. I have got a very, very large house. Some people say it looks like Balmoral, but it's a merchant's house from the 19th century. It was this government that introduced the Freedom of Information Act and it is this government that insisted on the things which caught me on the wrong foot."

As decades of financial abuse come to an end, MPs screamed like stuck pigs. Weirdly, some were defended in the national press by kowtowing members of the public who clearly relished the prospect of returning to a feudal system. The exposure of MPs' expenses threw up some wonderfully odd claims; Conservative leader David Cameron claimed almost seven hundred pounds on 'burning oil' (presumably for his Aga cooker). Others claimed for biscuits, jellied eels, a wig, orchids and a hedge trimmer for a helipad.

Susan Boyle, a middle-aged woman with a pleasant singing voice and a face that could send a dog under a table, became one of the most-viewed internet sensations of all time, but failed to win a television talent contest. Her overnight 'career', from rise to fall, ended with a breakdown and her admittance to The Priory clinic—a microlife that eclipsed even Jade Goody's.

Amidst global financial hardship, Turkey's £1 billion Mardan Palace opened its doors with the biggest Beluga and Bollinger party in history. Sharon Stone, attending with other fading stars like Richard Gere, Mariah Carey and, with grim inevitability, Paris Hilton, said it was a 'moment of potential profundity. We have come together to make the world a better place.' That's the beauty of celebrities; they'll say or do absolutely anything. The Russians found a way to punish their most rebellious oligarch hotel owner for spending his cash overseas; they closed down his revenue source, a vast Moscow market full of smuggled Chinese goods.

The line between PR and reality vanished with a staged tiff between Sacha Baron-Cohen and Eminem at the MTV Awards. (Cohen was dropped into Eminem's face dressed as a half-nude gay angel and the rapper called him a faggot before storming out.) Both were selling new products, and later confirmed the 'accident' as a publicity stunt. 'This is very exciting television,' said the show's presenter.

AEG, the promoters of London's 'O2 concerts which were to feature Michael Jackson's record-breaking forty-plus appearances, came up with a great way to save on refunds. Punters were offered replacement memorial souvenir tickets somehow 'inspired and designed' by the dead singer. Meanwhile, Jackson's death sparked a massive internet campaign of hoax celebrity death reports that included Jeff Goldblum falling off a cliff and George Clooney crashing a plane.

Oh, and Prince Charles gave the planet just 96 months left to survive.

But if the world ends, that's okay too, because it turns out there's an afterlife. The August 3rd issue of The Sun ran a front page headline announcing that Jade Goody, once so used to speaking through the medium of television, was now speaking through a television medium—from beyond the grave.

The title *Red Gloves* suggests, on one level, that like the woman who put the cat in the bin, we are all to some extent guilty. But don't think you can flee the city and live a life of pastoral tranquility, because the world has a way of catching up with you. As I hope these two volumes will show, whether you choose to stay behind or go abroad—you're fucked.

Writers are either paid very little or nothing at all for short stories, but a handful of commissioning editors remain constant, fair and loyal, so I'd like to take this opportunity to thank Pete Crowther, Steve Jones, Andy Cox, Maxim Jacubowski and Ellen Datlow. Their name on a book is your guarantee of excellence.

Every house has a rulebook. It's not an actual book, but it has rules you're not supposed to break. In our house the rulebook appeared after my Dad went away. Here are some of the rules:

- ◆ Put the lid down on the toilet seat when you've finished.
- ◆ If you want to get something down from the top shelf don't stack the furniture to reach it. Your cousin Freddie died like that.
- ◆ Don't touch the boiler in the kitchen, you'll burn yourself.
- ◆ Reading under the bedsheets with a torch will hurt your eyes.
- ◆ The internet does not replace real friends.
- ◆ Don't say Bollocks even though your Grandad says it all the time.
- ◆ Just because everyone else has got one doesn't mean that you should have one too.
- ◆ When you ask for seconds and can't finish them, remember there are people starving in Africa.
- ◆ Television doesn't go on until you've finished your homework.
- ◆ Pressing 6 on the speed-dial will call Auntie Pauline in Australia, she has verbal diarrhoea and it will come out of your pocket money.
- ◆ Every time you blaspheme, an angel gets a nosebleed.
- ◆ Don't touch the cat's tray without washing your hands afterwards.
- ◆ Don't ever put a lightbulb in the microwave again.

When we went on holiday, there was another set of rules:

- ◈ Don't go in the sea until an hour after you've eaten.
- ◈ Always keep an eye on the tide.
- ◈ Only go into an amusement arcade if you're prepared to lose money.
- ◈ A stick of rock can pull your fillings out.
- ◈ If you feel carsick tell Mum at once, don't leave it too late and do it down the window.
- ◈ There's no need to drop a brick on a jellyfish. It can still feel pain even though it hasn't got a face.

Soon I made up my own rulebook. These were rules I just seemed to know by instinct, or felt were probably true. Here are some of them:

- ◈ If you don't reach the bottom of the stairs before the toilet finishes flushing, the Thing That Lives In The Landing Cupboard will come after you.
- ◈ You can ruin next door's telly reception by throwing balls of silver foil at their satellite dish.
- ◈ Every time you squash an insect, God makes a mark in his book against you.
- ◈ If you die at home while your Mum is away there will be nobody to feed the cat, and it will eat your eyes.
- ◈ There is a horror film that can make you go mad if you watch it.

And:

- ◈ Dad is still checking up on you, even though he isn't here.

Then, in the winter of my twelfth birthday, I learned a new rule.

- ◈ Don't tell the neighbours that Mr Hill murdered his wife.

It was a game, really. I don't think I believed that Mr Hill had really murdered his wife, but I hated him because he had a dead grey eye like the guy in *Pirates Of The Caribbean,* and had painted all his flowerpots in Arsenal stripes, and he kept my football whenever it went over his fence. He probably had footballs enough to open a branch of JD Sports.

On Bonfire Night Mr Hill had a huge row with his wife. I heard her in the hall, yelling 'Do you know how painful this is, or what it's doing to me? I'm not going to stay in this house another minute.' Then she left. She dragged a huge suitcase out to the front step and climbed into a waiting taxi, and he slammed the door behind her. Two months before this I had heard a lot of banging and crashing in their house one night, so I figured they had been fighting for a long time.

I was the only one who saw her leave. When I told my best friend Andy about the row, I exaggerated the story a little bit. I told him that I had seen Mr Hill hit his wife with a shovel before burying her in the back garden while everyone else was watching the fireworks.

I told Andy not to tell anyone else, so by nightfall everyone in the street had heard the story, and as the days went on it became even more exaggerated to include all kinds of gross stuff. He'd cut off his wife's hands and buried them in his Arsenal pots, he'd used her spleen to decorate his Christmas tree, he kept her head on a stick in his shed and cast a spell on it to make it predict the football results.

I saw Mr Hill staring through his kitchen window with laser-vision that could have melted a hole in the glass, and I knew the story had reached him, so I stayed out of his way after that. I thought he might kill me as well, because by now I believed my own story.

'You mustn't go around telling people lies about Mr Hill,' said my Mum one day. 'His wife left him and he's very upset about that, without you making things worse by telling everyone he's a murderer.'

There had always been a damp patch on my bedroom wall near the ceiling. It was dark grey and furry, and shaped like the Isle Of Wight. One day there was an amazing storm. The rain fell sideways. Water came in through the back door and all our gutters overflowed, soaking my ceiling. The grey furry patch grew to the size of France and then part of the ceiling fell down, so my Mum called a company called AA-1 Roofs. They were called AA-1 so they would be the first people listed in the alphabetical telephone directory under Roof Repairs, but now that everyone used

Google they weren't at the top of the list anymore, so they were really cheap.

They came in to do the work, but told me and Mum to move out for Christmas because the air was unhealthy and the house needed to dry out for a bit.

'The good news,' said my Mum, 'is that Mr Hill has to go into hospital, and says we can stay there.'

'Why is he going to hospital?' I asked.

'He's having something done to his bladder.'

'Gross. Can't we stay in a hotel?' I asked.

'No, too expensive.'

'Bugger.'

'Mind your language.' My Mum collected the keys, and on Friday evening we went next door.

How can I describe Mr Hill's house?

The hall was as dark as a tunnel to the centre of the earth. There was a framed photo on the wall of a really old man that turned out to be a picture of Mr Hill's grandmother. The living room smelled of wet dogs. It was full of little china ornaments of poodles, dalmations, bulldogs, every kind of dog. There were piles of magazines about dogs and dog shows, and there were long brown dog hairs everywhere, but get this, *he didn't own a dog*. I could see why Mrs Hill had run away from him.

Every room was painted in a different shade of brown paint. Either he was colour-blind or couldn't be bothered to match up the tins. There was a clock in the hall that ticked very slowly, like someone hobbling painfully towards the grave. In the hall cupboard I found my footballs. He had let the air out of them and folded them on a shelf like pairs of pants. Weird.

Mr Hill had a son who had grown up and left home, and now that he lived alone he didn't bother cleaning up anymore. My Mum saw this as a challenge, and decided to give the place a spring-clean. I think she actually looked forward to our weekend of living next door, charging around with a mop and bucket.

'Think of this as a Christmas treat,' she told me, but Christmas is getting a RoboWarrior, not getting covered in dog hair in someone else's smelly, creepy house.

'You can play wherever you like,' she said, 'except in the room at the end of the upstairs hall. Mr Hill says you're not allowed to go in there under any circumstances. It's one of his rules.' So Mr Hill had a rulebook too.

I went out into the garden and stayed there, but there was nothing to do. Weirdly the garden was the opposite of the house, so perfectly kept that there weren't even any insects in it. Eventually it was time to go to bed. There were three rooms upstairs. The smallest was Mr Hill's son's room, which was now mine. Then came Mr Hill's room, which was where my Mum would sleep. Finally there was the big double room at the front of the house which nobody ever used and I wasn't allowed to go into Under Any Circumstances.

I stood outside this door and sniffed the keyhole. The dog-smell was coming from inside. I put my ear against the door and listened. I could hear faint breathing—in, gurgle, out, in, gurgle, out—like someone with a very bad cold and no tissues. I called Mum up and made her listen but she couldn't hear anything.

'Nothing at all?' I said, shocked. 'You really can't hear anything?'

'No,' she said.

'You wait till you want me to hear something.' Disgusted, I went to my room.

Mr Hill's son must have been about five when he left home to get a job, because his bedroom was full of stupid fluffy rabbits and realistic-looking puppies. I washed and got into my PJs and listened to the house. It creaked and clicked and rattled in the wind, so I couldn't get to sleep. My duffel coat on the door looked like a hunchbacked monster in the dark, and even though I knew it was just my coat, it bothered me. I must have drifted off for a few minutes, because I remember running through a jungle. Some kind of animal was after me. I heard claws scratching at the door.

At 11:45pm my Mum looked in and said 'Why are you still awake?' I don't know how she knew; she's sort of psychic like that.

'I can't sleep,' I told her. 'Listen to all the noise.'

She cocked an ear. 'That's just the rain falling on the dustbins.'

'It doesn't sound like that on our dustbins.'

She gave me a funny look. 'You okay?'

'I think I had a bad dream,' I told her. 'I was being chased.'

She came and on the edge of the bed. 'It's because you're in a strange house. Was my little soldier afraid?'

'No, I was fine.'

'Okay, I'll let you get some rest.'

'Can we put up Christmas decorations?'

'Mr Hill doesn't want pinholes.'

'I hate it here.'

'Give me a break, Paul. It's just for two nights. Go to sleep.'

The rest of the night I lay wide awake, watching the bedroom door. Finally I buried myself deep in bed with the pillows pulled up around my ears.

At seven o'clock it was supposed to get light, but it didn't. The rain had turned to thick wet fog. You could usually hear traffic outside but today there was complete silence. The fog had blinded and deafened the house, like someone had thrown a blanket over it. The street looked like it was made of mud, and someone on the radio was singing 'White Christmas'.

I checked the door for scratch-marks. Nothing. I got dressed when I smelled Mum burning the toast. Mr Hill's kitchen was bright yellow because it was the room where he smoked, and all the nicotine had stained the ceiling. I wondered what it made his food taste like.

Mum had tried to poach eggs in Mr Hill's microwave and they had exploded. She said 'You know I've never been good at breakfast. It's a horrible day. You'll be better off staying indoors.'

There was no way I was going to do that. I spent almost the whole day outside on my bike, but by the evening it was bucketing down with rain again, and thunder rolled in the distance. We ate beans on toast and watched some rubbish dancing show my Mum liked. The storm was getting closer because I counted the gaps between the flash and the bang, and they were shorter each time.

My Mum's mobile rang. It was Mr Hill. He needed some bathroom stuff to be brought to the hospital, so my Mum agreed to take it to him on her scooter. 'I don't want you coming with me,' she said, 'it's raining too hard. Do you want to stay up until I'm back? You've got your computer games.'

This was very good news, as it was already late. 'Drive slowly. Don't rush back,' I told her. 'I'll be fine.'

'Don't open the door to anyone, okay? And stay out of the end room. I know what you're like.'

'I don't know what you mean.' I tried to look innocent.

'Yeah, right. Butter wouldn't melt in your mouth.'

After an hour by myself, I got tired of blasting monsters on my game—actually I was stuck at the first boss and was fed up with repeating the same level over and over. So I went upstairs and had a nose in a few drawers. Mr Hill had a dressing table full of really good stuff, including a red penknife with about a million attachments, a huge ring of keys, some really weird comics in plastic bags called *Out Of This World*, several watches and a tobacco tin full of old metal puzzles.

I wanted to look in the room at the end of the hall, because I knew it would take an act of bravery to do so. My Dad used to say 'Are you a man or a mouse? Squeak up.' We'd laugh a lot about that one. When he told me not to do something, I didn't do it. With Mum it was different. Sometimes I deliberately did the opposite of what she asked.

Tonight was one of those occasions.

I wasn't scared, even though I was sure I could hear something breathing behind the door. Even though it smelled like something had died in the room. I stood outside the brown-painted door for along time, listening to the falling rain, listening for the in-gurgle-out breathing. I made a list in my head of all the terrible things that could be inside, so that I'd be prepared for the worst when I opened the door. I decided it could be any one of the following:

Mrs Hill had come back to the house to beg his forgiveness for leaving, and her husband had pretended to forgive her before locking her up in a cage and feeding her dogfood.

Mr Hill kept a pack of starving dogs in the room, and if I opened the door they would spring out and tear me to pieces.

Mr Hill had created a human being out of bits of dog, sewing all the parts together and bringing his creature to life with electricity. He had to keep it locked up because it was really angry all the time.

None of these situations were very likely, but they were all I could come up with. What else breathed and smelled like dead animals?

Finally I decided there was only one way to find out. Wrapping my fingers around the handle, I pushed down on it.

The door didn't budge. It was locked.

Then I remembered the keys in Mr Hill's desk. I went to the drawer and took out the great ring. Returning to the door, I tried each one in turn.

I tried the coolest-looking keys first, but none fit. Six. Seven. Eight. Nine. The tenth key was the smallest, and worked. The lock wasn't very big. Maybe there wasn't something trying to get out of the room after all. As I pushed open the door and tried to find the light switch, the animal smell overpowered me and I heard the breathing more loudly.

Then I saw it, a huge hair-covered outline against the rainy window. It had a bristly snout and pointed ears like an Alsatian. In the light from the streetlamp outside I could see the raised arms, the long curved claws, the great tongue that hung out from between yellow teeth. I knew the truth then;

Mr Hill was a werewolf.

He hadn't gone to hospital, he had tricked my Mum and lured her away, leaving me alone with him. He knew I would come to the room. He was going to catch me and suck the meat from my bones.

Then I found the light switch. The lampshade in the middle of the ceiling glowed orange, removing the dark from the room.

Mr Hill wasn't a werewolf after all.

The room was full of dead animals, and there was a huge book on his desk called 'TAXIDERMY FOR BEGINNERS'.

Mr Hill had a secret hobby. He stuffed dead animals. Lots of people used to do it. The noise I had mistaken for breathing was the hiss of a cooling unit which was breathing cold air over his creations.

I opened the book and began to read.

'Taxidermy Specimens—Preservation and Mounting. The taxidermist must remove the skin of the dead animal, then tan it and treat it. The animal's bones and muscles are posed in place with wires. The body is molded in plaster to make a cast, then re-covered with skin. Artificial eyes are then added as real ones would rot.'

I put down the book and looked around the room. A dozen dogs, a badger, four cats, some bats and foxes stared back at me with shining marble eyes. There was also an owl with no eyes and a duck without a beak. The big creature I saw by the window was a moulting brown bear, mounted on its back legs and frozen in mid-roar. There was another flash of lightning.

In jars by the window were some of the creatures' pink innards. No wonder Mr Hill didn't tell anyone about what he was doing.

Just then, there was a huge bang of thunder and all the lights in the street went out.

I watched in horror as the great head of the bear slowly turned its head toward me, its black eyes glittering with life. Its jaw slowly widened and it drooled saliva. I dropped the ring of keys.

A new sound took over from the hissing of the cooling unit. This time it really was breathing. A lot of breathing. I looked down and saw a bat creeping toward me on the tips of its wings. I jumped backwards in fright. A half-finished dog was coming up behind me, although it had difficulty walking because its legs were only wire and bone, and screwed-up newspapers stuck out from the gap in its stomach.

A huge centipede curled and stretched by my hand. Several rats dropped onto the desktop and scampered around me into the hall. Little patches of dried fur were falling off the bear as it lumbered toward me, shoving all the other creatures out of the way. A cat yowled in pain as he stood on its foot. The dogs whimpered. The foxes cried like babies. All these animals were hurting.

There was a crash as the stand that had been propping up the great bear fell over. All the animals were on the move. I could smell their stale breath, the sawdust and balls of newspaper than had taken the place of their entrails. I could feel their pain. They were creeping, hopping, staggering in terrible angry pain.

I stumbled backwards as the bear lunged for the door.

The house was in total darkness. I ran along the hall but caught the banister against my hip and fell onto my knees. I could hear the creatures coming out of the front bedroom. I heard scratching, scampering, thumping, whimpering, growling. They were coming closer every second. A perfectly preserved tarantula threw itself onto my back. I could feel its hairy legs pattering against the nape of my neck.

Knowing that I could not reach the stairs in time, I climbed to my feet and ran back to my room, but the animals were very close now. I dived inside and shoved the door shut, just as the bear wrapped its great clawed paw around the jamb and tried to push its way inside. He was forcing it open to let all the smaller creatures in. I kicked the door hard on his paw until he withdrew it with a great roar. And there I stayed, pushed against the door, until eventually the scratching and clawing stopped, and it sounded like they went away.

I didn't know what to do. Should I risk opening the door? I knew I'd be anxious until I had checked, so I slowly opened it and looked out.

The hall was empty. The door to the front bedroom was still unlocked, and the big ring of keys was on the floor, exactly where I had dropped it. But I hadn't imagined the stuffed animals. They filled the room, crouching or standing on every surface, and they still smelled bad. The bear was facing back to the window now, where it had been to start with. But there was something floating in the air—sawdust settling, like they had only just got back into position before I opened the door.

I went to the landing window and stared down into the street, or rather the nearest part of it, as the rest had completely disappeared in the fog.

As I stood watching, a figure slowly came into view and opened the front garden gate, but it wasn't my Mum. Whoever it was seemed to be having trouble walking, like they had sprained their ankle. A few moments later I heard the front door open and shut. Someone was climbing the stairs. I heard feet thumping and dragged on the stairs, coming nearer, and a strange *crick-crack* noise.

Mrs Hill was standing at the end of the hall in a green rain hat and Wellingtons. Her head was down. I couldn't see her eyes.

'I saw your mother go out, Paul,' she said. 'I want to talk to you for a minute.' Her voice was dry and whispery, as though her vocal chords had rusted.

As she walked toward me she dripped rain everywhere. She took off her hat and scratched her fingers through her hair. Mrs Hill was paler and bonier than I remembered, like she'd been dieting and hiding indoors for months. She stopped about three feet in front of me.

She smelled like mildew, like something that had been left past its sell-by date at the back of the fridge, and there was another smell too, the same dog smell about her like the bear, but I figured it was because her hair was wet. I couldn't move any further back, because the room of stuffed animals was behind me.

I didn't know what to do so I asked her if she wanted a cup of tea.

Slowly she raised her head. Her skin was as yellow and dry as an old newspaper. I looked in her eyes and saw glittering blue marbles, like a doll's. The left one was cracked. It had turned up and rolled in a little, so that I could see the damp blackness inside her socket.

'What have you been telling people about me?'

'Nothing,' I lied. 'It was a mistake.'

'You told the street that my husband killed me with a shovel on Bonfire Night and buried me in the garden. Don't lie to me.'

'No, I only told Andy, no-one else. As for the thing about your head being cut off and stuck on a pole in the shed, the story just got sort of stretched as it went around.'

She fumbled blindly with her handbag, snapping it open to dig out a handkerchief. Mopping the rain from her face, she smeared paint from her lips. 'You saw me leave on Bonfire Night. I didn't come back.'

'Okay.' I wasn't interested in what they got up to. Anything to make her go. Reaching down, she placed a hand on my shoulder and gripped it tightly. Her fingers were so bony that it felt like being pinched by crab claws. I was sure there was nothing in her that was still alive, no beating heart, no pulsing blood, just cold leathery flesh.

'Mr Hill saved me. Two months before Bonfire Night I had an accident. I fell down the stairs and nearly broke my neck, and he looked after me, even though things weren't good between us. I don't want to see him hurt. Do you understand?'

'I understand.'

Suddenly she bent down close to me. 'No more lies, Paul. That's one of my rules. No more lies or I will come back and find you. I will take out your guts and fill the space with straw and sawdust.' She stretched open her mouth and I saw right inside. There was newspaper at the back of it, sticking up out of her throat.

She released her bruising grip and turned to leave, her knees crick-cracking. When she went to put on her rain hat I saw the stitches, a neat dark row of them behind each ear.

She walked as if she was in great pain. As she slowly went down the stairs I noticed the uneven seams that ran down the backs of her legs. As she gripped the stair-rail with long red nails, I knew there were wires poking out of her fingertips. Her skin seemed to have been sewn back too tightly, like a cover on a sofa that didn't quite fit.

The front door opened and closed. I watched her hobble sadly down the empty street and disappear piece by piece into the fog.

The sawdust settled. The house was silent once more, as if wild things had returned to sleeping death. As I sat in the kitchen waiting for Mum to come back, I looked out into the foggy front garden, fearful of what I might now be able to see. I'd rather been hoping for a visit from Santa Claus, but now I didn't want to think what might come down the chimney.

When Mum came home I told her what had happened, but she didn't seem surprised. 'That Mrs Hill,' she sniffed. 'She's had a bit of work done if you ask me. And you—you've got too much imagination.'

But I knew the truth. The world has a rulebook. One of the rules is:

◆ The dead can't be brought back to life.

Sometimes the rulebook is wrong.

DEAD GROUND ZERO

To: William Barnsley, Cartographic Institute, Madrid
Cc: Dr. Daniel Thompson, Dept. Head, University College Hospital, London
From: Prof. Margaret Winn, UCH London
Subject: All Hallows Church

Dear William,

The department is insisting I use email now, citing the fact that it's faster and conveys more urgency, which is just as well as I have something rather urgent to discuss with you.

Sorry you couldn't make it over to the conference at St Alpheges. Just as well though, as all the usual imbeciles were there, blocking any progress that might be made. The members of the Catholic Council were barking up the wrong tree as usual, exercising themselves about birth control and women priests when they should have been commenting on the problem at hand, and the CoE synod weren't much better, wittering on about gay clergy, so little was achieved. Put a bunch of priests in a room together and they'll start planning the music program for the orchestra to play as the Titanic goes down. The fact that church attendances have all but disappeared in these troubled times seems to have completely escaped them. Don't get me started on that. I caught the PM's speech last night about how we must all pull together to overcome our economic adversities, and how Britain can teach the rest of the world how to survive the recession. He was speaking from a fact-finding trip to Texas. The GBP is now worth less than the Rand and he's hobnobbing with oil barons.

I attended the one-day event because I wanted to raised a question about All Hallows Church, but there was no time left at the end of the meeting to even touch on the subject. Do you know the building? It's a rather unlovely late Victorian pile in stained Portland stone, with flying buttresses and a collapsing spire, on Blackheath Road at the edge of Greenwich park.

I went there last month because there's an odd story about the diocese that keeps surfacing (in my world, at least; you know how much time I spend researching for the London Archaeological Society at the British Library). The architect Nicholas Hawksmoor had a raft of apprentices who took his more controversial views rather too much at face value. It's known that one apprentice, Thomas Moreby, worked on All Hallows, and while it's certain that he oversaw the construction of the crypt and undercroft, nobody knows how much of the above-ground part of the building he finished. It's a bit pointless to wonder now, because the upper section was completely rebuilt around 1850.

Anyway, as I arrived, I noticed a row of bright yellow JCBs lined up in the car park. There were also about a dozen protesters (mostly senior citizens) in rain-hoods hanging about looking cold and bored. One of them had a sign that read 'KEEP THE COUNTRYSIDE GREEN', like we were in the New Forest or something. Blackheath is the suburbs, for Heaven's sake. I know they mean well, but I think they enjoy being victims.

So I pulled over, hopped out and took a look, and sure enough they'd started to excavate the grounds immediately behind the church. Apparently, the idea is that the New Festival of Britain site is to have a tram-link to the Millennium Dome, which I supposed is one reason for the site's selection. Which brings me to the urgency of this note; you're a cartographer and know about these things better than I, but isn't there a long-standing government order not to dig up the East side of the park? Can they simply override it without consultation?

I'd appreciate it if you could get back to me as quickly as possible. I came past the site again yesterday and it looks as if they've already started digging.

Best as ever,
Prof. Margaret Winn

To: William Barnsley, Cartographic Institute, Madrid
Cc: Dr. Daniel Thompson, Dept Head UCH London
From: Prof. Margaret Winn, UCH London
Subject: All Hallows Church

Dear William,

Thanks for your prompt reply. That's what I thought. But I've checked, and no such consultation has taken place. On Saturday I visited the Museum of London and met with your old colleague Diane Fermier, who by the way sends her regards. Down in that dimly lit basement we pulled out the original mapping grid of the Blackheath area. The 17th century boundary lines surrounding the park and church are surprisingly unchanged from those of the present day. It seems pretty obvious to me that no-one has bothered to check up on this, a fact I find simply amazing.

Actually, the area between the park and the heathland has been disturbed on at least three occasions. Most recently, the largest ditches were filled with rubble from houses and factories bombed during the Blitz in 1940. Before that, George III ordered a number of large houses pulled down, and their remains were buried on the site in 1803 (this was at a time when the king was suffering from one of his lapses into madness—I imagine he thought the property belonged to raving Papists). Before that we find an estimated figure of almost 11,000 people buried on the site in the months directly preceding the Great Fire of London.

Now, although parish records do not extend to recording the deaths of London's poorest citizens, I'm pretty sure these were the earliest victims of the Bubonic Plague that swept the city in the year preceding the fire. Of the 100,000 who died, it would seem that over ten percent of the total were placed here on one site because the soft clay soil was easily removable. According to Diane, some of the rich were buried in lead coffins, but all the rest were placed in winding cloths or sacks, and here is my point; if they were then put in wet clay, surely this would act as a preservative?

I checked with an opposite number in Brussels, because as you know, the Belgian government has been heavily involved in the disinterment of animal remains from peat bogs on the borders of Northern France, and they have found that not only is skin and hair remarkably well preserved, but in many cases DNA sampling has shown that diseases we thought long-eradicated remained in stasis within animal carcasses.

If this is the case, what happens when the diggers reach London's dead? The sites in the centre of the old city have never been disturbed on this kind of scale. Do you know any epidemiologists who could offer advice about this? Clearly the government doesn't care to delve this deeply into the subject, but I think someone should make sure that there's no risk of contagion.

Best as ever,
Prof. Margaret Winn

To: William Barnsley, Cartographic Institute, Madrid
Cc: Dr. Daniel Thompson, Dept Head, UCH London
From: Prof. Margaret Winn, UCH London
Subject: All Hallows Church

Dear William,

I was surprised by your email yesterday. Can you really be so sure? I appreciate the point that centuries of low core temperature should have killed off the hardiest microbes, but no-one has ever tested a single site of this magnitude before. Now it emerges that the dig is to extend over forty meters down in order to incorporate several lift shafts and a large underground car park. This means disturbing a vast quantity of bodies.

I spoke with the site foreman, and he told me that he has been instructed to shift any 'debris' he finds into separate containers so that an archeological expert can sift through it, but he has not been told about the potential health risk posed by any finds, and has not been asked to quarantine any human remains. Indeed, he seems to have no knowledge about the history of the site. If you really feel this is an overreaction on my part, then I shall leave you to your work and seek advice elsewhere.

Prof. Margaret Winn

To: Professor Margaret Winn, UCH London
From: Dr. Marcus Hemming, Wellcome Institute

Dear Prof. Winn,

Thank you for your enquiry about the current excavation of the site at Black-heath designated for the New Festival of Britain. I had read about this in the press, but was surprised to hear that the land was formerly used as a plague pit. I must say I'm rather skeptical about this, as the distribution of the victims has been outlined in a number of historical records starting as early as 1667, and no-one has ever singled out this site in particular. It seems especially unlikely as we know the pathogenic route of the plague, from which this area is far removed.

Are you sure about your facts?

To: Dr. Marcus Hemming, Wellcome Institute
From: Professor Margaret Winn, UCH London

Dear Dr Marcus,

Let me set out my case. I hope you'll be able to understand my concerns after reading this.

In 2004, the London Metropolitan Archive in Clerkenwell received a set of large hand-drawn maps from the estate of one Oliver Whitby or Whichby (the spelling differs in different texts), who was the former Justice of the Rolls at Lincoln's Inn Fields. These items were found when the deceased's possessions were unparcelled from a lot sold but never examined by his great-grandfather. One of the problems faced by the LMA is the microfiching of material prior to disintegration, and as the maps were not deemed of sufficient public importance to receive preferential treatment they have sat in the basement of the LMA awaiting scans since their arrival.

In my researches, I met a young woman in charge of scanning these documents, and when she showed me the maps pertaining to the S.E. London area in question, extending across Blackheath to the edge of the church and the park. I made copies because I knew I had seen their outline somewhere before, but could not remember where.

I'm sure you know that the architect Nicholas Hawksmoor built six complex churches to his personal design, the nearest to the excavation site being St. Alfege's Church at Greenwich. While attending a seminar in that building recently, I was shown a layout dating from the period immediately following the Great Plague, which bore exactly the same borders.

Now, this is where it gets interesting; the Whitby family built and maintained a number of private burial sites around London. The first was constructed in 1642 at Blackheath, and the LMA's maps show a shaded section of the heath which, according to a coda found in Oliver Whitby's notes, had been set aside for the burial of plague victims.

So far as I know, this is the only evidence that has ever been uncovered pertaining to the burial of victims in this area. If it can be proven that these documents are real and not forgeries—and why would they be?—I think I have a case to stop the excavations before any real damage can be caused. What I need from you is some kind of testimonial which acknowledges the possibility that plague bacilli might be able to survive at low temperatures for long periods of time. Would that be possible?

I must point out that as the excavations are now well under way, time is of the utmost essence.

Yours,
Prof. Margaret Winn, UCH London

To: Professor Margaret Winn,
From: Dr. Marcus Hemming, Wellcome Institute

Dear Prof. Winn,

This is very worrying news. I can't provide absolute proof of what you want, but I can at least tell you what I know. To begin with, nobody has actually identified the Great Plague as definitely stemming from the Bubonic bacillus.

This was always assumed to be the case because the disease was thought to have originated in the Netherlands, from Dutch trading ships carrying infected bales of cotton. Bubonic plague is so-called because it causes swelling of the lymph ducts into 'buboes'.

The first areas affected in London were down by the docks. It was assumed that the plague was carried in miasma—poisoned air—and most London dignitaries beat a hasty retreat to the countryside, leaving their subjects to fend for themselves. The Lord Mayor, Sir John Lawrence, remained, but carried out his duties inside a specially constructed glass box. We now know that the disease was spread not by air but by blood.

The dead were buried beyond the city walls, one of the largest plague pits being situated in the so-called 'Dead Ground' at the Priory Hospital of the Blessed Virgin Mary Without Bishopsgate, known as 'St Mary Spital'. Burial here stopped when it was discovered that the plague bodies were being placed on corpses from earlier graves, and there was a fear that this denseness of humanity under the ground might cause a return of the contagion. It was a long-held belief that sheer weight of numbers could somehow caused diseases to multiply even among the dead. If the site at Blackheath had previously been used to bury the sick, it could well have been exposed and used again for plague victims—but why carry corpses across the river for burial?

The number of deaths in South London was quite small, so if, as you say, a sizeable percentage of the dead ended up at Blackheath, a proportion must have been moved from the North side of the Thames. Bodies were only shifted after dark—it was commonly said 'Grief by day, death by night'—and the journey would have required a great number of carts. But if the sites at St Mary, Charterhouse and St Botolph were full, the City officials may well have hired private contractors to rid themselves of the diseased under cover of darkness. I must say it has always struck me as odd that so many bodies could be placed in just three main sites, and I have wondered before whether alternative arrangements were made for their disposal without public knowledge.

I don't suppose the nature of the site at Blackheath was pointed on any maps of the time. The area grew extremely wealthy during the time of the slave trade, and it would have made the building of local property undesirable.

If this was indeed the case, and this Mr Whitby hired men to transport the dead to his pits, I start to share your concern, because the water table at Blackheath is surprisingly high given its elevation, and the preservation of the bodies requires two main factors, dampness and pressure (to create a vacuum). With both of these requirements being met, it starts to seem foolhardy to simply break open deep ground without expert advice.

There is something else that I am more loathe to mention, simply because it seems so damned peculiar. Two centuries after the Great Fire eradicated the plague (actually the plague burned itself by killing off everyone in London with weak immunity—the fire merely acted as a cleanser) the Victorians hired a team of Romanian boys to dig up the bodies at Charthouse. They chose Romanians because this race was thought to be naturally immune to plague; their nation had no history of coming into contact with the pandemic. When the pit was opened and examined, Queen Victoria's royal physician was summoned, and ordered the immediate resealing of the enclosure, but no official reason was ever provided for this act.

I've always wondered if he saw something there that disturbed him, something he could not make known to the general public.

I'm not in a position to make any further investigation into this subject, as you know. But I think you should continue to be concerned—for all our sakes. Do let me know how you get on.

Best,
Marcus

To: Michael Brooks
Site Manager, New Festival Of Britain Project
From: Prof. Margaret Winn, UCH London

Dear Mr Brooks,

I have tried repeatedly to contact you by phone about the excavation of this site (to the East of All Hallows Church) without success. I understand you were offered the services of an epidemiologist who could advise you about the safe removal of any human remains you might uncover in the ground. Apparently you turned him down and continued digging prior to receiving EEC health & safety clearance. If this is the case, might I enquire on whose authority you made this decision?

To: Prof. M Winn
From: M Brooks
Site Manager, NFOB Construction Ltd.

Dear Ms Winn,

If you have any objection to this company's code of practice, may I suggest you take it up with the Home Office, as they granted us permission to continue with the excavation in order to meet the construction deadline set out by the Home Secretary.

Yours etc
M Brooks

INTERVIEW TRANSCRIPT
Marek Schwarinski
Prof. Margaret Winn, UCH Health Advisor

WINN:
Could you state your name and position please?
SCHWARINSKI:
Marek Schwarinski, excavation worker, NFOB.
WINN:
This is the planned site of the New Festival of Britain.
SCHWARINSKI:
That is correct.
WINN:
Can you tell me what you saw at the site last—
SCHWARINSKI:
Thursday. We was digging out part of the site known as Quadrant 3—we're divided into teams to work on different quadrants—
WINN:
And yours is where the lift shafts will be?
SCHWARINSKI:
Yeah, that's right. We're down about twenty-three feet and the going suddenly gets much easier. The ground is softer, like. There's a lot of water down there, and we've got pumps in to drain it, so I'm thinking maybe we've hit an underground river, but there's nothing marked on any of the site maps. I talked to the lads, but they couldn't see nothing.
WINN:
What did you do?
SCHWARINSKI:
Got out of my digger to take a look. The ground under my boots was really soft and wet, it's deep brown clay, and—this was like a horror film, this bit—I see what looks like a bundle of squashed rags pressed into the soil, so I turn over the nearest bit with my foot. And it's a face. But really squashed, like, and the eyes was gone, but definitely a face, even with some whispy bits of hair on the skull. A girl I think.

WINN:
That must have been a shock.
SCHWARINSKI:
You see all kinds of shit on this job, but yeah, I bricked it. Now, we'd leveled out a good sixty square feet of soil at this depth, so I had a look across the area, and there's more of these brown lumps. It's wall-to-wall bodies, crushed in together, head to toe.
WINN:
What did you do then?
SCHWARINSKI:
I went to site Milco, the site manager, and told him what I'd seen.
WINN:
And what did he say?
SCHWARINSKI:
He told me to keep digging.
WINN:
He didn't suggest that you should stop work until an expert arrived?
SCHWARINSKI:
No, nothing like that. He told me not to say anything to the other workers.
WINN:
You didn't think of removing the bodies and setting them to one side?
SCHWARINSKI:
It ain't my job to do that. I only do what the site manager tells me.
WINN:
How long did it take you to clear the site?
SCHWARINSKI:
About three days, 'cause it was just me and two other blokes. The rest was taken off to another quadrant. When we got to the next level—
WINN:
How deep was that?
SCHWARINSKI:
About another ten feet—when we got there, the bodies stopped appearing and the soil was just clay again.

WINN:
What did you do with the corpses you'd found?
SCHWARINSKI:
They got dumped in with the rest of the outfill.
WINN:
They didn't go into special containers?
SCHWARINSKI:
No, nothing like that.
WINN:
And what happens to the outfill?
SCHWARINSKI:
It gets taken to the Thames estuary and dumped in the water. There's a land
project going on down there, a lot of building.
WINN:
Did everything get dumped?
SCHWARINSKI:
No, there was some stuff—
WINN:
Stuff?
SCHWARINSKI:
Bodies. The most complete bodies. They got removed and taken to a skip at
the back of the church.
WINN:
Who decided to do that?
SCHWARINSKI:
I don't know.
WINN:
How many bodies were there, would you say?
SCHWARINSKI:
A couple of dozen, maybe. They was all covered in mud, so it was hard to tell.
The rest of the stuff, well, it was all mashed together, so it was hard to tell
what all the bits were. I mean, there wasn't nothing worth saving. No valu-
ables or nothing.

WINN:
They were incomplete bodies. So the complete ones were removed. Do you
know what happened to them?
SCHWARINSKI:
No. When we came back to work the next day, the skip was gone.
WINN:
Did Mr Brooks tell you not to speak about this?
SCHWARINSKI:
No, not really. He just said there used to be a graveyard there—a long time
ago, like, and the land got built up over the years—he said it wasn't anything
to worry about, but it's been bothering me, like. And then when you turned
up—
WINN:
Mr Schwarinski, thank you.

From: Dr. Daniel Thompson, Dept. Head, UCH London
To: Professor Margaret Winn, UCH London

Dear Prof. Winn,

I have received a letter of complaint from a Mr Michael Brooks, the Site
Manager employed by the construction company of the New Festival Of
Britain, saying that you have been entering his site without permission, and
have attempted to conduct interviews with the excavation crew. Apparently
you've been citing the health concerns of this hospital, and have made all sorts
of wild accusations about what might happen should the construction
workers find human remains while they're digging. You've upset them so
much that several members of their workforce have threatened to seek union
representation over what they now see as breaches in the Health & Safety
laws.

May I remind you that you are technically an employee of this hospital, and that your actions must be made justifiable to our board of governors? There are proper channels for this kind of complaint. If you need advice about how to handle the situation, please come to see me and we can discuss the matter in private. I have no doubt that your intentions were for the best, but next time please talk to me first, before acting rashly and endangering a massive public project which—I'm sure I have no need to remind you—is of primary importance to the survival of this government and to the spirit of the nation.

Daniel Thompson

Letter sent to: Dr James MacMillan, Royal Archeological Institute

Dear James,

I can't believe you're still not on email, although given what's been going on lately, maybe it's a good idea that you don't keep a record of our conversation.

Since we spoke on the phone, my office has been ransacked and someone has broken into my car. Luckily, the most important files pertaining to this situation were not in my briefcase at the time. I actually had them with me. You know why I'm pursuing this, but I must admit that so far all I have is proof that health and Safety regulations were breached.

However, you can help me on a related but slightly different matter. Are you aware that an architect called Thomas Moreby was responsible for constructing the crypt and undercroft of All Hallows Church?

I need to know about this because Moreby was a man of strange beliefs—he thought the body lived on after death, that it was somehow inhabited by the spirits of those who had died of the plague—and that these undead beings would rise again if 'expos'd to pure humours'. In other words, if they were disinterred and exposed to fresh air. We have a situation where plague victims have been removed from a pit and—well, I can't tell you what happened to them, as nobody seems to know—I just wondered if you had come across any of Moreby's architectural writings?

I'm dropping this off at your house, but perhaps you could call me when you get this.

Ever,
Margaret

———————————————

Dear Margaret,

Forgive the scribble, and yes, I'm sorry about the lack of email but perhaps it's for the best in this case. I tried calling you but got your machine—hate the bloody things. To answer your question, Thomas Moreby did indeed allow his beliefs to affect his buildings. His convictions concerning resurrection can readily be seen in outlines for a City of London crypt (thankfully never constructed) which could be opened from the inside by its 'inhabitants'. He died in Bedlam, although it's rather hard to work out if he was mad or whether he just annoyed the wrong people.

Moreby believed that the newly revived would inherit the earth because, despite having been inhabited by the contagious dead, they would have purer souls (having seen the Other Side, I presume). Quite where he got this belief system is a mystery, although I detect the influence of Hawksmoor in his Pagan outlook. According to a colleague of mine, he left instructions in his personal effects to build such a crypt for himself beneath All Hallows church, but I suppose you already know that. I assume the idea was that when the time came, he would be resurrected along with his fellow 'pure souls'.

In his handwritten notes to the publisher of *Journal of a Plague Year*, Daniel Defoe—a dreadful writer, of course, but an invaluable witness to history—

points out that there were a great many strange beliefs among the survivors of the Great Plague and Great Fire of London. It's hardly surprising, given the circumstances. What's particularly interesting is that Moreby was also a closet Catholic with some highly influential friends in parliament. A conspiracy theorist would no doubt start to feel uneasy here. If, as you say, the remains of the burial victims were secretly removed (for a second time!) under the instructions of the Committee for the New Festival of Britain project and interred inside Moreby's crypt, it would suggest they were working within the guidelines set out by the Catholic church.

All Hallows is Church of England now, but the earliest building was not. Therefore, it's not such a wild surmise to guess that Moreby's crypt (if it still exists) has recently been opened and filled with the intact bodies of plague victims according to longstanding instructions lodged with the church. History has taught us that state and church are willing to collude openly when circumstances prove mutually beneficial. In this case, the government gets to expedite its plans for a feel-good event to improve national morale, and the church gets to keep taxes accruing from the property owned by Moreby which is still held in trust by the Duke of Leicester. Everybody wins.

This is of great academic interest, but hardly any help to you if what you most want to prove is that the health of ordinary citizens has been compromised by the exhumation.

Sorry not to be of more help. If there's anything else I can do to help, please don't hesitate to get in touch.

Best,
James

To: Janet Ramsey, Head of Current Affairs, Hard News
From: Prof. Margaret Winn, UCH London

Dear Janet,

Congratulations on your promotion. I hear the paper is going from strength to strength. I know you are no fan of the PM, and have a story lead for you that you may find interesting. There's a health scandal brewing over the Home Secretary's decision to waive public safety rules on the construction of the new Festival buildings. I didn't want to drop the details in this email, so I've mailed them to you under separate cover. When you get the envelope you'll find a number of interview transcripts I've recorded with the concerned parties. I have used false names in the document to protect their identities, as they would be at risk of losing their jobs should their views be made known. And in the current climate, who knows how long their opinions would stay on security files?

I also spoke to a friend of mine at the Royal Archaeological Institute, and it seems likely that the NFOB site managers removed bodies from the site and reinterred them under longstanding Papal instructions. What intrigues me most is that all of this information is on public file and readily available. It's just that no-one has bothered to fit it all together. Do you remember a time when we used to have proper investigative journalism in this country? The great hacks of the past all seem to have been replaced by celebrity children writing about shoes, restaurants and handbags. God, it's depressing.

I spoke to my superior here at the hospital, but he is a welcome caller at Downing Street and has basically warned me to leave the matter alone. I have spent eighteen years fighting ignorance and spin in matters of public health— my feelings about political interference are no secret, God knows—and I am damned if I'll stand by while risks of this magnitude are taken, simply to make the nation feel good about itself again.

Best,
Maggie

Janet,

Sorry, I've only just found this so it didn't go in the envelope. I'll post it separately. You should be able to see the relevance without comment from me.

Best,
Maggie

BIOSECURITY RULES WERE BREACHED AT DEVON FARM: OFFICIAL

The Devon turkey farm at the centre of the latest Avian Flu outbreak had been repeatedly warned about breaches in biosecurity, it emerged today. The latest World Health Organisation report is calling for a new international disease surveillance system to track mutating strains of Avian Flu, after it emerged that the virus has once again jumped species into humans, although in a relatively non-lethal strain.

The report states 'While there has not been a pandemic since 1968, another one is inevitable. Estimates are that the next pandemic will kill between 2 million and 50 million people worldwide and between 50,000 and 75,000 in the UK. Socio-economic disruption will be massive.'

Seventy five percent of all new human diseases originate from animals, but experts have warned they are currently identified only after infection has spread to humans. The committee chairman, Lord Wentworth, said: 'The last century has seen huge advances in public health and disease control through the world, but global mobilisation and lifestyle changes are constantly giving rise to new diseases and providing opportunities for them to spread rapidly. We are particularly concerned about the links between animals and humans. This is why a universal biosecurity code of conduct needs to be enforced on a global scale.'

Janet,

Just time for a quick note—call me as soon as you've had a chance to go through everything. I going to the site tonight to gather further evidence. My inside contact has arranged to get me admitted to the church grounds. The boy is taking quite a risk, but is willing to make a stand so that we can bring this matter to the attention of the public. Thank God there are a handful of people left with genuine moral convictions. I need to be sure of my facts before going public, but if I'm right, there is a very real danger to us all. I'll let you know how I get on.

Best,
Maggie

YOU HAVE REACHED THE ANSWERPHONE OF PROFESSOR MARGARET WINN. PLEASE LEAVE A MESSAGE AFTER THE BEEP.

'Maggie, if you're there can you pick up? I've been trying your mobile all morning but it goes straight to Voicemail. Where are you? I've been going through the contents of the packet you sent me, and there's something I don't understand—the stuff about church architecture? This guy called Thomas Moreby, the apprentice of Hawksmoor who designed All Hallows. I couldn't make a connection with what you were telling me about the public health issue, and I need to sort out—well, I need to know if all of this is on the level because it all sounds a bit crazy to be honest. Look, call me when you get this, okay?'

YOU HAVE REACHED THE ANSWERPHONE OF PROFESSOR MARGARET WINN. PLEASE LEAVE A MESSAGE AFTER THE BEEP.

'Maggie, I still haven't heard from you, and I need to fact-check if I'm going to run with this piece. I've been through everything now, and what you've sent me is potential dynamite. I'm not kidding, this could bring down the government. But I have to be absolutely sure of the facts. What did the police say when you reported the break-ins? We can't afford to make any mistakes if we're going to run all the way with this. If it's a deliberate cover-up, if the Home Secretary has given specific instructions to ignore guidelines and bypass safety checks just so that they can get the poor, dim citizens of this country whipped up in some kind of patriotic frenzy, then I think we have to cover our asses every step of the way. And I'll need photographic evidence, because great blocks of copy aren't going to shift papers. Hey, I'm still a hack at heart, what can I tell you! Call me now, the second you get this.'

FOR THE ATTENTION OF AUTHORISED PERSONNEL ONLY. THE CONTENTS OF THIS TRANSCRIPT ARE CONFIDENTIAL. THE DUPLICATION OF THIS MATERIAL IS STRICTLY PROHIB-ITED UNDER SECTION 19 OF THE NATIONAL SECURITY ACT.

[This recording was copied from the hard drive of a PDA belonging to J Ramsey, editor of Hard News online newspaper, and is the property of MI6]

SFX: (Background noise has been removed in order to clarify recording. Voice has been legally identified as that of the above user)

'Well Maggie, you're always complaining that there are no real investigative reporters left, so I'm doing this for you. And for myself, obviously. Although strictly speaking, our advertisers don't want to see any hard news on ours site. They'd be much happier if we stuck to reports about handbags, restaurants and shoes, as you always put it. Let me turn the engine off.

Okay, your Schwarinski guy appears to be waiting for me outside the church. There's no-one else around and the main site lights are off. I spoke to him on the phone earlier and he told me that the new EEC law covering light pollution in built-up areas means they have to switch off the power at midnight. It's—let me see, half past one in the morning. Let me go and see what he has to say. He looks quite cute. I might get a date out of it, if nothing else.

All right, Mr Schwarinski has gone off now. I was kind of hoping he'd stick around because it's bloody dark and I'm wearing heels. Not high ones, but the ground is really rough. He's given me his torch and spare batteries, but he took off like a shot as soon as he saw me through the gate. All I have to do is pull it behind me when I leave. I get the feeling his papers weren't exactly in order. He's taken a big enough risk just by letting me in.

I'm approaching the church. I think it's safe to wave the torch beam about because there's just the wall of the park on one side and the heath on the other. It's raining lightly and I can't see much traffic in the distance. The far road has been closed to vehicles in order to provide a works entrance to the site, so it's very quiet here and kind of peaceful, like being in the countryside. Not that I know much about countryside, unless you count the outdoor smoking area at the Sanderson Hotel.

I can see mechanical diggers lined in a long row like huge yellow beetles, all the way down one side of the churchyard. The main church door is locked— Schwarinski warned me that he wouldn't be able to get the key. But apparently there's a separate side entrance down here on the right, which he's left open. It won't take me into the main part of All Hallows, but I don't need to go there. This should—the door's stiff, but—hold on, there's a stone caught under the door.

I'm in. There's a small stone vestibule and a staircase leading down. Kind of narrow, like the staircase in the Monument. I hope it doesn't have as many steps. Very muddy underfoot—someone's been up and down these stairs a lot from the main site.

Okay, let's see what we've got here. Shit, I just bashed my head on the ceiling, which is really low. Hang on. Right, I'm in a brick-lined storage room that appears to run the width of the church, but not the length. Pretty boring so far. It's wet underfoot. Let me just—that's better. I can see more clearly now. Not much down here, some blue plastic crates, a bale of wire, a hosepipe, a stack of plywood against the wall. But there's another short corridor at the end, which according to your Irish pal leads to a second chamber. He thinks this is where they took the bodies, although if they did, they cleaned up afterwards as the floor here looks like it was recently washed down, and I can smell disinfectant. Yeah, there are puddles of the stuff all over the floor. I'm wearing Marc Jacobs shoes because I was out at dinner earlier. What an idiot.

Okay, nothing to report here except—hold on.

Interesting. Big wooden door rather like a miniature version of the famous 'Gate of Judgement' from St Stephen's Church, the one that was destroyed in the Blitz. This one has the same markings, the skulls and weeping putti, but it's in lousy condition. One side has been completely rotted through with fungus and woodworm. So much for the Catholic church preserving its antiquities for future generations. Smells bad, too.

Just so you don't worry, I've put on an anti-bacterial face mask, like the ones Japanese girls wear. I got it from someone on the travel desk. Not that I think there's anything down here to worry about. Maybe I should try to get the door open. Oh, it's not even locked. The hinges aren't attached on the other side. I can probably just push it out of the way—I have to put down the PDA to do this, so back in a minute. This is where gym classes come into use.

Right, I've shifted it a little to one side, enough to squeeze through. It's actually a lot heavier than it looks, and I don't think I'll be able to get it back in place by myself. I can't believe I'm doing this. Behind is—let me hold the flashlight up—a bit disappointing really. What we've got here is another room, about thirty by forty feet, the back of which appears to be unfinished— it looks like packed earth at the end. The smell is very bad now. I have to say it smells like something rotting. No sign of any bodies, though. If this really was Thomas Moreby's much-vaunted crypt of pure souls, it's pretty unspectacular.

There's something about the end all that's interesting, though. Going in for a closer look. It's bloody freezing in this part, and I can see my breath. Ah. Okay. Maybe I got a little too close. This is—yup, these are bodies all right, stacked floor to ceiling. All pretty squashed, dark brown and flat, just like the ones they pull from peat bogs. They're not going to be following Moreby's creed anytime soon, getting up and moving to their higher plane, mainly because I can't imagine that any of their bones are strong enough to support them. They're pretty intact, though. No smell from them—seems to be coming from somewhere else. Weird. Something down here smells—kind of alive, but rotten. Let me—no, definitely not the corpses.

Well, they've been moved here now so presumably the church will be happy about that. Not much else to report. I'm going to take a few shots of the body stack for the article, but I have to say I'm starting to wonder if this isn't much ado about nothing, Maggie. Okay, security protocol was breached, but these days that sort of thing happens all the time.

Something—I just saw something in my camera's flash. Shadows jumped. I probably imagined it. I'm going for another shot.

Christ. There's something in here—it moved really fast, just across the back of the camera frame. Okay, I'll just fire off the flash.

Jeez-*us*.

Fuck. Have to get back to the doorway but I can't see the gap. Fuck, fuck, fuck.

Oh. Oh God.

Oh God Maggie, I'm talking to you and I'm looking right at you.

How many days have you been in here? You poor—what's wrong with your— oh fuck—I can see your arms moving even though you're slumped against the wall so I know you're alive, but why don't you—what is that—

What is that? There's something all around you, like a red-brown mist. Shifting in and out of your skin. Oh Maggie, you have no eyes.

Something has half-eaten your eyes and there's something reddish-brown inside your mouth and you're still moving, what happened—

Fleas. They're fleas. Thousands and thousands of the fuckers. Christ, I've been an idiot. The Great Plague was caused by fleas that infested the Dutch cotton bales, then travelled on rats and jumped to humans. They bit into the flesh and spread the disease by sucking and transferring blood. Fleas. Simple organisms that are still evolving.

Everything you said makes sense now. No wonder Moreby believed the dead could walk again. They're not truly alive, just infested with fleas that have existed in a state of suspension until released into the air once more. But look at you. There's something more I can't see. You're moving almost as if you remember who I am. I can see the fleas shifting underneath your skin, but you look like you're in terrible pain—let me see—let me—

Oh God, your ears, there are thousands of them. They're sucking the blood from your brain, gorging themselves on your flesh, it must be a living nightmare for you. I'm going to go for help. Shit, the little fuckers can really jump. I can't see any on me but I feel itchy and you—you can just stay back there while I go back upstairs and make a call.

Christ, you made me jump, Marek. I didn't see you standing there. I'm glad you came back. I need to go upstairs and phone for an ambulance—what are you doing?

Don't put the door back! What are you fucking doing?!

The son-of-a bitch Russian fuck-bastard has shoved the door back in place. Let me out of here, you fucker! How much is he paying you? How much is your slimy boss paying you to do this? Open it, goddamn you!

Well, Maggie, it looks like you and me, old pal. Yeah, you can just stay over in that corner where your little parasites can't reach me. Do you even know what I'm saying? I can see you're dead, you're just not lying down. They own you now, your parasites have taken over their host. But what are they going to do once they've finished their food supply, eh? It's a pretty dumb parasite that kills its host. Fuck it, this was going to be the story that made my entire career.

Oh. So that's how it works. Just for the record, if anyone ever gets to hear this, my friend Margaret is coming toward me, and I think she means to drain me of blood in order to feed her parasites. She's cold and dead but the fleas are keeping her alive, so that she can feed on others. It looks like I'm about to join the pure souls, but I'm not going down without a fucking fight.

Not going down.

Christ, that hurts. Jesus, you bitch.

You living dead bitch.

Fuck, I'm down.

Down.

This would have made . . . a great . . . story.

RECORDING ENDS

From the Office of The Home Secretary To;
Dr. Daniel Thompson, Dept Head UCH London

Dear Dr Thompson,

This file has been watermarked and licensed to you only. Please read the contents, then destroy. We think our informant Mr Schwarinski attempted to collect the recording from Janet Ramsey's PDA, which he found on the floor of the crypt beneath All Hallows Church. However, he must have found both Ramsey and Professor Winn in a state of revived life. It appears that as he removed the door, they attacked and bit him, making their escape. We do not know their current whereabouts.

Mr Schwarinksi died of his wounds the following morning, but subsequently revived, attacking a hospital orderly. He has not been seen since.

I have to warn you that you may face prosecution for failure to pass on information vital to national security. This situation is out of control now.

Message ends.

THE WORLD, TAM DECIDED, WAS ONE LONG SERIES OF KEYS AND LOCKS, AND THERE WERE some doors that couldn't be shut once they'd been opened. The one that was giving her the most trouble that late rainy Saturday afternoon in October was painted seven shades of sea-green and wouldn't close properly—probably hadn't closed for years. She wedged her trainer against it and shoved with her shoulder, but it seemed too big for the frame, so she went downstairs to Mrs Hamalki and borrowed her husband's electric sander.

The rent had seemed a little too good to be true at four hundred a month, given the massive size of the apartment, and as she stood on a chair sanding half an inch from the top of the door, she started noticing problems. There was an odd smell of gas or possibly sewage emanating from the floor of the kitchen. The passing trains were close enough to rattle the windows, and there was some kind of basement nightclub next door that attracted slouchy chainsmokers beneath her bedroom window. The nasty stain in the centre of the lounge carpet looked like a dead pet had been left there for some time. A rainstorm revealed the biggest threat to her peace of mind; dribbling patches on the bowed bedroom ceiling in three different places. It was easy to imagine a Poseidon-type moment when tons of filthy water might suddenly fall in on her head while she was sleeping.

She got the door closed but it was still warped in its frame, as if it had been forced at some point in the past and would never be put right again. The flat on Caledonian Road occupied the second and third floors of a terraced Victorian house, and had survived a century and a half of expanding floorboards, shrinking mortar, falling roof tiles and rising damp.

But her sister Sophie had told her she would never forget her first flat, and she was right.

The door was finally closed with a satisfying thump, and Tam dropped into her very own second-hand sofa, knowing that she was at last beyond the reach of her well-meaning but annoying parents. She had a fixed space she did not have to share, a kingdom extending from garden to pavement in which she was free to be calm and quiet and alone at last.

According to Mrs Halmaki, the building had been owned by a single family for almost a hundred years, but had been turned into a boarding house at the end of the war, then carved into three flats in the early 1970s, to be reconfigured and repainted by dozens of tenants. If the ghosts of the original family still walked here, there was no easy way of sensing their presence beneath a dozen layers of cheap paint and paper. Tam would rather have liked to feel them pottering about the apartment, cooking or reading, or playing with their children. She owned a portable wind-up gramophone and a bunch of jolly 78 rpm records, but even the pre-war sound of Ambrose And His Orchestra was not enough to invoke their spirits. Too many drifters, drunks, loners and crazies had passed through the rooms since then.

Spreading her arms along the back of the sofa, she looked across at the three tall windows, the elaborate ceiling rose, the archway through to the weirdly stocked kitchen (three knives, two forks, four cheese graters—why?) and felt an overwhelming sense of freedom. Then she spoiled it all by answering a text from Lewis, her boyfriend, who was still living at home and wanted to come over. She told him he could visit so long as he always called her first and brought an inaugural bottle of decent wine.

Lewis arrived three hours later with a six-pack of lager and a giant can of cider. The simplest instructions always seemed to mutate in his brain. He had approached her a month earlier in a Shoreditch bar, and had spent the evening describing his unlikely adventures with a minor soap star more famous for her prodigious use of cocaine than her acting ability. Later Tam had discovered that Lewis was not the star's best friend at all, but was in fact obsessed with her, to the point where he had been warned to stay away from her house at night.

She should have marked him down as a stalker and fantasist, and have broken up with him right then. But somehow the moment had passed and she had found herself stuck with Lewis, worn down by his wheedling, moth-eaten charm.

When he rang the bell, she sleepily rose and twisted the door handle, but nothing happened. The jamb was stuck in the frame again.

'What's wrong?' Lewis called through the wood.

'You'll have to kick it from your side,' she instructed, and then he was in, staring up in concern as he passed through, rubbing his tattooed elbow. 'You need to get that seen to. What if there was a fire?'

'Maybe you can help me fix it.'

'I'm a tech-head, not a mechanic.' Lewis reckoned he designed websites, but had yet to show her any of his work. He circled slowly, appraising the flat. 'Not bad, funny smell, what's that stain? You need to give it a good clean. Have you got cable? Bit of damp there. Have you got anything to eat?' He dropped back into a kitchen chair, tilting it, putting his trainers up on the table.

'I thought you were going to bring wine?'

'They didn't have any. You got no dead-bolts on the windows. Someone could come up the drainpipe. Or down from the roof. I'm starving.'

She instantly wanted him out of the flat. He was an intruder, ruining every-thing just by sitting there. They went to the pizzeria next door, and it was as she watched him slowly chewing his pepperoni slice, lost for something inter-esting to say, that she decided to finish with him.

He accepted the news with good grace, which disturbed her more than if he had been hurt, because it suggested that he had either failed to understand or wasn't especially bothered. Sure enough, when she paid and they rose to leave, he asked when he could come around again.

'Lewis, were you listening? I don't want to go out with you, or anyone else for that matter. I just need to be alone for a while.'

Lewis played with the silver crucifix at his throat while he struggled with the concept of rejection. 'What do you mean?' he asked finally.

'I'm not going to see you for a while. I'm settling in. I've got a lot to think about.'

He looked blankly at her. 'Like what?'

'Well, I'm trained as a voice coach but the agency has yet to find me a job, my mother is subbing me rent so I need to pay her back, my dad's upset that I've moved out—' She halted, knowing that Lewis was already bored and thinking about himself. 'Forget it, let's just get out of here.'

She stood awkwardly outside while he smoked, watching the rain lace itself along the restaurant's canopy. 'I'll call you tomorrow,' he promised, bouncing off into the storm as she fled back to her apartment.

Lewis rang so often that she let her mobile go to voicemail without bothering to check who was calling. Luckily, she had not given him the number of the house phone.

It took a week to clean the place properly and repaint the lounge, replacing dingy magnolia with sunshine yellow, but soon the rooms were reflecting the morning light instead of merely absorbing it. Stains were removed and smells were banished, but the front door remained stubbornly stuck. She would have liked to scrape the layers of paint back to the wood, but knew that the work was too much for her. All detail had been lost over the years, so that the rooms were little more than blurred ghost-images of their former selves.

On Saturday morning she went downstairs to see her landlady, and found Mrs Hamalki's daughter coming out of the ground-floor apartment. There was a look of permanent exhaustion in Maria's eyes, as if the effort of merely remaining alive was too much for her.

'My mum was attacked last night,' she wearily explained. 'Someone tried to break in. I've told her before. I'd have her with us, only it's the kids.'

'That's awful. Is she all right?'

'They kept her in the Whittington overnight to see if there was concussion, but she's got a strong head. My dad used to knock her about. Me and my husband are just going to pick her up, but he's not been at all well.'

'What happened?'

'I heard someone at the door,' Mrs Hamalki told Tam an hour later, seated in her kitchen. She had a faint grey bruise above her bloodshot right eye, but otherwise seemed in good spirits. 'It was late, and I thought maybe you had lost your key. I went to answer it and there was a man—'

'What did he look like?'

'I don't know, early twenties, wearing a black hoodie, a white boy is all I remember. It was raining hard and the hall light was out, but I could smell drink on him. He shoved right past me and headed for your stairs. I told him he couldn't go up there and tried to stop him, just grabbed at his sleeve, and he whacked me and ran back out. It's that bloody club next door, they're all druggies and nutters in that place. I've complained to the council but they won't do anything.' She tipped some rum into her tea and gave it a stir. 'If he comes back, I'll take his face off. Fucking cheek, charging up my stairs. Where did he think he was?'

Tam's agent began sending her bookings for voice-coaching lessons. She had been hired to teach business managers how to handle presentations. The work required a lot of preparation, but was well paid. A week after starting in her new role, she returned home late on Saturday night and threw her coat onto the kitchen chair, only to realize that it had been moved a foot to the right. Nor was the TV remote where she had left it. A carton of orange juice had been taken from the fridge, finished and thrown in the bin.

Walking around the apartment she sensed the faint presence, a fading vapour trail, of someone who had passed through the flat room by room, touching, moving, assessing—invading. She could detect a faint citrus perfume. She examined the lock, but there was no sign that it had been tampered with. The windows were firmly shut.

She went to see Mrs Hamalki and asked, 'Does anyone else have a set of keys to my flat?'

'I used to have some, love, but the last tenant borrowed them and never gave them back. Funny little man he was, wrote for some weird magazine, didn't have any friends. I used to feel a bit sorry for him. I had to chuck him out when he couldn't pay the rent.'

'He never comes back, does he?'

'Not to my knowledge. Actually I think he died. Can't remember where I heard that. It might have been the one before.' Mrs Hamalki peered up the shadowed staircase. 'Anyway, what would he want to come back here for?'

Two doors along was Caledonian Road Bolt & Lock, a low-rent Aladdin's Cave lined with brass keys, toilet seats and door handles. The bloated, pale creature behind the counter wore old-school gold coin rings and had a seventies combover. He was pushing a battered chicken leg into his mouth and actually crunching the bones. He looked embarrassed about being caught with so much fried food.

'You need a London Bolt,' he told her. 'Know what that is? Fits into the floor, the ceiling and the door-jamb. Over there.' He waved a greasy finger at a length of galvanized steel that looked like a medieval torture device.

'I think it would make me feel like a prisoner,' she replied.

'Regular locks aren't enough, not around here. There's a big estate up the road, always a lot of trouble at the weekends.'

'I just need a new lock.'

'Know the easiest way to get into someone's flat? All you need is a screwdriver. You put the sharp end over the keyhole, like so,' he demonstrated. 'Then give the handle a good whack with your fist. It punches the lock right through.' He coughed and spat a sliver of chicken bone into his palm. 'You could have a French bolt, extends twice the length into the mortise.'

'I think I'd just like the regular lock replaced for now.'

'Suit yourself, but a child could open one of those.'

'Then give me one that a child can't open,' she said with impatience.

'Sixty quid, cash, includes the fitting. I can come round tomorrow morning.'

It was a rare fine day, so she opened all the windows. The locksmith duly appeared and cut a new mortise into the jamb. 'The wood's warped,' he pointed out. 'Must be draughty.'

'A bit,' said Tam. 'I just want to be sure that no-one can get in. Do you get many burglaries around here?'

'Not as many as we used to. Turnover's the problem. Too many short-let tenants take these places. They don't always hand back their keys. I can't tell you how many times I've changed this lock alone.'

'There've been a lot of people in this house?'

'Yeah, in this whole terrace. Because of the prison up the road. You'd get members of the family wanting to be near their loved ones. A lot of broken hearts. They'd come and go, but a few come back. There was this woman who broke into her old apartment, kept freaking out the new tenant. Never took anything, just quietly let herself in, stayed for a while and then left. Eventually they tracked her down and she explained why she was returning. Her son had rented the place before her, and had left all his old furniture and fittings behind. The boy had died of a drug overdose. His mother kept breaking in when she was drunk just to listen to her son's voicemail recording on the phone. The weirdest part is that the new tenant swore he had replaced the message with one of his own, but the mother reckoned she could still hear her son's voice on the line. Gives you the creeps, what some people get up to.' He rocked back on his heels and examined his work. 'Well, it ain't foolproof, but at least you're the only one who has the keys for it.'

'Can you do the windows as well?'

'You're not likely to get someone climbing up a century-old drainpipe, but I'll do them.' By the time he had finished, the flat was sealed tight.

Sophie called that night. 'I think you should have a word with Lewis,' she said. 'He's been having a go at you in his blog. It's a betrayal of confidence. He's talking about your sex life and everything. It's seriously out of order.'

It seemed to Tam that no matter how hard she tried to maintain her privacy, something always leaked out and became public; photos on phones, texts, emails, message boards, somebody could always find a way in to you. She called Lewis and warned him to take down the offending blog entries, which were not only explicit but described exactly where she lived. He promised to do so, but the very next day he cheerfully added the details of her phonecall to his blog, and there was nothing she could do about it. She should have known this was how he would be, given his obsessive tendencies with the soap star.

The new lock made no difference at all. She came home from work the following Saturday to find things moved again, this time in the upstairs bedroom—a pillow, a cushion, magazines, a hairbrush—trivial shifts, as if the apartment had been shunted slightly, or gently tipped, then righted.

Through her agent she met another voice coach, called Suzi, and invited her over for a revision evening, but they ended up drinking, surfing old rom-coms and complaining about boyfriends. Still, by consciously choosing who to invite to the apartment, she felt that she was in some way reclaiming her right to the space. Suzi had a vile mouth on her, but her criticism was mainly reserved for men she had dated.

'The worst one?' she asked, 'the very worst guy I ever went out with? No contest, I can win this hands down, nothing you say will be able to beat this.'

'Go on, then,' Tam urged with some trepidation.

'He used to live on the French Riviera, bummed around looking after boats, and I suppose he was kind of attractive in that woman's-magazine way, you know, a bit cheesy, all long wavy hair and narrowed eyes. He took me out to dinner and conveniently left his wallet at home, told me he didn't have a girlfriend, that he was too shy, too busy to date, the usual bullshit. We went back to his apartment but something seemed wrong.'

'What sort of thing?'

'I don't know, the place felt heavily trafficked, as if a lot of girls had been through there putting things right, tidying everything up for him. It wasn't how a man would keep a flat. Then his supposed best friend told me. He used to pick up women by writing the worst online contact ads in the world, really hateful stuff, like 'I'm an old-fashioned sexist and would never date a woman who didn't do exactly what I told them', or 'sometimes I've had to slap a girl around to keep her in line', and so on. And he'd get, like, loads of replies. He'd picked the most desperate answers and contact them, because he knew that the kind of girl who answered an ad like that would let a man do anything to her. Oh, and he once paid a mate to take an AIDS test for him. Some time later I found out his nickname. They called him the Cunt Of Monte Carlo.'

Tam was taking a swig of wine and laughed so hard that she spat Lambrusco onto the carpet.

Suzi rattled a bag of potato chips to find the ones that had the most salt on them. 'I heard he got fat and all his hair fell out, so he had to move back to London. When you let one of those creeps in you let them all in, because it reveals the shockingly low level of your self-esteem.'

'I think I have a ghost,' said Tam abruptly, surprised by her own admission.

'How do you know?'

'He comes in when I'm out and—rearranges stuff.'

'Maybe an interior designer died here.'

'No, really. Sometimes I come home and things are in the wrong place.'

'Then you need to change the locks.'

'I already did that, because my landlady says the previous tenant was a bit weird. But it's made no difference.'

'What about the windows?'

'I've had burglar bolts put on them. And there's a lingering scent—isn't that common with ghosts?'

'No such thing,' said Suzi with definite authority. 'It's either a past tenant, in which case you need to find out more about who was here before you, or it's a gay cat burglar. Mind you, I like what he's done with the place.' They both laughed, but Tam stopped first.

'Seriously, you don't believe there's a kind of—energy—in old houses?'

'I do, but it's not caused by the passage of phantoms. I trained to be an architect, and I can tell you this part of the street is late Gothic Revival, around 1865. You've got terra cotta sunflowers, scrollwork and sash windows behind all those plastic fascias downstairs. Your floorboards are 140 years old. They breathe and buckle according to heat and humidity. I've seen chairs tipped over and pictures knocked from walls. Houses of this age flex themselves.'

Tam hardly heard her. 'I changed the locks,' she said softly. 'There's no other way in.'

'No other way in.' Suzi rose unsteadily to her feet. 'Well, let's just check that.'

Together they went through the apartment room by room, knocking on the walls. Suzi provided a commentary as they went. 'Original lathe and plaster under lining paper. Two brick partitions, support walls from when this was a family home. Parlour, day room, corridor, bedrooms at the end, servants' rooms upstairs. Chimney breast here, bricked up now, can't move that without the house falling down. The windows at the back have been filled in. New doorway cut through here, and here. Hall and walls removed after the invention of central heating. No need for such small rooms now you can easily keep them warm. The landing's been opened out here, subdivided there. No secret passages that I can see.'

'Then it has to be a ghost,' said Tam.

Mrs Hamalki had kept a rent book for years, and had listed at least sixteen tenants. She remembered odd things about a few of them, but nothing of use about any of them. 'We had a murderer,' she confided. 'At least, everyone said he'd done his wife in.'

'He didn't tell you about it?'

'Of course not, nobody ever said anything to his face. But we talked about it behind his back, as you do. He said his wife had moved to Vancouver without leaving a forwarding address, but seeing as she was agoraphobic it didn't seem very likely. She just disappeared. Mind you, at that time we didn't have indoor plumbing, so he couldn't have dissolved her bones in an acid bath like John Haigh did.'

'Have the police had any luck with finding your attacker?' Tam asked.

'If they have, they haven't told me. I went next door and had a go at the club manager but he told me to fuck off. Nice way to speak to a lady. Did you talk to your boyfriend?'

'He's not my boyfriend, but no, I don't want to call and encourage him.'

'You got a picture of him?'

'I had one on my phone, but I erased it.'

'Only I might have been able to tell if it was the same man. I don't suppose he'll come back.' There was an element of wistfulness in the way she spoke, as if the intruder had performed some kind of useful service.

More uneventful days and nights passed before the visitor returned, and this time Tam was scared. She awoke from troubled sleep and looked at the bedroom alarm clock: 2:48AM. There was someone moving about on the floor below.

It sounded as if they were in the kitchen. She thought of leaving the light off and going to look—for about a tenth of a second. Then she flicked on the bedside lamp and crept out of bed to listen at the door. She heard the chink of a teacup, or a plate. China being gently tugged across wood. A tinkle of metal, a footfall, then another, an odd crunching sound, the creak of a floorboard, the crunching sound again. A shuffle, a thump.

Drawing a deep breath she threw open the door and went downstairs as loudly as possible. Then, her nerve failing, she stopped on the staircase to listen. All movement in the kitchen had ceased. Was her visitor waiting for her, or had he already disappeared? She looked around for some kind of weapon, but only found a travel umbrella, leaning against the wall like a bat with rigor mortis. It was better than nothing. Holding it like a lance before her, she charged into the kitchen.

There was rice all over the floor. A cup and saucer had been taken from the cupboard and placed on the table. The linen basket on top of the washing machine had been disturbed. Nothing had been moved according to any logical pattern. There was a faint trace of citrus in the still air.

She called Lewis's mobile, but it sounded as if she had woken him up. 'Have you been in my flat?' she shouted. 'Have you just been here?'

'I don't know what you're talking about,' he replied sleepily. 'I'm in bed.'

'What about the time before? Someone tried to push past my landlady. Was that you?'

'I just wanted to see you, babe. She grabbed me. I didn't mean to clip her. I was a bit pissed.'

'I knew it was you. I found your crucifix on the stairs.'

'Oh.' A pause. 'Can I have it back?'

The next morning she spoke to Mrs Hamalki, but decided not tell her about Lewis. Instead she asked her to write down the name of the previous tenant, a Mr Laschowisch. She searched for him on Facebook, and found him listed as the proprietor of a magazine called 'Gravestone—Online Journal Of The Fantastic'. She sent him a note and received an instant reply, as if he had been at his computer night and day, waiting for her. She explained that she was living in his old apartment, and asked him if he ever revisited it. His denial meant little; he was hardly likely to tell her if he had. But he talked to her about ghosts, and about the strange presence he had felt in the kitchen and lounge on certain rainy nights. However, Mr Laschowisch's experience was not hers; he said he had felt sharp temperature drops, heard the ringing of ghostly bells, and swore he had once seen the ethereal form of a tall woman in a white billowing gown pass through the wall between the bathroom and the hall. Tam decided he was nuts and deleted him from her Facebook contacts.

When she went to see the locksmith again, he was eating a piece of fried plaice out of the paper. His tiny office reeked of vinegar and pickled onions. 'I need the London bolt,' she said. 'Today, if possible.'

The locksmith sucked his fingers. He looked ashamed again, and shoveled the fish to one side. 'A much better choice. Tumble-locks can be picked. The modern versions have shallower indentations on the keys, which are much harder for thieves to open. But if you want to stop someone dead you need the bolt.'

She looked at the mess of paper and chips on his counter. 'Fried food is bad for you. I suppose you know that.'

'Yeah, but I love it. My wife thinks I have salads every day. She doesn't eat enough to keep a mouse alive.'

He fitted the anodized steel London bolt, which slammed into place with the finality of an oubliette being closed against a howling prisoner.

'I have a friend,' Suzi told her. 'She knows about this kind of manifestation and can get rid of them.'

'I don't need a pest controller,' said Tam.

'She's more of an exorcist,' Suzi replied.

'No,' said Tam. 'No, no, no.'

'Don't worry, she's not a Christian, more New Age.'

'I'm not paying for some crazy old bag to come around waving crystals over the furniture.' Tam was firm on that point. 'How much is she?'

'Let's get our terminology straight,' said the exorcist. 'I'm a sensitive. I can't see the future or tell you what you had for breakfast. But I can feel someone's living here apart from you.' The woman who turned up was a far cry from Madame Arcati; she looked more like a cross between a Pre-Raphaelite heroine and Kate Bush. She went by the unlikely name of Alicia Carbarendum, and opened a threadbare velvet carpet bag filled with small glass tubes of urine-coloured liquid. 'I make these myself,' she explained. 'I distill the essences from wildflowers. You know every flower has a meaning? The anemone is abandonment.' She raised a vial and checked it for sediment. 'Columbine is deserted love. Jonquil is violent sympathy. Lilies and orange blossoms are hatred and disdain, the petunia is resentment. I can tell that all these are present in your flat. We need to counter such disharmonies.' She unbottled two of the tubes and liberally sprinkled them. 'Don't worry, it doesn't stain.'

'Now what happens?' asked Tam.

'Well, that's it really. If it's a vengeful spirit he won't be able to get back in.'

'What do lemons mean?'

'That's a fruit,' said Alicia firmly, 'not a flower.' She snapped her bag shut. 'Can you write me a cheque?'

One week later, her ghost was back. Tam noticed he had a preference for Saturdays, after midnight. He was becoming more confident—the noises were louder and usually persisted until she reached the stairs. Alicia's sprinkled fragrances were quickly replaced with the bite of citrus, as if being overpowered by a stronger force. Tam was not so much frightened as made to feel persistently uncomfortable. The haunting forced her to ask questions about herself. What had she done to attract a revenant? Weren't they mostly drawn to damaged people? Was it trying to forge some kind of connection with her? Could it sense that she was lonely, that she had stopped trusting men, that she was, for all her protestations of independence, slowly becoming lost?

She asked Mrs Hamalki if she'd heard anything. 'No, love,' the landlady admitted. 'I take two Temazepam every night. I'm dead before my head hits the pillow. It's funny, 'cause I don't think we've ever had a problem with ghosts here before.' She made them sound like ants or mice.

Tam knew there was one way to discover the truth, but she was a natural coward and loathe to try it. However, after two more visitations she decided that something practical must be done. The following Saturday she armed herself with a carving knife, turned out all the lights in the lounge and dug under a blanket on the sofa. Then she waited for it to make an appearance.

She tried not to fall asleep, but the rhythmic ticking of rain on the windows and the slushing of cars on the wet street robbed her of consciousness. She drifted, then dozed, then descended into the deepest of untroubled slumbers.

She was brought back to wakefulness by a click and a scrape, a tinkle of metal and the faint smell of citrus. Something or someone—an amorphous dark shape—was in the room with her. Air passed wheezily through it. The black form wavered, but did not approach. Beneath the blanket Tam groped for the handle of the carving knife, but it had slipped from her grasp, down between the sofa cushions.

'I've been waiting for you,' she said matter-of-factly, sitting up.

'And I've been waiting for you,' came the reply.

'Why do you come here?'

'Because you're here.'

'Are you good or evil?'

'That's not for me to decide.'

'Do you mean to harm me?'

'That depends on you.'

'Can you walk through walls?'

'Yes, of course.'

'Why do you only manifest yourself on Saturday nights?'

'That's when my wife goes to bingo.'

The locksmith turned on the light. He was sweating heavily, and carrying his pass keys. 'She stays over at her sister's.' He admired her with dark, blank eyes.

'People trust locksmiths because they have to. Imagine if they didn't. I can get in anywhere.' He reached over and squeezed a catch on the London bolt. It sprang into place with an oiled click. 'This one's custom-built. There's a trick to it that no-one would ever spot. You can lock and unlock it from either side of the door. There now. You'll never get that open in a million years.'

'Lemons,' she said stupidly as he lumbered toward her. 'You use them to hide the smell of fried food from your wife.'

His hulking shadow fell over her.

The next morning, Suzi called at the flat, but there was no answer. She rang Mrs Hamalki's doorbell.

'I'm supposed to meet up with your tenant today,' she explained. 'She's not answering her doorbell.'

'Probably popped out to get something for breakfast,' said Mrs Hamalki, unconcerned.

'Can I wait for her?'

'I don't have keys, love. She changed the locks a couple of times. I think she got a bit paranoid about living alone. Her first time away from home. You can come in and have a cup of tea.'

By lunchtime, Suzi had worried Mrs Hamalki so much that she called her daughter's morose husband over to break down the door, but even he couldn't get it open. 'It's been bolted shut,' he confirmed. 'I've got a ladder on the van. I'll smash a window.' He looked as if he relished the idea.

Mrs Hamalki's daughter's husband broke the glass and climbed inside. The apartment was completely empty. There were no clothes in the cupboards, and the only sign of disturbance was a broken cup on the floor. The front door's London bolt still appeared to be locked from the inside. It had kept its secret well.

'Where did she get the locks changed?' Suzi asked him. 'It must have been somewhere nearby.'

As they were talking, they left the house and walked right past Caledonian Road Bolt & Lock, but the dark and narrow shop was closed up tight, and looked as if it would be for a very long time to come.

No, PLEASE, YOU WERE BEFORE ME. AGE BEFORE BEAUTY, HA HA. I'M IN NO RUSH TO BE
served. The barmaid knows me, she'll get around to looking after me soon
enough. This is my local. I'm always in here on special evenings. Well, there's
never anything on the telly and at least you meet interesting people here.
There's always someone new passing through.

I don't come in on a Saturday night because they have a DJ now and the
music's too loud for me. You'd probably enjoy it, being young. I haven't seen
you in here before. This place? Yes, it's unusual to find a traditional pub like
this. The Jack O' Lantern has an interesting history. Well, if you're sure I'm
not boring you. I like your Hallowe'en outfit; sexy witch, very original. This
place is a bit of a pet subject of mine.

We're on the site of an ancient peat bog. The strange phenomenon of gas
flickering over it was called *ignis fatuus*, from which we get the flickering of
the Jack O' Lantern. They built a coaching inn on the marsh in 1720. Not a
good idea. Even now, there's still water seeping through the basement walls.
Later it became a gin palace. That burned down, and it was rebuilt as a pub
called The Duke Of Wellington. Being on the corner of Southwark Street
and Leather Lane, the pub was caught between two districts, one of elegant
town houses and the other of terrible, reeking slums.

See this counter? It's part of the original bar. Solid teak, brass fittings. It
was curved in a great horseshoe that took in all three rooms, the public, the
snug and the saloon. But the Jack was caught between two worlds. The
drunken poor came in on that side in order to drown their miseries in cheap
ale, and the fine gentlemen ventured in to swig down their port while visiting

the brothels nearby. Oh yes, there were dozens in the backstreets. The area was notorious back then. It's all gentrified now. Urban professionals. They don't drink in here. Not posh enough for them. They'll be the first to scream when it's gone. Not that the area will ever really changed. You don't change London, London changes you.

Of course, there was always trouble in here on All Hallows Eve, right from when it first opened. One time, close to midnight, two of the king's horsemen came in and proceeded to get drunk. They mocked one of the poor ostlers who stood at the other side of the bar, and brought him over for their amusement. They challenged him to prove that he had not been born a bastard. When he couldn't do so, they told him that if he could win a game of wits, they would give him five gold sovereigns.

They placed a white swan feather on the one of the tables and seated themselves on either side of it. Then they produced a meat cleaver that belonged to the cook, sharpened it and challenged him to drop the feather into his lap before they could bring down the cleaver on his hand.

The ostler knew that the king's horsemen were employed for their strength and speed, and feared that they would cut off his fingers even though they were drunk, but once the bet had been made he couldn't refuse to go through with it. You never went back on a bet in those days.

They splayed his fingers on the table, six inches from the feather. As one of the men raised the cleaver high above his head, the other counted down on his pocket watch. The ostler held his hand flat and lowered his head to the level of the table, studying the feather. Then, as the countdown ended and the cleaver swooped, the ostler sucked the feather into his mouth and spat it into his lap. He won the bet. Unfortunately, the king's men were so angered that they took him outside and cut off his nose with their swords. The nose remained on the wall here for, oh, decades.

During the Second World War no-one was much in the mood to celebrate Hallowe'en. No female could come in alone, because it was considered immoral in those days. Well, so many men were off fighting, and most of the women around here were left behind. If they entered the pub by themselves it meant they were available, see. But there was one attractive married lady, a redhead, Marjorie somebody, who came in regularly and drank alone. None of the accompanied women would talk to her—they cut her dead. This Marjorie took no notice, just sat at the bar enjoying her drink.

But the whispering campaign took its toll. The other women said she was a tart, sitting there drinking gin and French while her husband was flying on dangerous missions over Germany. The pointed remarks grew louder, until they were directly addressed to her. Finally, Marjorie couldn't sit there any longer without answering back. She told the others that her husband had been shot down during the first weeks of the war, and that was why she came in alone, because it was his favourite place and she missed him so much.

The other women were chastened by this and felt sorry for her, but in time they became disapproving again, saying that a young widow should show remorse and respect for the dead. People were very judgmental in those days.

Then on October 31st 1944, when she'd been at the bar longer than usual, a handsome young airman came into the pub towards the end of the evening and kissed her passionately without even introducing himself. Everyone professed to be shocked. The women said it was disgusting for her to make such a spectacle, but their disapproval turned to outrage because she slid from her stool, put her arm around his waist and went off into the foggy night with him.

It wasn't until the barman was cleaning up that night that he found the photograph of Marjorie's husband lying on the counter. And of course, it was the young airman. He'd come back to find her on All Hallows Eve. Had he survived being shot down after all, or had the power of her love called him back from the other side, to be with her again? They never returned to the pub, so I don't suppose we'll ever know.

In the sixties they changed the name of the pub again. It became The Groove. Psychedelic it was, very druggy. All crimson-painted walls and rotating oil lights. Let's see, then it was Swingers, a purple, plastic, seventies pick-up joint, then in the eighties it was a gay leather bar called The Anvil, then it became The Frog 'N' Firkin, then it was a black-light techno club called ZeeQ, then it was a French-themed gastropub, La Petite Maison, and now it's back to being The Jack O' Lantern again. Always on the same site, always changing identities. But the nature of the place never changed, always the rich rubbing against the poor, the dead disturbing the living, the marsh rising up toward midnight.

See the pumpkin flickering above the bar? It's lit all year round, not just tonight. If you look carefully, it looks like you can see a skull behind the smile. It was put there one All Hallows Eve in the sixties. For months a sad-looking young man and his sick father would come and sit in that corner over there. The young man wanted to move in with his girlfriend, but her life was in Sheffield, and being with her meant moving away from his father. I would sit here and listen to the old man complaining about his illnesses, watching as his son got torn up inside about the decision he knew would soon have to make.

His father would sit there and cough and complain, and would catalogue the debilitating diseases from which he was suffering, but the funny thing was that he looked better with each passing week, while his son looked sicker and sicker.

I could see what was going to happen. The young man had to make a choice, and his decision coincided with his father's worst attack, although nobody knew what was wrong with him. The old man still managed to make it to the pub every night. The son made up his mind to leave, but he couldn't desert his father, even though Papa was slowly draining his life away. Finally he broke off with his girlfriend to look after his father, who looked so well in his hour of triumph that even the son became suspicious.

I heard the girl quickly married someone else. We didn't see the boy for a while, but when he finally came back in, he sat on that stool alone. It seemed the old man had fallen down the coal cellar steps at midnight on Hallowe'en, and had twisted his head right round. The son put the Jack O' Lantern up there that very night. It even looks like the old man . . .

The bar stool didn't stay empty for long. It was taken by a vivacious young woman who turned the head of every man as she pushed open the crimson curtains into the pub. Everyone loved her, the way she laughed and enjoyed the company of men so openly, without a care in the world. She came in every evening at eight o'clock. She drank a little too much and never had any money, but being in her presence made you feel like you'd won a prize.

She wanted to fall in love with a man who would bring some order to her chaotic life, and then one day she met such a man at a party. He held a senior post in American Embassy, and gave her everything she ever wanted, a beautiful house, nice clothes, money, stability. She stopped her drinking, bore him a son and became a model wife. His only stipulation was she should never again come into the pub. One evening he came home and found her hanging from a beam in their farmhouse. I think you can guess what night that was.

Of course, everyone in here has a story. There was a woman who used to come in once a month and get completely legless, but the landlord never banned her. I asked him why, and he told me that she was an actress hired to play drunk in bars for the Alcohol Licensing Board. They used to collect data on how often drunks were served liquor, and she came here to practice her act. The stress of her job got to her, though. One evening, she decided to have a real drink and got genuinely plastered, but the landlord thought she was just acting again. On the way home, she drove her car into a lamp-post and was beheaded. Hallowe'en again.

Look, it's like the lantern's laughing now, doesn't it?

You think this pub has endured more than its fair share of tragedy? I knew them all, and I'm still here. I sit here drinking while the tragedies of others unfold around me, and I can do nothing for them, any more than they can change me. And which of us is the main character in the story? Perhaps we only ever belong at the edges of someone else's tale. We suffer, we cry, we die unnoticed, and the people we consider unimportant fail to sense our suffering because to them we are merely background colours, minor characters in their story.

Of course, I could add my own story to the list of peripheral tales. I could tell you about the bizarre death of my wife, and what happened when the newspapers discovered where I had buried—oh, but that was so long ago.

Who am I? They call me Lantern Jack. I suppose I'm the pub mascot. Only here one night a year. And only ever seen by special people.

What's that? You can see me?

Yes dear, and I'll tell you why.

Come closer.

Closer.

Let me whisper in your ear.

It means you join me tonight.

Well, I should let you get on. I shouldn't have taken up so much of your time. I'm sure you must have many important things to do before midnight.

Cheers!

WE ALWAYS USED TO MEET IN THE INTREPID FOX, EVEN WHEN WE'D BEEN GHOST-hunting all night. Me, Shape and Ali would bed down for a long session with bottles of cider, and argue about London's pagan history, but as we got progressively more drunk the discussions about Wiccan mythology and Alistair Crowley and spirit dowsing would get blurred together with complaints about slashed student funding, climate change and the Labour party's lost idealogies. By the end of our evening nothing made sense any more, and we would totter back to our respective flats.

Shape was always finding a new crusade to fight and this month was no different. He'd heard that Ali and I sometimes went ghost hunting and announced that he wanted to join us. Having Shape on your side isn't always a good thing. He gets excited for a while but his enthusiasm ebbs just as fast and you get left with the wreckage he's created. As soon as he heard about our trips out to country houses, he wanted to find a revenant in a London house.

'Why is it that only abbeys and castles get visited by ghost hunters?' he asked. 'Forget the rich, we need to liberate the spirits of the poor and do some good in the world.' And for once he had an idea about how to find such a place. He had decided that spirits were probably most drawn to properties built on ley lines, those magnetic tracks that supposedly attract strange occurrences, and as there was a massive crossover point behind Euston Station which made the ground there more susceptible, that was the place to start looking.

So on Friday night, somewhat against my own will, the three of us met up and headed to Euston station.

Shape was striding ahead in his strappy Camden boots and long black leather coat, and Ali and I had to almost run to keep up with him. Now that he had joined us, he automatically assumed leadership.

'See, the area has always been really poor because the government needs to contain the working classes and deliberately trapped them here by forcing rents up in the surrounding areas so they couldn't move,' he reckoned, zooming along the centre of the pavement. 'And the poor are more prone to visitations by past spirits.'

'I don't understand,' said Ali, 'why would they be more likely to see ghosts? I thought ghosts appeared because of an injustice.'

'No, it's because the working classes are traditionally more superstitious,' Shape explained, as if talking to a child. 'The streets of ancient London followed the leylines, and they were traced over by hedgerows and canals. The low marshlands were poor areas largely because they flooded regularly. Water and fog brought illness, deaths created superstitions; that's why ghost stories were more associated with say, the poor East End and the areas around railway termini rather than the city's prosperous North.'

'Wow, I never thought of it like that,' said Ali. But she was always the first to admit she wasn't much of a thinker.

'I have some questions,' I said, because I knew how Shape got if you just let him have his way. He needed to be challenged, otherwise he would just walk over us. He was like that all through school, and he was like it once we were together on the same course at St Martin's. He's probably even worse now that he's in banking. We don't speak any more.

Shape sighed in annoyance. 'You always do have question, Max.'

'First, how are we going to find a house with a revenant, and second, how do we gather the physical evidence we need?'

'Look, are you on board with this project or not? You could get amazing material for your degree show.'

'Yeah, I'm on board. But I just don't see how we're going to pull it off from a practical point of view.'

'Don't worry, we'll have plenty of time to work out the physical side of things later. First we need to find the right house.'

I liked Shape then because I thought he cared about the world. He helped set up an innovative fund for earthquake victims at St Martin's and started a huge viral campaign to save the sacred white rhino—okay, so neither of those projects actually worked out, but the ideas were there. He always said he wanted to do some good in the world, like Bob Geldof and Bono. Shape's parents were uber-rich, but he said he never took a penny off them because they voted Conservative. They wanted him to go into banking right from the start but he defied them by taking up textile design, and now they were really angry with him, which made him really happy.

We were walking down a street called Coburg Street, going towards Star-cross Street. There were Indian restaurants and corner pubs, and rows of low two-floor Victorian houses with their ground floors converted into shops. I looked at the upstairs windows and saw dirty net curtains, rain-stains, ragged lines of washing on blue and red nylon lines, bicycles on balconies. Quite a lot of Indian kids. There was a big council estate just behind, ugly modern utility buildings sticking above the slate roofline of the terrace.

'According to the book, this is the spot where seven separate ley lines cross,' said Shape. 'We should start here. Ali, go up and ask those kids if they know of any strange occurrences happening in the houses around here.' He pointed to a hoodie gang in shiny blue track suits loitering outside a halal butchers.

I watched Ali hesitate. She didn't want to look like a wimp in front of Shape, because she was kind of in love with him even though he barely noticed her, so she went over to talk to the kids. We watched her talking to them for a minute or so. She came back.

'I couldn't understand a word they said,' she admitted. 'They have this funny accent.' Ali was quite posh and hadn't spent much time in London before she got accepted at St Martin's. She probably never had much of a chance to talk to Asian people in Norfolk, where her folks lived, not unless they were her mum's cleaners or something.

'That'll be the working class slang they use. You fail, Ali. Three fails and you're off the team, okay?' She looked shamefacedly at Shape, and mumbled an apology. 'Okay, I can see I'll have to sort this out. What we'll do is look for the houses that sit exactly on the confluence of ley lines. That's where the presence of revenants is strongest.'

It was grey and brown and drab around here, and just starting to rain, but I was intrigued about what we might find, and anyway we had nothing better to do today. We reached another row of houses (they all looked the same), clean and still and quiet, but these ones had black iron railings and brown brick basements you could see down into. The corner sign said Phoenix Street. Shape raised his eyes at me when he saw that. There was a shop at one end selling weird fruit and fat knobbly vegetables, most of which I wasn't familiar with.

'Go in there and ask the guy if they've had any spectral activity in this zone,' said Shape.

Spectral activity? I thought. *Suddenly he's the expert on ghost-hunting, and designating tasks out to his employees? Where was he when Ali and I spent a freezing night in Lesnes Abbey waiting for the ghost of a monk to appear?* This is how it always was with Shape. The night in the Abbey hadn't gone well. I thought the cold air might drive Ali into my arms for warmth at least, but all she talked about was him.

Shape peered through the window at the shopkeeper. 'He looks Indian, which means he'll be more spiritually in touch with such things,' he told us. 'There's no point in asking white people, they no longer have access to their souls.'

So I went into the Am-La Grocery Store. It was the most cluttered, overstocked store I'd ever been in. The bored boy behind the counter was barely visible under red and silver lottery tickets and chocolate bars. He was watching a blurry bootleg Bollywood film on the tiny monitor above his head. I bought a packet of mints because I felt a bit embarrassed, and asked him. 'Excuse me? We're doing some research for a student project? And we were wondering if you ever heard about there being any ghosts around here?'

He turned to me with sleepy eyes and realized he'd been asked something unusual. 'Ghosts?' he repeated, like he was trying out the word.

'Yeah, we heard there's a ghost in one of the houses.'

I had trouble understanding what he was saying because he had a strong accent and spoke so fast, but part of it was (I thought) 'The house down the street, man, the empty one. There's some old lady who haunts the place.' And he pointed back along the street. 'She's down there,' he said, emphasizing with a jab of the finger. 'We see her at the window sometimes. In the basement. Real scary.'

I was pathetically excited because I'd found our first lead. Why did I put so much store by winning Shape's approval? I went back out, where Shape and Ali were sheltering from the rain. 'He says there's the ghost of an old lady that appears just down here, they see her sometimes and she's really scary.'

'Well, of course I knew we'd find her,' Shape said casually. 'Doesn't he know which house?'

I didn't want to go back in the shop and ask him again, so I said 'Let's just take a look. Where are the ley lines the strongest?'

Shape took out his book and followed the scribbly map he'd made. 'Two houses from the end,' he said with absolute certainty, so that's where we went. We peered down into the basement but the room was dark behind the curtainless window and we couldn't see in.

'It doesn't look like anyone's living there,' said Ali.

'Maybe the living residents couldn't handle it,' Shape replied, opening the gate and going down. 'The manifestation probably drove them out. They didn't tell anyone because they were scared of looking crazy. That's what usually happens in these cases, you know.'

Shape always acted like he was the only living authority on these things, even though he was new to ghost-hunting. Ali and I had been doing it for ages, while Shape was off getting involved in lots of other stuff, student activism that mostly involved wildly unmanageable plans and half-hearted complaints rather than anything that instigated positive action. 'I must challenge the lies and expose the truth because I'm the only one who cares,' That was his mantra, but he never seemed to expose anything except his own inability to finish what he started. Basically he would try anything if he thought it would annoy his parents.

'What if it's got a burglar alarm?' I asked, worried.

'Max, these are working class people who haven't anything worth stealing, why would they have an alarm? All they have left is their dignity.' He reached the bottom and peered in through the dirty glass. He checked his book again. 'Yeah, this is definitely the right house.' He wiped the window with the end of his scarf. 'The rooms are empty, probably between rentals.'

We ventured down the stairs behind him and looked in. I could see a room lined in brown wallpaper and dirty wall-to-wall reddish carpet. A fireplace.

Some cardboard boxes and dirty rags on the floor. A ratty-looking sofa. An open doorway led into something darker, a hallway I guessed.

Shape was trying the front door, but of course it was locked. He shone his key-ring torch through the gaps. 'It's bolted. We'd have to go in through the window. That's just got an old-fashioned catch.'

'That's breaking and entering,' said Ali, concerned.

'No, not if it's empty, it's squatting and that's completely legal,' Shape told her. 'Besides, if there was a problem with the police I'd just tell them who my father is. We'd need some tools. We can come back another time for that.'

'We need to hold a proper watch first,' said Ali. 'We don't bring equipment for that because we need to verify the site. In other words, we have to see or hear something that will convince us the place has a spirit connection, otherwise we could waste weeks just hanging around at a dead venue.'

'Okay, we do that, then if there's any evidence of spirit manifestation, we come back and break in, yes?'

And suddenly we had a plan. We returned the same night at nine, went for a few beers in the corner pub and then headed back down to the house in Phoenix Street. A couple of Indian teens were hanging on the opposite pavement as usual, looking like they were waiting to pull drug runs. Shape opened the gate and we went down to the basement. We had these green nylon tripod stools that looked like small umbrellas but folded out, making it easier to sit for ages, and the main part of ghost hunting is sitting around.

We were in the greatcoats we took to Glasto last year, so we'd be warm and dry if the rain started up again. We set a small pocket torch beside the window and angled it so that the beam was shining into the room. Then we settled down to wait. It smelled of rotting vegetables down in the well of the basement, and I could hear rats snuffling about somewhere.

Nothing happened for the first half-hour. Then Ali said she saw something. 'Where?' asked Shape.

'Just in the corner, like a change of the shadow or something.' She tilted the torch and tried to see, but whatever there was, it wasn't there now. 'See, it was lighter by that wall and it went dark for a moment. Really, I saw a change,' she told him, anxious to be believed.

The thing about ghost-hunting is, just as you're about to give up for the night you always think you're about to see something, and you end up staying one more minute. You become convinced that if you pack up to go, you'll miss the moment. And that's what nearly happened here. Shape was bored, I could feel it, the rain had started up again and the last tube was going soon. Ali kept moving the torch around, and Shape kept telling her to leave it alone, and something caught Shape's eye. 'Turn off the torch,' he hissed at Ali, and leaned into the window, searching the room. And we unconsciously mimicked him, one on either side.

And then, suddenly and shockingly, we saw it. A woman's ghostly face, impossibly drawn, blank and paper-white, right in front of us, just an inch the other side of the glass, its mouth a dark 'O', hair wild, mad eyes wide—a textbook ghost. And something more—a sense of ancient tragedy, there for a second only and then gone, vanishing into nothing.

'Whoa!' We fell back off our stools, then packed up and shot up the stairs so fast that we embarrassed ourselves. We were shaken, but after a minute Shape was jazzed and wanted to go back down. 'We all saw it, didn't we? The manifestation? We should go and take another look.'

'No, I said, 'we have to get the equipment. We can come back tomorrow night.'

'But what if she doesn't reappear?' Ali twisted her rainbow-coloured braids anxiously.

'They're drawn to the life-force of the living,' said Shape, suddenly the expert again. 'Max is right, we'll come back tomorrow.'

We returned home and over the next day we collected what we needed. Infra-red equipment, night-vision digital recorder, barometer, EMF detector, hydrometer, spirit wind chime, motion detector, talcum powder, a decent clock. We'd have liked a thermal imaging scope to find cold spots but they were too expensive. Shape was impressed.

We arranged to meet at 11:00pm outside Euston station. Ali and I got to carry all the equipment. The rain had died down to a thin, greasy drizzle that made the sodium-yellow pavements slippery. We headed over to the house, and noted that neither of the houses on either side had their lights on, which was a good thing if we were about to take up house-breaking. Luckily, the bad weather had forced the hoodies off the streets.

Shape had brought a crowbar with him, and led the way down into the basement. He pushed one end under the rotting wood of the window sill and the catch popped, that easy, although we knew it would be harder to shut again. He had trouble opening the window, though, because the wood was damp and swollen, but eventually the three of us managed to work it up a little so that we could slither inside.

There was enough ambient light from the street to let us see the room in dim form. We put our bags down and took a look around. The basement had been divided from the rest of the house—the whole building had probably been sliced into flats. There was a rank-smelling galley kitchen still filled with dirty pots. No electricity, something green and reeking in the dead fridge. Further along the corridor we found two bedrooms, one devoid of any furniture, the wallpaper damp and hanging down in swathes. The other had a single bed with a pile of eiderdowns on it, and although I couldn't see much here at the back of the house, it looked like there was something shifting about.

'Rats,' said Shape. 'Don't go near them.'

In the main living room (the one by which we entered) there were a few odd items lying around; an khaki bag full of old toys, some framed photographs of a man in uniform, a box of mildewed newspapers, more photos, some women's clothes.

We set up the equipment. It was cold in here. 'Too cold,' said Shape. 'We're going to have to buy the thermal scope. I need to isolate the low temperature spots.'

We arranged the motion detectors (which we had swiped from the college) on either side of the lounge, and set two digital cameras in position. We tied the wind chime to the bulb flex hanging from the ceiling rose. Finally, we spread talcum powder over the floor. Then we popped open a few beers and settled down to wait.

After a while, inevitable, we fell asleep. But it was okay because the motion sensors were alarmed.

The next thing I knew, Shape was shaking me. 'What's happening?' I whispered.

'Listen,' said Ali.

Faint but clear, a small bell was ringing. I sat up. 'Is that the chimes?'

'No, it's coming from further away,' Shape whispered back. 'A classic sign or spirit arrival.'

'I don't know, it's sounds like it's coming from outside. It could even be an office alarm.'

'The room's got colder—can't you feel it?'

'Christ, what's that awful smell?'

I looked across to the red digital readout on the clock. Midnight. I tried to see into the thick shadows, but maybe one of the street lights had gone out because it seemed darker in the room now. I had brown spots swirling in my eyes, removing the distinct edges of the room. Ali was kneeling, straining to see. Shape was slowly rising, moving in a careful way that would not disturb the presence. He reached out and turned on the digital cameras. Then we waited. We waited for what seemed like twenty minutes, straining our ears, but nothing happened.

Ali rose and stretched her back. 'Well, that was a waste of—' she began when something rushed into the room with a banshee shriek, a white-wreathed, hunched apparition with a white screaming face and the wide black 'O' mouth and bony claw arms raised above its head, and all hell broke loose. The thing rushed up to Ali and she screamed and suddenly there was a slash and a shocking red cut had crossed the left side of her face, and Shape was backing up and knocking over one of the digital cameras. And then the apparition screamed something that sounded like words but its voice was so distorted that we couldn't understand, and we were bricking it and just wanted to get out of that awful reeking room. And just as quickly the apparition vanished and we were on our knees shoveling everything back into bags, and clambering out of the window and gone.

The next day we met in the student bar at St Martin's and ran the camera footage, but the cameras hadn't been pointing in the right direction and all you could see was a few frames showing a blur of white. The soundtrack picked up the creature's voice though. We played it over and over, filtering it until we could understand. It was saying something that sounded like 'Alanafga—terror' again and again, until Shape's shouting drowned it out.

'We need to do some research,' said Shape with an air of determination, 'and find out what these words mean.' Shape had a lunch date arranged at his father's club so he couldn't do the legwork, which meant that Ali and I had to head up to the London Metropolitan Archive in Clerkenwell to research the history of the house.

The archive's a great place. All the documents of London are kept there. There are medical records and high court rolls and maps showing where German bombs fell, but it's always empty except for a few old dears researching their family history. People don't seem interested in their own surroundings, or maybe they are but they're too busy to ever get around to checking them out. We had to leave all our belongings in the red lockers on the first floor, but then we headed upstairs and started looking up the housing history of the Somerstown area behind Euston, where Phoenix Street was located.

Turned out it was a weird old place. A long history of ghostly sightings in an area that was always been incomplete and on the move. Homes were always being torn down to make way for the railway. Even the newborn and the dead hadn't been allowed to linger in their cots and burial plots as the train tracks advanced over the land. Graveyards and hospitals torn up, the poor routed, Victorian philanthropists always ready to preach to the unemployed, the elderly and infirm, dumping a few moralizing Christian tracts on them before shoving them into workhouses to die.

No wonder the grey streets behind the station now housed a largely immigrant underclass. No gentrification here, no luxury lofts and gated communities for this chaotic backstage area of good old London Town, the part the tourists never saw.

It was Ali who found it in an old newspaper, the story of the jilted bride. Ann Matilda Barbary, due to be married at St Pancras Old Church on July 10th 1856, waited in vain to be collected by her father for the short walk to the wedding service, not knowing that her husband-to-be had been killed in a drunken fight at The Tap Inn, Euston, that very morning. She and her husband were going to live and raise a family in one room. From the picture, it clearly could have been the basement room in Phoenix Street.

'And that's why she appears in white,' said Shape. 'She waits for her groom who'll never come and she screams in pain when she finds out he's been killed.

This is dynamite stuff. We need to get better footage, though, if we're going to upload it onto a website.'

'I don't want to go back there,' said Ali. 'There was too much anger in her spirit. It's dangerous.' The cut on her face was no more than a scratch, but looked livid and sore.

'Then I'll go with Max,' said Shape, 'it'll be easier with just the two of us.'

The next night was a full moon, and although I had no idea why that would make a difference, Shape suggested it was the best time to witness another manifestation. So we headed for Phoenix Street once more, taking only one digital camera with us this time.

'If we can find out what the creature was trying to communicate,' Shape said, 'we'll have documentary evidence of a link between this world and the next. We could set up a website and make a fortune.' How he intended to do this remained an unexplored subject, but I went along with it.

We climbed down into the basement area and found the window still open, so we climbed inside and set up the camera once more. The moonlight had increased our vision in the musty room, and while we waited for a manifestation I went through the photographs in the one of the boxes. I turned over pictures of a couple married in the nineteen thirties, a man in a WW2 uniform, children, grandchildren—an entire family genesis left to warp and molder. The family name of Morgan kept cropping up in thin handwriting on the backs. Jack, Katie, Sally, Sam, Nick, cousins, sisters, aunts.

'The magnetic lines of the earth are holding her here, trapped at the spot where she died,' said Shape. 'We have to release this poor woman's spirit and set her soul free. Then we can blog about it.'

I could never tell if he was joking when he said things like this. Shape hardly said anything that wasn't intended as irony, so you never quite knew where you stood with him.

I turned over more photographs, some clearly recent. Soldiers messing around with a football in a sharp lunar landscape, except that it was brilliantly floodlit. Mailed from—

'I was raised an atheist but you know, we could find proof of Heaven, how cool would that be?' said Shape, and suddenly I realized he was just doing this to try and upset his parents again. He was thinking how annoyed they would be if he turned in a project based on proof of spiritualism in his degree show. That was all he really cared about.

I turned over another damp photograph of a young man in a sand-coloured uniform, squinting into harsh sunlight. Flipped it to the back and read; 'Alan Morgan Territorial Army Afghanistan'. *Alanafga—terror.*

Shape, I think you should see—'

And here she was again, wrapped in white, hurtling into the room, disturbed from her sleep, screaming in panic. 'Alan—Alan—my son is in Afga—' but she couldn't pronounce the word.

'Your grandson Alan is in the Territorials,' I said. But she couldn't hear, whirling insanely around the room. 'Mrs Morgan?' And she was running back to her bed on crippled arthritic legs, half-blind and deaf and crazed with fear.

'Not a ghost,' I told Shape, 'just an old woman. We're in an old woman's home. I think her grandson was looking after her but he's in Afghanistan now.'

'Jesus Christ.' Shape slammed the camera shut and grabbed his bag. 'Come on, let's get out of here.'

'No, can't you see she needs help? Something's happened. For some reason nobody knows she's here. Or if they do, they're not doing anything about it. She's been abandoned. Maybe her son failed to notify the Social Services before he left.'

Shape brought his face close to mine. 'Who gives a fuck? She's just some old bitch. A waste of time, a fucking waste of time.' He grabbed me and pushed me toward the window.

'You're the one who makes a big deal about caring,' I shouted at him.

'I don't care about her, she's alive. What good is that?' He climbed from the window and headed back to the street.

I wanted to stay and see that she was all right, but I didn't.

I didn't.

I couldn't call the Social Services either, not without leaving some kind of trace. If they tracked us down we could be arrested. I didn't know what to do. And in hindsight I did the wrong thing, I know that now. Instead of finding a way to leave an anonymous trail to Mrs Morgan's door, I thought I'd help her directly. Every evening on the way home from the college, I stopped at the

Indian takeaway in Phoenix Street and bought her a curry in an plastic tray, and left it just inside the basement window, together with a bottle of soda water. I pulled the window down as far as I could to stop the room from getting too cold, and every night when I came down again the tray from the previous visit had been emptied, so I just carried on doing it.

One night, I waited by the window to see if she would appear. After a while she shuffled into the room, still wrapped in the dirty sheets from her bed, and grabbed at the tray. Her bony arms were covered with suppurating sores. She dropped the plastic knife and fork on the floor and ate greedily with her fingers. I could not bear to watch a second longer. I was ashamed and confused by my own inaction.

Then, about a week after I had started bringing the food, the hoodie gang returned to the street and stood in front of me at the gateway to the basement, blocking my path. One of the Indian boys glowered from within his blue shiny track suit. He had huge brown eyes, and looked angry. 'You're not going down there with that,' he said with soft menace.

'Why not?' I asked, but they remained silent. 'Why not?'

Finally one of them spoke up. 'It's got nothing to do with you.'

'She needs the food, she'll die if she doesn't eat.'

'Walk away, man, there's nothing for you. Forget what you saw.'

'She's an old woman. What did she do wrong?'

'Not her, the grandson, disrespectin' us, innit.'

'What did he do to you?'

'Fuckin' us off, man. Shouldn't be here, should he. Wrong postcode for a white army boy, man. You shouldn't be here neither. Less you wanna get cut.' Their fists were in their pockets, but they were obviously carrying knives. I knew she was waiting in the basement room. I knew I was her lifeline. But there was nothing I could do. I could no longer reach her.

I went home and tried to forget, to shut out the sight of her desperate face. I tried not to smell that awful smell. I tried to pretend I had never seen her. I told myself it was nothing to do with me.

Two weeks later I picked up a copy of the local newspaper on the bus, the Camden Journal, and on page 14 I found a small article about her entitled 'Wartime heroine found dead in flat.'

The piece explained that Mrs Kate Morgan had been presented with an award for her outstanding work in a nursing unit of the WRAF in 1945 and had spent a lifetime caring for others. It said that her only living relative, her grandson, had recently been killed by friendly fire in Afghanistan. It went on to say that she had been dead for a week before her body was found. Local boys were being questioned. A woman from Social Services trotted out the usual line, that this was a failure of the system and must never be allowed to happen again.

I left St Martin's. I could no longer sleep. I dreaded the nights. Every time I lay in the dark and closed my eyes, all I saw was her terrified face. I never saw Shape or Ali again. If I'd have run into Shape, I don't know what I would have done. Something bad. Later someone told me he was running his parents' bank.

I was 21 when this happened. I am 30 now. The nightmares have lessened, but they never go away.

They say ghosts appear because of an injustice. Mrs Morgan was not a ghost before, but she is now. And all my life, she'll continue to destroy my sleep.

THE ADVENTURE OF LUCIFER'S FOOTPRINTS

I MUST SAY FROM THE OUTSET THAT THE SHOCKING BUSINESS OF LUCIFER'S FOOTPRINTS is something I cannot fully explain. And although there was a solution of sorts, it caused a rift between myself and my old friend that may never be fully healed. To this day, it chills me to the marrow to think of our foray into the dark netherworld that lies beyond the reach of rational science.

I have written elsewhere that although I recall the events laid out herein, I cannot place an exact date upon them, for I was not long married when I came to call upon Holmes once more.

I do remember the gutters of Baker Street running with melted ice and snow, the sky a sickly winter yellow above the chimneypots, which tempts me to place my visit on a Saturday in the late February of 1888. Should I venture to the vaults of the bank of Cox & Co., Charing Cross, and unearth my battered tin dispatch box, I would find among the many papers some notes which might be constructed into an account of what happened during our time in Devon. But I can still barely bring myself to believe what happened. And indeed, there is no logical explanation—I can only set down the facts as they occurred.

It began, as these things so often did, with a visitor to Holmes's rooms.

'This is really most inconvenient,' said my friend when he heard the door-bell and peered down from his front window.

'You don't know there is a caller for you,' I ventured, for it is true that my friend's suppositions sometimes seemed to me a little glib.

'Mrs Hudson does not take calls at this time,' he replied briskly. 'The butcher's boy is not due this morning, and the lady standing on the step is dressed in a style of finery that was at its height in London two years ago, which suggests she is up from the country—not a social call, for she would visit her milliner first, but a matter of urgent business.'

Moments later the door opened and Mrs Hudson requested to speak with Holmes. 'Sir, there is a lady for you who will not be put off,' she said. 'I have asked her to wait—'

'Mr Holmes, you are a consulting detective, are you not, and as such I should be able to call upon you as I would a doctor?' said the lady, coming into the room and removing her gloves.

'I have said as much myself, Miss—'

'Woodham, Lucy Woodham,' said the lady, as forthright as she was pretty.

'Please Madam, take a seat and pray tell me what I can do for you. This is Dr Watson, a trusted friend and confidant. You may speak freely in front of him.'

'I have travelled up from Devon today to see you because you came highly recommended to me by Miss A——-, for whom you handled a most delicate matter,' she began. 'My father is Major General Sir Henry Woodham.'

'A most valorous gentleman, Miss Woodham,' said Holmes, impressed. 'A favourite of Her Majesty's, I believe.'

'Indeed, sir, although you might not credit it to see him now, for he is a broken man.'

'Why so?'

'It began three months ago, when the footprints first appeared. And it has recently culminated in death and madness.'

I saw the sparkle in Holmes's eyes and felt his excitement like electricity in the room. He knew the game was afoot. 'Please be seated and tell me more, starting at the beginning,' he said.

'My father retired from the military world but found life hard to adapt to at Belstowe Grange,' Miss Woodham explained. 'He inherited the property from his grandfather, and upon his retirement we moved from Worcestershire to Devon, hoping to restore the house to its former glory. It wasn't long before we heard the stories.'

'What stories?'

'You must understand that Belstowe Down is a close community, Mr

Holmes. It centres around the rows of villagers' cottages, the parish church and the grange. It is quite ancient. There was supposed to have been a Roman encampment at the site. Storms often wash away the roads, keeping the village isolated and its residents prone to superstition. There is a legend that says when a terrible crime has been committed, the Devil sends his legions of the lost to take ghastly revenge upon the perpetrator.'

'And your villagers have recently had reason to believe this has once more come about.' Holmes tamped his pipe and sent aromatic blue clouds into the room. 'Please describe the circumstances.'

'On Sunday afternoon the head groom and his stable boy had been returning the horses from exercise when a sudden storm arose. The sky blackened and the wind howled, bringing squalls of rain that hammered at the house and flooded the grounds. I and my father watched from inside the grange. When the tempest finally passed, the stable boy was discovered in a state of shock from which he has not recovered, and the groom was found lying in the middle of the lawn with his throat cut deep from ear to ear.' Miss Woodham paused, quite overcome with emotion, but gathered her wits and continued. 'But that was not the worst of it.'

'What more could have happened?' I cried, feeling sorry for this fetching young lady who was clearly so distraught.

'I think we had better come directly to the grange with you to see for ourselves,' said Holmes.

A quick consultation of Bradshaw confirmed a train leaving within the hour. I suggested staying in the village inn, but Holmes felt it was wiser not to alert the local populace of our presence, and so took up Miss Woodham's offer of rooms on her father's estate.

The main body of the building at Belstowe Grange was Jacobean, wood-panelled, high-ceilinged and flagstone-floored, impossible to adequately heat and gloomy with shadows near the rafters. I imagined that Major General Sir Henry Woodham would be 'the Very Model' as Mr Gilbert might say, ramrod-backed and stern of countenance. His illustrious military career spoke volumes, and yet the gentleman who greeted us was but a shade of his former self. His sallow skin hung loose upon his stooped bones, his eyes were dark with approaching shadows and he started at the slightest noise.

'I'm glad you could attend us, Mr Holmes,' he said, shaking our hands in relief. 'This is the most confounded business, and I am deuced if I know what the answer might be. I can only think that the villagers are right, and the Devil himself has cursed this place.'

'There is no time to be lost. Perhaps we should start by seeing your stable boy,' Holmes suggested. 'Where is he now?'

'He is attended by a nurse upstairs,' said Miss Woodham, 'but I fear you will discover little from him. The lad has not uttered a single word since witnessing the death of his master.'

Jacob, the stable boy, lay pinned by hard white linens in a small room at the back of the house. His pale face stared straight up, his eyes unmoving, his lips dry. Holmes sat beside him while I shone a light in the lad's eyes to measure the contraction of his pupils. 'He is in shock,' I told the nurse. 'He must be regularly fed beef tea and kept warm. In time he will make a full recovery.'

Holmes was talking to the lad, speaking so quickly and softly that none of us could hear what he was saying. After a few minutes, the boy's mouth suddenly opened and he began to whisper the same thing over and over, something that sounded like 'Phantoms of the dead.'

'I fear we will get no more from him today,' said Holmes, rising sharply. He seemed hardly concerned for the boy's health, and only wanted more information. 'Come, Watson, we need to see the body of the groom. Perhaps Dr Watson might be allowed to examine him?'

'He is lying upstairs in the Barley Mow, awaiting the verdict of the coroner,' Miss Woodham explained. 'Mr Charlton can take you to him in the brougham.'

A short, barrel-chested man with luxuriant grey mutton chop whiskers and the sun-darkened face of an outdoorsman appeared beside the Major General.

'Mr Charlton can be trusted with anything you might have to say,' said Sir Henry. 'Like myself, he was a cavalry officer at the Crimean Peninsular. I have known him for well over thirty years. Many in our village fought for their country, but few were actively engaged with the enemy like Charles and myself.'

We made our way through scowling drinkers and climbed the worn stairs in the local alehouse, where we found the body of Elias Peason, the head groom, covered with a winding sheet that had grown dark with his blood. I removed the cloth and studied the wound at his throat. 'This cut was not made with a razor,' I exclaimed, 'but with a sword. It is too wide and deep, and was performed in a single sweep.'

'Bravo, Watson,' Holmes exclaimed. 'I knew I could rely upon your medical knowledge to help us out. But regard the look of sheer horror on his face. What did he see in the moment of his death? He turned his attention to Mr Charlton. 'Were the pair of them together throughout the course of the storm?'

'I am given to understand so. They were seen from the road by a passing ostler who insists that the boy ran off at the height of the storm, leaving his master alone.'

'He saw the groom die?'

'He says the man uttered an unearthly scream and fell to the ground, and that he was entirely alone.'

'You know this witness? He is reliable?'

'He is known to partake of strong drink upon occasion.'

'Do you have any reason to suspect the lad?'

'Not at all. He had the greatest respect for his master. You will see for yourself, sir. There is fear in his face, but no cruelty in his heart. During my time in the army I have seen men kill and be killed in turn, and I would swear the boy is innocent.'

'Then whom do you suspect?'

'I think you had better see the rest of it, sir,' said Mr Charlton, bringing us to the lawn where the body was found.

The half-acre of green behind the grange was still flooded from the storm. Around us the tops of tall beeches shook and whispered as if telling secrets. As we approached the spot where the groom had been killed, Holmes strode forward with a look of excitement on his face. Almost at once I saw what he saw, but could not make sense of it. 'What is that?' I asked.

There appeared to be hundreds of indentations surrounding the space where the body had fallen. The earth was as churned and broken as if a flight of stallions had been driven across it.

'Did the groom release your horses before he was attacked?' asked Holmes.

'No sir, these prints were not here before,' said Mr Charlton. 'The horses were affrighted in the storm, but were still stabled behind locked doors.'

'The prints appear to start at the edge of the lawn and lift away on the far side,' called Holmes. 'There are no other marks beyond them. It's almost as if they came down from the sky to attack the groom.'

'Whatever could have left so many hoof prints?' I asked, but no answer came.

'We have found them here before, sir, regularly for the last three months, sometimes numbering in their hundreds, cutting across the fields in a single flight.'

'There are no herds of wild horses in the area?'

'Not to my knowledge, sir, not since the grazing lands were fenced.'

'When was the last time the prints appeared?' asked Holmes.

'Two weeks ago to the day, sir.'

'And before that?'

'The Saturday previous, just after dark.'

'That is suggestive,' Holmes replied, but I could not see how.

Later that evening we joined Sir Henry and his daughter in the candlelit retiring room after dinner. Usually by this stage Holmes had a rough idea of what he was up against, but this time he remained uncharacteristically silent on the cause.

'Did your groom have any enemies?' he asked, stroking his thin nose thoughtfully. It was the kind of elementary question he usually had no need of raising.

'None at all,' said Sir Henry, pouring brandies. 'He was also a Crimea veteran. Military men form allegiances that last a lifetime.'

'Men without enemies are rarely found with their throats cut,' muttered Holmes, sinking into his armchair. 'I think I should hear more about this local legend of yours.'

'Then you should speak to Reverend Horniman,' said Sir Henry. 'I understand he is something of an expert on the subject.'

As we retired for bed, Miss Woodham stopped Holmes on the landing, anxious to speak to him beyond the hearing of Sir Henry.

'Mr Holmes, I do believe the Devil is at work here,' she whispered. 'My father is in fear of his life, and even Mr Charlton—usually the most stoic of gentlemen—seems to have taken fright. Something terrible is haunting this house, and you are our last hope.'

'I will do what I can, Miss Woodham, I promise you that.' Holmes laid a reassuring hand on her arm, but would say no more.

The next morning dawned bare and bitter, but dry at least. We walked to the parish church, planning to have a word with the reverend after his first service.

'We are honoured to have encouraged the attention of London's famous consulting detective,' said Rev. Horniman, welcoming us into the now emptied church, 'but this is a terrible business.'

'I was hoping you could enlighten us about your village's strange superstition,' said Holmes.

'I can show you something that has lately come to light concerning the legend, if that would help,' the Reverend offered. He returned from the sacristy bearing a parcel of oilskin cloth and carefully unwrapped it. 'This was found buried in the parish grounds. Our gravedigger was turning sods in preparation for a new grave when his spade stuck something hard.'

Inside the cloth was a glistening medal with an ornate clasp, being in the form of an oak leaf with an acorn at each extremity.

'But why would anyone bury such a thing?' I asked, looking up at Holmes. My companion seemed thunderstruck, and with barely another word set off in the direction of the village. It was all I could do to keep up with him.

'Really, Holmes,' I exclaimed, 'I think you might have been a little more civil to the Reverend, he was only trying to help.'

'Civility has no importance when lives are at stake,' came the reply. 'Come, my friend, we must head back to the Barley Mow.'

'Are we to view the corpse once more?' I ventured.

'No,' said Holmes, 'we must speak with the farmers who drink there.'

We found a surly group of red-faced men in dirty smocks seated around the bar. Holmes had realized that the best way to win them over was to stand a round of drinks, and soon had them talking. I had assumed he would want to prise gossip from them about the stable boy or the head groom, or perhaps about Sir Henry and his treatment of his tenants, but instead Holmes wanted to know about the patterns of the weather.

'This land is dipped between three hills,' said one of the farmers. 'The rain-clouds come a-sweeping over the trees and the air gets trapped, see, so we get more'an our fair share of storms—they start by swirling around in the vale and can't break back out.'

Holmes turned to nudge me. 'It is as I suspected,' he said. 'And can you stout fellows recall the most recent sequence of storms?'

We came away with a full record of recent bad weather attested to by the farmers. I could not see the relevance of this information, and as Holmes hurried us away in the direction of the grange I asked him what he hoped to find.

'I have a part of the puzzle but no more than that,' he admitted. 'To reach the true solution I begin to wonder if I must think the unthinkable. Let us catch up with Sir Henry, for I fear there is another storm coming in that could place him in great danger.'

'A storm?' I cried. 'I realize we are in the countryside where there is a greater risk in such meteorological events, but surely the Major General has nothing to fear from bad weather.'

'It is not the storm Sir Henry has to fear,' replied Holmes, 'but what hides inside it. Tell me, Watson, do you believe Our Majesty when she says that God has chosen the English people to lead the world?'

'Well, I believe she was elected by God to lead our nation, and as she is the head of the most powerful empire on Earth I imagine that gives us great strength.'

'Yes, but is it truly divine right? What if our belief is wrong?'

'It is something I cannot think about, save for the fact that, as a doctor, I believe that all peoples of the earth are created equal, and are just in different stages of development.'

'Hm. Wise words, my friend, but there are some who would find your opinions heresy. Come, we must find Sir Henry before another crime is enacted.'

'Surely you cannot think he is the culprit!' I interrupted.

'No, Watson, but I think the ghosts of his past are unleashing an unstoppable evil upon this estate.'

We reached the hall just as a fresh storm broke overhead. Divesting ourselves of our wet topcoats, we went to find the Major General, but were halted by Miss Woodham.

'There you are,' she said. 'My father was quite unseated by the rising storm and has gone out to await your arrival—did you not pass him? He was going to the top of the drive.'

Holmes uttered an epithet not suited for female ears and turned on his heel. I followed, running to keep his pace. We crossed the torn-up lawn and searched right and left. Sir Henry was standing between the lines of darkening beeches, but it was hard for me to keep sight of him. The rising gale was tearing leaves and even branches across our path.

'Can you hear that?' called Holmes. 'It sounds like voices.'

Indeed, I fancied I heard in the blast of wind that caught my ear the sound of crying voices, in great pain, terror and yes—anger. The sky was bruised in roiling shades of black and brown. 'We must get Sir Henry to safety!' I shouted. 'The stables are at our back.'

With a few long strides, Holmes had seized the old military man and pulled him away, but even as he did so I saw the hoofprints start to appear. They were puckering the soil directly ahead of Sir Henry, thundering toward him. 'This is madness!' I cried. 'It's as if the very gates of Hell are opening!'

The ground spat and tore all around us, clods of earth flying in every direction as the unseen hooves smashed and crushed the earth underfoot. There was a terrible slashing in the air, and Sir Henry flinched as if struck.

Reaching the stables, we tore open the doors and thrust Sir Henry inside. He offered no resistance, and collapsed on the hay bales as we battened down the entrance once more. It was then I saw that he had been cut—not deeply, as Holmes had been able to pull him back from harm, but enough to cause a fast flow of surface blood from his arm. I tore a horse blanket into strips and quickly staunched the bleeding.

As the wind and rain hammered the walls and clattered across the tin roof, thunder smashed so loudly that we could not hear each other speak. And so we remained for half an hour, until the worst of the tempest had passed and escaped to the hills once more.

'What devilry is this?' gasped Sir Henry. 'Please, Mr Holmes, go and make sure that my daughter is safe.'

Holmes went ahead, and I brought the Major General back to the house, but he was much depleted in energy. Upon arrival, I took the liberty of pouring him a brandy, and had one myself. Then I set about cleaning and bandaging his wound.

Feeling that we were safer in assembly, the five of us, Holmes, myself, Miss Woodham, Sir Henry and Charles Charlton gathered in the great room to wait for the clouds to clear, but by now night had fallen. Upstairs, the nurse sat with the mute stable-boy, whose dark eyes continued to stare at the ceiling as if seeing beyond into the blackest reaches of space.

A servant passed through with tapers and lit the room, dispelling some of our fears. We gathered around the fireplace, feeling stronger but no less disturbed.

'Some thirty years ago we all fought the Russians,' said Sir Henry. 'I believe the souls of our dead enemies have returned, to continue their war against us from beyond the grave.'

'I think not,' Holmes replied. 'I can explain in part what is happening, but there is one more piece of the puzzle still to place.'

'Please, Mr Holmes,' entreated Miss Woodham, 'shed any light you can on these terrible visitations.' As she spoke, we heard the wind begin to rise once more, and a fresh squall of rain hit the lead-light windows.

'The storm has circled and is coming back once more,' said Mr Charlton as the candles closest to the window guttered and blew out.

Holmes ignored the noise of the tempest and continued. 'It is said that the forces of nature have the power to open rifts between our world and the next. Each time the Devil's hoofprints have appeared, it has been during a time of natural disruption. This, after all, is the season of storms. As the possessor of one of the finest rational minds in the country, I cannot condone such thinking, you understand, but I appreciate how such beliefs arise. And then there was the matter of the little curate, Reverend Horniman, who set me thinking further.' Holmes dug into his jacket pocket and held up the gold medal. 'Three months ago, at the very time these attacks first started, the Reverend's gravedigger unearthed this medallion in his churchyard. In itself it is a rare enough piece, being awarded to those who fought in the Crimean theatres of war. But this particular one, with the ornate oak leaves on the cross-bar, is given only to those who had direct engagement with the enemy.'

'I have one in my possession,' said Sir Henry. 'My head groom was also in my regiment, and possessed another.'

'Indeed, sir. I took the imposition of checking. You may be aware that there are several other men from your regiment living in this village.'

'After the war, many of the men who had fought together chose to resettle in their old villages, and many recruits came from Devon.'

'But I believe there is another medal like this, with the oak leaf cross bar, held by someone in this very house.' Holmes looked at Mr Charlton.

'The one you found in the churchyard is mine,' said Mr Charlton in shame.

'But why, man?' cried Sir Henry. 'Why would you bury such an honour?'

'Because I could not bear to look at it,' said Mr Charlton. 'For what it represents, and the way it makes me feel. I hoped never to see it again. I determined to bury it soon after receiving it.' He turned to Holmes. 'The other old soldiers in the village don't know, sir. They are not a part of this.'

'A part of what?' coaxed Holmes.

'It was a secret held by only the three of us—and I am the most to blame for I carried out the order.'

'I think you had better tell us the truth now, Mr Charlton,' said Holmes, with urgency in his voice as the storm continued to rise.

'It sounds as if the wind is trying to tear off the roof,' said Miss Woodham, glancing to the ceiling with apprehension.

'You must understand the difficulties we faced, sir,' continued Mr Charlton, as more candles were snuffed out, and only the fluttering flames in the fireplace lit his face. 'The British army was poorly prepared to fight the Russians, and even more ill-equipped for the attack on the Crimean Peninsular. From the shore where we arrived to the battlefield was a lengthy and difficult journey by mule. Lord Cardigan and Lord Lucan were fools too busy baiting one another to take proper care of their troops. Food supplies were dropped at the dock and left to rot because we had no way of getting them to our men.

'It was I who made the decision to requisition the horses for the cavalry officers. I thought I could take them for our comrades, and the food supplies would be delivered by mule through the mountains. I did not know that most of the mules had died, and that without them there was no way of the food getting through.'

'I knew our comrades needlessly died of starvation when they should have lived to fight the enemy,' said Sir Henry, shocked. 'But I did not know of the part you played, Charles.'

'I'm sorry, sir. Believe me, had I known the results of my actions, I would not have acted thus.'

'Then these are not the spirits of avenging Russians, but of our own men!'

'Are there others in the village who are privy to this knowledge?' asked Holmes. 'It is vital that I am in full possession of the facts.'

'No sir,' said Mr Charlton, 'for I made sure that the requisition copies were destroyed. The secret resides solely with me, and now the deed is being punished. The dead do, indeed, return. And the lives of all those who survived in place of their fallen comrades are at risk.'

'Pish,' said Holmes. 'I do not believe in ghosts. You think the spirits of the fallen have been enticed by the Devil to take revenge against you? That they ride from Hades to take your lives?'

'Sir, I know this to be the case, and you have seen the hoofprints yourself, not made by horses but by the cloven-footed devils upon whom the soldiers of the dead must ride, for you see—*they had no horses of their own.*'

'It is madness to consider such superstitious nonsense,' said Holmes, but even as he spoke the wind howled down the chimney, blasting a great inferno of cinders out into the room, extinguishing the few remaining candles. Miss Woodham and myself stamped out the burning coals, but now the far window had blown in, as if the Devil himself was leaning against the walls. The full fury of the storm was attempting to enter the house.

'I must go out there and offer myself,' said Mr Charlton wildly. 'It was I who exposed my guilt before God by burying the medal, and now I must save Sir Henry while there is still time.'

'Listen to me, Mr Charlton,' said Holmes, 'I honestly believe you blame yourself for angering the dead, but it is a storm that caused the churning of the ground, and lightning that slashed the throat of your groom, nothing more.'

'That is not true, Holmes, and you know it!' I cried. 'I saw the wound for myself.'

'You are a man of science, Watson, you cannot believe this too!'

Mr Charlton ran to the door and flung it wide. We started after him, to pull him back into the safety of the room, but we were too late. Charles ran out onto the lawn and shouted at the sky, where a funnel of thick black cloud was spinning down towards the earth.

We felt the ground shake beneath us as great brown clods of mud were torn in a channel that roared toward Mr Charlton like a platoon stampeding through a valley. The 'Phantoms of the Dead', as the stable boy had called them, had returned. We watched in horror as Mr Charlton's body was slowly lifted in the air, punched and twisted this way and that, as if unseen creatures were pushing at him. Blood flew about his face and neck, then his chest and arms, and finally his limbs were torn and stretched until they broke. We could hear each crack and cry from below, where we stood. When he was eventually released and fell, we saw the slashes across his stout form that had parted clothing and flesh all the way to the bone, cutting him to ribbons. Mr Charlton was dead even before he had hit the ground.

A spectacular flash of lightning illuminated the scene. For a brief second I saw—or fancied I saw—the fiery horned devils who bore the dead on their backs, armed with unsheathed cavalry swords. And then they were gone, thundering back into the rolling clouds, born away by the tempestuous night.

'No more!' Holmes slammed the doors shut at his back, leaving the fallen man outside.

'No, Mr Holmes, now there is only me, and I am an old man whose time has come,' said Sir Henry, as his daughter ran to his side.

'Father, the Devil has had his due,' exclaimed Miss Woodham. 'Mr Charlton has made right his terrible mistake.'

'Perhaps that is so,' said Sir Henry, 'for there is no greater crime than when an officer has made his own men suffer.'

'You are wrong, sir,' said Holmes with some passion. 'The greater crime is to engage the enemy in the sure belief that God is on your side.' He turned to me. 'Come, Watson, I feel we should return to London tonight. There is nothing more to be done here.'

I had never seen my friend in a mood like this. He was angry. Not detached and analytical, but furious that he was being forced to face the impossible and consider it real. I felt sure that back in London he would bury his doubts once more in work and the syringe.

My last view of Sir Henry was as a sickly old man being comforted by his daughter, slumped in his armchair before the dying fire, disturbed by doubts that he might have spent his life believing in things that were not true.

Holmes and I returned to London, but during the long train journey home we did not speak of the case again, for fear that it might have awoken a chasm between us that no amount of reason could ever fill.

HONOR OAK RESERVOIR IS UNDERNEATH A GOLF COURSE IN Peckham, Thornhill reminds himself as he walks. That's the biggest subterranean vault he's ever visited, an inverted cathedral that's the largest reservoir in Europe, with four great chambers that hold 256 million litres of water, a great heart made of orange brick that ceaselessly pumps life into the metropolis. He would have liked to work on the new Brixton extension at Honor Oak but there wasn't a position, so he's back here in the tube tunnels beneath King's Cross, moving through the dead dusty air, looking for circuit faults. He comes down every night at midnight and goes up at 4:00am; that doesn't sound hard but there are meetings before and sometimes after, and while you're down you're on the move the whole time.

Looking back, he can see the unmistakable silhouette of Sandwich hopping nimbly across the rails. Sandwich's real name is Lando—he was named after a character in a Star Wars film, and hates it—his mates call him Sandwich because no-one has ever seen him eat, even though he's the size of a bear.

Thornhill has been down for three years now, and likes the job. The perks are good, his fellow workers are a nice bunch and he gets regular health check-ups chucked in for free. They're all outsiders, of course, men and women who work down here because they've joined a veritable foreign legion of employees who go below to forget.

But he doesn't forget. He goes down in order to remember.

'Early nineteen thirties,' calls Sandwich in that peculiarly high voice of his, 'Holborn Kingsway tram station. E/3 class double deckers. Wouldn't have minded driving them.' Everyone down here is a bit of an expert on some aspect of the transport system. Some of them could bore for England.

'Why didn't you become a driver?' Thornhill calls back.

'Couldn't pass the eye test,' Sandwich explains. 'Short-sighted. When I was a kid I always wanted to drive the 1938 red tube stock, varnished wood interiors, red and green finish, shovel lampshades. They've still got a few on the Isle of Wight.'

'That figures.'

'When they brought in the '67 Victoria Line carriages I reckon it took most of the fun away, anyway.' After that, drivers only had to press two buttons, one to operate the doors and one to start the train. Driving a train now was not much more than an exercise in staying awake.

'You've got an N3 up ahead,' calls Sandwich. 'First stop.' They're heading south on the Kennington branch of the Northern Line between King's Cross and Euston, checking all the junction boxes, looking for an intermittent fault that's showing up on the grid as an irregular power loss—inconsistent and too brief to disrupt service but a break all the same. Usually there's four of them working together, but tonight the other crew have been sent up to Highbury & Islington where one of the cleaners has found debris on the line. They've gone to see if any overhead cabling staples have come loose; it could be dangerous if they've fallen on the rails.

Thornhill is in boots and the orange boiler suit that makes him look like a Guantanamo Bay inmate. He raises his cage-lamp and aims the light on his helmet in the direction of the box, fixed on the wall at head-height where the main tunnel meets one of the side tubes leading away from the now-defunct Thameslink station on Pentonville Road. Such side-tunnels are rarely filled and capped. Most get used for equipment storage. Many just remain empty, and a few which run parallel to the main lines are kept clear in case of emergency, a euphemism for terrorist acts, and even the underground staff don't know exactly where these are located.

Digging his key from his tool-satchel, he unlocks the lid of the box and peers inside. Two rows of green LEDs tell him that all contacts are working perfectly. He's pretty sure that an intermittent fault would register as a flickering light or a red, in which case he'd simply replace the connector. 'Clear,' he tells Sandwich. 'How many more on this run?'

'Eighteen,' says Sandwich, checking his chart. 'They go all the way down to Goodge Street.'

'That's going to take us all night. What if it's something we can't fix?'

'Then someone will have to come down with specialist equipment and run a day-test on the line,' says Sandwich, who has caught up with him.

'Do you know where all the boxes are?' asks Thornhill.

'They're all on the main southbound except the ones between Euston and Warren Street.' Sandwich hands him a sheet with a diagram overlaid on their section of the tube map. He taps his thumb on the remaining pages thoughtfully. 'We could still finish on time if we split up,' he suggests. Crews are always supposed to operate in pairs, just in case one gets injured or suffers an attack of nerves. It doesn't happen very often; the LU workers know the dangers and are a pretty careful lot. Sandwich knows that if they take half the line each they can be back before four, and no-one will be any the wiser so long as they clock off together before the power is turned back on at 4:15am.

'I guess that would be okay,' says Thornhill somewhat hesitantly, knowing he will be in breach of contract by agreeing. Sandwich has spent his entire working life so far down here. The tunnels hold no terrors for him.

'You all right?' asks Sandwich. 'Only when you didn't come in last week...'

'I told you, I had a cold,' Thornhill quickly explains.

'I thought maybe—the cut on your hand.'

Thornhill hides his bandaged knuckles behind his back, self-conscious. 'That's nothing. I'd had a few. I get a bit angry sometimes.'

Sandwich is thinking it through, picking at the thought like a scab. 'Because Thornhill's not actually your name, is it? I only noticed because you left your mobile in the office and saw that it's registered in a different name. I know it's none of my business—'

'You're right,' snaps Thornhill, 'it is none of your business.'

'I mean, we all come down for different reasons. But there's also a reason why there are checks in place, you know? I'm not talking about terrorism or nothing like that.'

'I think I know what you're talking about.'

'You didn't get the Honor Oak job, so you came back down here.' It wasn't a question.

'I didn't mind where I went, so long as it was underground.'

'Fine.' Sandwich knows better than to ask why. As he says, everyone has their reasons. 'Look, I'll go down to Tottenham Court Road and start from that end, you work from here and we should meet up at Warren Street by about three thirty.' Without waiting for a reply, Sandwich nips over the rails to the far side of the tunnel and sets off, whistling something that sounds like 'It's A Long Way To Tipperary'. Moments later, Thornhill finds himself quite alone.

He has never worked alone down here before, but he's always known that the practice went on among the more experienced crews. He isn't frightened quite the reverse—but it still feels strange. Sandwich is a nice guy, a bit of a sad case since his girlfriend left him, but he never stops talking, never stops prying and asking questions, and the endless to-and-fro of vapid conversation never gives Thornhill time to be alone with his thoughts. Which is a pity, because there's still a lot to think about.

The faint swaying light from Sandwich's helmet in the tunnel ahead disappears, but there's still not total darkness. Somewhere further on to the left, in the curve of the ceiling, there is a grating that allows in a nimbus of pale luminescence.

He reaches the second junction box at a point where the main line meets a smaller service tunnel, and stops within the circle of darkness to listen. He can feel a cool breeze lifting the hairs at the base of his neck. The Tube is beset by these dark zephyrs that eddy and swirl where tunnels meet. You can faintly hear the passing air, but nobody knows where it comes from or why it disappears as suddenly as it starts. Before the 1970s, an army of women used to enter the system after the last train had run. They were called Fluffers, and their job was to remove all the dust-balls, flakes of skin and human hair that had gathered in the tunnels. People always leave traces of themselves.

Improved ventilation has removed the need for the Fluffers now, so that the only human beings who venture down here after the Tube stops running are the ones making electrical repairs or inspecting water damage. Most of the deeper stations have problems with underground wells, rivers, streams and conduits that periodically back up, and it's not a good idea to have water dripping onto electrical equipment.

The LEDs in the second box form two unbroken emerald lines. The fault lies further on, so he'll have to go deeper. All of the tunnels heading south descend toward the Thames, which is why the passages are fitted with flood gates. Thornhill can feel the temperature dropping as he sets off once more, passing beneath the dull glow of the grating, turning into the next great brick curve. The steel lines glint coldly in the beam of his lamp. Nests of mice, tiny brown bundles of fur that look as if they belong in country wheatfields instead of the London underground system, turn their black beads timidly up at him before scampering for cover. He approaches another tunnel entrance, D117 according to his diagram, and wonders if it's the one that was used as emergency headquarters for the wartime Railway Executive Committee. He's read a lot about the tube system since—he's read a lot. He can see there's no track leading inside, and the dust has settled thick and undisturbed, far removed from commuters and cleaners.

And there, standing in the tunnel entrance, swaying very slightly, is a young man of about fifteen or sixteen, his outline barely discernable. 'Can you help me?' he asks very politely, but in the kind of cockney accent Thornhill associates with old British films. He shines his torch on the lad's face, and is surprised to see that despite a neat short-back-and-sides haircut he is covered in dried mud. He wears a dirty collarless white shirt, braces and brown flannel trousers with thick turn-ups. The trousers are wet to the knees, as if he has been wading through water. 'Sir? Can you help me?' he asks again.

'What are you doing down here?' asks Thornhill, surprised to find himself unalone.

'I ought to be out of London,' he says apologetically. 'You know, like the poster.'

'What poster?'

'There's a drawing, a cartoon like, of a warden telling off a boy. *You ought not to be in London.* The Ministry of Health evacuation scheme. We didn't go. My old man thought it was for cowards.'

'I'm sorry, I'm not with you.'

'Where am I?'

'Euston interchange. I mean—you're underneath Euston Station. How did you get here?'

'Came up from Balham,' says the lad, dusting his sleeves. 'Cor, you should have seen the mess down there. A right old state. It bounced clear down the steps and into the northbound tunnel before it went off—buried the whole length of the platform in gravel, blew out the walls, ruptured the water mains and flooded the platform three feet deep. You should have heard the screaming. Shocking, it was. Hundred and eleven.'

'What?'

'Hundred and eleven dead so far. We was sheltering down there, six hundred of us kipping like sardines. The girl two down from me had both legs blown clean off. The escalators came down, then there was another bang and we looked up through the dust—we couldn't hardly see anything—and there was only a bloody bus, gone and driven right into the crater. I think the driver got out all right.'

'How did you get out?' Thornhill asks, puzzled.

'Well, we didn't.' The boy shakes his head in sleepy wonderment. His eyelids close and open again. There's dust on them.

'Do you need to get up top?'

'Can't. Staying down here now. But I thought you might know if I'm going the right way for Bromley-By-Bow. I've got relatives over there.'

Thornhill knows he should feel absurd giving directions to a dead man, but tonight it seems like a perfectly natural thing to do. When he's finished explaining the route, his companion smiles wanly and sets off once more with a little backward wave. Thornhill stands and watches until his form has faded into the dry black air of the tunnel. He admires the lad's determination.

The next junction box proves impossible to open. Water has calcified the lock, so he is forced to chip away with the end of a screwdriver for twenty minutes before he can unlatch it, and the wasted time sets him back. The connections are all functioning, though, so he closes it and continues downward.

Sometimes the dessicated air sets off an ache behind his eyes, but tonight he feels fine, rather light-headed and slow, as if he is sinking into a dream. He runs the tips of his fingers along the curving wall, over the sooty fat trunks of cables, heading toward the next box. It's darker now, no overhead light seeping in from anywhere, and the breeze is moaning faintly at his back. That's when he notices the sound of another man, deliberate footfalls planted behind his own. He turns and waits, staring into the dark until it pixilates into the fractured vision of a migraine.

He doesn't like this one.

'Oi, didn't you hear me?' the man calls, his voice an angry slur. Thornhill waits until he is approached, then steps back against the concave tunnel wall. Now he sees the reason for the man's strange speech; he has no lower jaw. He is as repulsive and ridiculous as a ventriloquist's puppet. His tongue hangs straight down, dry and useless, looking as though it belongs to a dog, or perhaps on a piece of luggage. He's dressed in a purple velvet jacket, tall and bony-featured, also missing his right ear and eye—the wounds don't look too bad because they've scabbed over—but he's salivating unstoppably as he shuffles closer, something Thornhill finds personal and vaguely embarrassing. 'D'you work down here?' the man demands to know, seemingly oblivious to his terrible injuries. It's hard to understand him.

Thornhill can smell strong alcohol on his breath. 'Yes,' he admits, 'but I'm not a doctor. I can't help you.' He assumes they only approach if they want something.

'I'd had a drink, of course I had, but it's the others you should be talking to.' He's very animated for a dead man.

'What others?'

'They were on the platform with me. Last train of the night from Bank Station, we'd all been drinking at the Christmas bash. I didn't slip.'

'You mean one of them pushed you?'

'I don't know, probably. Yeah, I mean yes they did.' It sounds like he's had plenty of time to convince himself.

'When was this?' Thornhill asks, starting to understand the nature of his visions.

'December 18th 1976,' says the man, shovelling his tongue back up into his mouth without much success. 'I hate it down here. I want to kill my mates for doing this, for pushing me. I want to go home.'

'Where is home?'

'West Harrow.'

'You'll need to follow the Metropolitan line from King's Cross,' says Thornhill. 'Go back in that direction.' For a moment he thinks the man will take a swing at him, but the poor creature turns around, almost overbalancing, and slams his hand into the wall, popping his knuckles. Then he heads away without another word. Something is leaking from his ragged jeans. Presumably he slipped from the platform and went under the incoming train. What a state to be in.

Thornhill had always half-expected this day to come. He had thought—hoped—that perhaps he would see them, but had not expected them to speak, or be able to hear him. His heart is beating faster and he feels even more light-headed. He wonders if he is having some form of nervous breakdown, alone here in the tunnels, going quietly mad while the rest of the crews plug leaks and check the tracks for debris.

He knows he should probably turn back and hand the remainder of the task to someone else, but he hates to leave a job unfinished, and besides—

For some unearthly reason he finds himself crying. Once the tears start, it's very hard to make them stop. He forces himself to think about the intermittent fault, checks the diagram and heads down beyond the Euston interchange in the direction of Warren Street. Plenty of tunnels around him now, gaping black mouths like bellowing monsters, who knows where they all lead? Some of them aren't even marked on his map, as if they're hiding secrets. They snake deep inside the soil of the city, burrowing beneath London in a dark carnival of stone. The arteries provide homes to who-knows-what, the dead lost and separated from the living.

It feels like he's been walking for hours. His boots are too tight and his legs are tired. He has checked eight boxes and found nothing wrong. Coming up to the ninth he starts to wonder if there really is a fault, or whether one of the controllers has simply misread a meter. But below this consideration is excitement and fear running like a fast-flowing river, the knowledge that everything he has dared to believe is being proved true.

According to his watch it's already 3:00am, and he has yet to locate the fault.

Something small and light brushes against his hair in the blackness, making him start. He swipes his right ear, batting it away, but there is another feather-shred flitting past, and another. And he can smell something now; the odour of cooking meat, as if he might enter the next tunnel bend and find a hamburger stand waiting to serve him. The specks touching his face and neck become more frequent. He grabs at one and rubs it between his fingers in the light of his helmet-torch. It is a smut, a drifting cinder. He sniffs it and knows at once that it is incinerated material of some kind, and his stomach shifts. He turns off the cage-lamp and his helmet-torch, and stands motionless in the pitch blackness, looking ahead. Sure enough, there's a parabola of flickering light around the corner.

It takes him several minutes to pass beyond the wide bend in the tunnel, and here the rails are tricky to negotiate because they pass through several sets of greased points. At first he thinks there are dozens of mattresses lying across the floor, but as he gets closer he realizes there are bodies wedged between the rails. Some are burning softly from within, like dying embers in grates. At the far end he can see a wall of twisted grey metal torn apart and fused with the surrounding brickwork, fires burning brightly inside. The exploded train carriage entirely blocks the tunnel. Even the trunking, the bundles of thick cables that form necklace loops along the tunnel walls, has been severed by the force of the explosion. Heading this way, ghostly in the pulsing firelight, hands upon each other's shoulders like Bruegel's parable of the blind leading the blind, the commuters seek a way to the surface, but as he approaches they disappear in whisps of burning dust. After all, they are the living, and have no place here among the dead.

Passing between the fallen bodies, ignoring the groans and the smell of roasting flesh, he walks on toward the source of the heat, knowing that it will disperse along with this apocalyptic vision. A temporal memory sealed beneath the streets in shafts of stone, forever trapped in the terrible moment of a July afternoon, the seventh day of the seventh month in 2005, when a terrorist bomb stole the lives of thirty seven passengers and injured seven hundred more. The dead must stay down here forever. Only the living may surface.

The present cannot exist for long with the past, and so the wreckage disperses, the wavering chain of survivors, each placing the next foot before the last with patience and determination, crumbles along its length and disappears, leaving only acrid dispersing smoke and the melancholy hubbub of departing spirits.

Thornhill stands alone once more. What shocks him most is not the scale of destruction but the sheer caprice of it all. He imagines a thousand families asking the same question he has asked over and over; why did it happen to us? Why were we singled out? But of course to provide an answer one needs to understand the workings of life itself. And life must remain unknowable for the spirit to survive.

Beyond the crash site the tunnel is clear. He can see the eleventh junction box in the halo of his torch. He unlocks the door and with difficulty, pulls it open.

There it is, right there, the fault. A winking crimson light on the second row, beyond which there are no more greens. Feeling in his tool-bag he locates a connector, snaps off the plastic end, flips the old one out and replaces it. Then he resets the switch and watches as the lines complete themselves. Job done.

He's running late. He'll have to move faster if he wants to reach Warren Street in time to catch Sandwich. He'd like to linger back here. He senses the others are drawn upwards, if not exactly toward the light then at least to a point where the layer between the living and the dead is thinnest. But he can't afford to keep Sandwich waiting.

One thing puzzles him. There has been nothing before this night, no sign that they might appear around him, no reason why they should all turn up now. Perhaps he wasn't ready before.

He's ready now.

He once read that those who die by the hand of another are the easiest to see. At the far end of the scale are those who die natural deaths—they can never return. But what about the ones whose departures are simply accidental? What does it take to see them?

The temperature is dipping lower and the air is slightly damper. He fancies he can smell the river, but at least four stations stand between him and the Thames. The tunnel twists to the right, then to the left. He is passing close to the southbound Victoria line and descending fast. That's when he understands, of course. Finally knows what he is doing. He's known all along but denial is a powerful drug that can erase almost any other feeling. He reaches the Victorian line sub-junction and descends via the service tunnel to the lower line.

Time is getting short, but he dare not run; there are transverse pipes that can trap your boot and twist it. After three years of travelling through this subterranean maze he always knows exactly where he is. Right now he is branching off beneath Tottenham Court Road, moving in the direction of Warren Street. Above him are a pair of pubs, a shabby terrace of shops and houses that lead to Fitzroy Square. He remembers how the square looked when he was working nearby on an electrical installation in a bank; the pavements were all dug up. One had a hole running all the way down to the underground line.

Down.

It comes to him in a flash. The answer has always been right in front of him, but the time had never been right until now. He finally understands, and is ready. He looks at his watch. 4:23am. The power is back on throughout the underground system. Sandwich will be up by now, angrily wondering where he is.

Thornhill looks down at the rails. Without hesitation he steps up on them and hops from one to the other, crossing the track to the far side of the tunnel. Halfway across he stops, balancing on the third rail. Slowly and deliberately he plants his right foot down on the ground. He has a strange sensation, unpleasant but momentary. It leaves him with a feeling of transformation, of departure and arrival. Then he continues to the opposite wall and waits.

It isn't long before she appears on the other side of the line, outlined against the wet black brick. She has round brown eyes, dark hair cropped in a French bob, a chequered skirt, a navy blue sweater and knee socks, just as he remembered. So like her mother. She looks over and gravely acknowledges him.

He loves the way children do that, the way they look when they're counting and concentrating, taking everything at face value, being very serious. 'Hello,' he says.

'Where's Mummy?'

'She couldn't be here, Amy. She had to go far away. She lives in another country now. But I'm here.'

'I thought you weren't coming.'

'I didn't know what to do, but I'm here now.'

'It's boring. All the tunnels looks the same. I can't find Jasper.'

'Jasper wasn't with you when—Jasper was back at the house.' Jasper is Amy's teddy bear. On the day she had accompanied him to his job, he had made her leave it at home. *There's no room for Jasper and your bike in the car*, he had told her. If only he had made her leave the bike behind instead.

She had not been allowed to enter the bank's hard-hat area, and had gone to cycle in the little green park, the one at the centre of Fitzroy Square. He remembered thinking there was something wrong and running out into the street. Her bicycle lay on its side, next to the workman's hole. She had dropped something—a pendant from her bracelet, just a cheap little thing—it had fallen in, and she had gone to pick it up. At first he couldn't see her. It didn't seem possible she could have fallen so far.

'Where have you been?' Amy asks.

'I've been working down here, looking for you.'

'But I've been here all the time.' Her tone is reproachful.

'I know, sweetie, I just couldn't reach you. If my boss knew I'd taken the job just to find you, he wouldn't have let me come down tonight.'

'Why do I have to stay here?'

'The world above was just a dream,' he murmurs. 'I think this is where our real lives are.'

'Are you going to stay with me?'

His heart swells to bursting as he rushes back toward her. 'Yes, of course I am. That's why I'm here.' He takes her hand and it feels just as it did when she was alive, warm and dry. Her touch completes him. 'Where would you like to go?'

'I don't want to go any further down.' She tips her head on one side, considering the question carefully. 'Up perhaps. Can we go up?'

'I don't know,' he admits. 'We can try.' Sweeping her into his arms, he holds her close, letting her warmth envelop him. Then he sets off with his lost daughter, heading back up the tunnel, toward the world that will always be just above, and only slightly out of reach.

THE STRETCH

WE SHOULD NEVER HAVE GOT THE STRETCH.

It was meant to be a ten-passenger stretch Lincoln limousine with chrome wheels and opalescent pearl white paintwork, but the thing outside Sofie's parents' house in her street looked like a chop-job, even though it took up three parking spaces. Sofie didn't notice. When she saw it she screamed and batted the air with her arms and jumped up and down. Sofie screamed a lot, sometimes when she didn't get her own way, and other times when she did. It was kind of confusing. She screamed to us in the lounge, where we'd been doing the photos.

'Oh my God!' Her high voice rose to a level that could attract bats, climaxing on the added first syllable of God. 'It's here, the car's here!

Her best friend Bethany joined her in a descant scream. She also waved her arms and jumped up and down at the window.

'Aaaaah! It's here!'

The pair of them reacted to everything as if they'd just won a fucking game show, I swear. It was as if they thought there were cameras on them and five million people were watching.

'This is going to be the best birthday ever after my own fifteenth, which was just so awesome.' Last month Bethany went to Disneyland Paris dressed as an angel, albeit one with a bare midriff and a septic belly piercing, and she wasn't about to let anyone forget it, ever.

I could see Sofie toying with the idea of reminding her that this was just one part of the week-long celebrations paid for by her father, but then she decided to be gracious, which was a first for her. The pair of them copied their nanosecond-popular TV heroines in every way. This particular month they were over Hannah Montana and into The Veronicas, over the Jonas Brothers and into Black Eyed Peas again, over Pink and Beth Orton and into Ryder, over Twitter and into Kjangi, still loving Lady GaGa, back into Scott Pilgrim and hating everyone over twenty. They knew more about hair care, fashion, dating and the rites-of-passage rituals of teenaged girls than any style magazine could ever know in a million years, because style mags employed burned out jackal-skanks who were like twenty two at least, and besides as teenagers it was their job, it was what they did, even though they were from Dulwich, a shitty composition of commuter-belt boredom arranged for angry families in mock-Tudor mansions.

Sofie and Bethany were dressed in shimmering icing-pink and white, and thought they looked so hot. I mean. What they looked like was underage hoes in need of parental deprogramming.

See, girls like Sofie and Bethany aren't cutting-edge, they're not looking for the next big thing, they're the majority. Individually they have no power, but they're victorious through sheer weight of numbers. Like the Nazis almost were.

Unfortunately they had to take me with them for the evening. We didn't exactly relate, mainly because I wore black eye-shadow and read books. I was going through a phase where I liked movies with subtitles and German-sounding bands, and I guess I looked a little blankly at them when their conversation turned to boys or new methods of delivering lip gloss. I had to go along because my mother was getting frisky with Bethany's father, if I can say that without having to stick my fingers down my throat, and her old man wanted someone sensible in attendance. Believe me, I wasn't too thrilled to be going along with the Scream Sisters, either.

The plan was to hire a stretch limo, drive around London and go to the Buddha Bar on the embankment, but it turned out we weren't old enough to be admitted to a nightclub serving alcohol, so the itinerary had to be changed to include a stop at the Tropical Café and a visit to Glitterball, a skanky teens-only disco at the butthole-end of Camden Town.

I could see the driver watching our approach with horror in his heart. He said his name was Korfa, which sounded like a Greek starter. He was tall and bony, and had a treeline of beard growth, and wore cheap-copy mirrored shades, and looked bored to death, as if he hated his work intensely, except I kept catching him admiring himself in the wing mirror. He looked Somali—I knew what Somalis looked like because I used to see them when I had a summer job in the supermarket. We don't have black people in Dulwich.

Unsmiling, he held open the door while we climbed into the stretch. The interior reeked of furniture polish. Sofie took ages to settle herself because she wanted the whole street to see us, but there was no-one around. The men paid for living in Dulwich by working a sixty hour week, and the women were always off waxing themselves. I got this particular stretch from the internet because it was fifty pounds cheaper than anyone else's. Most of Korfa's clients were booked for hen nights or teenage birthday parties. It was probably a great job if you were a pedophile, but this guy looked as if his only fantasies involved getting off work early.

I stared out of the Lincoln's tinted windows with a sinking heart. I just hoped nobody could see me in such an embarrassing car. I would have thought it was cool once, but in the last few months I'd begun to feel separated from the others. I guess I was becoming more serious-minded and adult in my outlook. The antics of my so-called girlfriends were sweet and silly, but they belonged to a childhood I was leaving behind. There were probably still good times to be had together, but my interest in their world had evaporated. The endless chatter about sex, music and clothes seemed repetitive and pointless because they never drew any conclusions from what they were saying. I could see their futures; they would marry and remain in the neighbourhood, but I wanted to go far away as fast as I possibly could. I knew there would soon come a time when they'd look at me with total disdain, conveniently tagging me as part of a world to which they didn't belong. But I thought, why shouldn't we have fun for now? They were sweet kids underneath the makeup, kind of flirty, kind of flighty, but it was their age—the gap of a few months between us had become a huge desert, enough for me to look upon them as children. They knew it, and I knew it. I just hoped Sofie hadn't worked out why it had happened.

The driver showed us how to turn on the intercom, how to unlock the laminated drinks cabinet (soft beverages only) and how to operate the sound system, but none of it felt right, like the interior had been stripped out and poorly rebuilt. Then he slipped inside and sat in the heat of the car's interior, waiting for Sofie and Bethany to calm down.

'It smells like somebody died in here,' Bethany complained. 'Hey, can you turn the air-con on?'

The driver pressed a button, then slid the partition shut so that he wouldn't have to hear Sofie's excited screeching. I could tell by the look on his face that he was thinking *Shit, the one with the blonde bunches is really annoying.*

Sofie had swiped vodka from her mother's cupboard, and had even printed out some cocktail recipes so we knew which mixers to use. Bethany had filched a joint from her brother, although there was nowhere to smoke it. She plugged in her iPod and jacked up the sound, a girl band mix that even I liked. The stretch coasted over the cambers of the suburban roads like a carnival float, and joined the evening traffic to the West End.

It was 6:00pm on a hot, muggy and slightly wet July night, the clouds clamped in a brown lid over the buildings, but we were girls on the town and at least two of us were dressed to make men weep. In photographs I took before we left the house, Sofie and Bethany were devastating; there was a still-ness in their knowing eyes. They had slightly parted lips, swept-back hair, limp pale arms, long thin thighs. Their outfits had the accidental effect of making them look like Victorian schoolchildren in a divinity play, at least until they opened their mouths. Me, I stayed out of the frame. I don't do pictures. I don't want something to turn up on Facebook twenty years later, thank you.

'The driver's seriously fucking sexy,' said Bethany, 'but I don't think he speaks any English.'

'He doesn't need to speak, does he?' said Sofie. 'I saw him looking at your legs as you got in. He's a bit old for you, though, twenty at least.'

'Fuck right off. I'd have a go on him. He's got massive feet.'

'That's because he's—' She mouthed the word 'black'. 'They're used to walking around without shoes.'

I tuned out of their trash-talk. Mostly, they copied stuff they'd seen on TV. I watched the street slide past the window; takeaway, betting shop, pizzeria, pub, Oxfam, café, minicab firm, the same drab parades endlessly reordered like a playlist with a limited selection of bad songs, the same dumpy figures loading white plastic bags into their homes. I looked back at the others, who were waiting to hand me a glass with some lurid pink concoction in it.

'Come on Jennifer, wish me happy birthday,' said Sofie, raising her drink. She toasted us, but the glasses were plastic and couldn't provide the ring of celebration.

The partition slid open. The driver leaned his head back and tapped a long forefinger on a notice taped to the glass; 'Do not spill drinks on seats'. Sofie pulled a face and giggled once the partition closed. She had a nervous energy that unsettled me, like an actor finding little bits of business to perform in the background of a play, and the more she did it, the more nervous she made everyone else. There's a tension around a birthday that can break like the end of a hot day.

We were finishing our third drink as the stretch hit the great grey field of Trafalgar Square. Bethany opened the window and yelled at passers-by.

'Beth, don't be such a chav,' said Sofie, pulling her back into her seat.

'What's the point of having a limo if they can't fucking see you?' The vodka had flushed Bethany red to her bleached blonde roots. She shimmered and shook with slender threads of Tiffany jewelry, gifts granted by her parents in exchange for buying time away from her. Bethany's folks had a pool they never swim in, a sauna they never used and two children they preferred to forget. I think Bethany wore their presents to remind them she was still there.

We sat among the plastic ferns of the Tropical Café and ate tough, dry pineapple burgers while electronic bird-calls bleated around us. As I chewed and tuned out the chatter, I studied the dust-caked tops of the fake palms and figured that the cleaners were probably Filipino, because they obviously couldn't reach the tops to clean them. Half the restaurant's space was taken up by a retail outlet peddling winsome ethnic tat to children. The whole enterprise struck me as cynically manipulative, but nobody else seemed to mind. I finished my shake and the conversation faded back in.

Bethany was explaining some kind of complex arrangement with her sister. 'Danii said she was going to stay out with him, because he's got a car, and Mum said if you do you needn't come back, so she said you can't tell me what to do anymore, it's just because you don't approve of Jack, and Mum goes as long as you live under this roof—'

Then I drifted away again. I was sitting under a freezing air-con unit, so I started thinking of polar reaches, of blue translucent ice rising in wind-sculpted scoops above a dark and violent sea. I tried to imagine being so cold that you couldn't feel your body. What would it be like to become stranded at the top of the world, with nothing and no-one to save you? The arctic wind cutting across the floes and stinging like needles, scouring away everything except the moment, the water a sharp blue glass that could draw me in and suck me down into its depths. And then I was back at the table, watching Bethany suck a glittery pink soda from a blue plastic parrot. I wondered what they put in it to make it sparkle like that, iron filings perhaps.

'Jen? Come back, honey, we're about to be sung to.' Sofie and Bethany were staring at me. Three waiters wiggled between the tables with a sickly chocolate cake covered in sparklers. They sang, but it turned out two of them didn't know the lyrics to 'Happy Birthday', so they just mumbled along. The third carried the song, then encouraged the other diners to applaud, but nobody could be bothered. If they couldn't wish someone happy birthday, I wondered what they thought about the rain forests.

By the time we finished the cake and Bethany had queued to buy a cuddly gorilla for £19.99, we were running late. It had started to rain. Korfa was seated in the stretch around the corner from the restaurant, half asleep. He flashed a look of annoyance when Sofie knocked on the window, but smartly stepped out to let us in. Bethany made a show of entering the Lincoln, but nobody was looking at her. It was hot and oppressive, rising toward a rainstorm, the way London always spoils things on a summer night.

'You know what we should do,' said Bethany, 'we should pick up a cute guy and invite him along with us.'

'So not happening.' Sofie waved away the idea with her fingertips, as if drying her nails. 'This is a girls' night out, remember?'

'Okay, whatever, only don't complain that you didn't have anything to remember your birthday by, yeah?' Bethany snapped back. 'Pour us a drink, for fuck's sake.'

We arrived at Glitterball, an old warehouse with a fake stressed-steel frontage, to find a queue of sour-faced inner city teenagers who scanned us as if we were dirt. Sofie had instructed Korfa to drive right up to the club's entrance, so that we could disembark in front of the crowd, but the bouncer made us stand behind everyone else, which took the edge off our big entrance.

Korfa picked his nails and read the paper, ignoring us as we stood in the softly falling rain waiting to get inside. 'I fucking hate him,' Bethany told Sofie. 'We're the clients and he looks at us like we're fucking trash or something.'

'He's got a boring job,' I pointed out, 'I don't think he means any harm.'

'If it's so boring, why doesn't go back to his own country and tend cattle for a living?'

'Let it go, Beth.'

'No, you let it go, Jen-if-ferr,' Bethany barked back, her hands on her narrow hips. 'You've been looking down your nose at us all evening like we're shit on your shoes, honey. It's all so beneath you, isn't it? I don't know why you wanted to come in the first place.' Bethany wasn't really angry; she just enjoyed finding drama in situations and acting as if she was in some kind of crappy American rom-com.

'I came because it's Sofie's birthday,' I explained.

'You don't really like her, though, do you? Ever since—'

'What?' I dared her.

Thankfully the line suddenly started to move, and we found ourselves inside. The club was chocolate-box gaudy and overheated, a smart racket created by someone with an ugly empty building and an angle for sucking money out of teenagers. The ancient DJ cranked up old Girls Aloud hits that no-one wanted to dance to. They couldn't have been more badly mixed if he'd used a plastic bucket and a stick. We stood at the edge of the floor making fun of the boys while Sofie tipped vodka into our Red Bulls. Bethany sulked because Sofie had taken over a conversation with a cute boy, and had been so charming and attentive that she'd driven him away. But then Sofie met another boy called Jamie who looked like a black wig on a stick and who tried to convince us that he was an art student at Goldsmith's, and within a few minutes they were feverishly snogging.

By the time we returned to the stretch with the godawful Jamie in tow, it was almost 10:00pm. Sofie's father had instructed her to be home by eleven. Her mother lived in Wimbledon with an Indian property developer, and hadn't been in contact since the previous Christmas. By now it was so muggy that I could smell my body beneath my signature scent, and I wanted to go home for a shower. The entire evening had been my idea of Hell.

By now, Korfa had dropped all pretense of civility. He didn't like having an extra passenger on board and he stared at us in his mirror as if we were aliens. The stretch grazed through bleak streets on its way back to the suburbs, and the mood in the car was downbeat. We were on our second bottle of vodka and Jamie was virtually chewing Sofie's face off when Bethany slid to the front of the compartment and opened the partition, and started desperately chatting up Korfa, and I was just wishing it was over.

Jamie spoke, but I couldn't understand a word he said. He had a coolness impediment that stopped him from being able to talk properly or make any sense. Sofie translated; she wanted to go with him to buy some dope. She was fifteen and wanted to do a drug run. Classy. I asked her if perhaps she would like to go and have some facial tattoos while she was at it. By now we were running through the kind of neighborhood where you expected to see the odd burning car, but Jamie was apparently from around here, and tried to convince us it was OK. I asked what had happened to the joint we had, and they just looked blankly at me, dissolving into giggles.

By now Bethany was hanging her thin arms through the partition, keeping up a non-stop barrage of conversation with Korfa. Sofie's mouth was occupied with Jamie's slug-like tongue, so that left me by myself, which was fine in my book. And Sofie broke off the tongue-wrestle to command Korfa to stop the car.

We were between a Seven-Eleven that was a cross between a rubbish dump and a needle exchange, and a block of council flats that had steel grilles riveted over the ground floor windows. Jamie announced that this was where he lived, and he'd just run up to his apartment for a minute 'to get something'. Sofie looked at the street, pulled a face and said no way, do you think I'm mad or something, so we drove on to a shopping parade with bleached strip-lighting and plenty of people.

Then I noticed Sofie and Jamie were conspiring, and she suddenly announced that they were going to the off-license to buy beer, and they'd be back in twenty minutes. Twenty minutes to buy beer? But before I could argue they were laughing and getting out and gone, and I looked through the store window but couldn't see them. A moment later, Bethany was whispering something to Korfa, and he reluctantly got out of the car and held the door open for her, and she smiled secretively at me and said they'd be back in a few minutes, and the pair of them went off down the skanky alleyway at the side of the parade. She knew I wouldn't complain, otherwise she'd tell Sofie that I had sex with her ex-boyfriend, and that he told me she'd never done anything more than kiss him because she had intimacy issues.

So I was left stuck in the stretch by myself. I couldn't get out because he'd shut the door and locked it—I think he just did it without thinking—but at least we were parked legally, so there was nothing I could do but sit back, turn up the music and wait for them.

Another ten minutes passed, and there was no sign of anyone. I looked out at the streets and just saw crew boys hanging around looking in their baggy white pyjama-clothes, and a queue of wobbly drunk loners at the chicken outlet, and I started to get worried because I was shut in the car, and then, twelve minutes later, Sofie and Jamie reappeared with the beers, so I figured they just went for a smoke. Whatever else Sofie was, she wasn't a slut. But she demanded to know why I let Bethany out of my sight, like I was her keeper. I explained that I hadn't been put on earth to take care of her, and that she'd be back in a minute because Korfa would want to get us home and go off duty. I expected to see her coming round the corner any second.

Bu when Korfa reappeared, he was alone. Sofie was very stoned, and Jamie had fallen back on the seat and looked like he'd checked out of his head without paying the bill, and Sofie asked where Bethany had gone. And Korfa replied, in his funny, heavy accent, that she'd got all weird on him and had gone off.

'What was she doing going off with you anyway?' she wanted to know. 'You should have gone after her. We can't just sit here and wait for her to come back.' She was thinking about herself as usual.

'She said she wasn't going to come back,' said Korfa. 'She said not to wait for her.'

'You're lying,' Sofie snapped back, holding up a spangly Tiffany purse. 'She would never leave her stuff here.' She called Bethany's mobile, and a moment later it rang in the car—it was in her bag, 'What happened?' Sofie demanded to know.

'I told you,' said Korfa laboriously. 'She pretty much pulled me into the alley. She started kissing me.'

'Yeah, like you had to be dragged. She's fifteen! You broke the law—we can have you sent back to your own country.'

'This is my country,' he replied. 'I'm from Leigh-On-Sea.'

'I thought you were from Somalia,' I said.

'I am, originally. It makes the time go faster if I act like I don't understand English.'

'What did you do to her?'

'I told you, she started kissing me, then suddenly said she wanted to go and ran off. I know how it looks.'

'Believe me, you don't know how it looks. It's going to be worse for you than you could ever imagine.' Sofie waited for this one to pass over the footlights. She was acting now, wobbling her head and playing to the balcony. She'd been too young to grieve in public for Diana's death, but she'd laid flowers outside the O2 when Michael Jackson died, although two hours later she was texting jokes about him.

I noticed she had no intention of getting out of the stretch to look for her best friend, so I suggested we search the alleyway.

Korfa agreed, and let me out. I took a walk into the trash-strewn gap between the buildings and had a look around. One end opened out into a neat little children's playground with grass and two swings. I figured there had to be another way into the playground, but couldn't see it.

'That's where we sat,' says Korfa apologetically. 'On those swings. Then she went off.'

'Why did she leave?'

'I don't know.' He shrugged.

'Did you try it on with her?'

'No, I swear! She was all over me. Then she just kind of went blank and stopped. She got up, said she had to go and ran off in that direction.' He pointed to the far end of the alley, but there were no lights down there, and suddenly I was afraid of going into the dark with him.

We headed home. What else could we do? Sofie was stoned and needed to sort herself out before hitting her parents' house. The mood was damaged now, everyone was antsy and upset. Even Jamie had roused himself and was blearily looking around, as if he realized that something was wrong but couldn't put his finger on the problem. Sofie explained the situation to him.

We'd been driving through the darkened streets for a while before I realized Korfa was rattled and lost. 'You don't know where you're going, do you?' I asked quietly. He didn't reply, but kept glancing at the Sat-Nav and tapping the side of it.

Sofie decided to stage her next WTF moment by shouting 'Where are you taking us?' over and over. 'Take us home now! Now! Fucking idiot doesn't even know how to use a Sat-Nav.'

'They're complicated,' Jamie offered uselessly, siding with his fellow male.

'What are you doing?' Sofie was panicked. She kept picking up her mobile and toying with the idea of texting someone, then changing her mind. She didn't want to talk to her parents in case they had a go at her.

'Stop the car! Stop the car!' she screamed suddenly, and kept doing it until, in annoyance, he did.

He slowly turned to look at her. 'What do you want me to do?'

'We have to find Bethany.' She was whimpering and demanding, trapped between personas, trying to behave like a demanding pop-star but turning back into a little girl.

'Does she have enough money on her to get home?' I asked.

'I don't know, do I?' Sofie's tone was vicious. 'How am I supposed to know?'

'She must have known what she was doing, even if she ran off.'

'Thirty quid,' said Jamie out of the blue.

'What?'

'That's how much she has on her. She told me, change from a gorilla or something?' He was right. Her father had given her a fifty pound note. We'd split the restaurant bill on credit cards and she'd paid cash for the gorilla.

'She'll calm down and get a taxi back,' I said.

'What makes you so sure of yourself, Miss Know-It-All?' spat Sofie. 'You think I'm going to trust you after you fucked Ryan, and don't try to deny it because Bethany told me.'

So there it was, out in the open. Sofie was breaking up with him, Ryan and I hit it off—or at least I thought we had—and I lost my virginity to him. Then he went away to uni. And Bethany knew because I'd stupidly told her.

'You're so fucking pompous, you know that?' Sofie yelled at me, 'thinking you're so cool because you wear black and read and you're a Goth, but you're just the same as the rest of us really!'

'I am not a Goth,' I told her, 'I'm an individual.'

'Yeah, all your friends are. A big identical gang of fucking individuals.'

I was going to protest about that, then changed my mind. Sofie had spiraled into a major arm-flap. 'Turn the car around, we have to find her! He tried to rape her, then she probably fought him off and he killed her, shoved her into a skip or something!' The idea was stupid but it set me wondering; perhaps he'd taken her up on her offer, she'd chickened out and he'd somehow knocked her out or something.

Korfa had had enough. He restarted the stretch and pulled out into the traffic. We got to the third set of lights on a blank, bright ribbon of road studded with discount computer outlets, B&Q barns and closed supermarkets when everything suddenly went quiet and we coasted to the side of the road.

'What's going on?' Sofie's voice was in a permanent state of scream now.

'I don't know.'

Korfa popped the hood, took off his jacket and got out to take a look. Sofie pummeled her mobile but got no signal. 'Jamie, do something, don't just sit there!'

Jamie shrugged and got out of the stretch.

'Where are you going?' Sofie screamed.

'Going to find a signal.' He ambled off up the road, moving out of the streetlights. I think he really wanted to get away from her.

'Come back, you can't do this!'

He ignored her and carried on walking.

'This is crazy!' she kept shouting, as if she did it long enough someone would come. 'I don't believe it! This is fucking crazy!'

Korfa slammed the hood and got back into the stretch. He tried the engine and it turned over. Slamming the doors, ignoring Sofie, he drove off.

Now she wanted him to stop. 'We can't leave Jamie,' she shrieked, 'turn around!' Then to me; 'He's faking it, it's all a trick, he's a fucking nutter! He's trying to kidnap us! Stop the car, you black fucker! Stop the car!'

And before I knew what was happening she had half-thrown herself over into the front passenger seat and taken something from his discarded jacket, opening the window and throwing it out.

'What was that?' I asked, but I already knew it had been Korfa's wallet. He slammed on the brakes and she crashed forward, banging her forehead on the half-opened partition.

Jumping out of the car, he stopped to lock us in and ran back up the road for his wallet. Sofie was screaming and crying, tugging ineffectually at the door handle, but I noticed her eyeliner hadn't smudged. When Korfa came running back she fell suddenly silent, fearful for the first time that she might really be in danger.

He remained silent as he started up the stretch once more, squealed the thing in a great big turning circle and slammed off up the road, cutting back and forth, bouncing across the sidestreets so that Sofie and I were rolling from one side of the great leather seating units to the other. I tried to make out where we were going but saw blank bright shops and deserted pavements. Sofie was crying and mumbling and smashing her mobile against the arm rest, and there was nothing I could say or do that would calm her down.

I had no idea where we were; there was nothing outside I recognized. Suddenly he braked hard and reversed, looking over his shoulder, muttering something to himself. Then he slowed to a stop.

'What are you doing, Korfa?' I asked as calmly and clearly as I could. Ignoring me, he was about to place the stretch in Park when Sofie flew at him, slamming his back with her fists and trying to scratch his face, his neck.

He hadn't been expecting the attack. The stretch jumped back in gear and reversed violently. There was a horrible wet thump and we rocked to a stop.

This time, we all got out. We'd reversed into the wall by the off-license where Bethany had gone missing. Korfa had been using his Sat-Nav to find the fastest way back to the spot where we'd lost her.

Bethany had been coming out of the off-license.

She was under the car with a box of KFC still gripped in one hand. I guess she'd been waiting for a cab. The rear bumper had crushed both her legs so badly you could see white shards of shattered bone sticking out. She looked a bit like her fried chicken meal. She looked up at us from under the exhaust pipe, open-mouthed and kind of surprised. I remember noticing her designer trainers for the first time and wondering if they would fit me if she didn't walk again.

And she didn't. I mean, she had a lot of operations and got a lot better, but when she got out of her chair she could only do a kind of rolling spazz-walk, and after about thirty seconds she had to sit down and rest.

Her parents were really pissed off, because first they had to cancel their holiday in Florida to look after her, then they pretty much had to cancel everything else forever. Which meant that her father quickly broke off with my mother, and she married an alcoholic who beat her up and now we're all in rehab together.

I heard Sofie ended up on some cable channel selling perfume. Apparently she made a lot of money. Then she had a facelift that went wrong. It left her looking like the Elephant Man. She spent all her money fighting the doctor in court, and still lost.

Bethany never explained what really happened that night. Personally I think she got him excited, then panicked and ran off, but if she ever talks about it, it won't be to me. When I visited her, she hadn't been out of her bedroom for a year. I only went once. It was too depressing to go back.

Korfa had to pay for the repairs to the stretch out of his salary. When the vehicle went to the insurers' garage, they discovered it was a reconditioned hearse that had been badly converted into a party limo. It had never been granted a safety certificate, so Korfa got deported, which must have been a bummer.

At school we did this course on Victorian literature, and how the women suffered from a kind of hothouse hysteria whenever they were all together, and they kept having fainting fits because they wore tight corsets. I think what we had that night was a similar thing, caused by us all being together in the hearse-stretch. I thought of all those corpses it had carried through the years, and wondered how many people had gone angrily to their deaths, and whether all that pent-up furious death-energy had somehow charged the atmosphere inside the car that night, affecting our behaviour.

Or maybe we just naturally brought out the worst in each other.

I know it's uncharitable, but I kept thinking. If only Bethany hadn't come back from the alley, if only she'd been found dead, everything would have been all right for the rest of us. I mean, is that so wrong?

I saw the hearse-stretch once more, cruising up Charing Cross Road with a new driver at the wheel, and all the girls inside it were screaming as if they were being killed, and I wondered if something bad was going to happen to them too. I'll admit, part of me hoped it would. Just so I'd know that there was another more sinister force at work, and it hadn't just been our fault.

Because if it *had* just been us, it wouldn't make us very nice people, would it?

THE DECEIVERS

THIS IS A POLICE STATEMENT, BUT THEY SAID I COULD TELL IT IN MY OWN WAY. SO I'M not writing it down, I'm dictating it into the desk sergeant's laptop, like he even knows how to operate it. He sticks Post-It notes on the lid, the keys are filthy and there's software on it from before I was born.

I'm not worried. I'm going to get out of here because there's someone coming who can prove what really happened.

They want me to put everything down, so first I have to explain about the hill.

The boundary line between Devon and Cornwall is dotted with small villages that pretend they're towns, but they're not. For a start, everyone who lives in them is either really old, over forty at least, and has lived there all their lives, or they're from London and only come down at the weekends. The locals all hate them, although my Dad says we should smile as we charge them double, like the French do. There's no-one of my age to hang out with here, and nowhere to go if you do find someone. If you travel to one of the bigger towns with your mates, there's a good chance you'll get beaten up just because you're from somewhere else.

My folks are obsessed with getting fresh air. 'Let's go for a walk and get some fresh air', like there's ever anything else to do. 'Let's go up to the hill.' We live in a village called Trethorton Hill. It consists of a short high street, about a hundred and twenty houses, two pubs and a hill. That's it. There's nothing even remotely interesting about the hill, it's just a huge pimple of grass and scrub with a single white rock set in the top, not even a proper standing stone, and when they get up there hikers say things 'You can see all the way to Dartmoor from here', as if that's a good thing. I hate hikers, with their billy cans and red knees and woollen hats, and their rulebooks and guidebooks and hard little eyes. But that's what everyone around here does every Sunday. On Saturdays they go to Liskeard for their shopping, and on Sundays they go up the hill. I used to think that was boring until I realized that people actually come here from other towns to go up the hill, and what does that make their villages, if it's more interesting here than staying where they are?

The locals think they're cool and that they've been around, but they haven't. I heard some old guy in the supermarket telling the cashier that he'd just been up North, and she was reacting in amazement, like he'd just told her he'd been to Alpha Centauri. Then he added, 'yes, I went all the way to Tintagel', and I realized he meant North Cornwall. Jesus.

I have an older sister, and she got out while she could. I say 'got out', what she did was get pregnant by some docker who'd gone to work on container ships out of Liverpool, so now she's stuck in Swansea with two bulldog-faced kids, in a hell of her own making.

Not for me. Once I get a job offer you won't see me for dust. I'm smart, I'm awake, I've got a mind. But it doesn't pay to be too clever in a village. People get suspicious of you. Best to keep your mouth shut and stay indoors mucking about on the internet, taking to smart people on the other side of the world. Someone asked me if we had Wi-Fi, and I had to explain we don't even get decent mobile phone reception here. The internet stops you from getting too lonely, because there are people in places with exotic sounding names, and they're just as bored as you are, so it makes you feel better.

I made one friend but he's not my friend anymore, a kid called Daniel who came from the next village. I met him at IT club, and then at the Trethorton Charity Climb—we weren't taking part, we were just hanging around—and I thought 'We're alike. He's awake too.' Daniel lives in a damp shadowy dell called Crayshaw. It's a village which loses its sunlight before lunchtime even at the height of summer. Daniel's parents are rich—his old man had invented rubberized flooring for factories and had sold it all around the world. So Daniel got an amazing allowance but had no-one to share it with, because he had a gimp leg which meant he couldn't play football, and the flybrains at school treated him like dirt because he was from the wrong village and couldn't do sports. He never told them he had money, but he told me after I stuck up for him in a fight.

Daniel got excused from double games on Fridays (he only did the midweek swimming) and I didn't go because I hated it. I once forged a doctor's letter to Mr Phelps the gym teacher saying I had a defective heart valve and couldn't do contact sports, and the moron never even bothered to check it out with my folks. So every Friday afternoon we kicked around Trethorton Hill looking for ways to annoy the hikers. Once we tied fishing wire across the grass and filmed them all falling over on our phones.

Although Daniel had money he couldn't really spend it. He was only allowed to catch the bus as far as Liskeard because of his leg, so it wasn't like we were going to whip off to Ibiza for the weekend, but we bought stuff online, and for a while we had a lot of fun hanging out together.

My old man says when things go wrong there's always a woman involved, and in this case it was a girl called Tara Mellor. She was in our year and had been suspended twice for wearing an incorrect school uniform. She was tall and thin with cropped blonde hair, and I was nuts about her, but for some incredible reason she seemed to prefer Daniel. But at the start the three of us hung out together a lot.

The lardy desk sergeant just came by, saw what I was writing and said could I get to the point. I wanted to say 'could you get to the gym?' but he'd already waddled off.

I think the problem was that Daniel and I kept trying to impress Tara. To his credit, he never flashed his cash at her—he was too cool for that—and besides, she wasn't interested in money. She wasn't like the other girls we knew from school, who spent all their spare time planning shopping trips to town on Saturdays. She read a lot, and was interested in ancient history. The trouble started on the day she dragged us to Liskeard's 'Man, Myth & Magic' Museum. The locals wanted to get rid of the word 'man' because they said it was sexist, and rename it 'The Liskeard Early Civilisation Centre'. We wrote in to the Liskeard Gazette with a suggestion of our own, but I guess they worked out that the acronym we suggested would be pronounced 'Dogs' Cocks' and they didn't run our letter.

We were in the museum and there was a section on local legends, the usual guff about ghosts, human sacrifices, phantom hounds and highwaymen, and Tara said there was no proof that any of the stories were true, they were just made up by drunk old publicans, and she pointed out that Trethorton Hill didn't even have any decent legends attached to it, that's how lame the place was, and that's when we decided to make one up.

We decided it had to be a believable legend, something with evidence to back it up. It also had to be something that could scare the hikers off the hill. So Daniel said how about aliens, and I said no because crop circles had been discredited years ago, all you needed was a couple of dopeheads armed with a piece of rope and a plank. We needed something more sophisticated. I thought we should create a plausible unsolved mystery, so we decided on a desperate sailor who had come ashore after murdering his violent captain in a mutiny, and who for some unknown reason dragged a local girl up the hill and cut her throat. Then we added a supernatural element that would provide proof of the legend, a ghostly wailing you could hear on certain nights when the air was still.

PC Porky just came by again and asked me if I was writing a novel, and I told him if I was I'd let him know so he could hire someone to read it to him.

Daniel knew quite a lot about sound technology, and figured we could rig outdoor speakers around the hill, running from two synced-up MP3 players. We decided to record the ghost crying and phase the sound so that it appeared to circle the hill, and preset the time so that we wouldn't have to be there when it happened. I didn't involve Tara in this because I wanted to surprise her, to show I was interested in myths and stuff. We ordered the components we needed on Daniel's Paypal account, and when they arrived we tested everything in the fields beyond Trethorton, down near the river.

Next, we needed to record the sound of the crying woman, and Daniel said he had a bit of software that could replicate the human voice but also distort it. We aimed for something between a child in pain and a fox at night. It had to be haunting and other-worldly, and after a weekend of experimentation we had mixed it to perfection. The effect was so spooky it made the hairs on my arms stand up.

Then it was time for the trial run.

Late one night we loaded the equipment into our back-packs and set off for the hill. It took over three hours to set up the sound parameters because we hadn't allowed for the wind noise up there, but we eventually got it so that the crying echoed from one speaker to the next. The effect was subtle, so that you weren't aware you were being directed between the speakers. And Daniel had recorded it a dozen times, switching the equalizer settings so that you never heard the same sound arrangement twice. He was also able to vary the start times, so we set the switch-on at different hours between 11PM and 2AM. We figured the battery charge on the MP3 players would hold for a long time because they were only being used for a few minutes at a time. Then we sealed the players in plastic bags and buried them. The four speakers were more of a problem because we needed them to be above ground. We put one deep inside a hawthorn bush and another in a wet ditch, after first making sure that the connections were all covered. The other two we hid in clumps of grass, hoping that no-one would stumble across them.

Then we went home to write the letters. We targeted both of the local papers, the Gazette and the Chronicle, and used false names. We assumed different identities, becoming hikers and pensioners, fathers and kids, and varied the content of the letters. One said he'd heard a sound like trapped animal on the hill, another said it sounded like a woman being tortured, and so on. Daniel thought there was a risk the paper might check the senders' addresses, but I said why would they? Two weeks after the first letter appeared, we hooked our first outsider—some old guy had been walking his dog and heard the sound for himself, and wrote in to the Gazette.

After another two weeks had passed and a handful of letters had been published, describing the eerie sounds on the hill, we hit them with Phase Two—the legend. This letter appeared to have been sent from a retired schoolmistress, now living in Wales (I got my sister to post it, but I didn't let her read the contents). The schoolmistress explained the source of the strange sounds on Trethorton Hill. She repeated the bare bones of our legend about the sailor and the girl, and the Chronicle published it as their star letter of the week.

I know what you're thinking. How bored did we have to be to do this? Pretty damn bored, I guess, but it was fun winding up the locals. Soon, the hiking club members were taking turns to check out the ghost of Trethorton Hill, and created a chart detailing exactly when and where the ghost could be heard, according to which direction the wind was coming from. They put it up in the village hall and asked others to add to it with different-coloured marker pens. Hikers like stuff like that.

The main thing, from our point of view, was to get everyone in the village to believe in it before we exposed the whole thing as a hoax. It was our revenge on everyone for being so boring and sheep-like. With each passing week, the letter pages became more polarized between huffing walkers who refused to believe the legend, and others who said they'd heard it for themselves.

Daniel and I went up the hill at the weekends and found whole groups of drunk Emos hanging around waiting to hear the cry of the murdered woman. We thought they'd start poking about, trying to find out where the sound was coming from, so Daniel periodically turned off the system from his remote, because we were worried they might start digging up the ground and tearing the bushes apart, but most of them seemed content to lie around on the grass drinking and making out. I think they really wanted to believe.

The week after this, Tara suddenly became much more friendly with me, and was cooler around Daniel, to the point where it seemed like she didn't want to see him. They'd obviously had some kind of falling out, but neither of them was prepared to talk about it. Maybe he'd tried it on with her and she wasn't having it. Daniel acted like he wasn't bothered and it didn't affect our friendship, and then I realised that Tara and I were kind of going out, so everything was okay.

Hang on, the sergeant is waving his stubby sausage fingers at me.

It turns out he just wanted to offer me a cup of tea. Bless.

So. Then one Friday—this was about six weeks after the whole thing had started, I opened the Chronicle to find a letter from a genuine school-teacher—some retired guy in Portsmouth, citing precedence for the legend.

Dear Sir,

I have been following the discussions about Trethorton's Sobbing Woman with great interest. When I was a child, I well remember my late father taking me to the top of the hill to hear the cries of this poor tortured soul. He told me that she was a local Liskeard girl who had been murdered by her swain some time in the 1800s. Whenever I think of my holidays there, the memories of our trips to the 'Black Hill' send shivers down my spine.

Yours sincerely,
Arthur Parkyn
Schoolteacher (retired)

Black Hill? It was never called the Black Hill. What was he on about? Not to be outdone, a builder from Likeard wrote in and put a lot more meat on the bones. I still have the cutting here;

Dear Chronicle Letters,

Concerning the legend of Trethorton's Sobbing Woman, the name of the victim was Ennor Maddern. From the age of eight she worked at what was then called the Anchor Inn (demolished in 1893), where she eventually met and fell in love with a sailor named Carne Greenway. Carne was a sailor on board the HMS Sans Pareil. He served under a cruel, violent captain named either Sambourne or Sanborn, and led the mutiny against his captain in March of 1827. The captain was killed and thrown overboard to general approval of the long-suffering crew, but as Greenway was the leader of the mutineers, he was hunted by the local sheriffs as soon as he set foot on land.

The horrors of the mutiny affected this young man dreadfully. He was hounded from one county to the next and became a smuggler in order to survive. When he was finally able to make his way back to see his beloved Ennor, he discovered that she was about to marry the corrupt town magistrate. Carne came calling at her window one wild night, and she pretended to be thrilled to see him, and arranged to meet him later at Trethorton Hill. But when he arrived there Carne found that Ennor had betrayed him, and had rallied a gang of ruffians to join with her from Portlooe, where the HMS Sans

Pareil was docked. These men sought revenge for the death of their captain. In the ensuing fight, Carne took the girl as a hostage, and as the men came at him he took a knife to her throat as punishment for this act of betrayal.

The ghostly cry that can be heard on the Black Hill is not the sound of Ennor's death, but her sobbing in contrition for her own foolishness in ever doubting her beloved. It resonates from the standing stone which appeared after her death, placed there by villagers in commemoration, although there are those who believe her spirit resides within it. I hope this clears up the mystery surrounding this phenomenon.

Yours,
James Talbot, Liskeard

Needless to say, Daniel and I were pissing ourselves. The following week brought another letter, this one from a vicar who added a new detail to the story. He said 'When a local magistrate identified the disguised sailor, Greenway kidnapped his daughter and brought her to the Black Hill, demanding that the magistrate deliver money and a horse, but the magistrate betrayed him, and in desperation Greenway killed the woman he loved'.

It was inevitable that this point of view should be quickly revised. A woman called Dr Megan Stander, an academic from University College London, wrote in. I didn't keep a copy of her letter, but it said something like;

'Typically, Mr Parkyn twists an important piece of local history to a patriarchal viewpoint in which Ennor Maddern takes the hag-role of the traditional Cornish witch or siren, luring an innocent sailor to his doom, and Carne Greenway is whitewashed to become the dominant male-hero of the story.'

Another letter agreed with her, pointing out that Parkyn had reversed the legend, as the cruel sailor had in fact kidnapped Ennor and raped her on the hill, cutting her throat in a state of frenzied blood-lust. Meanwhile, the myth was taken up by a local reporter in the Gazette who reckoned he'd uncovered the truth about the 'Sobbing Virgin of Trethorton Hill'. According to records she had indeed been 'cruelly violat'd upon the Tor' and had cut her own throat with a straight razor out of shame. He suggested the town should erect a statue to her on top of the hill.

It was all too good to be true. Daniel and I could see that everyone was just getting in on the act, each challenging the next to come up with a new addition to the story, but I wondered; was there a possibility that they actually believed what they were saying?

The Gazette's reporter was the worst; he kept adding all kinds of details to the myth, citing unspecified 'local records'. But even he never explained what this girl was doing on top of a hill at midnight with a straight razor in her pocket, or why she'd become known as the Sobbing Virgin if she'd been violated. It was the most exciting thing to happen in our village in years. Even Tara became fascinated by the legend; it gave us something in common to talk about. I was dying to tell her the truth, but I decided to wait until the time was right.

The next time Daniel and I went up to Trethorton Hill, we realized that the time had come, because the entire hill was covered with people. The white stone had been roped off by the council, and there was an incredible party atmosphere; kids were selling beer from cold-bags and there was even a guy serving overpriced hot dogs. So, early the next morning, before anyone was around, we went there again and dug up the speakers. We had to go in daylight because my mobile didn't have a flash. I took shots of every step, the unearthing of the wires, the MP3 player being removed from the plastic bag, then we wrote a long letter to both the Gazette and the Chronicle about how we'd done it, and how we'd wanted to prove that people were gullible enough to believe anything. We included pictures of us removing the equipment.

The only thing I forgot to do was tell Tara about the hoax.

That was when things started to get weird. I don't think either of us had realized the effect of what we'd done. The first sign of trouble was an editorial in the Chronicle, which was now engaged in a circulation war with the Gazette, thanks to each side's determination to get to the truth of the legend. The piece was entitled; 'Local Youths Deny Historic Past', and pointed the finger of blame at me and Daniel. I remember one section vividly. It said;

'The story of Ennor Maddern and Carne Greenway has touched the hearts of everyone in the South West. Their tragic romance stands as a symbol of an extraordinary time in our history. It has proven to be both inspirational and instructive. For some, it is a tale of honour and oppression, a classic example of machismo and the subjugation of women, for others it is a dire warning about the way in which class and status corrupts innocent lives. And yet in these celebrity-obsessed times, it seems that whenever new light is thrown on our past, someone tries to push into the spotlight by refusing to believe that it ever happened.' The article named us and printed our pictures, saying that we were using the legend to try and claim some fame for ourselves.

It didn't stop there. So many people swore they'd heard the sound of the sobbing woman—and of course, they had—that the story was picked up on the national news, and even more visitors arrived to see what the fuss was about. The next Saturday night, Daniel and I went back up onto Trethorton Hill and found dozens of people still up there, waiting to hear the climax of the legend being played out. And even though the speakers were no longer hidden around the stone, several of them swore they'd heard her crying. The legend was out of our hands now. It was bigger than us, and all we could do was sit back helplessly and watch it grow.

The next morning I answered the front door and was punched in the face by some mad hiker who swore at me for 'trying to ruin the reputations of the Trethorton Three'. I'd read somewhere that this was what they were now calling the legend, as it was suggested that there had been a love triangle between the captain of the HMS Sans Pariel, the sailor and the woman who loved them both. One school of thought was that Ennor Maddern had killed herself for the love of the captain Carne Greenway had killed. The legend was open to so many different interpretations that you could fall in with a group standing for any one of them.

Overnight we became outcasts in our own village. My parents had their car defaced. Someone spray-painted the word LIARS over our garden wall. Daniel's father stopped his allowance after some people accused him of conspiring with his son at a PTA meeting. But worst of all, Tara came around one evening to tell me that she didn't want to see me anymore.

'I identified with Ennor Maddern,' she told me. 'As soon as I heard her story, it was like something inside me became more complete, like I'd discovered a sister. I could feel her pain.'

'I don't know how you can say that, because she doesn't exist,' I told her angrily. 'We made her up. There's no such person.'

Tara shook her head, close to tears. 'Why you would lie like this?' she asked. 'I know Ennor was real. I researched her life, I even saw her picture.'

'Where?'

'There are websites dedicated to her story,' she told me.

'Yeah, and they've all been put together by the kind of stoners who lie on the hill at night thinking that passing satellites are space ships. Believing in something doesn't make it come true. They're just trying to make their lives more interesting.'

'That's not fair,' she said. 'You can't disrespect us by calling us stupid. I don't know why you would want to hurt us all like this.' And she walked away from the front door without once looking back.

I had to prove I wasn't going mad. I searched the websites and found a number of them using a coloured lithograph of a baby-faced girl in a linen smock, labeled 'Ennor Maddern, aged seventeen years, just before her tragic demise.' It took me a couple of evenings to trace the picture back to an old painting of a French peasant girl which hadn't even been produced in the right country or the right century, but that didn't seem to matter to anyone. A bit of proper research should have cleared the whole matter up, but no-one wanted to do it. I thought about pointing this out in another letter to the press, but decided against it. I knew that anything I said now would just make people angry.

Then Daniel got beaten up by a couple of kids in masks who stopped him on the way home from school. He came out of Liskeard Infirmary with nine stitches in his face, and said he'd had enough. We decided to make one last ditch attempt to clear our names by sending the CD with the recording of the sobbing woman to the press. We posted it to the Chronicle and the Gazette, and sat back to see the result. I think we believed that in the worst case they'd just say we were making it up again, trying to get our names in the papers. But I had this pathetic fantasy that some smart young journalist might show enough initiative to get a few witnesses together who'd agree that this was what they'd heard, and then discredit the recording by having it broken down into component parts.

I think, on the whole, I over-estimated the intelligence of the press.

What happened instead was something entirely unforeseen. The journalists were happy enough to believe that the transcription was genuine, and had us both taken into custody. According to them the sound is real, and it's a series of callous real-time recordings of a girl being raped.

Both my parents and Daniel's have admitted that to their knowledge the only girl we ever hung around with was Tara Mellor, so now it's down to her to clear our names. I'm sitting here in Liskeard police station with this shitty computer and my father outside smoking himself to death, waiting for Tara to come and provide a witness report.

Okay. The sergeant says I have a chance to amend my statement now, in the light of what I've just heard.

All I can tell you is that I don't know why Tara would say this—that Daniel raped her. She says that the week after we saw the Emos on the hill, we took her up there and Daniel pinned her down on the stone, and begged her to have sex with him, and when she turned him down he held her by the throat and raped her. She says she thinks I must have been there as well to record the sound, which makes me an accessory. She says I covered up for Daniel because he was my best friend.

Part of me knows she's lying because I wasn't there, and because Daniel has a gimp leg and she's tall and strong enough to look after herself. Besides, he just wouldn't do something like that, even though he can be strange and diffi-cult sometimes. Also her timing is out, because why would I be recording the sound if we were already playing it to visitors by that time? She says I was trying to replace the recording with a more realistic version, like that makes any sense.

But part of me also remembers how she changed toward Daniel around that time, and started to shudder whenever he came near her, like she was scared of him. And I can't get rid of the feeling that perhaps he did do some-thing bad to her.

The worst part was in the last section of her statement. She says that ever since then, she's been going up on Trethorton Hill at night and she hears the sound of the crying woman, and the sobbing is real, and she can't tell if it's the anguished cries of Ennor Maddern, or if it's her, and it was her all along.

I don't know if Tara was raped or not. I don't know who the deceivers are anymore. But there's an easy way to sort it out. Take me up to the hill at night and I'll show you where the speakers were planted, and you'll hear there's nothing there now except the wind. Going up the Black Hill is the only real way to prove my innocence. Even though part of me is terrified that I'll hear the sound of crying.

'I'M IN LOVE WITH YOUR TOILET,' I TOLD HILARY. 'THE GERANIUM WALLPAPER IS A REAL finishing touch with the walnut veneer.'

'Stained faux-beechwood,' Hilary pointed out. Hilary is tall and wears a shade of coral gloss lipstick I'm sure they've discontinued everywhere except Africa. She's my next door neighbour. 'And have you noticed, June, we've matching air freshener?' She showed me her spray can. 'You can't beat floral top notes in a downstairs loo.'

'I find a cedar and cranberry *pot-pourri* pleasing, but you really need citrus fruits to mask some odours.' I ran a surreptitious finger along Hilary's dado and checked it for smearage. 'How is Richard, by the way?'

'In line for promotion, something about taking over the whole of the South East, but it's none of my business of course, so long as he remembers the housekeeping money.' I knew she was trying not to look out of the corner of her eye to check that I was admiring everything thoroughly.

'Doesn't your husband already supply the whole of the South coast with bolts?' I asked, keen to know what their house was worth and approaching the subject in a roundabout manner. 'You'll be able to afford another property.'

'We can afford another property now,' she snipped back. 'You must have been glad to move here, June. Gordon told me about your old house. It must have been so *exhausting* living in such tiny rooms, but that's the problem with Victorian back-to-backs. They used to be called slums, of course.'

My lips thinned with supressed anger. 'Actually we never really needed the extra space.'

'That's because you don't get out much. You must feel so *trapped* at home.'
Hilary smiled sweetly as she ushered me into her vast kitchen, trying to look
entirely innocent, even though I suspected she'd spent the previous afternoon
being bent over the kitchen table by the Ocado delivery man.

Twenty minutes later I returned to my own inferior house to prepare
dinner. I began to assemble ingredients, trying not to think about Hilary's
insulting remarks.

I was so fucking tired of competing.

Setting the cookery book before me, I began to read.

'I do so abhor those grim little boxes with pre-tenderised meat you find in
supermarkets,' said Nigella, leering out of the book with a sultry smile, 'but
they'll do in a pinch until you can reach a decent poulterer.'

What the hell is she talking about? I thought. *Poulterer? Is that someone who
just sells chickens, or does he actually shoot them as well?* The word conjured
those sepia Victorian photographs of men in straw boaters standing outside
cluttered shops holding gigantic feathered birds up by their legs. But I
soldiered on, turning over another page of Nigella's cookery bible, perfectly
described by the term *lavishly illustrated*.

'Of course, you don't have to choose Chateau Yquem when you're making
lemon balm jelly.' I wracked my brain. Nothing. Nigella might as well have
been writing in Swahili. I tried another page. *Fish pie, I think, that's nice and
simple.*

'The saffron redeems the bland, cottonwoolly fish you buy in those plastic-
wrapped polystyrene trays at superstores; useful when you can't get to a
fishmonger.'

Did people really speak like this? I turned more pages.

'Bacon lifts the flabbiness of farmed salmon.'

'There's an authenticity to the waxy nut.'

'Luscious, honeyed creaminess.'

On and on it went, the burbling of a madwoman wandering the halls of
some forgotten culinary insane asylum.

I slammed the book shut. *What fucking planet is this woman living on?* I
wondered. *We live in Hamingwell. It's a commuter estate. We don't have a poulterer, we have a Waitrose half a mile out of town, or shops like Greggs where*

dumpy girls with doughy faces that disappear into their necks serve sausage rolls to morbidly obese children. We have stubbled dole-scum on park benches hammering the Tennant's Super at eight in the morning. Down by the bus station there's a bowlegged crack-whore with needle-marks behind her knees who takes a dump in the gutter and talks rubbish to frightened old ladies outside Argos. There are mad tramps having shoving fights over bottles in playgrounds, and drunks in pyjama bottoms pissing with one hand against the window of Iceland to steady themselves, and stoic African traffic wardens pimp-strutting around vans, and pasty teenaged burnouts with neck tattoos and baggies kick-lifting skateboards in car parks, and the Eastern European bloke who crouches in the corner of the building next to Somerfield glaring at everyone through his facial hair. We do have one specialist shop in the high street. It used to be a funeral parlour, and now performs tattoos and piercings.

I looked at Nigella Lawson's face on the cover of her cookery book. Her recipe for fish pie was called 'Blakean Fish Pie' because the dye in it reminded her of a sunset in a fucking painting.

I would have loved to live on Nigella's planet. I imagined the kitchen goddess at dinner parties, those dreaming, sensual eyes recalling a golden memory of scented Provence hills as she ruminatively chewed a chive-tinted flake of monkfish. Her lightly frosted lips parting slightly to allow the entrance of another morsel. *Should we be drinking the Chateau Yquem tonight?* I wondered, *although as it says here that Chateau Yquem is a Sauterne that goes with sweet puddings I guess the answer is no, we should be on a Pouilly Fume.*

On page 164 of Nigella's 'How To Eat' (stupid question, you just open your mouth and shovel it in) there was an artfully minimalist picture of a sardine can with the lid graceful bent upwards. *Funnily enough,* I thought, *there's a tin just like this hanging from the tree outside my front door, although I don't think it was put there by a photographer's assistant, and the pool of sick at the tree's base with the discarded Sunny D bottle stuck in it somewhat mitigates the mise-en-scene.*

Looking through the cookbook I realised with a shock that there were no food pictures in it at all, just ladles and spoons on dynamic backgrounds. *That's the proof I needed,* I decided, *Nigella actually hates food and the mess it*

*makes. She hates screaming kids and dirty hands and girls without tights and
betting shops and nuisance drinkers because in her world there is only the fecundity of blossoming buds and the firm ripeness of hand-picked white peaches.*

*I'm not supposed to cook from this book at all. I'm meant to keep it on a kitchen
table with a sprig of dried lavender on top like some kind of votive ornament.*

Fish pie it is, then.

I couldn't be asked to go to Waitrose. I went to the Am-La 24 Hr Super-
Mart and asked the girl behind the counter for one of the ingredients to the
fish pie, crayfish. The girl pronounced the word back at me, trying it out on
the tongue, then shook her head in confusion. No, it clearly didn't ring a bell.

'You want 'addock?' she offered with a hopeful smile, pointing to a tray of
luminous yellow filets that might have been irradiated during the Chernobyl
meltdown. The checkout boy was a cute-faced Eurasian called Sunii. He was
helpful and kind and laughed in my face when I asked him where the fresh
nutmegs were kept. I returned to the underground car park and briefly found
myself trapped between two unbreakable glass doors smeared with pieces of
burger. I knew it was a Macdonalds' burger because I could recognise the
machine cut of the dill slice stuck to the overhead neon tubing.

Shouting through a sheet of filthy glass, the parking attendant explained
that I needed have my ticket punched by the checkout clerk, then swipe it
through the safety box, then re-validate it in a machine, then enter it into
another machine before a pole barrier and a set of yellow steel grilles would
swing open to release me. When I had the temerity to ask why this was, he
laughed and said 'Where do you normally shop then, love?'

Now I understood the appeal of Nigella-land, where Pooh still sat on an
oak tree branch and vicars doffed their trilbies to nurses with perambulators,
where there was honey still for tea and the empire sun could never set on
those who truly believe in fairies. Nigella wasn't baking cakes, she was selling
reveries of a hopelessly misremembered past.

A woman stopped me and tried to get me to sign a petition to save a horse
trough. The trough had been empty for years and was used as a litter bin by
the local kids. She wanted it planted with flowers.

People are always trying to save things, I thought. *Save our post office, save
our church hall, they collect a hundred signatures, paint some banners, then*

march down to the town hall to present their petition. They're wasting their time because all the places they march for are doomed. They've been unprofitable for years, because the people who march to save them never used them when they weren't under threat. Oh, they like the idea of such places, picturesque contributions to the old-world charm of England's village past, but in truth, the shops and streets and monuments they try to save are too useless, too slow, too busy, too old. To make any business successful these days you have to deal in bulk, in mass output, in fast turnaround, in unit throughput.

So they buy Nigella's books instead. Abasing themselves at the feet of the kitchen goddess is the least they can do.

I realised that this must have been the moment when I decided the kitchen goddess of the aspirant middle classes must die. Then I thought; *Her house will be protected, she probably attracts stalkers with those come-hither buttered fruit dumplings that must be made with real cream, sinful but so gorgeous of a summer evening.* She spent her whole time feeding us fantasies we could never fulfil.

Maybe the problem wasn't Nigella at all but the whole race of people like her, people who complained about speed-bumps and traffic cones from the space-hogging absurdity of their 4X4s, people who moaned about the difficulty of finding a really good private school for Harry and Charlotte, by which they meant that most of the schools were full of ethnic kids, and they didn't want their darlings to start speaking with glottal stops and getting TB, people for whom the state of luxury was a given, not an aspiration.

When you actively decide to hurt someone, I thought as I queued for a bargain bunch of shop-soiled daffodils, *you must assume that you are damned at the moment you act.* The sense of relief that followed this knowledge was intensely liberating.

I wanted to plan a crime. Ideally, I would have kidnapped a rich little girl from a Chelsea nursery school and subjected her to an upbringing on a sink estate, but the wealthy have the power to mobilise unseen forces against you, so I abandoned the idea even before I got home.

Then I read that Nigella would be signing copies of her latest cookery manual at Waterstones bookshop in Kensington High Street at midday on Saturday morning.

The good thing about bookshops is that they don't have metal detectors, but just to be on the safe side I took a 22 centimetre anthracite ceramic utility knife I bought on Amazon. As I shuffled forward in the long queue of adoring acolytes I knew that nobody would suspect me because I looked like any other downtrodden, knackered housewife pretending that quality cookery had liberated her from the drudgery of married life.

When I reached her signing desk– which I noticed had snowdrops on it in a little pink vase—I looked up and saw that Nigella was, in fact, beautiful. Her complexion was probably the result of using apricot facial scrub and tropical vanilla pod essence. I knew then that I couldn't hurt her, any more than I could have stuck a knife into the Virgin Mary.

Nigella was looking at me expectantly, with smiling eyes, her beautiful fountain pen raised, her assistant delicately pinning open the book at the first page. 'How shall I sign it?' she asked sweetly.

I thought about my days, the diurnal passage of sun and moon that brought nothing, absolutely nothing at all that I would want or could afford. There was only one thing in the world I needed, and that was freedom.

'Sign it in blood,' I said, withdrawing the knife and sticking the white point deep into my bare throat. So white—I do so adore the whiteness that lifts the flabbiness of farmed salmon and adds a luscious, honeyed creaminess to the authenticity to the waxy nut. So red, a red that redeems the blandness of the cottonwoolly fish you buy in superstores.

To say that Nigella was quite surprised is a bit of an understatement. A perfect parabola of crimson arced across her sweater, as if it had been hand-stitched in by nuns working for Agnes B. There was an awful lot of screaming, but Nigella was as calm and helpful as Florence Nightingale.

I don't remember much after that. It wasn't Nigella's fault; I know that now. It was me—I simply didn't measure up. My ambitions ended at stained faux-beechwood when they should have been set much higher, at Blakean Fish Pie.

They tell me I'm not very well.

I like the food here. It comes in white plastic trays with a little white plastic implement called a Spork, a combination spoon and fork that's so blunt it won't even cut a Brussels sprout that's been boiled in the hospital kitchen for over an hour. Everything tastes exactly the same, like soft potatoey chicken. Or chickeny potato. There are brown swirls that might be blancmange or swede, and green swirls that might be peas or jelly. I can usually detect top-notes of turnip or lard. It's perfect. My life is finally perfect.

Although they have to take me out of the Day Room when Nigella's on the television.

OH I DO LIKE TO BE BESIDE THE SEASIDE

Toby pushed the nail deep inside the piece of bread, placed it in his steel catapult and fired it high over the side of the pier. A seagull dropped from the steel-grey cloudscape, its yellow beak agape, and swallowed it.

'Choke, you fucker,' Toby yelled. He turned to Harry. 'Got any more?'

'That was the last one,' said Harry. 'We're wasting our time. They can eat broken glass without dying. They've got special stomachs.'

'What about barbed wire?'

'Same. My dad's got some rat poison in the shed. He saved it from when he was in the military. They're not allowed to sell it in shops.'

'Nah.' Toby kicked at the railing until a chip of blue paint came off. 'Do you think the pier would burn?'

'The one in Brighton burned.'

'Let's get something to eat.' He cast a cheated look back at the gull, which had alighted on a post further along the pier. It gave a healthy shriek as he passed. He threw a pebble at it and missed.

The funfair was empty. A boy with a Metallica tattoo across his shoulders was mopping patches of rainwater from the steel plates on the bumper car floor. Everyone teased him because the tattooist had spelled the band's name wrong, with two Ts and one L.

'Oi Damon, you wanna be careful, you'll electrocute yourself,' Toby called.

'Fuck off,' Damon shouted back. 'It only works if you touch the ceiling.' He raised his metal broom handle and thrashed the mesh above his head, spraying sparks, forgetting he had bare feet. 'Fuck!' He hopped back and swing the broom at them.

'What a moron.' Toby and Harry laughed together. Damon had ingested so many drugs during his clubbing years that he could barely remember his own name. They passed Gypsy Rosalee the fortune teller, who was actually a secretary at Cole Bay Co-Operative Funerals, making a bit of money on the side by building sales pitches for lay-away burial plans into the predictions for her elderly clients. Once he had paid to have his palm read, and she had told him he would go to the bad. 'You're not satisfied with your lot,' she had said, sitting back and folding her arms. 'You think you're too good for us. Lads like you always come unstuck.'

'You're not a real fortune teller.'

'I know enough to someone living under a curse when I see one.' She dug out his money and threw it back at him. 'Go on, fuck off.'

Now he skirted the helter-skelter, where rain had removed so much lubrication from the slide's runners that it was common to see someone getting off their mat halfway down and giving it a push. Ahead was the big dipper that had been closed ever since a pair of toddlers were catapulted into the sea when their carriage braking system failed. Apparently one of them was still in a coma. He hated the pier even more than he hated the rest of the town.

Cole Bay, population 17,650, former fishing village, was like a hundred other British seaside resorts, a byword for boredom, a destination that might have amused the Victorians, but was hopelessly outpaced by the expectations of modern daytrippers, who wanted something more than rip-off amusements, a few chip shops, some knackered beach donkeys and a floral clock. By day sour-faced couples huddled in shelters unwrapping sandwiches and opening thermos flasks. By night every teenager in town was out in the backstreets, getting pissed and goading their friends into punch-ups. Where the land met the sea, all hopes and ambitions were drawn away by the tide.

Ahead, a bored girl was rolling garish pink spiderwebs of candy floss around a stick. Her name was Michelle, and she had originally planned to work at the fair on Saturdays until she could get away to London, but now she seemed to be on the Pavilion Pier every day. As she blankly swirled the stick, strands of reeking spun sugar flicked onto her bare midriff.

'What the fuck are you lookin' at?' she said, popping a pink bubble of gum at Toby.

'Why do you keep making that shit when you haven't got any customers?' Toby stuck his finger in the tub and allowed sugar to cover it.

'It gets bunged up if I stop. We get flies in it and all sorts. The punters don't notice. I'm not going out with you so don't ask.'

'Wasn't going to. You're too old for me, and you're getting fat. Anyway, I thought you were leaving Cole Bay and going to London.'

'Changed my mind, didn't I. Went full time. It's easy work 'cause there's no-one here midweek.'

'Boring, though.'

'Not as boring as being at school. Which is where you and your mouthy mate are supposed to be.'

'Double games period. We bunked off. We're going to see a horror film.'

'The living dead thing? You don't need to watch a movie for that, just hang around here. And you ain't gonna pass for eighteen, neither of you.'

'The ticket guy goes out with my sister. If he doesn't let us in I'll put the blocks on his chances.'

The first fat drops of rain spattered on the pier's floorboards. 'Go on then, take your grubby fingers out my tub and fuck off to your film.' Michelle tugged at the striped awning of her stall, dismissing them.

They ran back along the pier, past pairs of shuffling pensioners in plastic rain-hoods. They still had an hour to kill before the film started.

The Punch & Judy Man was on the beach packing up his theatre. They called down as they passed. 'No show today, Stan?'

'Fucking weather,' Stan called back. 'I'd make the effort and stay open, but we had a gang of kids in earlier, right tearaways, the little bastards were making fun and chucking stuff. Puppets not good enough for them now there's videogames.'

'You should try putting in some new material,' said Toby.

'I've tried that. Blue jokes, new songs. I had Mr Punch perform a yodeling number, but the last time I tried it I swallowed me swozzel.'

They headed up to the promenade, where the old folk sat in hotel greenhouses trying to ripen like tomatoes. The air reeked of doughnut fat and seaside rock. Outside the Lord Nelson, a drunk fat girl in a tiny halter top was sitting on the kerb, stoically attempting to be sick between her spread legs.

Dudley Salterton was sitting on a bench outside the Crow's Nest play-house, looking more than ever like a tramp. He pulled the withered roll-up from his lips as they boys stopped before him and coughed hard, spitting a green globule onto the pavement.

'You all right, Dudley?' asked Toby. 'You got a piece of cigarette paper stuck on your lip.'

'Fuck off, will you? I'm on in a minute.'

'You're not in the panto, are you? I thought it started ages ago.' Toby looked up at the poster for Aladdin, which starred someone from Steps and a runner-up from Big Brother. Dudley was the resident compère at the Crow's Nest's variety nights, filling the gaps between acts with lame magic tricks and banter he had first used in the years after the war, half-heartedly updated to include jokes about modern TV personalities. Not that his elderly audience cared; they came to catch up with each other, to wave and eat and chat. They came because it was raining, because there was nothing else to do in Cole Bay on a wet Wednesday afternoon, because they were afraid of dying alone.

Dudley was ancient and yellow with nicotine, but vanity required him to dye his hair and eyebrows a peculiar shade of chestnut. He never shaved properly, and had been living in a single room in a bed & breakfast joint on the front ever since his wife killed herself. He smelled of sweat, rolling tobacco and Old Spice.

'I'm doing a guest spot in the second act because their comic got fired for always being pissed during rehearsals. But I told them I'm not doing it Chinese, I'll play it straight, thank you very much. I sing *Windmills of Your Mind*, do some newspaper tearing and balloon animals, let Barnacle Bill tell a couple of off-colour jokes, then I'm off over the Lord Nelson for a pint.' Barnacle Bill was Dudley's ventriloquist's dummy. Quite what he was doing in Aladdin was anyone's guess. With its lascivious wink, rolling eyes, peeling lips and dry, startled hair the dummy tended to have a terrifying effect on children. Lately, Dudley had been dying his hair darker and was starting to look like his dummy than ever. Both had been at their peak of popularity during the war, and were soon to be shut up in boxes.

'What's it like, being in a panto?' Harry asked.

'Fucking awful. Widow Twankey went to prison for child molesting a few years back. How he got the job here I'll never know. Must know someone on the council. It's not right. We have to get children up on stage and make them do a dance. Barnacle Bill shouted at one of them last week and the little fucker pissed himself. I gave his arm a right good pinch as he left the stage. It stinks up there.'

'Do you get comps?'

'I wouldn't bother, there's nobody in except a party of spastics from Rhyll, and they're making a hell of a noise. I don't think they're getting any of the jokes. They're probably throwing shit at each other by now.'

'You're not supposed to say spastics.'

'Who fucking cares down here? It's not exactly the London Palladium, is it?'

'Is there an orchestra?'

'No, Eileen's on the piano and there's a bloke with a drumkit. But he's only got one arm.'

'Shark?'

'Thalidomide. There's a wiggly little hand at the end. Gives me the creeps.'

Toby and Harry kept walking. They passed the rock shop, where stretches of sickly peppermint folded back and forth on metal spindles like elasticated innards. The window was filled with edible novelty items; giant false teeth, bacon and eggs, an outsized baby's dummy, a bright pink penis. Behind the counter an enormously fat girl in hoop earrings and a tiny skintight top stared at them as if she was wondering how they might taste.

At the next corner, four old people stood watching while a fifth attempted to park his car. The car was small and the space was huge, but the driver managed to hit both the vehicle behind and the one in front several times over. The pensioners stood there watching, without offering any advice or help. Finally the car was parked two feet from the kerb and the group crept on, their excitement over.

'You know that Morrissey song, *Every Day Is Like Sunday*?' asked Harry. 'Do you think he wrote it about Cole Bay?'

'What, 'the coastal town they forgot to close down'? Yeah, probably. How much longer?'

Harry checked his mobile. 'Forty five minutes. Wanna go in the funfair?'

'Not really, but we're here now.' They walked in beneath the broken coloured bulbs of the Cole Bay Kursaal and headed for the ghost train. The Kursaal used to be called Funland, but the council changed the name after too many accidents gave the place a bad reputation.

The ghost train's plywood frontage had been painted with crude copies of Scooby Doo characters, along with some skeletons and demons cribbed from old Marvel comics. From within came a shriek of un-oiled metal and a wail like a ghost calling through a hooter. Toby and Harry bypassed the deserted ticket counter—Charleen, the girl who worked there, was round the back having a fag—and flicked on the power as they passed the ride's main junction box. Jumping into the first narrow carriage, they rolled off, banging through the doors into darkness. An acrid tang of electricity and damp cloth filled their nostrils. The car twisted about on its miniature track, its wheels crackling with errant voltage as they passed a dummy of Dracula that looked more like a leprous orchestra conductor.

'So, are you in?' Toby shouted as they juddered around a day-glo graveyard.

'It's up to you,' said Harry, who always followed Toby's instructions. 'I guess so. Are we really going to the pictures?'

'No, of course not. Go home and get your stuff, then meet me at the arcade.' That was it. Toby's mind was made up. Harry felt a pitch in his stomach, and knew it was real now. They would run away and leave this miserable cemetery behind for good.

When the ghost train carriage returned to its station at the front of the ride, it was empty.

Harry knew what he had to do. He ran back along the street toward his parents' house. Meanwhile, Toby walked into the Paradise Penny Arcade. He passed the old man who spent his life rhythmically shoveling coins into the Penny Rapids, passed the Skee-Ball slides, the Driving Test, the Flick-A-Ball slots and came up against the creepy Jolly Jack Tar in its wooden case. The damned thing was a museum piece, and had been giving him nightmares ever since he was a baby. Its skin was just plaster, its rictus smile mere painted wood, but it looked leathery and cancerous, like an embalmed corpse. When a ten-pence piece was inserted, it rocked back and forth squealing with laughter while a crackly organ recording of *I Do Like To Be Beside The Seaside* played. The sailor grinned and eyed him from the side of its head, as if to say *I know what you're up to.*

He carried on past banks of beeping, squealing money-stealers and jerky out-of-date video games, to the change booth. He knocked on the scratched, filthy glass, startling Winfrey.

'Fuck off, Toby, you nearly gave me a fucking heart attack,' Winfrey complained, wiping mustard pickle from his T-shirt. He set down his sandwich and stared blearily through the glass. He had a red spiderweb tattooed across his forehead and had several teeth missing, so that at first glance it looked as if he had fallen through a plate glass window. 'What do you want?'

'What time are you cashing up?'

'My shift ends in twenty minutes, but Michelle can't get here until half past. You gonna mind the booth for me?'

'What's it worth?'

'I'll give you a quid. If you're gonna hang around, don't fuck up the machines with plastic.'

'Yeah, all right. I'm waiting for Harry anyway.' He made his way over to a one-arm bandit, watched until Winfrey had turned his back and inserted a coin-shaped piece of plastic into the slot. He waited for the tumblers to trip, then removed it. While he was playing, he checked the railway timetable in his pocket.

He became aware that a gigantic woman was standing beside him. She looked like something from a seaside-postcard. She was wearing a red and white spotted cap the size of a Christmas pudding above a shiny purple wig, a billowing green and yellow gown with metal saucepans fixed over breasts like beachballs, union-jack bloomers and striped leggings. She pursed bee-sting lips and batted her false eyelashes at him. Her doughy face was coated in belisha beacon-coloured makeup that ended in a line across her wobbly chin. 'I hope you're not trying to cheat the machines, little boy,' she said in a bizarre falsetto.

Toby turned to look at her. 'Who are you supposed to be?' He took an involuntary step back.

'I'm the Widow. All the little boys and girls come to see me. Haven't you been to see me?' Widow Twankey fluttered and simpered, waggling her padded hips. She had come off stage between numbers to have a couple of ciggies and a few slugs of scotch from her hip flask. 'Aladdin's singing his ballad. He'll drag it out for twenty minutes at least. Thinks someone from the telly will spot him and make him a star. Fat fucking chance.' Twankey's voice had dropped to a normal male register now, but still retained an unpleasantly theatrical sibilance. 'Show me what you've got in your hand.' Pudgy beringed fingers slapped his knuckles. Toby opened his fist to reveal the clear plastic coin.

'Perhaps I should tell old Winfrey what you're up to, stealing his money.'

'No, don't.'

'Then come and give your old auntie a kiss.'

'You're not my auntie.'

'No, but you can fucking pretend for a minute, unless you want Winfrey to call the cops on you.' The widow came close enough for Toby to smell whisky on her breath. She wetly pursed her lips. Toby grimaced and allowed her to plant a kiss on his cheek. As she did so, she slid her hand over the top of his right thigh and the crotch of his jeans. 'You've got some good muscles on you for a young 'un,' she hissed, giving his cock a squeeze. 'Big for your age. Come and see matron after the show and I'll take you backstage if you like. I keep special presents there for my favourite boys and girls back there.' The widow gave a slow, exaggerated wink and released him. 'Now run along and play.'

Harry running in with the duffel bag and was holding it high. 'I've got it,' he said excitedly as the pantomime dame sailed past him.

'For Christ's sake stop waving it around.' Toby snatched it away and pulled him into the shadows behind the machines, beyond the range of Winfrey's convex ceiling mirrors. He pulled opened the bag and checked its contents.

'It belonged to my brother. Do you know how it works?'

'Of course I know. Give me a minute, will you?'

'I brought you something else as well. It's at the bottom.'

Toby pulled up a rusty tin and examined the label. It read; *Government Issue Imperial Brand Rodent Exterminator. Caution: Contains Warfarin and Caustic Soda.* 'How old is this?'

'Really old. But it should still work on seagulls. Are we going back on the pier to try it out?'

'No,' said Toby. 'We're never going back on the pier.'

'Never? But I thought we could kill loads of them before we left.'

Toby ignored him. He pocketed the items he needed and passed the bag back to Harry. 'Come on.'

Stepping from the shadows, he made his way over to Winfrey's booth. Winfrey was picking his way through a pile of filthy ten pound notes that had been softening with overhandling. As soon as he saw the boy he snapped a red rubber band around the bundle and slid it into his bank bag. Winfrey's takings at the arcade weren't high, but his lads sold amphetamines around the town and used him to launder the cash for a cut.

'If you want to get off, I'll cover for you,' said Toby.

'Hang on, I haven't finished me tea yet.'

Behind them, Harry was banging on the Penny Falls to make the coins slip from the steel shelves. 'Oi, you little fucker,' Winfrey shouted, fumbling his way out of the booth.

Toby slipped inside and pulled the lid off the rusty tin Harry had brought along. He thrust his hand into the white powder, emptying as much as he could into Winfrey's tea, which reeked of whisky. The powder went everywhere, but he managed to blow it off the counter and wipe the rim of the mug before Winfrey came back. The cashier grabbed his nylon jacket and pulled it over his shoulders. 'Your little pal is going to get into trouble and end up inside, like his brother,' he warned. 'Fucking rubbish, that whole family.'

As Winfrey drank down his tea, Toby watched blankly, wondering if he could taste any difference. Apparently not. He couldn't imagine the cashier had any tastebuds left, given the amount he drank. Winfrey drained his mug completely, leaving a rime of white powder around his cracked lips.

Toby retreated to the far side of the arcade, keeping one eye on the booth. 'Unbelievable,' he muttered, 'he can't even taste rat poison. I put half the pot in.'

Harry hadn't heard. He had been hypnotized by a two pound coin that was hovering on the edge of a narrow metal platform in the Coin Cascade machine. Toby craned back at the booth, watching for signs of pain and death.

'Hello Toby.' He whirled around to find Michelle standing beside him. 'I thought you two were off to the flicks.'

'There's still time. You're early.'

'I was looking for you. I now you're up to something, both of you.'

'I don't know what you mean.'

'Don't fuck me about. You're going somewhere. You're getting out.'

'Who said that?'

'I hear everything that's going on. Take me with you.'

'What?'

'Take me with you. I have to leave this place, Toby. I'm going mental. I can't stay here any longer. I can't even go home because of my folks.'

He looked at her bare midriff. 'Aren't you cold?'

'I'm trying to get air on it. My belly button ring went septic. Of course I'm not cold. I'm never cold anymore. I'm fucking pregnant.'

'I didn't know.'

She looked to the sky, blinking. 'That's a surprise, everyone else in this shit-hole town does.'

'Who's the father?'

'What am I, psychic? Maybe I should go and ask Gypsy Rosalee.' She shifted her weight to the other foot and looked at him with desperation in her eyes. 'So what do you think? Can I come?'

'I can't, Michelle. Especially not if you're pregnant.'

'But you and Harry are going.'

'I'm not taking Harry with me.'

'Does he know that?'

'No. I just decided.'

'But you can't leave him behind. He worships you. What's he going to do without you?' She peered over at the booth. 'Shit, what's wrong with Winfrey?'

Toby looked around and saw Winfrey's face pressed hard against the glass, as if he was trying to force his way through it. He was drooling and spitting, grinding his forehead.

'Stay here a second,' he said, panicked, and ran over to the booth as Harry picked up that something was wrong and followed after him.

Toby knew exactly where to kick the booth door to open it. Winfrey had thrown up over himself, the counter, the till, his paperwork. He must have eaten a couple of pizzas earlier, because everything was red. He clutched feebly at Toby as the boy tore the bank bag from his grip and popped it open. The takings weren't inside.

'Where's the money?' Toby asked.

'My guts are killing me.' Winfrey spat again. 'Give me a hand outside.'

'The takings. They're gone.'

'No, I gave 'em to Eddie to bank for me.'

'Eddie? Who's Eddie?'

'The widow. Widow Twankey.' He coughed and licked at his lips, wiping up the remains of the powder. Dark blood leaked over his lower teeth, onto his T-shirt. He tried to stand and slipped from his stool. There was a terrible smell. Winfrey had soiled himself.

'What are you doing?' Michelle called, 'what's going on?' But before she could reach them Toby had grabbed Harry's hand and was dragging him away toward the rear exit.

The boys found themselves in the stinking trash-filled alleyway behind the arcade that was meant to be kept clear in case of fire. 'Toby, you're taking me with you, aren't you?' Harry asked anxiously.

'I can't, Harry. You're too young. You'd get us caught.'

'I'm only two years younger than you.'

'I'm sorry, mate.'

'You said I could come with you.'

'Listen.' Toby stopped in the alley and squeezed his eyes shut, not turning around. 'You can't come because I don't want you with me. You're just a kid. You'd be a drag on my style, all right? Go on home.'

'But Toby—'

'Look, just fuck off, will you?'

He bit his cheek, waiting and listening, refusing to turn. He heard a whimper like a dog being kicked, followed by footsteps stamping away. Part of his heart went with Harry.

He pushed open the unguarded fire door of the Crow's Nest theatre
and climbed the concrete steps in darkness. The show had finished; he had
seen the clusters of homebound children drifting past the arcade. The
building smelled of fresh-cut wood, cheap scent, mildew. He followed
the only light source to another short staircase and found himself in the backstage area. Passing between the flats of Wishee Washee's laundry house, he
entered an artificial forest that owed to the Sussex Downs than the China
steppes.

'There you are, you little scamp,' drawled Widow Twanky. She was sitting
on a giant polystyrene toadstool leisurely smoking a cigarette. She wore a hat
with a miniature line of union jack knickers suspended across it. 'This is the
only time I can bear this fucking place. When the tinies have all fucked off
home. It's the screaming that does my head in. It sounds like pigs being slaugh-
tered in here some afternoons.'

Toby looked about. A backpack sat beside the widow's stockinged right
ankle. The dame was studying the glowing tip of her cigarette. 'I suppose
you've come for your gift.'

'Why are you still in that outfit?'

'Aladdin's fucking Cinderella in my dressing room. Well, she's the Emperor
of China's daughter in this production, but if she thinks she's doing
Cinderella at Christmas she's another thought coming. The bitch couldn't
carry a note in a bucket. Besides.' He hitched up his bosom. 'I like being in
drag. It's a good place to hide.'

Twankey rose to his feet. 'Christ, my knees are fucking killing me. Come
on then, let's go to Ali Baba's cave.' She sailed back into a darkened area of the
stage. Toby followed and found himself surrounded by plywood treasure
chests filled with gold-painted plastic trinkets, as if the genie's fabled cavern
had fallen on hard times and had been reduced to a pound store. 'Winfrey
lent us this lot from his arcade. What a load of shit.' The dame plonked herself
down on a stack of money bags marked with cartoon dollar signs. 'Come
here. Want to see what the widow's got for you?' Twankey pulled him close
and began fumbling in her red, white and blue bloomers.

Toby pulled the gun from his pocket, took aim and shot the dame in the
balls. It wasn't a very powerful weapon and made hardly any noise, but

Twankey released an incredible scream, so Toby made sure to aim the next shot into his mouth, which shut her up.

Her purple wig skewed over her left ear, revealing a sweaty bald pate. She thrashed about on the money bags, spitting crimson teeth, her pudgy fingers digging into the bloody patch between her legs. Toby emptied the remainder of the clip into her stomach and face, then snatched up the backpack and checked its contents. The money was inside.

The dame had torn down his union jack bloomers and was scrabbling blindly at his flopping scarlet cock, as if trying to recover his original identity in his dying moments.

Toby crashed out of the stage door and passed the rear of the arcade. It was raining in hard squalls as he emerged from the end of the alley and dashed across the empty road, heading toward the station. The promenade was completely deserted now, the pier lost behind grey skeins of rain. The only living thing in sight was a single bedraggled donkey on the beach, tethered and facing stupidly into the downpour. He swung his arm high and threw the gun far into the grey sea.

The train to London was due to leave in just over seven minutes. In London no-one would ever find him. There, he could be anyone he wanted to be. He increased his speed but the pavement was dangerously slick, and he did not want to risk a fall. The town would try any old trick to keep him back.

He was getting soaked. Ahead he could just make out an odd figure approaching through the downpour. There was something about it he recognized. It was short and stumpy, and was walking as if it had broken its legs. At first he thought Harry had come after him. But as its appearance became more defined, Toby's thumping heart rose in his chest.

The thing crystallized from within the hammering clouds of rain, and he saw now that it was a truncated sailor the size of a child, dressed in navy blue, its hands flapping uselessly at its sides, its knees rising and falling like a puppet's. The peals of recorded laughter grew louder as it approached. It rocked from side to side and rolled its eyes. The awful Edwardian seaside song warped and wavered through blasts of wind as it ran faster toward him. The music was distorted and sinister now, less a celebration of holiday pleasure than a Satanists' chant.

The Jolly Jack Tar slammed into Toby, winding him, sending him to his knees. As it threw its arms around his neck. He felt wood through coarse material, then realised that its wooden limbs were held together with wires that were cutting into his skin. He could feel them in its fingertips as it tightened its embrace, digging into his flesh.

The dummy's eyes rolled and its grin widened. It rocked back and forth, knocking against Toby's head with a look that said *I told you so*. It was a museum piece, a doll, nothing more, but how like a living thing it was, filled with ancient sea-wisdom, preserved and trapped in a glass case for the amusement of others.

Toby rolled over onto his side, the dummy clinging tight, then tighter still. He dropped the bag as its death-grip stopped his breath and the wires from its wooden fingers jabbed into his chest, as if trying to worming their way to his heart. It bit him with a strangely flat wooden mouth, but bit down hard and would not be dislodged, and he knew he was destined to fall and remain here beside the seaside, beside the sea.

His last clear sight was across the desolate beach to the tethered donkey standing stoically in the rain, doomed like the rest of them, in the arcades and ticket booths, in the filthy glass cases and crumbling beach shelters, to live out its days at the end of the land.

Look here, I'm not a bad chap. I was educated at a minor public school, and I don't pretend to be especially bright, but I'm not afraid of telling a story against myself. However, this is pushing the envelope a bit. I mean, suppose it wound up on Facebook or something? I'd look a perfect fool. But I have to get it off my chest.

What happened to me was down to fate and inevitability, because of my background, because I was born out of my time, because I just wanted to make a good impression. I'm telling you because you're young and you might have the same kind of night that changes your life.

Here's what happened.

I, Elliot Sandhurst, son of Claude and Margaret Sandhurst, both late of Her Majesty's Foreign Office, self-proclaimed chinless wonder, was born into the top two percent of the population, but like so many of the upper ranks these days without a pot to piss in, had to go out there and find paid employment—which I did, at something called an 'event promotions company', the sort of media joint where you don't actually do anything except sit in meetings full of gobbledygook congratulating each other. I was always slightly amazed to see that a salary had been put in my bank account at the end of each month.

After three years in the same department, I foolishly assumed I was next in line for promotion when I discovered that Renata, my boss, had hired a fellow ten years my junior to fill a position that was equal in stature to my own.

The new boy was called Tamar. I assumed he was foreign or his name was an anagram or something, who knows. Tamar had street-cred, spiky hair, many pairs of Diesel jeans and a sense of entitlement that could cut through concrete. But to me, he appeared to be little more than a fetus with cheek-bones. And he started on a higher salary than my current level of pay. Meanwhile, I had just been told that I would not be getting a bonus this Christmas.

I knew I'd been rumbled. I was being sent a clear message; improve my game or be overtaken by somebody faster and hungrier. Tamar moved slowly, talked slowly and seemed inarticulate to the point of imbecility, but he was tall, dark and ludicrously handsome. It wasn't fair; there were job applicants who shelled out for special courses that taught them how to hone their CVs, not realizing that someone like Tamar could drift into reception with bed-hair and half-shut eyes, and casually step over them straight into a great job, all because he looked good in a cheap jacket and ironic shoes.

I did not look good in a cheap jacket. I owned several expensive bespoke Jermyn Street suits that were cunningly designed to hide my nascent paunch. I had my hair cut at an exclusive Mayfair salon where they knew how to cover up bald spots and disguise thinning follicles. The Sandhursts are not rich; my father insisted I did these things because his father did before him, just as I was expected to apply for membership at the Garrick and spend my weekends in the freezing Buckinghamshire countryside repairing the rotted windows of our draughty, leaking stately pile.

Tamar was twenty three and lived in the kind of London suburb that was so unfashionable, most people couldn't find its station on a tube map if you asked them to point to it with a stick. Everyone said he worked hard and was diligent, never left early and tried his best to make money for the company in what was apparently a loss-making department, although I never saw any sign of it. He usually came in with a Powerpoint presentation that consisted of a lot of media toss-words like *Brand Teasing*, *Cloudworking* and *Rightsizing*, coupled to colourful but insanely complex bar charts that reduced everyone in the room nursery school infants, having to raise their hands to ask questions. And they loved it. They loved him. He could do nothing wrong.

Whereas I lived in Belgravia and spent most weekends listening to the threats of my gout-ridden father, and had been warned that if I failed to make this career work, the old man would decide once and for all that I was a useless wastrel and would cut me out of my so-called inheritance, which consisted of a mortgaged-to-the-hilt mock-Georgian monstrosity with half a roof and a few acres of knotty grass that stank of pigs.

I felt I deserved a little more respect at work, so I needed to win my colleagues over. I had to give myself some credibility. I considered the options.

What could I do? Take them to a new cool nightspot? No, because I didn't know any. I just had my club, which would never allow them all in. Besides, my fellow office workers wouldn't be very impressed by the sight of a room full of drooling old duffers asleep in leather armchairs.

How about some kind of sporting event? I'd never even made it onto my school cricket eleven, and anyway most of the group got tickets for corporate bashes at Ascot, Twickenham, Wimbledon and Henley.

Dinner in a fancy restaurant? I couldn't afford to pay for all of them, and besides, knowing Renata's tastes, she would most likely suggest the kind of restaurant that only took bookings once every six months and specialised in novelty dishes that involved freezing crème caramel in nitrous oxide.

However, unbeknown to them, I had a secret weapon. My sister Daisy. She was a surprisingly good cook. Daisy and I had grown up travelling with our parents through various Foreign Office outposts in the Far East, and she had regularly attended hotel cooking classes because it got her out of netball practice.

I was pretty confident that if I could get my boss and her cronies over for dinner, I could impress them. Daisy loved cooking and would be able to provide a meal that would prove really memorable. I would just have to heat it up. I wouldn't want her there on the night, because she was nuts and would scupper my chances of regaining a foothold in the company if she so much as opened her mouth, but I thought that if she could deliver the meal earlier in the day, I would be able to do the rest.

There was the other problem. If Renata saw my Belgravia apartment she might feel less inclined to reward me at work, so I would have to borrow an apartment in an insalubrious part of town. Luckily, I had a friend, Will, whose father used to groom at my mother's stables, who lived in King's Cross. He was going away for a few weeks and needed someone to water his plants.

I drew up my guest list.

Renata could bring her husband, Lucio, who was a famous Italian graphic artist and, by all accounts, a total coke-monkey. Simon, the group account director, was responsible for looking after the agency's key clients, and could bore cats into comas just by describing his day to them. There was no need to invite his partner, presuming he had actually managed to attach himself to another human being so desperately lonely that she was prepared to spend time with him. I would pointedly snub Tamar by not inviting him, but would ask Cheryl, the company's lawyer, who was an extremely attractive Caribbean workaholic currently being groomed for a directorship by the managing director. Perhaps she would be so impressed by the meal that she'd suggest getting together again, and the next time it would be just the two of us.

The apartment was perfect; a loft of black slate, stripped brick and low lighting, edgy and cool enough to suggest that Will had style but not great wealth, near the station and taxi ranks, so that no-one would have an excuse for failing to turn up. It took three weeks of cajoling to get them all to agree to come over, and I had to bribe Daisy to pre-cook the meal, but finally the date was set and everyone accepted.

I spent a small fortune on purchasing several bottles of decent French wine. I memorized the layout of the kitchen so that I would not make any mistakes, and laid a stylish table. On the Saturday afternoon, Daisy delivered several cardboard boxes containing a complete Thai feast arranged in numbered foil cartons, although she stayed long enough to down one of the bottles of vintage red and have a drunken shrieking fit about her ex-boyfriend.

Then things started to go wrong. I managed to burn a lemongrass chicken dish while I was reheating it, a candle set one of the curtains on fire and the stunning Cheryl turned up with Tamar on her arm. Judging by the liquid warmth that filled her eyes every time she caught sight of him, she had fallen in love. It looked like she was wearing one of his shirts. He was so fashionably skinny that he could swap clothes with girls. Every time he made an ironic remark, she laughed. Everyone laughed. He'd been working at our place for less than a month.

Lumpen Simon appeared without a date—no surprise there—and Renata arrived with Lucio bearing a very acceptable bottle of Chateau Lafitte. 'Well, this is fun,' she said, eyeing the tiny, cluttered kitchen with suspicion as she waited for me to take their coats. This was all bit of a comedown for me. In India we'd had servants, for God's sake, and here I was being piled with outer garments while my boss wandered about pricing the ornaments.

'It's been ages since I went to a dinner party,' she said. 'I honestly didn't think anyone held them anymore. I suppose most people think it's a bit old school now.' She was fond of giving out the kind of backhanded English compliments that made you wonder if you'd just been insulted.

'This is a great flat,' said Cheryl admiringly. 'We'd love to get something like this in town.' I thought *We? You've known him for thirty seconds, woman, at this rate you'll be going through swatch-books for the nursery before I've had a chance to serve dessert.*

It's amazing what a difference good food and fine wine can make to your guests' spirits. At first there was just a polite exchange of information, like pupils attending some kind of evening language class. But after a while the drinks kicked in and we sat around the cramped lounge table picking bits of wax off the candles opening our hearts to one another. I found out, in no particular order, that;

Renata had spent her gap year earnings on an abortion.

Lucio had tried out for the Lucchese football team and had been propositioned by the girlfriend of a famous Italian racing driver.

Cheryl took pole-dancing lessons to keep fit.

Simon belonged to a society that re-enacted historical British battles.

But Tamar beat all of them. First he let slip that he had been in a boy band that had achieved Top 100 success. Then he mentioned in passing that he had once modelled for Dolce & Gabbana. Finally, he sent his credibility rating through the roof by telling us that he came from one of London's worst housing estates.

There was no way I could compete. All this *opening up* was alien to me. I had nothing to offer back. I realised that I simply didn't fit in. The Sandhurst family revelled in their ability to keep everything secret. That was what the British did best. As I opened more wine and cleared the dinner plates and served fresh fruit salad and Eton Mess, Tamar was telling the rest of the table about the day he had saved a policeman's life. His story had just the right amount of tousle-and-shucks modesty to it, and at the end, everyone went 'aaaah'. He'd shared the love and made them all feel warm. I felt my pole position slipping away as Tamar roared past me toward the job-promotion finishing line.

It was then that a funny thing happened. It took me a couple of minutes to pick up on the hint, but I realized that Renata wanted something, she just wouldn't spell it out.

I'm not very attuned to hints about drugs. To tell the truth, I hadn't much experience of them. I'd taken one lungful of a joint at Oxford on Guy Fawkes Night and had fallen into the bonfire like a poleaxed elm. My roommate had been forced to put me out by rolling me on the lawn. That was the sum total of my chemical experience. So when Renata and Lucio eyed the glass table top and obliquely suggested I could make it a perfect evening by breaking out something for them to enjoy, I looked at them blankly. Then I saw Cheryl smiling knowingly, and realized that I was expected to have bought in some coke. Everyone seemed to perk up at the idea except Simon, who was going on about railway timetables.

I actually found myself apologizing for not having bought anything special in, but I was careful to make it sound like I usually did whenever I had friends over, and it was just an oversight that I had forgotten this time. Incredible.

'Well, that's easily rectified, darling,' said Renata, smiling at the rest of the table. 'We're in King's Cross after all. Why don't you just pop out and get some while we finish this bottle?' She made it sound as if I'd run out of milk and could whip over to the supermarket.

Having made a bid for credibility in this field—I may have overdone it by suggesting that I regularly partied at the local night spots, something I could tell they didn't believe even as the words came out of my mouth—I now found myself back-pedaling frantically. Renata started to look pouty, so I hastily donned my suit jacket and told them I'd be back in fifteen minutes, trying to sound as though this was the sort of thing I did all the time. As I left the room, I looked back and saw them drinking and laughing, barely aware that I was no longer in the room, quite happy to sit there and wait for my return. Londoners.

I stepped out into the street and looked about. The station was brightly illuminated, but the side streets were dark and mean. Where to start on my quest?

I noticed the tramps were back. Several of them were having a party in an alley beside McDonalds, pouring the contents of one can into another as if making cocktails. Outside the nightclub next door, a huge gang of fairies—girls in pink glittery wings and little pink ruffled skirts—were queuing to get in, shoving and swearing at each other like pissed sailors. The area around the station was really busy. Businessmen were heading home after a night in the pub with their satchel straps slung across their chests like off-duty postmen.

A couple of coppers were talking to a young black man, all in seeming good humour. If I was going to successfully buy drugs, I had to get down with my homies, except that they weren't my homies, my homies were men with flat tweed caps who sat on tractors blocking narrow country lanes.

I tried to get the lay of my new hostile territory. Who, around me, looked like a drug dealer? Not the girl sitting on the kerb being sick between her legs while her friend held her hair out of her face. Not the two perfectly square skinheads who kept shouting something in an incomprehensible Scottish dialect at passers-by between slugs of Special Brew. Not the wobbly man having a wee against the window of Nando's, steadying himself with one hand on the glass.

Would it sound racist if I said I was looking for black men?

Ah, it would—okay—as you were. Well I did, and I'm sorry for it now, it's a cultural problem and all I can say is that I'm better than my grandmother, who screamed and ran off when a black man touched her arm at Victoria Station. He was trying to return her purse, which she'd dropped on the concourse.

I suppose I'd seen too much American television. And as it turned out the drug dealer was white, not black, and looked like the sort of cherubic, overfed, shaven-pated teenager you'd let into your home to assist with the repaving of your patio. He was dressed in a scuffed brown leather jacket with a grey hood, and jeans that were slightly too long at the back, so that they had frayed. He looked like he had been born with his hands in his pockets. He spoke out of the side of his mouth in barely more than a mumble.

'What you after?'

I supposed lads like him were always hanging around stations, invisible to all except those who were looking for them, so I said 'I'd like some cocaine please.'

And he said, 'One or two?'

And I said 'Well, I'd better get two,' as if they were eggs and I wasn't sure about the recipe's quantities.

And he said, 'One twenty.' I must admit that I felt rather chuffed about discovering the street price of cocaine. I suppose it made me look a bit less clueless. Now, as luck would have it I'd been to a cashpoint earlier in the day and had taken out £200 to buy things I'd needed for the dinner, and I had £150 left because I'd ended up putting the wine on my Visa card. He asked to see the money, I showed him, then he told me to follow him.

'Can't I just wait here and let you bring it to me?' I asked, and it turned out this was a bit of a naïve question because he screwed his face into a ball and said 'You're 'aving a larf, incha?' And of course when I thought about it I realised there were police and cameras all over the place, so I meekly followed him down Pentonville Road to an alley that reeked of urine, and into a back-street full of council flats. It was just thirty seconds from Will's apartment, but it felt as if we had been suddenly flown to Afghanistan.

I'd never been in a council flat before, and I hope I never will again. It was quite, quite ghastly. We threaded our way along an underlit terrace covered in bicycles and dead plants and plastic lawn chairs, past gangs of very thin Indian boys standing around with their hands in their pockets like they had nothing else to do. It was all most peculiar. Every single one of the front doors we passed was fire engine red, which I thought an odd coincidence. As we skirted around them, the Indian boys made derogatory remarks and sucked their teeth, for absolutely no reason that I could see.

My drug dealer gave a complicated knock on the door and after a minute it was opened by an emaciated girl in a black vest and baggy grey trousers. There were no social niceties, no introductions. I simply followed him in. You'd think she would have checked. I could have been anyone.

The hallway smelled of fried chicken and something less sanitary.

'Go in there,' said the Cherub, holding open the first door off the hall. I found myself in an incredibly small room filled with the kind of brown leather sofas they always advertise on Boxing Day. You know the type, very common and vulgar-looking. Wedged into the sofas were four men and two girls. The girls looked like beauticians from a provincial department store, the kind who appear to be wearing their underwear on the outside of their clothes, all legs and makeup, and the men looked like various versions of Frankenstein. The walls were covered in film posters attached to the blotchy silver wallpaper by drawing pins. I noted *Reservoir Dogs, Inglorious Basterds, Bad Lieutenant* and rather less explicably, *Toy Story 3*.

Very complicated-looking bits of drug paraphernalia were scattered over the tiled table in front of them. Don't get me wrong; I wasn't a total hick. I knew what cocaine looked like; I'd seen *Scarface*. But there were glass pipettes and blackened beakers and rolls of silver foil and other bits and pieces that mystified me. Oh, and for some reason, a big stack of X-Men comics, council house literature.

The TV in the corner was showing a movie I vaguely recognised. The colour was turned up too high. The group seemed to be playing some kind of game involving the film they were watching. On the screen, a man in over-developed pectorals and a nappy yelled something about the honour of Sparta and shook his spear. Suddenly everyone in the room made a guttural roaring noise, reached forward to the table and threw back a small glass of clear liquid, followed by a swig from a black bottle. A moment later, the nappy-man said 'Sparta' again and everyone roared again.

'It's a drinking game,' the Cherub explained as he returned, 'tequila and a Guinness chaser every time Gerard Butler shouts 'Sparta.''

The Cherub threw me a beer. No-one had ever thrown a beer at me before. I even managed to catch it. Seating himself on the arm of the chair, he unfolded a rectangle of newspaper, handed me a shortened section of a McDonald's plastic straw and said 'Check that out, pal.' I was his pal now.

I hadn't thought about this. Suddenly I realised that I would have to try the merchandise, just like drug lords did in crime films. There was no way out. I jammed one end of the straw up my right nostril and sucked hard.

'Fuck!' shouted the Cherub, snatching back the paper, which was now empty. McDonald's straws are quite wide, and I assumed he meant that it hadn't all been for me. 'You'd better make it one fifty and I'll get your gear,' he said, holding out his hand.

'What do you mean?' I asked. The girls imitated the way I spoke and tittered.

'That wasn't your coke, was it,' the Cherub replied. I had to stop and work out whether he was asking me a question.

'Then what was it?' I asked. The inside of my nose was really starting to burn.

'Some kind of MDMA cocktail we cooked up in the kitchen. Pukka designer stuff, no rubbish.'

'MDMA? What's that?' I asked, but everyone just looked at me and started laughing again. The Cherub was waiting, and the best Frankenstein in the room, a teenaged monster who had a curving row of crimped stitches running around his right ear and over his cheek, glared at me so hard I feared he might have left a burn hole in the wallpaper, so I dug out my wallet and handed over the contents before he decided to hit me.

'Okay, let's go and get it,' said the cherub, rising.

'Is it not here, then?' I asked.

'No, it's at the Baron's.'

'Who is the Baron?' Everyone laughed again, quite rudely I thought.

And we were off once more, but now some of the Frankensteins and one of the girls came with us out of curiosity, following behind like some kind of Victorian concert party gone horribly wrong.

This time we went through the rear of the building to a black-painted fire escape, and up several floors to the flat roof. Looking down, I could see the road I had walked along earlier. If I leaned over the edge, I could probably have spotted my dinner guests patiently sitting around the table.

The cherub pushed open another red door and led us into a bare rectangular concrete room lit in each corner with a fat black candle. On the breezeblock wall opposite was a really terrible painting of a woman having sex with a crocodile.

In the centre of the room crouched an enormously fat man in a top hat covered in gold Christmas tree decorations. He had a mad frizzy grey beard and was wrapped in a woman's red floral bathrobe, and wore matching red wellingtons. An iPod had been docked into a speaker on the floor, and was playing something that sounded like a radically decelerated version of the theme music to *Doctor Who*.

'Is it hot in here, or is it me?' I asked, loosening my collar, and everybody laughed again, like court jesters paid to guffaw at the king's jokes even when he didn't say anything funny.

I noticed that there was something wrong with the candles; their flames were leaving fiery trails whenever I moved my head. The Cherub said something to the bearded man and they shared a private moment of covert laughter. One of the beautician girls wandered over to me and ran her hand down the front of my shirt. She seemed to be moving in slow motion. Everything was. Suddenly, without any kind of warning, she pulled open her shirt and released a pair of astonishing, pendulous white breasts. Thinking back, it must have been done up with press-studs.

I found myself feeling simultaneously threatened and excited. Leaning forward, she held long, dark nipples between her thumbs and forefingers and rubbed them back and forth across my chest like battery contacts. She said something, but it sounded like a radio someone had placed a pillow over. I stuck a finger in my ear and wiggled it, but still couldn't hear.

She slid her hands inside my shirt and ripped it open. Buttons landed on the floor, very slowly and loudly. I felt my trouser zipper opening and my tumescent member being removed from its safe nest.

'Now look here, hang on a minute,' I said, 'I came here for a legitimate reason—' I had trouble saying the word *legitimate*—'to collect two portions of cocaine.' But I don't think any of the words came out very clearly.

I felt my member being enveloped in something wet and hot. Closing my eyes, I saw myself flying backwards and up, like a child on a tall playground swing, higher and higher, my stomach rising and falling. When I looked back down, I found Father Christmas's face attached to my groin, his fat lips glued over my private parts as if he had swallowed them whole. He looked up at me and rolled his eyes. I think I might have screamed.

I certainly jumped back. Everyone was laughing, and by now I was hot and angry. The Cherub appeared to think that I'd been a good sport and slapped me on the shoulder, as if I had passed some kind of revolting initiation ceremony. His face loomed close to mine. His lips were a mile across, and as he spoke I thought his mouth would swallow the universe. 'I'll get your coke, don't worry,' he said, speaking very loudly and distinctly, like a teacher dealing with a truculent child. I was trying very hard not to think of the Father Christmas-man who had been attached to my testicles. He was still kneeling on the floor grinning.

There was a fire burning in the middle of the next room on a rusty old barbeque grill, and the only piece of furniture was a ratty old Ikea sofa with the springs poking through the cushions. Another pair of Frankensteins sat side by side on it. These ones were wearing matching Elizabethan ruff-collar shirts and black leather jerkins, and were drinking lagers. They continued to talk across me very quickly, as if I wasn't there, like some kind of peculiar burlesque hall double act.

'London's wildlife is tragically under-appreciated,' said one.

'Murderers are the most elusive and mysterious of all the creatures that appear in conurbations after dark,' agreed the other.

'They're shy nocturnal souls who leave their spoor in various parts of our fair city, especially in the section christened Murder Mile, from outside Camden Town's *Pret A Manger*—'

'A trainee rabbi was found hacked up in bin-bags,' interjected the other.

'Past Royal College Street—'

'Ladies of the night were chopped into pieces there and dumped in bin-bags, identified by their breast implants.'

'And the Regent's Canal—'

'Where the American tourist was slashed in half with a machete.'

'Along Kentish Town Road—'

'Adam Ant threw a carburettor through a pub window and threatened patrons with a fake gun—'

'To Kentish Town tube—'

'A man was beaten to death by gang members for doing nothing more than politely asking the way.'

'Up to Tufnell Park tube station—'

'Home to at least half a dozen recent assorted gunshot victims all under the age of seventeen.'

'Bin-bag murderers are civic-minded. They'd never dream of shoveling guts and limbs into gutters, and at least allow the dustmen some faint hope of recovering the victims' jewelry.'

Now they both spoke together in perfect unison. 'And so the city's Hogarthian spirit, vengeful, feral and packing serious heat, lives on.'

It was quite a performance. The Frankensteins fell silent and turned to look at me as if waiting for a round of applause. Their heads were moving around, leaving phosphorescent traces in the air, as if they had become radioactive. The fire was whizzing about all over the place.

I pointed at a can of lager. 'Could I have some of that?' I asked thickly. 'I seem to have a terribly dry throat.'

One of them gave me his can and I drank greedily, spilling most of the beer down my shirt.

The Cherub was grinning and beckoning. I stumbled toward him, forced to follow, partly because I was having terrible trouble maintaining an upright balance, partly because he had all my money, and partly because I still had a dinner party full of guests waiting to be served a dessert treat.

'What's wrong with those two?' I asked, looking back at the Frankensteins. 'I think I need to get what I came for now. Would that be possible?'

'It'll just be a couple more minutes,' the Cherub told me, maintaining eye contact as he walked backwards. His crimson pupils were Loris-sized in the candle-light. There were flames waltzing in them. 'So, what's a posh ponce like you doing here?'

'I needed—I need to prove—I just need—' I was finding it hard to concentrate, because the two Frankensteins on the couch were now singing showtunes very loudly, very off-key, something about a lonely goatherd.

'There are no addicts on the streets of King's Cross anymore,' said the Cherub sadly. 'You used to feel you were providing a useful service.' He pushed open the door and stepped out onto the roof. He span around and stared into my eyes. 'Have you ever seen your heart beating outside your body?'

'I have no idea what you're talking about,' I admitted.

'Have a drink of water.' He passed over a two-thirds empty bottle of Evian.

Without pausing to think, I drank. 'It tastes funny,' I said.

The Cherub gave an apologetic shrug and held up a little white pill. 'I dissolved some of these in it.'

'Why do you keep doing that?' I asked, angry with him now.

He grabbed the back of my head and held me still. 'You're going to feel very strange in a minute. Are your feet tingling?'

'Yes, that's funny, they are.' I held out my arms, which seemed to be about four feet long. 'And so are my fingers. Oh.'

As I watched them, my fingers slowly turned green with the kind of suppurating rot I saw around the bases of elm trees on my father's estate. The nails blackened, cracked and fell off like old paint. I could see pale points of bone sticking through the tips of my ragged digits, although they didn't seem to be sore. I remember thinking that I would have wear gloves from now on. I looked down at my retreating feet. The same thing was happening with them. Somewhere along the line I had lost my shoes and was walking about in bare feet. With each step, I left behind another rotted toe.

'Problem with your feet?'

'You could say that,' I mouthed at him. 'I don't want this to happen when I'm old. All this falling to bits.' I grabbed the back of his jacket. The leather felt so nice that I never wanted to let go. 'Please don't let me get old. It's all squishy. I will stay young if I have your jacket.'

'You can't have my jacket.'

'Can I just stroke it again?'

'We have to go down now.' He pointed to the fire escape, but it looked like a roller coaster, stretching off into the far, far distance, somewhere in the inky darkness several hundred miles below. 'What are you doing?' he asked me, clearly concerned.

'I'm getting in the car,' I told him, as if it should be obvious. The roller coaster car was shiny red, with chromium lightning bolts on the sides and fat chrome bumpers. I climbed in and hung onto the side rails as he released the handbrake and we fell sharply, the wind punching my breath from me. We raced down the lethal steel slope for an age, far beyond sight of the ground.

'Let go of the bannisters,' the Cherub was shouting in my ear.

'What bannisters?' I asked, looking back at my white-knuckled, rotting hands gripped tightly over the sides of the roller coaster car. I shook my head, unable to speak at all now. There was a terrible noise inside my brain like the mountain sliding down onto the tracks in *The Railway Children*, and I realised what it was; I was grinding my teeth. I could taste blood.

'Okay, I can see we're going to have to try something else,' said the Cherub. 'We have to fool the cider's jail.'

'What?' I bellowed in his face.

'We have to pull the tiger's tail.'

I shook my head violently, dislodging a number of buildings.

'Come with me. Just hold my arm and turn around. That's it.' I looked behind me. Sitting on the gravel of the undulating roof some kind of mythical creature was sitting on its haunches, breathing heavily. It was tiger-striped, yellow and brown, with an immense jawbone and leaking yellow eyes. It lumbered blindly to its feet and sniffed the air. Around his vast bull-neck was a great steel chain.

'My God, what on earth is that?'

'That is the Were-Tiger,' said the Cherub, reaching up to stroke the creature's chest. 'It's father was a werewolf and it's mother—'

'—was a tiger, I get that,' I said anxiously, watching it crunching something in its mouth. 'What's it eating?'

The Cherub pulled something from between its bloody teeth. I caught a blast of stinking meat. He was holding the top half of a baby, probably no more than about six months old. Horrified, I stumbled backwards.

'Why are you feeding it babies?' I asked.

'Highlights are his tutors,' he replied.

'I'm sorry?'

'He likes them as chew-toys.' The Cherub began to undo its chain.

'Look, do you think that's wise?' I asked.

He brought the end of the chain over to me and looped it through the belt of my trousers, at the back. 'How long would you say this is?' he asked, holding up the chain.

'Oh, I don't know—about ten feet?'

'So you've got about five seconds head start, haven't you?' He reached around the back of the Were-Tiger, raised his boot and stamped hard on its tail. The beast threw back its head and roared, spraying me with bloody flecks of baby-meat. Its little baby arm bounced bloodily off my chest.

A moment later the Were-Tiger rose up on its hind legs, surprisingly agile, and threw itself at me. I fled back to the roller-coaster, slung myself into the car and launched down the next dip with the creature forced into close pursuit, attached to me by the length of chain.

The speed of my descent was tremendous. I plummeted down the rusted iron rails, up over a hump that lifted my stomach and down again, steeper than the last, as the ground rushed up toward me. My speed had increased so much now that I was pulling the Were-Tiger in my slipstream, and its hurtling bulk threatened to crash forward on top of me. Its immense teeth closed over my left ear and tore away a piece of my lobe, but now the pace of the car increased again and the chain was pulled taut, and he fell back.

The ground was racing up to meet my face, closer, closer, and I crash-landed with a tremendous smash. The infuriated creature landed on its head and rolled aside in a spray of blood and spittle, knocked unconscious. And there was the Cherub again, laughing as he unbuckled the great chain from my trousers and reattached it to a drainpipe, holding the Were-Tiger in place.

It felt as if every bone in my body was broken. Luckily my face had landed in a pile of small soft black rocks that had protected my fine good looks from damage.

'You're going to bleed in Sitges,' said the Cherub.

'I'm sorry?' I cupped my bloody ear at him.

'You're going to need some stitches.' The Cherub hauled me to my feet and poked me in the ribs. 'Does that hurt?'

'Yes, quite a lot,' I told him, dripping earlobe blood onto my shirt-front.

'I think you've cracked a couple of ribs. Can you see your heart now?'

'Yes, I think I can.'

'Come on, let's get you sorted out.'

'Do you think I could have a lay down?' I asked. 'I'm suddenly feeling rather tired. Can I go home?'

'I don't know. How many fingers am I holding up?'

I counted them. 'Fifteen,' I replied. 'Can I collect my purchases now?'

'Better give it another couple of minutes. You'll start to feel peckish soon.'

We walked through a thick jungle filled with glossy ferns, and I gingerly stepped over a sleeping boa constrictor, its iridescent scales sparkling in the night air. Something that looked like an enormous armour-plated mosquito landed on my arm and stung me. I yelped, although the cry turned into laughter.

The Cherub kicked open another door—also painted red—and led me inside. A runway of flickering candles led to a very attractive Hawaiian scene. There was a beach, and a distant waterfall, and that strange Hawaiian music that sounds like a banjo being repeatedly stretched, and a girl in a grass skirt and coconut shells came over and draped a necklace of brightly coloured artificial flowers around my neck.

She traced her hand delicately across my back, and passed me a beautiful bag made of woven reeds. 'Here are your purchases,' she said, smiling.

'Thank you, you've very nice. I like your Hawaiian island,' I told her, and she laughed.

'He needs some fresh hair,' she said.

'I've got hair.'

'No, fresh air.'

My clothes were soaked in sweat, and I suddenly started to feel cold and very hungry. The bright colours had begun to fade down to drab greys and browns. I blinked and opened my eyes wide, then blinked again. I wasn't on a beach, I was in a basement full of builders' sand, and the waterfall was a tap running noisily into a floor drain. My mouth felt as if it was full of wool. I realised the Cherub was talking to me.

'I told you, there's no addicts out there on the street now, and I need to test the effects of this shit. Thanks for your feedback. Sorry the dog bit you.' He gave a pleasant smile. I looked around, taking in my surroundings. The great Were-Tiger had been replaced by a brindle bull mastiff on a bit of string. It was chewing happily a child's plastic baby doll. Oddly, the girl in the grass skirt and coconut shells was still dressed that way. I imagined she was going out later. I tried to speak but no sound came out.

'We had a laugh trying to get you down the fire escape,' he said. 'Well, it was nice doing business with you. You'd better get off now.'

'Wait,' I said, 'who was Father Christmas?'

'Oh, the Baron. My old man. It's his flat.'

And he shut the basement door in my face. Outside there was no jungle, just weeds and dirt and an old green plastic hosepipe curled on the floor. I climbed back up to the street and out into the alleyway. My arms and legs felt as if they were made of lead.

It felt as if the temperature had dropped to below zero. Back on the main road the tail lights of cars and taxis were still leaving faint vapour trails, but the effect was much more muted now. I seemed to be carrying a white plastic Tesco bag. Everything seemed suddenly scratchy and real and rather boring.

When I got back to the apartment, I checked my watch and realised that I had been gone for over two hours. Worse, I had unthinkingly locked the downstairs door with the chub key when I left, shutting everyone in. With a growing sense of dread, I made my way upstairs. Even as I was putting my key in the lock, I heard someone say 'Thank God'.

As I pushed open the door, I tried to be nonchalant. 'Sorry about the delay,' I said cheerfully. 'Had a bit of a problem, but it's all sorted now.'

All the wine had gone. My dinner part guests had the trapped look of prison inmates and lay slumped around the room. As I came in, they sat up and stared at me with their mouths open.

'What the fucking hell happened to you?' asked Renata. 'Your ear is all torn up, you've got blood and bits of coal stuck all over your face, someone's written WANKER across the back of your jacket in white paint and a chunk of your hair is missing.'

'And you locked us in, you dick,' said Lucio, which was a bit rich coming from him.

'Yes, sorry about that, I ran into a spot of bother.' I stepped further into the room. Everyone gasped.

'Your junk, man,' said Tamar, appalled.

'I'm sorry?'

'Elliot, your penis is hanging out,' said Cheryl, 'and you've got no shoes.'

'Thank you, Cheryl, well done for noticing.' I tucked myself back in. I'd thought it was a bit draughty walking home.

'And Jesus! You've got a fish-hook in your arm!'

'So I have. Well, never mind. Don't worry about me, I wasn't raped or anything, but I did fight a were-tiger on a roller-coaster. Just so you could enjoy yourselves a little bit more. Sorry about locking you in.'

'No that any of us are in the mood now,' said Renata huffily, 'but did you get what you went for?'

'Oh yes, absolutely.' I held up the bag, then emptied it out onto the table. I found myself staring at a large bunch of bananas. 'Ah. Right. Not cocaine then.'

'Who said anything about cocaine?' said Renata incredulously. 'I thought you went to get chocolate.'

'So did I,' said Tamar. Everyone else agreed with him.

'Did you now. Well, I must have misread that signal. Never mind.' I dumped the bananas on the table before them. 'Enjoy.'

I dropped down and fell instantly into a deep snoring coma.

Tamar got my job, which was probably just as well. I imagine he's a lot better at it than me. He's probably a CEO by now. Me, I'm a gardener on my father's estate. I'm paid a pittance and it's not exactly taxing, but I quite like the work. The natural order has reasserted itself. There's a moral here somewhere, but I'm not entirely sure what it is.

I do know one thing. If you're ever in King's Cross and see an angelic-faced skinhead with a bull mastiff on a bit of string, don't buy any bananas from him.

BRYANT & MAY IN THE SOUP

It was the thickest fog London had ever seen.

Acrid and jaundiced, it rolled across London on the 5th of December, 1952, and lasted for four days. It was impossible to keep at bay; yellow tendrils unfurled through windows, crept under doors and down chimneys until it was difficult to tell if you were inside or out. The fog stopped traffic and asphyxiated the cattle at Smithfield's Market. At Sadler's Wells, performances were halted because it invaded the auditorium, choking the dancers and the audience. Down near the Thames, visibility dropped to nil. Cars crashed into pillar boxes, cats fell out of trees and pedestrians became lost in their own front gardens. On the low-slung Isle of Dogs, it was said that people could not even see their own feet. Only the highest point of Hampstead Heath rose above the dense yellow smoke. From there, all you could see were the hills of Kent and Surrey.

This bizarre phenomenon had been caused by an unfortunate confluence of factors. The month had started with bitterly low temperatures and heavy snowfalls, so the residents of London piled cheap coal into their grates. The sulphurous smoke from their chimneys mixed with pollutants from the capital's factories, and became trapped beneath an inverse anticylone. The resulting miasma caused over 12,000 fatalities and stained London's buildings black for fifty years. The young and the elderly died from respiratory problems. Their lungs filled with pus and they choked to death.

The thought of suffering in so horrible a fashion clouded Harry Whitworth's thoughts. In the last few minutes he had found it difficult to catch his breath. Cramps were knotting his stomach, and he had to keep stopping beside the gutter to spit. When he reached his place of employment, the coachworks in Brewer Street, he was surprised to find the place almost deserted.

'Where is everybody?' he asked Stan, the skinny young apprentice who helped the mechanics tune the engines.

'Ain't you heard, Harry? The place has been closed until the fog lifts. We can't take anything out in this, not without someone walking in front of the vehicle, and we ain't got the staff. Charlie was supposed to phone you and tell you not to come in.'

'We're not on the phone,' Harry explained. 'Why are the engines running?'

'Maintenance. A couple of them are dicky. I thought if we couldn't take the coaches out, I'd at least be able to get some soot off the pistons.'

'I think my ticker could do with a decoke,' said Harry, patting his chest. 'I feel proper queer. I was sick a few minutes ago, and I've got a chronic pain in my guts. I've been coughing like a good 'un. Can't catch me breath. Let me get the weight off my feet, at least.'

'You know you're not supposed—'

Too late. Harry had climbed up into the driver's seat of the nearest coach, sat down and placed his hands on the wheel. With a weary sigh, he closed his eyes.

Two minutes later, he was dead.

Arthur Bryant realised how bad the fog had become when he tried to post a letter in a pensioner. Earlier that day he had asked a lamp-post for a light.

He was on his way to meet John May, his fellow detective at Bow Street police station, but had somehow lost his way in the few short streets from Aldwych. Luckily, knowing that his partner was capable of getting lost inside a corset, May had come looking for him. Bryant had a distinctive silhouette, like a disinterred mole in a raincoat, and was easy to spot. When a hand fell upon his shoulder, he jumped.

'Ah, there you are,' said Bryant, as if it were he who had found the other. 'You left a message at my club?'

'You don't have a club, Arthur. It's a pub, and not a very nice one either.' May linked his arm in Bryant's and steered him out of the road.

'Perhaps not, but at least they've managed to keep out this blasted muck.'
Bryant was lately in the habit of frequenting a basement dive bar underneath
Piccadilly Circus that served high-quality oysters to low-quality clientele.
'Your note said something about a coach garage.'

'That's right, it's nearby.' May wiped his forehead and found it wet with
sooty black droplets. 'I'd keep your scarf fastened tightly over your mouth,
there's a lot of dirt in the air. You know you've always had trouble with your
lungs.'

It took them ages to feel their way to Brewer Street. 'I got a call from my
sister,' May explained. 'Her neighbour's boy, Stan, told her he had a dead body
on his hands and didn't know what to do.'

The main gate to the coachworks was shut, but there was an unlocked side
door. The interior of the building was wreathed in mist, but at least it was
thinner than the air outside. A gawky boy with a face of crowded freckles ran
toward them. He waved behind him, distraught. 'He's over here, sir. Come
with me.'

They found Harry Whitworth behind the wheel of the green and cream
coach. His skin was blanched to a peculiar shade of khaki. 'Did you find him
like this?' asked May.

'No sir, he came in for work late this morning, about nine o'clock. He
normally starts at eight but I think he had trouble finding his way because of
this fog.'

'Did he complain of any health problems?'

'Yes sir, he told me he was having trouble breathing. He'd been sick, and
had a sore tummy. And he was coughing a lot.'

Bryant climbed into the seat next to Harry Whitworth, reached over and
opened his mouth. 'He's got a tongue like a razor strop.'

'Flat, you mean?' asked May.

'No, dry. Anybody else here?'

'No sir,' said Stan, 'they've all been given the day off.'

'So none of the coaches were running their engines?'

'Two of them were running. I was making some repairs, so the day wasn't
wasted.'

'Any fog get in here?'

'Some, sir. It's difficult to keep out.' Stan looked distraught.

'But the doors and windows were all shut?'

'Yes. On the radio this morning they were telling everyone to stay indoors and keep everything sealed.'

'But you're in an enclosed space, lad. Did you not think about the exhaust fumes?'

'No sir. Couldn't be any worse than the fog.'

'Actually it could.' Bryant eased himself out of the coach cabin. 'I think this chap died of carbon monoxide poisoning.'

Stan's thin hands flew to his mouth. 'You're not saying I killed him?'

'Not exactly,' said May, anxious to placate the boy. 'It would have been an accident.'

'Surely you knew the danger of running the engines in an enclosed space?' asked Bryant sternly. 'You could have asphyxiated yourself. The engines are off now, though.'

'Yes sir, I turned them off to attend to Harry.'

'How old are you?'

'Seventeen, sir.'

'In good health?'

'As far as I know. I've always been good at P.E.'

'And Mr Whitworth?'

'He had a bout of pneumonia last year.'

'He's a driver, yes?'

'No sir, not anymore, not since his illness. He does the driver's rosters.'

'So Harry Whitworth had a chest weakness, which is why the lad survived and he didn't,' May told Bryant. 'Open and shut case.'

'Do you know how we can contact Mr Whitworth's family?' Bryant asked.

'That's easy enough,' the boy told them. 'His son Clive works over at the ABC cafe on Wardour Street.'

'Come on.' May tugged at his partner's sleeve. 'Let's get it over with.'

'I won't go to prison, will I?' Stan was wringing his cap in his hands.

'No. But you're not to go anywhere until our men get here, do you understand? You're on your honour. They'll only be a few minutes.'

Bryant was still hanging around the coach as May made to leave. 'What's the matter?' he asked.

'Nothing,' Bryant decided finally. 'Only it's funny.'

'What's funny?'

'If Harry Whitworth has a desk job, why did he get behind the wheel?'

The two detectives left the coachworks and made slow progress through the thickening fog. Their hearing became almost as muffled as their sight. May was forced to yank his partner out of the path of a recklessly driven taxi.

'Do you mind?' Bryant complained indignantly, 'this is my best coat.'

'You were nearly buried in it,' May snapped back. 'There's the cafeteria. On your left. No, your other left.'

Ahead was a soft glowing rectangle of glass. Bryant felt around, located the door handle and pushed. The pair tumbled into the café, which smelled of boiled cabbage and roly-poly pudding. The radio was playing, its thin treble making Winifred Atwell's honky-tonk piano sound even tinnier than usual. Less than half a dozen customers sat at the tables; the fog was keeping everyone out of the West End. A pretty waitress stood listlessly examining her painted nails. Bryant went to the kitchen counter and rapped on it with his knuckles. 'Anyone at home back there?'

A tired-looking young man in a chef's hat appeared. One glance at his nose in alarming profile told the detectives that they had found Harry Whitworth's son. 'Are you Clive Whitworth?' May asked. When the young man cautiously nodded, he continued. 'I'm afraid we have some rather bad news for you.'

They seated him in the kitchen and gave him a tot of brandy from Bryant's hip-flask. 'When did you last see your dad?' May probed gently.

'This morning.' Clive looked down at his hands. 'He often comes in for breakfast. Mum died a couple of years ago. He doesn't cook for himself.'

'You live in the same house?'

'I'd like to get my own place, of course. We normally come in together from East Finchley. Not today, though. I had to start early.'

'How did he seem to you?'

'He was coughing a lot. I think the fog was getting to him. I told him he shouldn't have come in.'

'How did he get here from the station?'

'He'd have walked, I'm sure. In spite of the fog. He was stubborn like that.'

'Well,' said May, waiting for a suitable break in the conversation, 'we should be getting along. We'll make all the necessary arrangements for your father, you needn't worry yourself about that side of things.' He gave Clive Whitworth a comforting pat on the back and led the way from the kitchen.

Bryant was unusually quiet as they returned to Bow Street through the sickly yellow fumes. May knew better than to assume it was simply because he was heavily muffled.

'All right,' he said as they unwrapped themselves back at the police station, 'what's the matter?'

Bryant regarded him with innocent blue eyes. 'What do you mean?'

'I always know when there's something on your mind. Out with it.'

'Well, it's really unimportant.' Bryant dropped behind his desk and began to doodle aimlessly on a blotter.

'Really, getting information out of you is like pulling teeth some days. Are you going to tell me or not?'

'I've been thinking. Harry Whitworth had weak lungs, and had been out in the fog. The bloodless dry tongue is a classic sign of oxygen starvation, consistent with carbon monoxide poisoning. In both cases it's a form of hypoxia leading to death, but which of the two causes of death was it?'

'Does it really matter?' asked May. 'Most likely it was a little of both.'

'He told the boy he had an upset stomach when he arrived. Perhaps we should wait until Oswald Finch has had a chance to conduct a post mortem.' Finch was the coroner used by the Bow Street police.

'Well, it's terribly sad, but I'm sure there'll be similar cases before the fog lifts.' May opened his report folder, happy to fill it in and move on.

They worked quietly until lunchtime. At ten to one, Bryant rose and knotted his scarf around his face once more, leaving only his eyes and the tops of his ears exposed. He looked like Wilfred from the Bash Street Kids. 'I thought I'd pop out and get something to eat,' he mumbled. 'I'll bring you something back.' And he was gone. This in itself was extraordinary, as May knew his partner always brought sandwiches in gruesome combinations that involved cheese, jam and sardines. Sure enough, today's greaseproof paper packet was still in the top drawer of his desk. *What's he up to?* he thought.

Half an hour later, he received a phonecall. Bryant was ringing from the blue police box on Shaftesbury Avenue. 'I wonder if you'd be so kind as to meet me back at the coachworks?' he asked.

Harry Whitworth's body had been removed, but Stan the apprentice was still seated glumly in the manager's office, waiting to be released. He rose in anxiety as the detectives arrived. 'Will it be all right for me to go home soon, sir?' he asked. 'It's been a terrible morning.'

'Of course, Stanley, I just want you to repeat what you told me a few minutes ago.'

'About Harry and his son?'

'That's right.'

Stan turned to John May. 'I was telling Mr Bryant that they don't get on. Ever since Harry's wife died he's not allowed Clive out of his sight.'

'Not that part, the part about why Harry seated himself behind the wheel of the coach.'

Stan looked sheepish. 'He misses it, see. He's been banned from driving.'

'And why was he banned? Tell Mr May here.'

'After his wife died, Harry started drinking. He had an accident. He's been here all his working life, though, so Charlie put him in charge of the rosters. You don't need to drive for that position. He misses taking the coaches out.'

'And that little tidbit of information was of interest to me because?' asked May as he was virtually dragged back into the shrouded street by Bryant.

'Next stop, the ABC café,' said Bryant, ignoring him. When they reached the restaurant, Bryant prevented his partner from going in. To May's astonishment, Bryant knocked on the window and the pretty little waitress slipped out. She sucked her crimson bottom lip and widened her eyes at May in a way that reminded him of Betty Boop.

'Our prearranged signal,' Bryant explained. 'Dolly, tell Mr May what you told me.'

Dolly was clearly excited to be part of an investigation. 'Just that Clive and the old man had a terrible bust-up the other day, right in the middle of the restaurant.' May couldn't help noticing that she had upgraded the ABC from a mere cafeteria. 'Clive and me went out to the dancehall last Saturday and got back late, and the old man was furious, told him he couldn't go out no more, and Clive said 'I'm twenty one, I've got the key of the door and can do what I like', and the old man said 'Over my dead body', and Clive said he wished the old man would hurry up and die.'

Released, Dolly reluctantly returned to her station in the café.

'What is the point of all this?' asked May tetchily.

'Harry Whitworth was already sick when he got to the coachworks.'

'Yes, so you said.'

'He hopped on a bus from the tube. Dolly was arriving for work, and saw him getting off at the bottom of Wardour Street. So he wasn't out in the fog for very long at all.'

'What about at the other end, from his house?'

'He lives right next door to the station, and leaves a minute before the train arrives. She's a mine of information, Clive's little lady.'

'So you're telling me he didn't die of either cause?'

'No, but I think somebody would like us to think he did.'

'Not Stan.'

'No. Stan was at the coachworks an hour before Harry, and had been running the engines all that time, so there couldn't have been enough carbon monoxide in the air to hurt either of them.'

'Then what made him sick?'

'Harry came to work separately from his son this morning. I think they had another argument, either this morning or last night. The only thing he did before reaching his place of employment was have a bite to eat.'

'You think Clive poisoned him?'

'I'm just saying that I think we should search the kitchen.'

Harold Whitworth had eaten some scrambled eggs and had drunk a bowl of Brown Windsor soup, his favourite. His son watched in dumbfounded amazement as the two detectives checked every canister of ingredients. Rationing meant that powdered eggs were still in use, but May tasted them and found nothing wrong. Bryant tried everything from the lard to a piece of mutton shin that had been used for the soup.

'This is ridiculous,' May complained. 'Dolly, how many eggs and Brown Windsors have you got through serving today?'

Dolly check the larder and returned. 'About two dozen eggs and six soups,' she told them.

'And did Harry Whitworth's come from the same place as all the others?'

'Oh yes, sir.'

'There you have it.' May threw up his hands in despair, but he knew that once Bryant was convinced of something, nothing would disabuse him of the notion until every last particle of doubt had been combusted.

'Clive, did you have words with your father this morning?'

'No, he had one of his sulks on. Barely said a thing, just ordered from the menu, ate and left without even paying.'

Bryant turned to Dolly, the waitress. 'Where did Harry sit?'

'Over there,' she said, pointing to a small formica-topped table in the corner.

'Does he always sit in the same place?'

'No, of course not. We do have other customers, you know. We're very popular.'

'I can't imagine why.' Bryant wandered over to the table, tasted the salt, pepper and tomato sauce, and returned more dissatisfied than ever.

'Well, I'm sorry to have taken up so much of your time,' he told Clive finally. 'I'll let you attend to your customers.'

The moment they stepped outside, Bryant slapped his partner in the chest and brought him to a standstill. 'I need you to stay in the doorway opposite and not let that young man out of your sight until I get back,' he said.

'In this fog? You must be joking.'

'Then take my scarf.' Bryant unwrapped it from his own neck and began to mummify May before he could protest.

Helplessly, May was forced to install himself in the shadowed doorway of a tobacconist's shop, but found he could barely see across the narrow road. The city had entered a state of limbo. Trucks and taxis hove into his blurred line of vision like prehistoric beasts, only to vanish just as suddenly. He could see black particles floating in the air. He wondered how much poison the people of London were being forced to consume, and how it would affect them.

The bell on the door of the cafeteria tinkled with each arrival and departure. The customers appeared as little more than phantoms, and it was hard to keep track of them all. May stamped his feet and wiped the beads of black water from his brow. He readjusted the scarf, and was alarmed to note that the patch covering his mouth was thick with grime. He wanted to go home and climb into a hot bath.

Two hours and ten minutes after he had left, Bryant returned. His stumpy figure was as unmistakeable as ever in the gloom. He was panting. 'Sorry to leave you so long,' he apologised, 'but I had to get a preliminary result from a friend of mine who runs a the chemist's shop in Oxford Street. Has he come out?'

'Who, Clive Whitworth? A result on what?' asked May.

'I tipped some of the salt and pepper into my handkerchief before I left the café. Dolly told me the old man didn't like ketchup, so I thought it had to be in the condiments.'

'You mean poison?'

'What else would I mean? The pepper was fine. The salt has been cut with an industrial chemical that causes hypoxia. But it's a very low dosage, too low to do any damage, no more than one grain to every thirty of salt. Hang on, someone's coming out.'

They both peered across the road. 'I can't see a blinking thing,' Bryant complained.

'It's Clive.'

'Damn, he's leaving early. I've arranged to have him placed under arrest, but the others aren't here yet. This blasted fog. We'll have to follow him.'

Tracking their quarry through the chaotic backstreets of Soho would have been tricky enough without the obscuring murk. But at least if they could not see him, Clive Whitworth could not spot that he was being followed. At one point when he disappeared behind a stack of fish-crates, the detectives feared they had lost him, but he emerged from the other side, crossing into Greek Street and then to Soho Square. The watery sun threw shafts of strange green light through the branches of the plane trees, as if London was in the throes of an apocalypse.

'He's heading for St Peter's,' Bryant pointed out. The red-brick tower of the Roman Catholic church rose in the East quadrant of the square. The detectives followed their suspect inside.

Even here, blossoms of yellow mist were unfolding beneath the doors of the church. Fog hung in the air like the manifestation of some unholy spirit. Clive seated himself at a pew and dropped forward onto his knees in fervid prayer. The detectives crept into the row behind him and quietly listened.

After a few minutes, Bryant stood. 'A confession of guilt, I think,' he told his partner. Clive turned to look at them and started.

'I am arresting you for the murder of Harold Whitworth,' Bryant began, placing a hand on his shoulder. He liked to do things the traditional way. 'Anything you say . . .'

Clive tried to bolt, but was restrained by May's rugby-strengthened arms.

'Come on,' said Bryant, 'hold him tight and let's get out of this fog. I've had enough poison for one day.'

Back at Bow Street, Clive Whitworth did not attempt to rescind his confession. He looked utterly defeated. The detectives retreated back to their cluttered first-floor office. It was so gloomy that they had to turn on the lights. May placed a kettle on the gas ring, and Bryant filled his pipe.

'You're not going to smoke your navy shag in here, are you?' May complained. 'The air's thick enough as it is.'

'I'm replacing the coal smoke with the healthy aroma of high-grade tobacco.' Bryant tipped back in his chair and began to puff. 'Come on, then, I know you're dying to ask me how he did it.'

'All right then. I can't for the life of me see how.'

'Clive and Harry Whitworth had a fight last night. Harry told his son he would never have the house. Clive took a powerful poison from his garden shed and carried it to work. He added a tiny amount to the salt. Harry always came in for something to eat before the start of his shift, even when they had argued.'

'But surely he couldn't know where the old man would end up sitting.'

'Precisely. So he measured out the poison and added it to each of the salt cellars in the room. It didn't matter where Harry sat.'

'Then why didn't any of the other customers become ill?'

'Harry used more salt than anyone else. Clive knew he would.'

'I really don't see how he could know that.'

'After the argument, Harry went down the pub and got drunk. You heard what Stan said; since the death of his wife he had become an alcoholic and lost his license. Excessive drinking removes the salt from your system. Alcoholics always oversalt their food. Harry had no choice but to do so—it was a biological necessity. For every thirty grains of salt, he consumed a grain of poison.'

'Well I'm damned,' said May. 'I wonder what gave him that idea?'

'Look out of the window,' Bryant replied. 'The city poisons us all. It's just a matter of degree.'

He blew a satisfying cloud of smoke into the air, and watched in amusement as John May had a coughing fit.

.

RED GLOVES VOLUME 2: INFERNAL
The World Horrors

To celebrate his 25th year of writing award-winning horror stories, Christopher Fowler has created two new collections totaling 25 tales.

This second volume contains stories set in exotic locations around the world, where deceptively ordinary events like a holiday in the Far East or a trip to the French Riviera cause terrifying fates to unfold. Here you'll find innocent travellers beset with accidents, tragedies, murders, nightmares and epiphanies as they wander far from home. And to top it off, there's a short story featuring disreputable detectives Bryant & May.

It's an infernally dangerous world out there. Step out into unfamiliar lands of darkness, derangement and deadpan laughter with the nation's most sinister storyteller.

"Through his black sense of humour Fowler crowbars open middle-class anxieties. These are imaginative, bleak cautionary tales which shed their little pools of perverse candlelight on both new and familiar places."

—*The Guardian*

Christopher Fowler was born in Greenwich, London. He is the award-winning author of thirty novels and a dozen short story collections, and creator of the popular Bryant & May mysteries. He worked in film, creating movie posters, trailers and documentaries, fulfilling several pathetic schoolboy fantasies, releasing a terrible Christmas pop single, becoming a male model, posing as the villain in a Batman graphic novel, running a night club, appearing in the *Pan Books of Horror* and standing in for James Bond.

He has written comedy and drama for the BBC, has a weekly column in the *Independent* on Sunday, is the crime reviewer for the *FT* and has written for *The Times, Telegraph, Guardian, Daily Mail, Time Out, Black Static, Smoke, Big Issue* and many others. After living in France and the USA he is now lives in King's Cross, London. He recently wrote the *War Of The Worlds* videogame for Paramount, starring Patrick Stewart. His books for 2011 are the supernatural thriller *Hell Train*, and a Bryant & May book, *The Memory Of Blood*.

In the past year he has been nominated for eight national book awards. He is the winner of the Edge Hill prize 2008 for *Old Devil Moon*, and the Last Laugh prize 2009 for *The Victoria Vanishes*.

RED GLOVES

VOLUME 2

RED GLOVES

VOLUME 2

THE WORLD
HORRORS

Christopher
Fowler

2011

Published in October 2011 by PS Publishing Ltd. by
arrangement with the author. All rights reserved by the author.

FIRST EDITION

ISBN
978-1-848631-98-4
978-1-848631-99-1 (Signed Edition)

Story credits appear at the end of the book.

Design and layout by Alligator Tree Graphics.

Printed in England by the MPG Books Group.

PS Publishing Ltd
Grosvenor House
1 New Road
Hornsea, HU18 1PG
England

e-mail: editor@pspublishing.co.uk • *Internet:* http://www.pspublishing.co.uk

CONTENTS

Unheimlich 5

The Eleventh Day 9

Piano Man 31

The Girl On Mount Olympus 47

Halloween Dog 59

Poison Pen 63

The Conspirators 93

The Boy Thug 111

The Velocity of Blame 127

Arkangel 139

The Mistake at The Monsoon Palace 165

Beautiful Men 187

Bryant & May's Mystery Tour 201

RED GLOVES

VOLUME 2

For Sue Gibson, our gal in Oz.

UNHEIMLICH ████████████

IT COSTS A LOT OF MONEY TO BRING A BODY BACK FROM OVERSEAS.
When my best friend died in France, we had to decide whether to ship him back or have him cremated on the spot. We opted for the latter option. Some of him was sprinkled from the back of a boat in Monte Carlo, some of him came home to a cemetery in England and some of him remained in a duffle bag under the stairs, and in a friend's handbag. As a man who was known far and wide, he would have appreciated the irony of being in so many places at once, even after his death.

I love travel, but I'm not a loner. I don't understand people who travel alone—how do they share their experiences? So I end up waiting for my partner or friends to become free, so they can travel with me. Plus I'm a liability, the tourist most likely to board the wrong train/ plane/ boat in any given situation, so it's good to travel with somebody sensible. I have a history of being in the wrong place at the wrong time. I was in Mumbai during the bombings and in Sri Lanka during the floods. But if you followed the Foreign Office guidelines about overseas travel, you'd never go anywhere. Part of the thrill is not knowing what will happen next. London is never a boring city, but for the majority of us it's surprisingly consistent and safe. I worry that this nice warm safety net will dull my senses and make me a boring writer, so I travel whenever circumstances allow.

Oddly, I've never felt very safe in America—the guns bother me. I'm talking about the coast cities, but one day I hope to travel to the parts that Europeans rarely visit. There is a wonderful German word, *unheimlich*, meaning 'uncanny', which has deeper connotations because it suggests the

5

unease that is caused by being away from home, literally un-home-like. The Jewish word *shpilkes* catches how I feel in the USA—to be on *shpilkes* is to be jittery, walking on needles, unsettled.

Europeans travel to more countries than most because the distances are smaller. I can get to Paris more quickly than I can get to Manchester, because I live beside the Eurostar terminal, and being able to switch into a less familiar society so easily refreshes the senses.

As is always the case, some of the stories were written as commissions and appear in other volumes. There's a general idea that you should try not to overlap stories in order to maximize your readership, but launch dates slip around like molasses, and overlaps can occur. However, I strongly believe in looking at collections and anthologies in their entirety. I'm a collector/listmaker, and it's important to me that I assemble my stories in chronological order in my own collections, so that readers can see how stories evolve and influence each other. For that reason, I try to make them as definitive as possible. In fact, I usually rewrite commissioned stories before including them in my own collections, so even if you've chanced across any of them elsewhere, you may well find these versions to be different. This is the first time any of them has appeared in one of my own collections, and this double volume will bring you up to date with my work as a whole.

The following stories take place in Poland, America, France, Russia, the Middle East, India and Thailand. I rarely write about any place where I haven't been, because I like to get the details right, although I tend to concentrate on the atmosphere more than the minutiae of exotic locales.

My parents never travelled much. I count myself lucky that I'm part of the generation that is able to move about, but I'm still appalled at how little of the world I've really seen. We are creatures of habit and tend to stay in our tribes, so we'll pick hotels in destinations where friends have been before us, because it reduces anxiety. But a little anxiety can be a good thing, as I hope you agree after reading these stories. And if you read both volumes, you'll see that whether you stay home or go travelling, bad situations are never very far away.

Apart from owing a debt of gratitude to Pete Crowther for getting this

collection into print, I'd also like to thank editor Steve Jones, who has frequently commissioned my stories over the years, and whose name on an anthology is a seal of excellence.

—Christopher Fowler, King's Cross, London

THE ELEVENTH DAY ▰▰▰▰▰▰▰▰▰▰▰

THE FIRST DAY

MIA TEREBENIN WORKED IN THE ST PETERSBURG INTERNATIONAL ARCHIVE, cataloguing documents pertaining to postwar Russian-American oil initiatives. She was twenty two years old, a little too slender, pale and blonde, with ice-blue eyes and a translucence to her skin that gave her a haunted quality that men either found attractive or disturbing. Her colleagues joked that during the season of white nights she all but disappeared in the dull glare of falling snow.

For the past eighty years the archive had been situated in a grand municipal building to the south of the city on Moskovskly Prospekt, but now it was gradually being transferred to a vast, impersonal data facility some fifteen kilometers further out of town. Mia had worked in the gloomy maze of corridors for nineteen months, and was looking forward to being in an office that had sunlight and reliable heating, It meant she would no longer have to cross half an kilometer of icy marble to find a functioning toilet, or arrive at the office to find the radiator pipes frozen solid.

The archivists with whom she worked were mostly older, unsociable academics from Moscow who had chosen the job so that they could work uninterrupted by the demands of normal life. Here they could hide themselves away with their documents in an isolated building that protected them from the intrusions of the world.

At 6:48PM on the last Friday evening in September, Mia cleared her desk, packed her suitcase and locked her office. Masha and Andrei, her two colleagues, had moved to the new building at the end of the previous week,

and although they had not been great friends she missed hearing someone else's conversation, because there was nobody left on the seventh floor except a couple of young men who were being employed to check the contents of document boxes and tape them up, ready for removal.

She never took the elevator because it was supposed to be unreliable, but she decided to do so tonight because the lights were out on the staircase, and because she was wearing heels and the marble steps were treacherous. Usually she had boots or trainers to change into, but this morning she had overslept and did not have time to pack her bag with everything she needed.

When bad things happen, who is to say where their roots lie? In the days to come Mia found herself saying 'If only I hadn't . . .' and 'Things would have been different if . . .' She should have had an early night, she should have changed the batteries in her alarm clock, but later she realised that fate is simply an implacable predetermination, the disastrous consequence of destiny's journey. She came to understand that there was nothing she could have done to prevent this chain of events from occurring, and was reconciled by the thought.

She was crossing the marble landing, looking apprehensively into the darkened stairwell that lay ahead, when she heard the loud, tinny ping of the elevator arriving. She looked up above the brushed steel doors to see its triangular red light flick on. The doors slid open and because there was already someone inside the car her apprehension evaporated and she ran to catch it.

The doors closed and she checked the panel to make sure that the stranger was also going to the ground floor. He was, so she stepped back and held her briefcase with both fists closed over the handle, and stared at the floor as people do, out of modesty and awkwardness, and a desire not to attract attention to themselves.

The elevator passed the fifth floor. It had mirrored walls of mottled gold, a fake-wood frame and ceiling which was actually painted steel, and a scuffed metal floor. According to the sign on the wall it could hold eight passengers, and was equipped with an intercom in the event of emergency. She glanced into the mirror and caught sight of the other passenger. He was tall and slender, with a long, high cheek-boned face, a strong nose and eyes so deep-set that from the side they just looked like holes in his head. His sleek black

hair was cropped to a line above his ears. He wore a thick red check shirt, a cheap, generic brand of jeans and dirty trainers. His briefcase was metal and hard-edged.

She looked back at her shoes, thinking she needed to save up some money and buy a new pair because these had scuffed toecaps, when the lift came to an abrupt stop between floors five and four. Mia's knees absorbed the brief buckle in gravity and she righted herself. The lights flickered once but remained on.

'What the hell?' said the man. He had been leaning against the panel, which was set into the side wall of the elevator, and now he jumped back as if he had been bitten.

'Did you press something?' Mia asked.

'No, I wasn't touching it,' said the man. 'Anyway, the buttons are recessed. It's probably a break in the power.' He pressed the ground floor button again and raised his head, listening, but nothing happened. 'That's not good.'

'What?' asked Mia.

He held up a finger. 'I can't hear any machinery. If it's an electrical fault it might have tripped the circuit.'

'What does that mean?'

'Well, the system would have to be reset.'

'But the lights are still working.'

'They're on a different circuit.' He studied the wall panel.

'You seem to know a lot about it,' Mia said, watching him.

'I'm an electrician. I'm installing trunking in the new building. I came here for a meeting to see if we can take any of the old telephone equipment with us.' He seemed to notice her for the first time. 'Hello, I'm Galia Sokolov.' He had to bend a little to shake her hand.

'I'm Mia,' she said. 'I'm in records, but I'm moving out next week. I hope the new building has better lifts than this.'

'Don't worry, they're super-modern. I'm surprised this thing is still in service. I just hope the intercom has been checked lately.' He pressed the speaker button and kept his ear close to the grille. There was a distant crackle, like a faraway radio station being tuned, but the sound ended abruptly. 'See, there's a hard line to a response station, but if the line isn't regularly tested it

can kick off.' He listened again. 'No, that's completely dead. Sounds like someone hasn't been doing their monthly check.'

'Wait, there's a helpline to call.' Mia pointed to the number printed at the base of the panel. She fished in her briefcase for her mobile, then studied the screen. 'It says *No Access To Network*. Can you try yours?'

'I haven't got mine on me,' Galia admitted. 'It's still on my desk. I was going downstairs for a smoke. Wait, maybe it needs a hard reboot. Try turning it off, taking the battery out and putting it back in.'

Mia unclipped the mobile's back, shook out the battery, slipped it back in and turned it on. A minute later the same message came up again.

'Wait, it might just be a dead spot. Let me try.'

'I can manage,' said Mia.

'I've got longer arms.' He took the mobile and held it up to the corners of the elevator, then down at the base of the door. 'Nothing. Not even a weak signal.'

'I've been meaning to get it looked at.'

'I don't think it's your phone. There's a lot of sensitive data on the fourth and fifth floors. The rooms are probably shielded. If we were just one floor further down—'

'Well, we're not,' said Mia testily. 'What do we do now?'

'I don't know,' Galia admitted. He tried the intercom button again, but the line was definitely dead. Mia reached around him and stabbed harder at it. She had no fear of enclosed spaces, but it was getting late and she was supposed to be cooking her mother a beef stew tonight. The shops would soon be closed. Besides, the building was emptying out and would be shut up for the weekend. She studied the button panel carefully. 'Is something supposed to be in there? Look.' She pointed to a small rectangular hole in the panel that looked as if it should house a fuse or a button.

Galia shrugged. 'It's made by a Russian company. You never know which buttons are supposed to be there and which ones aren't. They take out broken ones, then find the replacements don't fit.'

'Should we bang on the doors? The caretaker might hear us.'

'I doubt it, but we can try.' Galia balled his fists and pounded the doors hard. They shouted, directing their voices to the slender join in the far corner

of the door. Galia produced a strong, loud bellow but it made no difference.

They took turns to shout for about an hour. Galia pulled a screwdriver from his back pocket and inserted it between the door and the wall. He tried to lever open the door, but gave up after a few minutes. 'I think it has a metal catch that prevents the door from being forced,' he said finally. 'It's pretty solid.' He almost sounded impressed.

Mia sank back against the wall, frustrated and angry. 'I suppose we'll just have to wait until someone comes,' she said finally.

'Someone will come,' he told her. 'We can't be the last ones out of the building.'

'What if we are?'

'Then we'll be stuck here overnight. There are always people in the place on Saturday mornings. I sometimes get called in for the whole day. Hopefully we won't have to wait that long. Someone will come.' He gave her an optimistic smile.

That was the first day.

THE SECOND DAY

The contents of her briefcase were laid out neatly across the floor. They included an almost empty bottle of water (it was unsafe to drink from the taps at the archive), an apple, a nutrition bar, various pots and tubes of makeup, her useless mobile, its battery now almost dead, a comb, a nail file and some documents she had been planning to work on over the weekend. She separated the items with precision. 'My mother has Alzheimer's,' she said. 'My brother thinks it's quite a useful disease. Sometimes he says he's been to visit her and he hasn't, but she can't remember. She relies on me, but I don't suppose she rang anyone when I didn't turn up,' she said. 'Later today my brother is supposed to look in on her. She'll tell him I didn't come and he'll call me.'

'You think he'll figure out what's happened?'

'I don't know. He's not very smart. Probably not. He'll just think I've gone to visit friends, and our mother forgot to tell him. I was due to look in on a

colleague today, but Masha only has my mobile number.' She studied the contents of her briefcase. 'Okay, now it's your turn.'

'Are you okay?' Galia asked, concerned.

'No, of course not, but there's no point in panicking, is there? What have you got?'

Galia sighed and began to sort through his case. He found a handful of boiled sweets underneath his papers.

'Ah ha! A treasure trove. You've been holding out on me.'

'I didn't know they were there.' He unwrapped one and passed it over. Mia examined it and made a face. 'Yuk. Butterscotch. Oh well, beggars can't be choosers.'

It was cold in the lift, but at least Mia had a thick fleece jacket to sleep beneath. Galia had curled himself up on the floor and dozed. It was 4:20AM.

At half past seven Mia awoke and saw the contents of Galia's case laid out at her feet like votive offerings. A screwdriver. A penknife. A pencil. Some rubber bands. A tube of glue. A lottery ticket. A scarf. Some unopened letters that looked like bills. An entry form for a marathon run. It wasn't a very inspiring collection of items. 'I'm sorry,' he said, sweeping them back in his case, 'if I'd have known we were going to get stuck here I'd have brought better equipment with me.'

'Look, you're an engineer—'

'Electrician.'

'You must know what to do in a situation like this.'

'The lift is jammed because the brake-shoes have come on, so there's no danger of us falling. They're programmed to spring out and lock into place if there's a power failure, but I think what happened here was a current surge that tripped the circuit breakers. The system is old and they probably have to be reset manually, and if there's no-one around to do it, it doesn't get fixed. There's another possibility. Maybe somebody forced the doors on one of the other floors; that would also cause the lift to stop. We can't call out on the intercom because the fixed line is dead, but there should still be an alarm—a light and a buzzer—working somewhere, even though we can't hear it. We just have to stay calm and wait.'

'What if nobody comes? They're closing down the building.'

'Not yet, not for good. There are people coming in and out all the time,' Galia assured her. 'Those men with the boxes, they're bound to need to use the lift. They can't carry everything down all those flights of stairs.'

'But they're just temporary workers, they don't know who's in the building and who isn't. There's no reason why they should care. If the lift's not working they'll find another way down. Maybe there's a goods lift.'

'You worry a lot.'

'That's what my mother says.'

'What happened to your father?'

'He died of lung cancer. His own fault. Chain-smoker.'

'Do you have a boyfriend?'

'No.'

'Why not?'

'I don't know. I never go anywhere where I'm likely to meet one. I'm always working.'

'But you're very pretty.'

She gave him a cool look and raised her hand. 'Look, don't—just don't, okay? This is not the time or place.'

'I'm sorry, it was just an impartial observation.'

'Galia, I need to pee.'

'Okay.' He looked around. 'Finish the water in your bottle and use that.'

'Shouldn't we save the water?'

'We'll be out soon. It can't be much longer. Here, look. Now we make a funnel from the plastic cover on my paperwork.' He took out his pen-knife and expertly carved a small cone, neatly locking the edges together.

She looked at it. 'That's amazing. What are you, a survivalist?'

'Putin is a survivalist. I'm not a fan of the president.'

'Quite right, keep your shirt on. Face the door.' She turned away from him and squatted, filling the bottle.

'Okay,' he said when she had finished, 'now give it to me.'

She looked suspicious. 'Why?'

'I'm getting rid of it. It'll start to smell.' He pushed his weight against the door and carefully emptied the bottle down into the gap between the door and the floor. 'Let's hope neither of us needs to do anything bigger.'

'I doubt it. I've been on a diet all week. The apple and the nutrition bar are my lunch from yesterday.'

'Why are you on a diet?'

'Have you seen what happens to Russian girls?'

'I didn't eat either. I forgot the time. I usually have sandwiches in my case. Try and get some sleep. There won't be anyone here before nine at the earliest, not on a Saturday.'

'Okay.' She settled herself back in the corner of the elevator. 'This floor's hard.'

That was the start of the second day.

THE THIRD DAY

'What's the problem?'

'It hurts. Let me take a break for a second.' Galia dropped back down on his soles and rubbed his thighs. 'Okay, let's try again.' He reached up onto tiptoe and fitted his screwdriver into the screwhead, carefully scraping at the layers of paint that covered it. 'Russian workmanship,' he said through gritted teeth. 'They'd rather keep painting over it than bother to sand it once.' The screwdriver skidded across the ceiling, hitting the neon light panel. 'Support my legs, will you?'

Mia had no desire to touch him. Her skin was coated in a layer of sweat, her eyes were gritty. They had finished the apple and had agreed to eat the nutrition bar later. Neither of them expected anyone to show up on Sunday, so they would have to hold out at least another twenty hours, until the remaining members of the archive's workforce came into work on Monday.

'Got me?'

'Yes.' She gripped harder. His legs felt surprisingly muscular; she had figured he was a weakling—it had taken this long for him to think of climbing out through the roof. In fairness, neither of them had been thinking rationally, because until now they had expected to be released any minute. The ceiling panel was small and unpromising, not at all as it might appear in a film.

At his fifth attempt, one of the screws holding the panel began to turn and eventually came out. The second one gave more easily, the third easier still. But the thread on the fourth had torn, and there was no way of removing it. 'I don't believe it,' she said, staring at the ceiling panel. 'Can't you just force it?'

'How?' Galia asked. 'I can't get any leverage up there.'

'Then let me try. You can hold me up, can't you?' They switched roles. Once he had balanced himself, Galia raised her above his head, balancing her on his thigh. He let her hammer at the panel with the butt of the screwdriver. One half of it slowly lifted, but the metal was folding diagonally, raising only a triangle that was not large enough for a cat to climb through.

'It's no use,' she said, 'I can't move it back any further.'

'What can you see?'

'Nothing, just black and a bit of the wall. Wait, lift me up a bit higher.' She pushed her arm through the hole and felt something wet. A small amount of water was dripping into the shaft.

'There must be a leak somewhere above us.' She cupped her hand and carefully brought it back through the hole. The water was iridescent with petrol contamination and looked grey in her hand. She touched her tongue to it.

'I don't think you should drink that,' said Galia.

'We haven't got anything else. It's a bit brackish, tastes like water though. Take the lid off my facial cleanser and pass it up.'

He handed her the plastic lid, and she pushed her arm through the space once more, waiting for the cup to fill. 'I heard about a cleaning woman in Samara who got stuck in a lift and survived for thirty days by drinking the water in her mop pail.'

He was exhausted from holding her so high, and nearly dropped her. It was hard work, and took several trips just to fill the little lid of her makeup case. 'I hope I don't get sick drinking this,' he said, eyeing her doubtfully as he sipped from the container. 'So, how come you don't have a boyfriend?'

She rolled her eyes and dropped down into the corner, retreating behind her furry coat. 'I don't want to go into it, okay?'

'Do you think we'll be on television when we get out?'

'I don't know, I don't care, I just want to go home and see my mother.'

'It's weird that no-one's come looking for us.'

'They're not worried.'

'You usually go missing?'

'No, it's just—we don't check in with each other much. I take turns caring for my mother. That's part of the deal.'

'What deal?'

'My brother and I don't really get along, so we don't overlap our visits.' She pulled the jacket tighter around her. 'Anyway, you're always asking me questions. What about you? You live here?'

'I just moved to St Petersburg. I'm from Moscow. And before that, a small town you won't have heard of.'

'Do you have family here?'

'You mean am I married?' He shook his head as if enjoying a private joke. 'No, I don't have family. Here or in Moscow. My father died, mother's family emigrated. There's nobody left. There's nothing to say.'

Mia knew how private Muscovites could be, and did not press him for details. There was no point in trying. Getting personal information out of them was like tearing out fingernails.

'You're pretty good,' he said.

'What do you mean?'

'No tears, no screaming fits, no tantrums. I mean, this is a pretty nasty situation, and you've handled it very calmly. That's impressive.'

'It doesn't mean I'm not having a very bad time. My back aches. I really need to walk around soon or it'll seize up. And I'm fighting the urge to scream. Could you try the door again with your penknife?'

'I told you, it won't open. This thing's a cheap knock-off. I'll only snap the blade.'

'Just try it again for me.'

Galia opened out the longest blade of the imitation Swiss army knife and inserted it into narrow gap at the edge of the door. Gently leaning his weight against it, he pushed. After a minute there was a crack and he swore, snatching away his bloodied hand. The blade clattered to the floor. Mia jumped to his side. 'What happened?'

'The damned thing broke. I told you it would.' He sucked at the heel of his hand.

'Show me.'

'It's okay.' He pulled away, dripping blood. She could tell by now that he hated to be touched. It was odd, considering how small the space was, that they had shared so little intimacy, not a hug of comfort, little more than the accidental brush of a hand. Last night, while she had been forced to defecate into a plastic makeup bag, they had shifted to the far corners of their cell in denial of their own humanity.

'It's just a surface cut.' He shook his hand out, turning aside. She noticed that he hardly slept. Whenever she dozed, her last sight was of him watching her.

'Why won't you let me touch you?'

'I don't need to be comforted. I know how to handle a cut.'

'I'm not saying you don't. It's just that you won't let anyone help you.'

'I don't like being fussed over.'

'By anyone? Or just me?'

'Go back to sleep.'

'Well, we'll be out of here in the morning,' she pointed out primly. 'Then you won't have to worry about me after that.'

THE FOURTH DAY

Something had gone wrong. It was 10:00AM. There should have been people in the building by now, but they had not heard a sound. And it had become cold in the lift.

'The main boilers are in the basement,' said Galia. 'It's always hot down there. I think they've been saving money by turning off the heat to the occupied floors. It's a stupid system.'

'Why can't we hear anyone?' Mia asked. 'Someone must have noticed by now that the lift is stuck.'

'The fourth floor has been cleared. Maybe the fifth as well, I don't know. I never have to go there.'

'Me neither. I don't see many people going in and out of the building, but I figure there has to be staff still working on other floors.'

'Maybe not. Maybe they managed to clear the building on Friday. But even that shouldn't make a difference. There must still be people here, and everyone has to pass the elevator bank.'

'I don't know,' said Mia wearily. 'Nobody tells me anything, I'm just a junior. I can't shout anymore. I have no voice left.' It was true. Both of them were now speaking in hoarse whispers. She threw a desultory kick at the door, but as usual it barely registered the sound. Some things built by Russians were liable to fall to pieces overnight, and others were built to last a century. It appeared that the lift belonged in the latter group.

'Are you hungry?'

'No, not really. I feel spaced, but then I've been on a permanent diet for the last three years. I'm used to feeling like this. I'm thirsty, though. Can I climb up again?'

Galia rose and waited for Mia to get to her feet. He allowed her to climb up on his bent leg, noting that she seemed to feel lighter, but perhaps that was his imagination. He was still uncomfortable about physical contact. She reached through the bent panel with her cup and waited for water to drip, but none came. 'It's stopped,' she called down. 'Maybe the leak was fixed.'

'Or maybe it only leaks when the heating system is turned on. The heat might expand the pipe joints and cause them to leak.'

She lowered herself back down. 'I can't believe you brought nothing to eat in that toolcase.'

'I didn't know this was going to happen.'

'Try the intercom again.'

'I've tried it a hundred times, Mia.'

She gave him an odd look. 'That's the first time you've used my name.'

'Well, I like to get to know people first.' He gave a small smile.

She laughed. It felt good to laugh again. She had to fight to stop it from turning into tears.

THE FIFTH DAY

'I think it stinks in here,' she said, lolling her head to one side and looking at

the plastic sack of shit in the corner. 'I mean, I can't smell anything but it must stink, mustn't it? Like when they open astronauts' capsules. They say the smell is terrible.'

'I don't know.'

'My hair needs washing.'

'After two weeks, your hair starts cleaning itself.' Galia was idly rearranging the papers in his case. According to his watch it was 4:45PM but there was no sound of any activity from outside. They were still taking turns throughout the day to hammer on the door and yell for help, but their energy was fading. Mia looked unwell. Her skin was greasy and pale, and she seemed to be having trouble focusing her attention on anything for long. She stared from half-shut eyes, in a muffled limbo-land between sleep and wakefulness.

'Do you think your mother is okay? Do you think your brother went to see her?'

'I hope so, he's kind of unreliable.'

'Is that why he hasn't tried to find you?'

'I don't know. Probably. He disappears every now and again with some girl he's just met in a bar.'

'But why hasn't anyone else come for you?'

'I don't fucking know, Galia, okay?' she shouted, her patience suddenly broken. 'Because we live in a world where people don't give a shit. Because my own mother doesn't even recognize me. If I'm honest—if I'm really honest—there's no one out there who cares if I live or die. No-one.'

'I'm sorry,' he said, reaching out toward her.

'Don't touch me. Don't fucking touch me.'

'All right,' he said. 'All right.'

They sat in the respective corners of their cell and listened to the silence in the shaft. Then they heard it. The unmistakable sound of a woman in heels, walking across marble. And a man's footsteps, heavier, wider, very close. They were talking. Their conversation faded and grew in a fluctuating wavelength. Galia pressed his ear to the door. Mia tried to get to her feet but had to be assisted.

'Help! We're here! We're inside! Call someone! Please help us!' They kicked against the door with their heels, then listened. The voices and the

footsteps had stopped. Were they looking at the elevator, trying to hear who was trapped inside?

They called and hammered and listened, but there was nothing more from beyond the steel walls. The silence was palpable and overpowering.

'What's wrong with people?' she said, sliding slowly down the mirrored wall. 'What the hell is wrong with these people?'

THE SIXTH DAY

'My period should have started. That'll be nice, won't it? I have no tampons. Pity, they would have been something else we could have added to the pile in the corner.' She nodded at the plastic bag of excrement.

'Your period can stop in times of stress,' he said. 'I read that somewhere.'

'Know a lot about women, do you?' she asked belligerently. 'When was the last time you went with a girl? Have you ever even had a girlfriend?'

He looked down at the floor between his knees. 'It's none of your business.'

'Really? Well, we've spent a lot of time together and you ask plenty of questions about me, but you never talk about yourself, beyond the fact that you resented your mother remarrying and moving to France. Do you even like girls?'

'Of course I do.' His voice was barely a whisper. 'I love them.'

'Well, I would have thought this was a perfect opportunity for you to get to know one really well, but all you do is stare at me. I've seen you watch me while I'm trying to sleep.'

'I don't have anything to say. Men don't talk as much as women.'

'So now you understand all women. I didn't know you were such an expert.'

'I know what you're trying to do, Mia, you're trying to goad me but it won't work. I'm not angry.'

'Really? Why not? You should be. If you'd taken the stairs, if the power hadn't gone off, if the lift hadn't broken down, if the building wasn't being emptied, you'd be home right now having a wank in front of your computer.'

'Why are you being like this, Mia? It won't solve anything.'

'Exactly, nothing I say or do is going to make any difference. If someone was going to come, they'd have been here by now. Something is wrong out there—I don't know what, but it's not normal. What's going on outside is not just another working day, it's something bad or weird or—I don't know, it's just not right. We can hear them, they must be able to hear us but they do nothing. Maybe the world came to an end. Maybe Martians took over. Maybe we're already dead.'

'Don't talk like that,' said Galia angrily. 'You mustn't say that.'

'Why not? Face it, we might as well be. Nobody's going to rescue us, we're going to die in here, a pair of pathetic, pointless deaths. It's over.'

'You're just being crazy because you're upset. It's dehydration. Our bodies are made up of two-thirds water. We need it for circulation and breathing, and to build energy. If you're losing more water than you're taking in, you dehydrate.'

'But it's cold in here. I'm not sweating.'

'No, but the air's dry. You only have to lose just two and a half percent of your body weight to lose a quarter of your power. I mean, for a hundred and seventy five pound man that's only around two quarts of water. Then your blood gets thicker and loses volume, your heart has to work harder and your blood slows.'

'What happens after that?'

'Then you die.'

'How long do you think we've got?'

'I don't know. We last had water the day before yesterday. You can survive without food for four to six weeks, but water . . . we've got maybe four, five days tops.'

THE SEVENTH DAY

A new fatalism had settled in the elevator. They tried the leak again, but found no more water, and besides, Galia was no longer able to lift Mia close to the ceiling. The floor was littered in debris from their cases; everything had been torn up and examined for the possibility of providing nutrition. The door

was covered in scratches but they had not been able to move it even a quarter of an inch. Occasionally they heard a noise outside that might have been a person or a rat—it was hard to tell the sounds apart from each other.

Mia could no longer think clearly. Her thoughts were a jumble of faded memories and half-formed notions. In her lucid moments she thought of her mother alone in her apartment without food, not remembering how to use her telephone, and of her brother out somewhere partying with some crazy girl, oblivious of his responsibilities. Then she would drift into the world of her imagination, remembering her childhood at the red-walled apartment in Kirovsk, her grandmother's patient smile, the puppy that died of distemper at Christmas.

When she awoke, Galia was cradling her head on his thigh and stroking her wet hair from her eyes. 'What are you doing?' she asked.

'You have a fever. I found two headache pills in my jacket. Do you think you can swallow them without water?'

'I don't know . . .'

He pressed the pain-relief tablets from their foil blister-pack and folded them into her hand. 'Think of a knife cutting a fresh lemon in half, and imagine the juice running from it into your mouth.'

She looked up at him and smiled. 'It's working. My mouth is wet.' She ate the pills but could not swallow them, and crunched them instead.

'Tell me about your family,' he said gently. 'Tell me about growing up. Tell me who you hope to fall in love with.'

She spoke in a faint whisper, but her thoughts did not hold for long and soon she was asleep once more.

THE EIGHTH DAY

It was late afternoon when they heard the laughter, a woman screeching in what sounded like a helpless fit of hysterics. She had to be drunk. The noise was a burst of mundane life in their strange cocoon. Galia made a show of shouting but knew by now that there would be no response. In the last few days they had heard several others walking and talking, but there had been

no reaction to their hammering. Mia briefly opened her eyes at the sound, but vaporised into fitful sleep once more. Her skin had turned a strange shade of yellow-grey, as if she was becoming bruised from within, and she looked even more translucent than usual, fading into her surroundings, sinking within the sweat-drenched folds of her reeking clothes.

Galia stared at his thinning reflection in the opposite wall, noting how they looked like a couple long familiar with each other. It was a peaceful image to hold in his mind as he allowed himself to fall asleep.

THE NINTH DAY

The lassitude of their becalmed world deepened like a mantle of snow or dust, thick and museum-silent, so viscous that it was virtually unbreathable. Galia reached out and pressed his fingertips against the mirrored wall, wondering if he might somehow be able to pass through it now, for it felt as if some fundamental metaphysical change was occurring, in the same way that the atoms of corpses eventually mingled with the wood of their coffins.

He found a few crumbs of something—possibly brick-dust, hopefully the remains of a wholemeal biscuit—in the inside pocket of his jacket, and gently forced them between Mia's lips, trying to make her eat them, but they remained on the tip of her dry tongue.

At some time in the course of that endless, neon-lit evening, Mia's fever broke and she appeared a little healthier. The sweat dried on her brow, and she was able to sit up. She was too dry to speak, and Galia knew she needed water or she would die in the next few hours.

Slowly and painfully he rose and wedged himself in a corner of the lift, reaching up inch by inch until he could reach his fingertips through the panel. He retracted them in wonder. They were cold and wet.

'Mia, the water's back. I think I can get us some. But I'll need to stand on you to reach it.'

'I can't—everything hurts. Please Galia, no.'

Ignoring her, he pushed a foot onto her back, jumped up and reached the plastic cup through the panel until she cried and sharply rolled away from

him, causing him to fall with the cup, spilling the precious droplets. 'You idiot,' he rasped, 'I can get you some water, you can last out longer.'

'What's the point?' she croaked back. 'No-one is coming. Why should I bother to try lasting for a few more hours?'

'Because it's not over yet,' he answered. 'It doesn't end like this.'

THE TENTH DAY

They lay together like old lovers. Galia pulled himself up and stared back at the smeared mirror. Mia was curled over him with her arm around his waist. They looked posed, as if they were having a portrait painted. He listened to her soft shallow breath, and then at the distant thumping on a floor somewhere above them. With infinite patience and care he arranged her hair back over her ears and forehead, and adjusted the coat that was her bed, so that she looked like any normal girl asleep in her partner's arms. Even though her eyes were sunken and her lips were the colour of paper, she was beautiful. After a few minutes her eyes slowly opened and she saw him. She managed a faint smile.

'Hello, you.'

'Hello.'

'You're always there.'

'Yes, always here.'

'I was dreaming of fruit—fresh fruit and chocolate. The chocolate was so real I could smell it. And there was a great lake of fresh water.'

'That sounds like a nice dream.'

'Maybe we always dream about things as they should be, you know—in an ideal world.'

'I don't know. I've had too many nightmares in my life.'

'Your life wasn't good? Is that why you don't talk about it?'

'My life has been as bad as some very bad dreams. But that's what nightmares are for. They prepare you for the world.'

'I'm sorry.'

'Don't be.'

'I'm sorry you won't get a chance to put it right. To enjoy the good part.'

'You think every life has a good part?'

'It must do. Otherwise why else are we here?' She snuggled into his bony waist, enjoying this oasis of lucidity. 'There must be a part which makes you feel this is why you're alive.'

'I hope you're right. I would like to feel for a moment that everything was perfect.'

'We're all selfish, I know that. We want grat—' She stopped to cough. He tried to calm her but she wanted to talk. 'Gratification. Pleasure. That's human nature. It doesn't make us bad. But we must give as much pleasure as we want to receive. Don't you think that?'

'Yes, I suppose I do.'

'Good.' She was happy that the matter seemed settled. There was no point now in talking of escape or rescue or survival. They had reached a calm plateau where a purity of thought passed easily between them. 'I only wish—'

'You should try to rest,' he said, noting that her last coughing fit had produced specks of blood from her lungs.

'I feel okay. My throat hurts less when I talk. That doesn't make sense, does it?'

'Nothing makes sense in this world anymore, Mia. Maybe it never did,'

'I only wish I could have experienced more. Gone travelling. I've never been to a really good beach, a tropical beach, you know? Like the ones in the brochures. I've never been to the kind of parties you see in films. Never had champagne. Never been to China or India or the West. Never got out of a car at a nightclub and walked to the front of the queue, all the photographers trying to take my picture. Not that I'd want to do that, it's just the idea that's nice.'

'What were you going to do when you left this job? Get married, have children?'

'No. I was thinking of leaving to teach in an African village. I knew a girl at school who did that. A job you'd look forward to each day, with children and sunlight, lots of sunlight.'

'That's nice.'

'What about you?'

'I don't know. It's not been easy for me to overcome unhappiness. All I can ever do is make it go away for a few months at a time.' He looked at his watch. 'It's one minute past midnight. Another day just started.'

THE ELEVENTH DAY

'You've been keeping track.'

'Yes,' he admitted. 'Can I ask you again?'

'Go on, then.' She held his gaze in the mirror and nodded permission.

'Why didn't you find a boyfriend?'

'Because I never met anyone who deserved me.'

'Do you think you could ever have—fallen in love with me?'

She thought for a while, and it seemed that she had drifted back into sleep, but her eyes slowly opened once more. 'I think I'm in love with you now,' she said.

And there it was, the simplicity of the admission, without irony, kindness or dishonesty, stripped of any other meaning, a calm and perfect statement of love that appeared like a boat on a flat, still sea. The boat held hope.

'And I am in love with you.' His eyes held hers. 'I have always loved you.' There was nothing else either of them needed to say anymore. He watched her unchanging face as she fell asleep with his image imprinted upon her retinas, and remained quite still as her breath became shallower until it was imperceptible, and the minutes turned to hours, and her coma deepened, and the day ticked silently away, slowing to ever tinier proportions of the clock, and he knew she had finally passed into across the threshold of death. He checked his watch: 7:45PM. The building was empty once again.

He set her body gently on the floor and tucked the collar of her coat around her neck, wanting her to be comfortable and beautiful now more than ever. He had difficulty rising to his feet.

He dug into his tool case and found the red plastic rectangle, and carefully reinserted it into the hole in the lift's control panel. Then he pressed the ground floor button.

He heard the machinery and cables moving above him. The elevator

started up and descended to the ground floor. He cleared the detritus from the lift and picked up the chocolate bar wrappers that had fallen from his pocket.

When the doors opened, he removed the taped signs that said 'Elevator Maintenance In Operation For Two Weeks' and put them in his case.

He was tired and thirsty, but it had been a moving and truly wonderful experience. He had experienced the most perfect form of love. Flooded with an overwhelming sense of satisfaction, he made his way toward the exit and the outside world.

PIANO MAN ▇▇▇▇▇▇▇▇▇▇▇▇▇▇▇▇▇▇▇▇▇▇▇▇▇▇

I KNEW I WAS RIGHT TO HATE JAZZ, BUT NEW ORLEANS GAVE ME A REASON TO FEAR IT. For years I figured it was black-sweater-and-goatee music that appealed to aged hipsters, but in the Big Easy that image is only part of the story. There are plenty of jazz-funksters and rapmasters around that town now, but you can still find bars where the music hasn't changed in eighty years. The real trouble is that old jazz can be twisted into easy listening and piped into elevators like soap bubbles that burble through the overheated air at a volume just loud enough to cloud your thoughts. A reworking of Weather Report's *Birdland* was playing in the lobby of the Marriot hotel when I arrived, and a horrible, plinky electro-version of Miles Davis's *So What* issued from the speakers as I handed my key in to the concierge.

Every city trades on its image, but in parts of New Orleans it works because they've still got the old range of religions. The *Vieux Carré* was romantic in a rundown way, although it was smaller than Soho and really just a few old streets of shops and bars geared around fleecing tourists, housed behind wrought-iron balustrades. And though it traded on its old movie image, the French Quarter was still kind of cool. But after I'd done it there was the rest of the place to deal with, about the most scarred-up ugly-ass concrete city I've ever seen in my life, and post-Katrina you can still see tidemarks on some buildings, warnings of what could happen again if the levees break in some other place.

It hadn't stopped raining from the moment I stepped off the plane, and the forecast predicted worse to come. Everyone was talking about how it reminded them of August 2005, just before Katrina found its full force, which

was no comfort at all. But the people were friendly enough, and I was only planning to be there for a couple of days until I could hook up with Ren, the photographer who was coming down from Memphis to take me on the last leg of the trip, if he ever bothered to sober up and return my phone calls.

For a couple of days I checked out locations for good copy and moody shots, and although I quickly got tired of traipsing around with a yellow slicker dripping ice-water onto my knees, the dry hotel air made me feel sick. So, forcing myself back into the rain once more, I headed from Canal Street in the direction of Bourbon.

I was meant to be revealing 'secret New Orleans' from an insider's perspective, but I wasn't an insider. I wasn't even from the same side of the country. I was working for a low-end travel supplement based out of Fresno and had, I suspect, been chosen for the assignment by my boss because I was willing to work below standard rates and leave at short notice. But I needed the cash right then, and freelance writing assignments had been pretty thin on the ground lately. I figured I could scrape by with some guff about jazz clubs and voodoo rituals, the ones that still get staged for tourists, and catch myself some good times in the process.

First I needed a funky dark-wood sawdust-floor bar with a peanut barrel, a pianist and candles in colored pots, a place where life had been restored to how it had been before the hurricane, but the coolest joints wanted to charge me a fortune for the privilege of a story, and my editor felt the bar should be paying the magazine for the free publicity. Except nobody had ever heard of the Fresno Freedom Travel Guide here and was like *who the fuck are you?*

But then I turned off Bourbon into one of the narrow cross-streets where the shops beneath the verandahs were smaller and darker, and found myself outside an open-fronted bar called Stormy's, where one hell of an argument was hammering. As I peered through the folding front doors into the beer-musty dimness of the bar, I saw a tall, bony old dude in a blue Zephyrs cap and collarless shirt shouting at someone who could only be an official, because he wore the kind of suit no man would ever purposely choose for himself.

'So what did you *evah* do for me, huh?' the dude shouted. 'All this talk, all these promises. The last time we had a flood around here, when we was bailing

out the basement trying to save th' only supplies we could lay our hands on, where the *hay-ull* were you? We couldn't even raise your damn office on the phone. Now you come in here and give me shit about breaking regulations, well you can kiss my skinny black ass before I take it down, and that's the end of it. Now you turn yourself around and get out of my bar.'

'Mr Beauregard, I have every respect for you—my father used to greatly admire your piano playing—but the fact remains that you cannot simply remake the rules on this. Now I can give you seven days to remove that thing before my boys will be forced to come in and take down.'

'You ain't stepping one foot into my bar, Marchais. Your father and his pals was nothing but trouble, and all you doing is tryin' to follow in their foot-steps. You come in here again, or you send any of your little butt-boys in here to do your dirty work, I'll set my dog on all of you. Now start marching.'

The owner was no spring chicken but feisty as hell, I had to give him that. I got talking to LaVinna, the waitress, who told me he really was called Stormy, and he always lived up to his name. 'I'll introduce you,' she said, 'but if he starts cursing and getting all heated up you'll have to go, because one day that vein on the side of his head is going to pop.'

Stormy was riled because he'd rebuilt the bar after Katrina with his own hands, and now the official was telling him he didn't get proper permission for the work.

'What I did,' he told me later, 'was build a new platform out back for the piano, but to put it there I had to build a roof over it where the yard had been. Hell, it weren't even no yard, just waste ground some crazy woman across the way uses for her damn' chickens, and it ain't even legal to keep chickens around here no more, 'specially when you're killing 'em in some damn religious ritual. In the forty years we've been here we never needed no building regulations.'

He took me to the rear of the bar to show me his handiwork. I guess he was pretty proud of what he'd achieved, even though it was technically illegal. The centerpiece of the new room was a piano in an upright teak case chased with silver designs, acanthus leaves and lilies. A pair of ornate silver candle-sticks stuck out above the keyboard, which was reversed from the usual layout, white notes raised out of black. It was a thing to behold, and Stormy

had done the instrument justice by housing it on an octagonal stage in his covered yard.

'The piano used to belong to Warena Samedi, told me she built it herself,' he said proudly. 'What I want to know is, how'd Don Marchais get to find out about me rebuilding the bar?'

I'd read in a local magazine that Warena Samedi had been some kind of hot-shot voodoo priestess back in the sixties, which I guessed meant she sold potions and rag-dolls to the easily fooled. The fact that she wore red leather miniskirts and looked more like a centerfold than a witch didn't hurt business, either. I didn't have too much time for people trying to perpetuate primitive black mythology, just because it suited them to believe there was something more exotic about people of a different skin color. But if she'd really built the piano and could play it like a dream, she at least had the soul of an artist.

'Maybe one of your customers saw it when he came in here, and bears a grudge against you,' I suggested. 'Know anyone like that?'

Well, of course he did. Everyone who owns a bar has a few enemies. Stormy thought hard for a minute and made a connection with Marchais. I got all this from LaVinna, who told me that Marchais had appointed a guy called Sam Threefinger—they called him that because he got stupid-drunk one time over in some Creole bar in Metairie and shot up his own left hand—to take down any property extensions he couldn't pull extra cash out of. Point is that Threefinger had been running a rival bar to Stormy's across the street, and they'd had a big old falling out. Threefinger knew about the piano because he was a believer, and had bought up most of the items Warena Samedi once owned. Someone had written a book about her scandalous life, and as a consequence, her stuff fetched top money from collectors. Now he and Marchais were working Bourbon as a team, shaking down owners and helping themselves to whatever they liked.

I did *not* want to mess with this. It wasn't my turf, and it wasn't what my editor wanted. But maybe some part of me, the part that had once wanted to be a real journalist and not a features hack, sparked back into life when a story fell at my feet. I told myself I'd see if it went anywhere, write it up and then check around to find a buyer. I asked LaVinna what she thought Stormy was going to do about it, but I must have been staring too hard at her wide, deep,

smooth cleavage because she told me she was ending her shift at six and maybe we should discuss it over dinner. Except that she came back to my room and we never did get that dinner.

Next morning the weather had worsened and it was hard not to think of Katrina as I fought my way up Canal Street. The NHC had pegged the little bugger swirling past the Florida coastline as a storm, not a hurricane, and weren't even going to the trouble of naming it, but they'd been wrong before. I wanted to grab a meeting with Sam Threefinger, and picked up his address on the internet because he was using his nickname as a URL, like he was proud of it. He was running an antiques business on the side, and it didn't take a genius to work out where he was getting his stock from. I figured if he was that much of a lush I could snag an interview with him in exchange for a couple of bottles.

But he wasn't at his house. My timing was off; he was already on his way to see Stormy and make him take down his new patio. Most likely, I thought, he had designs on that piano, although he must have been pretty dumb not to think folks would put two and two together when they saw it in his store. So I retraced my steps to the bar, but the rain was sheeting off the rooftops like needles, and I'd only managed three blocks before my eyes were burning. I waited in a café as the tail of the storm hit hard and the girls on the next table started to share their memories of Katrina, how one had been forced to hide from looters, how another had her baby airlifted out without a name tag, and how she'd gone crazy trying to find it. It was all background for me; I took notes and kept quiet.

The streets didn't look like they could get any wetter so I finished my coffee and pressed on. But I'd lost valuable time. When I arrived at Stormy's, I was late again. This time the cops were already there, tying yellow plastic ribbons around the back of the bar. LaVinna came over as soon as she saw me. 'I told you that temper of his would do the job,' she said, shaking her head.

'What happened?'

'Sam came in here and told Stormy that he and Marchais were getting a court order to close down the bar, and that he was impounding the piano.'

'I knew it,' I said, 'he's after that damn relic.'

'Not any more he ain't. Stormy took the shotgun down from behind the

bar and pulled it on him. Short version is, they got in close and the damn thing went off.'

'Jesus, is he hurt?'

'He has a hole through his brain the size of a nickel so yes, I guess it pinches a little.'

'You don't sound too upset.'

'Listen, I liked him, I worked for him, but he was an old lech and he never raised my wages in four years. I have a little boy stuck at my grandma's house going crazy with boredom. I was about to find myself a better job. But this ain't gonna look good on my resume.' She nodded back at the mess behind her. 'After the bullet left Stormy's head it went through the keyboard of the piano, then he fell back on top of it and the damn thing collapsed. The police got a blown-up body and an exploded piano back there to sort out. Now I got to stick around for witness statements instead of making tips.'

I looked over her shoulder to the mess on the patio. I could see Stormy's legs sticking out from a pile of wood sticks and shattered veneer panels.

I'll be honest here, I didn't know LaVinna had a kid and it put me off seeing her again. But I wanted to flesh out the story, and she seemed the best way through it. I knew I could probably get to Sam Threefinger too, because he had the law on his side and had been attacked, and innocent parties like that were always happy to kick off about how badly they'd been treated. There's something about knowing you're in the wrong that makes you want to tell everyone you were right.

I missed something LaVinna said. 'That is, if you're going to stick around for a few more days,' she was saying, like she had plans for us.

'I don't know,' I told her. 'I got to wait until Ren gets here and do the shots, but after that I'm gone.'

'Right.' She gave me a cool, steady look. 'But you may end up getting caught out by the storm. It ain't blown out yet.' She made sure I knew what she meant.

I called Sam Threefinger but he wasn't picking up, so I left a message for him to call my cell phone. Next, I rang a few local contacts and dragged prom-ises out of them to at least read anything I wrote on the subject; seems there was plenty of interest in any story that included mention of Warena Samedi,

so I decided to do a little more research. I started online, but kept hitting the same three or four sources, so it was necessary to put in some face-time with people who knew her.

Now, I don't mean to be rude, but a lot of women find God when their men leave them, know what I mean? And Ms Samedi's friends had found religion big time. Not just Christianity, though. I met up with Tamasha Woodfall, an old follower who lived in an apartment full of plants by the river, where she sat on an overstuffed stripy sofa watching the boats, her corkscrew copper hair piled on and around her head, her beads and bangles and bracelets clattering every time she moved her arms. Her plumpness protected her from being dated to any era, but I figured the stuff in her apartment went back at least sixty years. I liked her a lot, but she was crazy as a loon.

'Warena didn't just have knowledge of the old religion, she was a living part of the process,' she told me. 'Come over here and sit by me, boy.'

Frankly I didn't know what she meant at all, and admitted it. And I wasn't going to sit beside her either, because I could tell the old broad had wandering hands. 'Are you talking about love potions, curses, stuff like that?' I had to ask.

'Oh, that's just front-of-house sales,' she said, waving the idea aside. 'And nobody needs love potions, they just need to get in touch with themselves and their sex-u-al-ity, you know?' She smoothed her fingers down the side of her breast, and I could see she'd be big trouble after dark and a few whiskies. It's the old ones you have to watch out for.

'So what did Warena do that other people couldn't?'

'All kinds of things. But her biggest talent? She could restore a form of life.'

'You mean she could bring someone back from the dead?'

'I wouldn't use those words exactly, 'cause it's not like that. I mean, the corporeal remains stay behind and go down to the grave, bless the Lord. It was more—a conjuration.'

I wasn't sure there was such a word, but gave her the benefit of the doubt. 'You ever see this happen?'

'Oh sure, plenty of times.'

'How did it work?'

'The usual way. There was a service, songs and prayers, a series of incantations, rituals to observe, certain powdered herbs and minerals scattered in a proscribed sequence—sometimes she used the blood of a chicken, but I think some of that was for show, you know, so the clients felt they was getting value for their money.'

'And what did they get? I mean, at the end?'

'A restoration of the spirit, like I said, entirely separate from the body, but a kind of—' she watched the wide grey river for a minute, carefully formulating her words, '—essence of the departed. It wouldn't stay long, a day or two at the most, but it was most definitely visible. When my Sammy died she brought him back to me, just for a few hours.'

'Sammy was your husband?'

'No, my dog, praise Jesus.'

'But what was the point?' I wondered if I was missing something obvious. 'Why bring someone's spirit back at all?'

'Bless you, to bring peace to those left behind, of course. How many times have you wanted someone back, just for a few moments, for one last look of tenderness?'

I realized that she was staring intently at me. 'But you've never lost anyone, have you?' She made it sound almost sad.

'No,' I admitted. 'No-one really close. I don't know much about death.'

'Then you don't know about love, neither. You should testify to Christ the Lord and find the love.'

The conversation closed quickly after that, but I promised to look in on her again if I heard anything more. The other woman I went to see was Missy Allbright, who was nothing like her name, and lived on the first floor of a rundown apartment out in Metairie. The stairs were dark, the room was dark and she was dressed in black. The floor was covered in cats, some of them stuffed, and I couldn't tell which ones were alive as I stumbled through them to her guest chair.

'I'd give you some tea but I don't really want you to stay that long,' she announced, seating herself opposite.

'Well, at least you're honest.'

'I have to tell you no good will come of mentioning that woman,' she told me straight off. 'Warena Samedi—her real name was Miriam Fellowes but that didn't sound so enticing to the press—underneath that pretty hide she was a vengeful, messed up, mean old bitch.'

I remarked that she didn't look so old in the pictures I had seen.

'That's 'cause she never again let herself be photographed after she was thirty. She played with fire all her life and got old real fast. You don't race an engine without wearing down the parts.'

I asked Missy if she'd read the book about Warena. 'I did, and I can tell you there wasn't one word of truth in it.'

'But did she really have a gift?' I asked.

'I can't deny her that, but the way she used it—well, that wasn't how we were taught.'

'You have it too?'

She caught the rise in my voice. 'Why is it everyone thinks she was the only one with special abilities?'

'She had good PR and prominent tits,' I ventured.

That got a laugh from Missy. 'Maybe you and I'll have some ginger tea.'

We talked until it got even darker. I thought the storm was going to suck the windows clean out of the room. 'There was only one man she ever really loved,' Missy told me. 'You should have heard the sweet music they made in that bar of a night. Stormy worshipped her, but he couldn't give her what she needed.'

'What did she need?'

'More. More of everything. The problem was that by this time she couldn't turn it off.'

'Turn what off?'

'The sex energy, the power, the darkness that channeled right through her and kept on going until she became its slave. It destroyed everything around her and it finally killed her. After she was gone old Stormy lost around a hundred pounds, like something was eating him from the inside out.'

'How did Warena die?'

'She and Stormy were fighting all the time. She'd go out and stay missing for three, four days at a stretch, and he'd always take her back. Then she finally

left him for good, and nobody saw her around here again. All I know about
her death is what I read in the papers, but it was ugly. No-one really found
out the truth. The cops got a call late one night to a filthy house with a bunch
of dead men in it, and the story goes she was sleeping with all of them. Of
course, there was something weird right at the end. The city coroner got
himself fired for incompetence, because he swore the men died after she did,
even though they'd been killed with her knife and her prints were all over the
handle.'

'That's an incredible story,' I replied. 'Did the state ever follow it up and
find out what really happened?'

'They had their hands full, son. Katrina hit the shore five days later.'

I thought about Missy's story all the way back to the hotel, and how it
fitted with Stormy's death. It seemed I was missing something, and that something was probably connected with Sam Threefinger, so that night I sat down
at my laptop and did a little digging. Sam's real name was Laurent DuChamp.
He'd been in a soft-touch annex of the Louisiana State Penitentiary a couple
of times for fencing stolen goods, and it seemed he hadn't learned his lesson.
He'd set up his antique shop in 2002, after his last stretch. I wondered if he
had approached Stormy about buying the piano before, so I called LaVinna,
who told me it had been in storage for years. And that meant the first time
Sam saw it after Warena's death was when it appeared on the new stage.

The thing that struck me most was how Stormy had managed to cheat his
old rival by destroying Warena's most coveted possession at the moment of
his demise. It was a kind of justice, but I wondered if there was more to it
than that. I admit I wanted an ending; I had the material for a good article,
but needed to give it a more satisfying punchline.

The next morning it seemed the storm had blown itself out, but Ren called
me to say his plane had been grounded because Louis Armstrong Airport was
in the eye of the storm, and the worst was yet to come, so rather than sitting
around cooling my heels waiting for Sam Threefinger to call me, I decided to
take a cab over to his store.

The sign on the door said CLOSED and the place was locked up tight. I
cupped my hands and peered through the rain-streaked window. The interior
was so murky it could have been filled with pond water. It was mainly clut-

tered with 1960s furniture and musical instruments, but looked as if no-one had been there for days. I talked the cabdriver into taking me out to Sam's house. He didn't want to go there, complained it was beyond his working area, the weather was too bad and he wouldn't wait around for me to come back, but by this time I was getting desperate. Ren was delayed, I'd already spent my fee for the piece just holing up at the hotel, and there was no other work on the horizon. I needed to sell the story, period.

The rain was thundering loud enough to drown out the cab's radio. We came off the I-10 at Lovola, left the main strip and turned into a chain of tree-filled avenues. The house had an antebellum grandeur that seemed out of place. It reminded me of pictures I'd seen of the old Rosedown Plantation outside St Francisville, with Greek Revival-style wings and a long verandah, only scaled down to fit a modern neighborhood—because this house was freshly painted and no more than ten years old. I rang, then knocked on the screen doors, but there was no answer. By that time the damned cab driver had slammed into reverse and beaten a retreat from the property.

I could do nothing but circle the house and see if Threefinger was out back somewhere. Although the lawns were neatly trimmed, water was pooling fast on the grass and I was quickly covered in mud. The rear screen door was bashed in, the nets torn, the door hanging off its hinges. I tried to see inside but it was too dark to make anything out. I should have called the cops right then, but just didn't think of it. There was no-one around, and I couldn't see across the street, so I went in.

The house lights weren't working but I had a lighter in my pocket. It looked like there had been a fight of some kind in the downstairs rooms; a chair lay on its side, and what I thought at first was torn up paper proved to be broken white crockery. The rugs were squashy with blown-in rainfall. Not wanting to risk getting shot as an intruder, I called out Sam's name a couple of times, but there was no answer. I was about to leave when I heard the ceiling floor-boards creak.

I figured maybe Threefinger had been attacked by someone from Stormy's who blamed him for the old man's death and wanted to make a point about it. You get that feeling about New Orleans; there are plenty of nice people, and plenty of crazies looking to get back at the world. Wherever you get old-

school religion, it follows you find old-school vengeance. I wasn't thrilled about the idea of looking upstairs with no lights and no weapon, but I had no other choice. Besides, I had no personal beef with Threefinger, and for all I knew the guy could have had a heart attack. I fantasized a heroic race to the hospital, where the recovering old man would pour out his heart to give me a nice dramatic wraparound to the story.

I could smell something acrid, like burning paper that had been put out. As I climbed the stairs, the rain pounding on the roof grew louder. It was hard to see, but I could make out a long brown corridor leading to several big rooms, most with their doors open. I figured the one at the front was the master bedroom. I could see something moving beneath its windows, wrapped in a grey blanket. As I came closer, the pile shook a little and shifted backwards.

'Stay away,' it suddenly warned, 'don't get any nearer.' The room stank of whisky. A red, puffy face emerged from the blanket cocoon and stared blearily back. Sam looked like shit. 'Who the hell are you?' he asked, pushing to his feet.

I explained I'd been leaving messages for him, and wanted to talk about what happened at Stormy's. I figured he could at least give me some background to their feud, and I'd be able to give the article some shape. I had the end, I just needed the beginning, or so I thought until Sam said, 'He's back,' and I knew he meant Stormy, that somehow his guilt over the old man's death had manifested itself in the kind of magic the old women professed to believe in. I didn't buy the voodoo end of the deal, but it gave me a great angle.

'He's dead,' I said, 'I saw them take Stormy off to the morgue. What happened here?'

'Nothing.' Sam had suddenly sensed he was talking to a stranger and shut his mouth. 'This is private property. You should go now.'

'You've had some storm damage downstairs. Back door's blown in.'

'That weren't no storm, fool, it was him.'

'Stormy.'

'Who else?'

'Tamasha Woodfall told me that Warena could bring people's souls back from the dead, but only for a short time. If Sam's spirit returned and you

think you saw him, he's gone now. It's over.' Disabusing people of their notions is no way to win friendship, so I was trying to go along with him.

He gave no reply. Shuffling over to the liquor cabinet, he filled a tumbler, keeping the blanket hitched around his shoulders. 'See, that's the problem, right there,' he said. 'Outsiders never see the full picture. You think he'd just turn up and go away again? Revenants come back for a reason, and they stay until they've done the job. Most appear so they can give the living some comfort. You get a hug like a warm breeze, they dry away a tear, then they're gone. Sam's back to do some damage.'

'Why would he want to do that?'

'Don't fuck around with me, sonny. You been speaking to people, you know damn well why he's come back.'

'Well, there's no-one here now.'

'You can't be sure, with this rain keeping up.'

I didn't understand what the rain had to do with it. 'Look, I'll go and I'll close the back door on my way out.'

'No.' Suddenly I knew he was terrified of being left alone. 'LaVinna told me who you are. You want an interview, I'll be happy to give it to you, but downstairs where I can keep an eye on the place.'

We moved to the front parlour, but couldn't get the power up. It really looked like there had been a fight in the room. Sam was twitchy as hell, shifting back and forth, checking both sides of the house. 'He wants to give me the piano,' he said, and now I knew I was dealing with a crazy man.

'The piano's gone,' I reminded him.

'No, you don't understand.' He held up his hand and cocked his ear. 'Listen, damn it. You hear that?'

And there, behind the drumming rain, I swear I heard something like a piano being played. No, not played, *jangled*, like a cat was trapped inside it and was rolling around on the wires. 'What is that?' I asked.

'So you do hear it.'

But now the rain renewed its strength and the sound was lost once more. We both stood in the middle of the room listening like a pair of crazies. I knew I was being a fool, half expecting a snaggle-toothed corpse to coming walking through the porch door with its arms outstretched like a character

from an old EC comic, but the dark house, the storm, the crazy old man all got to me.

Then I heard it again, closer this time, a sound like a harpsichord being dropped on its side, discordant high notes and bass echoes that underscored the movement of something shifting hesitantly outside the walls. With each step there was a glissando, as if someone was dragging a piano, bumping and crashing it.

'You *do* hear that.' Sam was triumphant but terrified. 'Give me your car keys, I'll get you out of here,' I told him.

'They're upstairs on my dresser.' He couldn't take his eyes from the front door, which was strobing with the shadows of the storm-beaten trees.

'I'll go get them.'

'No, don't leave me alone!'

'Then you get them.' He was spooking me now. This, I knew, was how voodoo worked, spreading its fear like a contagion, turning skeptics into believers. I followed his eyes as he turned his gaze toward each of the windows, listening. He was tracking its path around the house. The blinds were all down, but I could see a shadow passing from one bay to the next. I ran for the stairs. I found a set of Oldsmobile keys and grabbed them, then headed back, but halted on the landing. The terrible jangling was inside now. I looked down and saw that the doors I had propped shut had been kicked apart. Something had dragged itself inside. I tried to find Sam, but figured he had retreated into a corner behind the stairs.

As I came down, I looked between the banisters. I had only met Stormy alive once, and I suppose the thing below represented him. It was tall and bony, and still wore a baseball cap, but it walked as if moving on broken stilts. The piano's wires were threaded through its wasted body, and where its stomach should have been keys and cables were strung with bits of dried-out gut. Wires stuck out everywhere, through staring red eyes, elbows, leg-bones and vertibrae. The fingers looked like piano keys, but it was hard to tell where meat and wood met. Warena's revival power lived on, but Stormy's spirit had been mashed with the piano in such a way that both had come back as one tortured creature. It stumped and staggered toward Sam, who was scrabbling away in a corner of the parlour, whimpering and pleading.

The strung-up keyboard fingers tore at his face and throat, wires slashing and stinging across his flesh, ripped at his soft stomach until I couldn't tell where Sam ended and the piano-man began. The whole thing was a bloody mess of flesh and wood and steel, and although it tried to pull away at the end of the attack, I could already see it unraveling and falling apart. The keys bounced to the floor, the wires lost their tautness, and the spirit of Stormy Beauregard evaporated, leaving behind a few sticks of varnished wood and the splintered remains of a man who looked like he'd been pistol-whipped with piano wire and eviscerated. And as the last of Stormy faded, I swear I heard a few chords play out in perfect harmony, before they were swamped by the drumming of the rain.

I took stock of my situation. My fingerprints were all over the house, and just in case the cops were too dumb to find me that way, I threw up all over the floor, leaving them plenty of DNA. I knew the bitches had set me up, pushing me toward Sam Threefinger, knowing that Stormy would reappear and take him down. They needed somebody stupid to carry the can, so that they would be left alone and unsuspected, free to continue practicing their damned rituals.

I'm driving out of the state on the I-10 now, trying to outrun the rolling storm, but I had to use my credit card to hire a car, and it's only a matter of time before I get hauled in for the murder of Sam Threefinger. They'll probably already have spoken to LaVinna, who'll place me in the bar near the corpse of her boss. None of it will make any fucking sense at all, but from what I heard the Louisiana police aren't going to be too bothered about that. Besides, what am I going to say in my defence, that I stood by and watched as the man whose house I had broken into tried to fight off the spirit of a half-man, half-piano? That's one piece of music that's *never* gonna play.

Man, I knew I was right to hate jazz.

THE GIRL ON MOUNT OLYMPUS ▬▬▬▬▬▬▬▬

Aɴɴᴀ ʜᴀᴅ ʙᴇᴇɴ ꜱɪᴛᴛɪɴɢ ɪɴ Sᴛᴀʀʙᴜᴄᴋꜱ ꜰᴏʀ ɴᴇᴀʀʟʏ ʜᴀʟꜰ ᴀɴ ʜᴏᴜʀ ᴡʜᴇɴ ꜱʜᴇ ʙᴇᴄᴀᴍᴇ aware of two things; one, that the dead heated air was starting to make her feel sick, and two, that someone was reading over her shoulder. Vaguely annoyed, she turned the page but felt the eyes lingering on her book. She turned around, ready for an argument.

'I love that novel,' he said before she could give him one of her hard looks. 'I didn't think anyone read it anymore.' He was dark and cute, about twenty one, with olive skin, brown eyes and heavy black eyebrows. His hair was thick enough to hold pencils in. She closed the paperback and examined the cover as if considering it for the first time. 'I found it in a charity shop,' she admitted.

'Which version is that?'

'I didn't know there was more than one.'

'John Fowles revised it years later. He added new stuff but didn't really improve on the original.'

She searched the cover of 'The Magus' for clues. 'I guess it's the first version. It's pretty old. I like the setting. You know, the Greek island.'

'I'm from an island.' He smiled. He had very white teeth.

She looked at him more carefully. 'Cyprus.'

'Of course Cyprus. You're in a Cypriot neighborhood. Everybody around here is from Cyprus. Our parents and grandparents came here after losing their homes during the Turkish occupation in 1974.'

'So you were born here.' She could see him more clearly now. His beautiful black hair was a little too crafted, his silver jewellery a little too heavy. He was

a little too sure of himself. She could see him memorising a few book titles to impress girls, when he actually preferred to be popping wheelies on his scooter in a pub forecourt, leaning too close to a girl in a bar, knuckle-knocking his mates behind her back, not being mean, just being male. Having locked her assessment in place, she grew subtly cooler. 'And you've never been there.'

'Yes of course. I go every summer at the start of the season.'

'To Aya Napia.'

'No. That's just for English and German kids looking to get laid. I visit my brother Tony in Nicosia. He owns a bookstore. In my family, we all read.' He smiled again. 'That's Fowles' best book, I think.'

This time she smiled back. She indicated the novel. 'It's very strange. Unsettling. Don't tell me how it turns out.'

'I think I've seen you in here before,' he said, leaning forward and proffering a tanned hand. 'Always with a book. I'm Nick.'

'Anna.' They shook rather formally. She self-consciously pushed back her hair, aware of how thin it looked when it needed washing. She hated the thought that someone else might be listening in and noting how easily she could be picked up by a stranger, so she pushed her stool back slightly to create some distance between them.

'Anna,' he said, trying the name out. 'Tell me Anna, do you like Greek food?'

She didn't want to insult him by pointing out that she found it rather overcooked, but again he continued before she could reply. 'I don't mean kebab takeaways, I mean real Greek food, octopus and cuttlefish, shrimps and feta in coriander and pine nut salads.'

She must have been staring at him in surprise, because he felt the need to explain. 'I'm a chef. That is, I'm training as a chef at The Real Greek, you know those places? It's a chain, but a good one.'

'That's different,' she admitted, warming more. 'I've been to the one by the river. I really liked it.'

'Then you must come to the one near here. I'll cook for you. It would be my pleasure.'

The thought crossed her mind that he was simply touting for business,

but it seemed an unnecessarily elaborate approach to winning customers. She decided not to answer until he presented her with further clues to his intentions.

'Ah, now you're thinking he needs customers for his restaurant.' His smile became a laugh. 'Yes?'

'No, certainly not.'

'You want to know the truth? I work unsociable hours. It's difficult to meet anyone, so I figured if I offered to cook for you, I could work and you could eat, so it we both get pleasure and it would be like a date.'

'You're asking me on a date?' asked Anna, genuinely amazed now.

He thought about it for a moment, then nodded vigorously. 'Yes, that's exactly what I'm doing.' And he laughed again.

Before she replied, Anna made up her mind to accept his offer.

It took them ages to find the place. Lily had a tourist map the car rental company had provided, but it mostly consisted of adverts for as-yet-unbuilt luxury apartments and terrible-looking nightclubs, all of which were clearly marked with photographs, while half of the island's the major roads were missing.

'Well, it has to be around here somewhere,' Paul said for the third time. 'It must be enormous.' He pointed to the passenger window. 'Keep a look out on the other side.'

'There.' Lily pointed at a gap in the hibiscus bushes. 'I can see the top of a water slide.'

'Great. Watch for the car park,' Paul instructed. 'Are you sure you still want to go?'

'No, of course not. But I'm being a good girl and facing my fears. I didn't even learn to swim until last year. Anyway, it's not fear of the water, it's—'

'What?'

'Nothing. We're here now. Look.' Lily pointed to the sun-faded blue sign across the entrance that read *Aqua World*.

Paul pulled the Nissan to a halt and studied the posters. 'God, it's 32 euros each, that's steep.'

Lily checked her watch. 'And it's only an hour and a half before they shut. Maybe we shouldn't bother.'

'It still gives us enough time to go on every ride.'

'Everything? Even the really tall ones?'

'Sure—you have to do them all if we go in, I told you, that's the deal.' Paul noticed her hand. 'You didn't take your ring off when we went in the sea.'

'You only just gave it to me, Paul. I'm superstitious. If I took it off and lost it, you might tell me we're not engaged anymore.'

'Why would you even think something like that?' Paul placed his arm along the seat and backed the car into a parking space. Switching off the ignition, he turned to her with questions in his eyes.

'I told you. I've not had much luck with guys in the past. I was always optimistic, though. I thought I'd meet someone decent, but it turned out a good attitude wasn't enough to protect me.'

'Well, you don't have to worry any more, do you?' he said. 'Everyone gets hurt by bad romance at some point. You have to develop a thick skin.'

'I never want to do that,' Lily explained. 'I want to keep the feeling of unconditionally being in love, I want everyone to see it in my face, shining out like a suntan.'

He brushed her cheek with the back of his hand. 'I can see it in everything you do. You wouldn't be able to hide it if you tried. Come on.'

They studied the great map at the entrance. When they saw that it displayed twenty different vertiginous water slides, they became as excited as children. Passing through the turnstiles, they placed their shorts, flip-flops and T-shirts in a locker and headed into the park.

Inside, chlorinated cyan water sluiced through white plastic channels that snaked across sculpted emerald meadows. The park was themed around characters from Greek mythology, and was dotted with risible statuary. Ahead of them, a vast trident-wielding Poseidon rose from plaster waves, looking more like a sinister nude Santa Claus than the god of all the stormy oceans.

It was the third week of the summer season, and the grounds were still only half full. A strong wind had risen, and two of the more extreme rides had been closed for safety reasons. Each slide was flanked by a stone statue and an only slightly more human lifeguard. The humans were bronzed, toned and

bored. As they directed the screaming children who emerged from the flumes, guiding them out of the pools as quickly as possible, they tried to maintain their Grecian poses.

Lily watched a group of young girls climbing the tower of the Aphrodite Drop, higher and higher up the staircase until the wind whipped their hair about their faces. Listening to their delighted screams, she took pleasure in their happiness. Soon they would become women, and face the thousand tests that adulthood would bring. She hoped they would always remember the moments when they had no cares in the world, as she did right now. Being aware of her own happiness made her feel strangely guilty, as if she would somehow have to pay for it later.

A sudden cool breeze buffeted her bare back, making her shiver.

Nick dragged his chair across the narrow third-floor balcony and sat down beside Anna. Ahead, the cool grey-green sea faded into night mist. There was so little air that the waves below sounded like someone gently unwrapping a sweet. 'I'm glad you decided to come with me,' he said, setting two bottles of Keo beer on the balcony table. 'I hate not seeing the sun in London. I thought you were going to change your mind.'

'I was probably looking for reasons to say no,' said Anna. 'I mean, we haven't known each other very long, and when you go on holiday with someone, well, you're kind of stuck with them, aren't you?' She had surprised herself by coming, after three years of steadfastly refusing every offer to enjoy herself. Finally she had realised it was time to let go of the bad experiences of the past, and start trusting again, although it took longer to do so now.

So, do you feel better about it? I could tell you were having second thoughts.'

'Of course I was, trotting off to Cyprus with a stranger. I hardly know you.'

'That sounds really old.'

'I can't help it; that's how I am. Look, I guess I was more stressed than I realized in London. I hate my job. My office doesn't have any windows, and the people in my scheduling department are all married with kids, out in the suburbs. I have nothing to say to them.'

'Then you need to get out of that place and do something you enjoy.'

'I don't know what that is.'

'You never just take a chance, throw everything away, start again?'

'God, no!' Anna took a swig of beer. 'I'm a planner. Charts and achievement lists, all my life. I worry too much about what might happen.'

'Maybe that's why your boyfriends never worked out.' He saw her stiffen slightly. 'I mean, maybe you just need to relax more into yourself.'

'I'm quite relaxed enough, thank you.' He could hear the tension in her voice, and decided to change the subject. She sounded prim and even older, and he could suddenly imagine the kind of woman she would become. They were only on Day Three of the holiday and she was already starting to irrationally annoy him.

The screams echoed up to the mouth of the blue plastic channel. Paul stood at the top of the tower next to Lily, waiting for the signal to jump in. The lifeguard was balancing between the two tubes, waiting for the last riders to clear. Although he wore shorts and was bare-footed, he was wrapped in a heavy red plastic windcheater, protecting himself against the late afternoon winds that swept in from the sea and blew across the fields surrounding the water park.

'Hold onto the bar until I say,' he recited mechanically. 'When you let go, cross your arms and your ankles, and leave the pool at the bottom as quickly as possible.'

Lily looked across at her lover and smiled nervously.

'It's all right,' Paul mouthed at her. 'I'll see you at the bottom.'

The guard turned back to them. 'Okay—go.'

Lily stepped into the tube, seated herself and was catapulted down the terrifying, stomach-dropping shaft.

'I can't hear what you're saying,' Anna shouted into Nick's ear. An Alicia Keyes track was playing so loudly that she was drowned out by bass distortion.

'I said my brother Tony is the manager here,' Nick shouted back.

They were in a shoreline nightclub in Limassol where tattooed Russians in

sleeveless vests sat slumped at the bar slugging watered cocktails. The moment they had stepped through the tacky steel doors, Nick knew it had been a bad idea suggesting they should come to the club. He hadn't been here since the makeover.

'It's awful,' Anna called back as two beached blondes with burned shoulders and corkscrew chimney-cuts tottered past them on sky-high heels. 'Can we get out of here?'

'Don't you want to stay for one drink, just to meet my brother? Tony will be here in a few minutes. We always hang out together.'

'No! I can't hear myself think. I'm going outside. You don't have to come with me.'

'Of course I do.' He cleared the crowds ahead of her and pushed open the doors. Outside, the full chaos of Limassol on a Saturday night hit them. A dozen different club tracks created arrhythmic heartbeats, providing the street with a mutant soundscape. Young men were screaming up the promenade on the rear wheels of their motorbikes, restaurants buffered the night sky with red and blue neon, fat tourists waddled past with sunburned arms and bitten legs.

'Could we go somewhere quiet, where we can just be together?' She gave an anxious smile, always ready to think the worst. Nick was so beautiful and uncomplicated, the world seemed simple to him. She fretted and panicked and over-analysed—it was just that she wanted to be confident. She would give herself unconditionally if she could just be completely sure that she trusted him.

Nick flicked back a smile, and led her to a quiet bar overlooking the sea where just a couple of elderly Cypriot women sat with coffee. It was colder here, but calmer. He went to the bar and returned with a bottle of wine, marvelling at how little it took to make her happy. They sat and drank in silence. The streets behind them shed too much light to unsheath the stars, so they watched the stately passage of tankers, lit like grand hotels.

Tony found them, eyed Anna with a leery laugh and ordered himself a beer. He had lived on the island all his life, and looked nothing like his brother. Tony was squat and sweaty, but the biggest difference was in his behaviour; where Nick was attentive, Tony ignored her and only addressed his brother.

Anna had been dismissed from the conversation. She had met his type before, and already hated him. Pushing back her chair and folding her arms, she longed for this part of the evening to be over.

After a while she rose and walked to the edge of the beach, leaving the brothers to talk together. Looking back at Nick and hearing his laughter, she considered the possibility that she might have fallen in love, and once that happened she would be little more than a fish writhing on a hook.

'How was that for you?' Paul burst out of the pool and hauled Anna to the edge of the pool, laughing.

'A nightmare!' Lily shouted back. 'I don't understand how kids do it without flinching. I've got water up my nose.' She shook herself like a spaniel.

He found it hard to take his eyes from her slender pale body. She was so beautiful it made his eyes hurt. No matter what anyone said about beauty being skin deep, physical attraction was important to him. He wanted to feel proud with her. 'Come on,' he said, 'let's do the big one. Up there. Mount Olympus. Looks like they're reopening it.'

He pointed to the immense slide, a white wooden tower consisting of ten spindly staircases. From its peak protruded a covered plastic pipeline descending in a series of terrifyingly tight loops. On its highest landing a lone lifeguard stood motionless between fluttering flags, looking out across the sun-bleached fields.

Lily shielded her eyes against the searing light and studied the lone figure, the empty ride. 'I don't think it's open,' she said, willing it to be shut.

'The wind's dropped a little. Let's go and see if we can get on it. I said all of the rides, didn't I?'

'Do we have to? It's higher than all the others.'

'Don't be a baby.'

'I'm not—it's just—'*The darkness*, she wanted to add. *The thought of being trapped inside that crushing pitch-black tunnel, falling down to an unknown fate. The darkness pressing in all around like death. It's the unknown that frightens me.*

'Come on,' he said, 'you're not scared, are you?'

'No,' she said, 'of course not,' and followed him up the staircase.

Nick's apartment was above a rowdy nightclub called *Glam*, a misnomer if ever there was one. Below, the English were cheering the football on a vast screen with the colour turned up too high. Leaning on the balcony wall, Anna looked back at the flat. It had three perfectly square white rooms filled with books, and you could see a sliver of sea if you went to the bathroom window and stood on tiptoe, but it was clean and caught the cool night breeze from the shore.

Nick lit fat red candles and set them in saucers on the floor, and they drank more white wine, thick, sharp-tasting local stuff that made Anna's stomach burn. She talked too much and then felt unbearably hot, and stood at the balcony with her shirt loosened, feeling the sea air on her collarbone. Nick listened and waited, as if expecting to hear some signal in her voice, and when he realised she was talking for the sake of it, led her to bed.

As Paul and Lily climbed the stairs, the wind began to pick up again. They reached the fourth landing, and Lily stopped to look out over the parched fields dotted with tubular hay bales, the distant black sand beach, the tankers passing endlessly beyond.

'What are you looking at?' asked Paul.

'When we're married,' she replied, 'can we travel? I mean really travel, not like those couples who say they'll do things and then start working and just lapse back into behaving like their parents?'

Paul's laughter contained puzzlement. 'Yeah, of course, we'll go around the world.'

'You won't go off me when I lose my looks, like my dad did with my mum?'

'You can't foretell the future. Nobody knows that, not politicians, not priests, nobody, because nobody's been there.' He reached down and seized her hand, hauling her up the next flight of stairs, and she knew she would go anywhere with him. She knew that from the top of the tower, the whole world would be able to see their love.

Above them, the stoic lifeguard looked down from the railing, a black silhouette against the deep blue of the sky.

Nick had kissed and caressed her, and put her into bed. Then he left the room. Now Anna waited for him in the darkness. The cool night air from the shutterless windows ruffled her hair and chilled her shoulders, so she rose and closed the glass. As her head was swimming, she lay down on the pillow and thought about what would happen in the next few minutes. She had kept him at bay for long enough. She didn't want him to know that she was just as anxious to sleep with him. But by doing so now, would she spoil the holiday? She tried not to evaluate her options, as she did in everything else. Her mother said she was not normal. It was time to be normal.

She looked up and saw a tiny, whiny bug perpetually hitting itself against the ceiling. Presumably Nick was still in the bathroom. She tried to hear him brushing his teeth, but there was no sound. She had almost fallen asleep by the time the door opened once more.

'You were a long time. I think I drank too much.'

'Shhh.' He climbed into bed beside her. His hands felt cold and rougher than she had imagined. He ran his fingers lightly over her nipples. She froze. As he fondled her breast with practiced ease, she could sense that he was manoeuvring himself into place, ready to hoist himself on top of her without wasting a moment, without so much as a kiss or caress. It all felt so wrong. She hardened against him, and the more he pushed at her, the more she resisted.

She felt his stubby penis, wet at the tip, jabbing into the top of her leg, and shoved him away in shock. Climbing out to the edge of the bed in panic, she fumbled for the light and flicked it on. Tony, Nick's brother, raised himself on one arm and squinted at her. 'What the fuck's the matter with you?' he asked, 'Nick said you'd be cool with it.'

Lily and Paul reached the top platform of Mount Olympus. The wind was snatching plumes of water from the open mouth of the chute. Lily could see

the drop of the water tunnel, the way it wrapped itself around the staun-chions, the final open section of torrenting water. She could hardly see anyone else in the park. The sun was dropping low now.

Paul turned to the lifeguard, a frozen-looking girl who glared blankly at them from beneath her plastic Aquapark hood. 'Can we go down together?' he asked. 'My girlfriend's a bit scared. I should look after her. We just got engaged.'

The lifeguard remained motionless while she assessed them. Then she indi-cated the left tunnel and unclipped the rope that had been placed across it. 'The lighter one in front, the heavier one behind, place your legs under her arms. Keep your hands and feet tucked in.' She sounded English, distant and odd.

Paul turned to Lily and kissed her. 'You heard the young lady. In you go.'

Lily peered into the darkened tunnel mouth, then climbed into the red plastic step and lowered herself into the water. Paul enclosed her from behind. 'Don't worry,' he said, 'I've got you. I'll always be here for you.'

The lifeguard was holding them back from the edge of the tunnel with her bare foot. After a few seconds, she raised it and let the pumping water shoot them out into the tunnel. A moment later, they were gone.

Anna lowered the *Aquapark* hood from her face and stepped to the railing, searching below. She felt nothing but hatred, for men, for the world, for lovers. She had long since blotted out the memory of the fight with Tony, and Nick's clawed face, the accusations and the police—it had all happened so long ago. But sometimes she still wondered why she had decided to remain on the island, lost and invisible, unable to speak to another human being. It had crossed her mind on several occasions that she might not be well. Her mother was probably beside herself with worry. Her mother, who had never felt she was normal anyway.

Was it normal to ignore everyone who spoke to you? To seal yourself away from the world, to go to work and come home to a box-room behind the motorway where no-one would ever find you? To long for some closure to the consuming hatred you felt?

Last night she had gone to the supermarket in Limassol and bought ten packets of old-fashioned razorblades. This morning she had carefully cut

them in half, and gone to work two hours early. Then she had taken the blades from their packet and embedded them longways in the mastic joints that held the tunnel sections of the Mount Olympus ride together, working from the top of the tube, going all the way down to the bottom.

So much for the mystery of love.

She leaned over the railing and listened out for the screams.

HALLOWEEN DOG ▆▆▆▆▆▆▆▆▆▆▆▆▆▆▆▆▆▆▆▆▆▆

Fᴇᴡ ᴘᴇᴏᴘʟᴇ ᴋɴᴏᴡ ᴛʜɪs, ʙᴜᴛ Hᴀʟʟᴏᴡᴇᴇɴ ᴅᴏᴇsɴ'ᴛ ᴊᴜsᴛ ʀᴇᴍᴏᴠᴇ ᴛʜᴇ ʙᴏᴜɴᴅᴀʀɪᴇs between the living and the dead. The Druids skinned animals for their heads and pelts before sacrificing them to Celtic deities on huge bonfires, and as a karmic consequence, all lowly creatures gain human sentience once a year. Most of them waste the opportunity. Some are in cages. Some have brains so small that it makes no difference whether they can think or not. Jellyfish and canaries get a particularly raw deal. Dogs and monkeys tend to have the best time, provided they're not being experimented on.

Unfortunately, the first conscious realization to form in the brain of Butch, a bowlegged English bulldog whose new teenaged owner, Walt, eked out a pathetic living as a bar cleaner at the Five Aces on Neil Avenue in Columbus, Ohio, was that his master was a complete idiot. Well-meaning and innocent, maybe, but still an idiot. Walt had just been tricked by a group of friends into becoming the driver for a local robbery.

'All you have to do is sit in the truck,' said Heath, his supposed buddy from the Five Aces bar, 'but bring your dog. We need him to intimidate the guard.'

'Let's leave him behind,' pleaded Walt. 'He's not too smart.'

Thanks a bunch, thought Butch. *Right now I'm smarter than you.*

'He looks fierce, and that's all we need.' Heath hadn't been able to get hold of a gun, and figured a scary-faced dog would do in a pinch.

The gang ran into Hester's Deli, Butch bit the checkout boy in the nuts, and much to his surprise, despite being chased half a block by an eighty-year-old woman, they successfully pulled off their first-time heist. But moments after Heath reached the corner and threw the money bag into the truck, Walt

stepped on the gas and hightailed it out of town, leaving his fellow gang members on the sidewalk.

'Finally I'm not a loser anymore,' Walt told his dog. 'You and I have made it, pal. We can make a new start, do anything we like. We're going places.'

Butch felt that Walt had somewhat misunderstood the concept of achievement, but he also recalled gaining human feelings last Halloween, and becoming disgusted to discover that he was a dog, sitting around a ratty apartment licking his balls and eating leftover hamburger meat. Actually, the ball-licking part hadn't been so bad. But this was better.

'This Halloween is gonna be the best you ever had,' Walt promised. 'What would you like to do?'

Find me a hooker and get me wasted, thought Butch. *Order some Cristal champagne. Anything just so long as I don't have to sniff any dog assholes.*

They ditched the truck, changed some of the large denominations at the Great Western Shopping Centre, drove for a while, then checked into a motel. Butch wished he'd been given human vocal chords, just for the night of Halloween, but when he opened his mouth only barks and whines emerged.

Walt explained that he knew a girl from the bar called Jenni, a real hottie he could trust because she'd told him she was nuts about him, and to come find her if he ever made enough money to buy her for the evening.

'So let's go see Jenni, have a party and get totally wild,' said Walt, rubbing Butch between the ears.

Finally, thought Butch, *six Halloweens spent watching some old bitch sleeping in front of the TV, the seventh spent running around the streets trying to find a new owner, now it looks like I'm finally gonna get some human action. Thank you, Samhain.*

Walt called Jenni and told her he had money. Half an hour later they arrived at her front porch. When Jenni opened the door in her low-cut white shirt and tiny cobalt-blue skirt, Butch got a cross-species boner, then reminded himself it was okay because, for this night at least, he was an honorary human. And he knew that the best part about being human was that, even though he was in the body of a dog and still wearing a collar, he could briefly attain a state of grace and experience something lost to him the

rest of the year. He could finally feel the respect and admiration of his human peers. Instead of just standing around with his tongue hanging out, whimpering for his lead or begging for food, he could show intelligence with his eyes and make a connection with other human beings. He could feel what it meant to be a man, not just some four-legged creature admired solely for its ability to fetch sticks from lakes.

Jenni invited them in. It looked as if the entire contents of the Pottery Barn catalog had been emptied into her little house, especially the section on flounces and frills. But he could tell she loved him. She squealed and scratched his belly, and fed him a steak, and Walt poured him a bowl of champagne. Jenni bent close and looked deep into his eyes. 'Walt told me you helped him make some money today,' she said, 'so I'm going to do something special for you. We're meeting up with some of my girlfriends tonight, and they all have dogs. You are going to have the best night of your life.'

Jeez, am I gonna get laid as well? Butch dared to entertain the thought. Okay, it was sex with another dog, but he had to take it where he could get it. He gazed soulfully into Jenni's eyes, then into Walt's, and felt the connection grow strong. *Tonight*, he willed them to hear, *I am truly one of you.*

Butch looked around the room in disgust. There were five other dogs. Gonzales the mad Mexican Hairless Chihuahua had been dressed up as miniature Superman. Jackula was a Jack Russell and had been kitted out as a Bela Lugosi-style vampire. His mistress had stuffed false plastic fangs into his mouth, so that he was permanently baring his teeth. He even had a squawking budgerigar on his back disguised as a bat. Suzi the Pekinese had been dressed as a cat, the ultimate humiliation. Buddy the Labrador had been tricked up like a pilot in a biplane, with goggles and cardboard wings sticking out from his ribcage. Otto the German Shepherd was dressed as Adolph Hitler, complete with little jackboots and a toothbrush moustache.

Butch checked his reflection in the window. He had been dressed as little Bo Peep in false eyelashes, a pink French empire bonnet and dozens of pastel bows. He was a Halloween Dog, and he looked fucking ridiculous. Ahead of him, the adults cavorted about in red plastic devil outfits.

Butch silently cursed the pagan festival that had granted him the mind of a human, while leaving humans with the brains of animals.

POISON PEN ▰▰▰▰▰▰▰▰▰▰▰▰

ANDREW BAYER

Uncle Andrew played the Stock Exchange and used his gains to fund his passions—but what were his passions? Nobody knew. He told his friends that he was a collector, but there were no collections at his Buckinghamshire mansion or his London flat.

Now he was in Southern France, tearing along the Grande Corniche in his classic white 1968 Mercedes convertible, and the curving emerald hills had just parted to reveal the port of Monaco below. The autumn air was cool and smelled of pine and lavender. The morning sky was the same aching azure as the Mediterranean, and a few thin grey clouds still hung like spiderwebs in the trees below the road.

Andrew pushed his speed to fifty, the most he could risk on a road with a forty metre drop on one side and no crash barriers. He was late for lunch with Lycus Gerolstein, his lawyer, who would be waiting for him at the *Salon des Etoiles*, ready to celebrate their latest purchase with a glass of fine champagne.

Coming from the opposite direction, a Nicoise estate agent was lighting her cigarette with one hand and arguing on her cellphone with the other, which didn't leave her any way of controling the wheel of her Porsche Boxster. She was trying to arrange for some Russians to view a *pieds dans l'eau* property in Fontvieille but they were being very difficult about the appointment times. She argued, threatened and cajoled but they wouldn't come earlier, and she sensed she was losing the sale.

What she should have been doing was watching the central divider as she

rounded the bend, because moments later she blithely crossed it, forcing the car coming from the opposite direction—a classic white convertible Mercedes—off the tarmac and out into the clouds.

The great vehicle sailed as gracefully as a galleon for a few seconds, then seemed to realise that it weighed over a ton, and dropped into the valley below. Andrew might have been able to get out, except that his hand-stitched 1968 seatbelt had not been manufactured for speedy removal. He was still trying to unbuckle it when he hit the cliff face and bounced all the way down to the roof of the rococo Banque de Grimaldi building on the Avenue des Citronniers in Monte Carlo. The noise was so loud that it made diners briefly stir themselves from their lobster salads.

Andrew Bayer's classic car was stuck out of the bank's roof with its rear wheels still spinning. Inside the grand financial institution, his corpse, tethered by the effective seat-belt, dripped blood over piles of banknotes. The accident made the front page of *Nice Matin* next day, right next to a car insurance advert. The irony did not go unnoticed.

In England, 23 year-old Mark Bayer heard about the death of his favourite uncle, happy-go-lucky Andrew, and was heartbroken. He had been closer to Andrew than he was to his own father, who had worked in loss adjustment all his life and treated Mark as if he was a failure, just because he had chosen to become a graphic designer and get some pleasure from his career.

Mark had inherited Uncle Andrew's easygoing attitude. Recently he had spent more time than usual with old man in London, for his uncle had been undergoing sporadic treatment for lung cancer at the Harley Street Clinic. Uncle Andrew was wealthy and knew how to enjoy himself, which made the rest of his serious-minded family regard him as a wastrel. Two years earlier he had retired to his grand country manse with his second much younger wife, a woman who had appeared on his arm after a trip to Boston, where he had been attending some kind of collectors' convention.

But what had he been doing in the South of France when he died? Nobody seemed to know, not even his wife.

Mark and his family attended the cremation service, which was held in Monte Carlo. Uncle Andrew had a brother and a sister of similar ages, a daughter from his first wife and the aforementioned much younger second

wife. The family was therefore split into three separate interested parties, and at any time at least one of these was arguing with the other two. Their loyalties shifted and switched like warring states in an Eastern European nation.

All in all, it was not the best recipe for a happy send-off.

The much younger second wife turned up in a tight-fitting Dior trouser suit and a white hat better suited to Ladies Day at Ascot. She outraged Mark's family, who were looking for any excuse to take umbrage.

During the service, a vicious argument escalated between Andrew's first and second wives, during which the first wife, whose name was Cheryl, questioned the second wife, whose name was Catherine, about her motives for marrying a wealthy man who was almost twice her age. Catherine replied that she had fallen in love with men like Andrew before. 'Tell me,' spat Cheryl, 'at precisely what moment do you usually fall in love with your elderly millionaires?'

The family members quickly became embroiled and lined up on either side, carping across the divide. At a drinks party afterwards there was another fight when Mark's father, who was paying for the wake, had his credit cards humiliatingly rejected by the venue's management. Money and inheritance were openly discussed—subjects Mark's mother regarded as vulgar in the extreme. The English, she remarked pointedly, did not expose their financial affairs in public. This last remark was clearly aimed at Uncle Andrew's second wife, who was American and regarded the entire Bayer family as a bunch of bitter limey snobs with very little, as far as she could see, to be snobbish about. The wake ended on a very sour note indeed.

A few days later in London, the entire family attended the reading of Andrew's will at Lycus Gerolstein's office. Here, seated around the lawyer's boardroom table, they heard that Uncle Andrew's possessions, including another classic car, a boat, a country house, jewellery, a London apartment and bequests of cash, were to be divided up between various family members. It seemed that everyone's wishes had been catered for. Only one of the children had been deliberately and notably excluded from the will—Mark.

The young designer was surprised by the fact that he had been left nothing, as it contradicted what Uncle Andrew told him when they'd last met. In fact, Andrew had gone out of his way to promise that he was leaving something

very special to his favourite nephew. 'You were always the one I liked the best,' Andrew had confided. 'I know you'll make something of yourself. I want to ensure that you'll be truly happy in your life, so I'm leaving you the greatest of the gifts in my possession.'

But he had left nothing. There was not even a mention of the boy in the will.

Mark was upset at first. He thought the old man had loved, trusted and confided in him. Perhaps he had caused some offence over their final lunch and hurt his uncle's feelings? Even Mark's younger brother Ben had been bequeathed some money. Mark thought back over their last meeting, breaking it down into moments, but could think of nothing he had done to upset Uncle Andrew.

The family was very sorry to lose their patriarch. The amiably disreputable old fellow had been a touchstone for them, someone they could go to for advice and help, always kindly, always fair, a calm centre to the frequently bitter whirlwind of Bayer family spats, recriminations and alliances. Now that he had suddenly been taken from them, they felt as if they had been cast adrift. There was no-one to whom they could turn. Gabriel, Andrew's younger brother, was flaky and neurotic. Joan, his sister, was a melancholia-prone hysteric. Life without their mentor would be very different indeed.

At first the Bayers sought to pursue proceedings against the estate agent driving the other car, but she was in a Nice hospital with a broken neck, and Lycus, the family lawyer, advised them not to start an action against her in a French court of law. The process, he warned, would be protracted and constricted by red tape, and would probably last, Jarndyce-style, until there was no money left, but that was the French for you.

With conflicting emotions, Mark listened to his family's growing grievances. The complaints were petty; why had Uncle Andrew left Mark's parents jewellery but little money? Why had he only bequeathed his brother a classic car? Nothing quite made sense. Soon, a poisonous pall began to creep over the formerly happy family, and the things Uncle Andrew had left behind began to be evaluated, coveted and compared.

Mark looked on in discomfort as his parents pored over their copy of Uncle Andrew's will, endlessly reinterpreting every word. He had never thought of

them as greedy people, but now it seemed they were becoming obsessed with the amounts they had been left. He had heard that this was the common result of losing a senior family member, but the process still disturbed him. Worse, it traduced his memory of the avuncular old man and made him think more harshly of the surviving Bayers. Assuming that these ill humours would be short-lived, he returned to work and family life, albeit diminished, continued as before.

GABRIEL BAYER

Exactly one month after his uncle had died, Mark received a phonecall just as he was starting to fall asleep at the keyboard of his computer. He had been putting in long hours, trying to drum up business for his ailing design practice.

'Mark, is that you?' asked a familiar voice.

'Uncle Gabriel?' Mark liked his other uncle, even though Gabriel struck him as emotionally unstable. Gabriel was 47 and twice divorced, and had a difficult relationship with his two unruly children, but his heart was in the right place.

'I'm sorry to call you at this time of night, Mark. I know you always keep late hours.'

'Are you okay?' It was unusual for Gabriel to call.

'I don't know. I don't think so. Look, I know how close you were to my brother. You were always his favourite. I thought you might understand.'

'Understand what?'

'I just saw Andrew.'

'Yeah, I keep thinking I see him too.'

'No, I mean I really saw him, alive.'

'What are you talking about?'

'I know this is going to sound ridiculous, but I was driving back from the office this evening and passed him standing on the side of the road. He was waving at me.'

'Uncle Gabriel, you know that's impossible.'

'I know, but I swear to you it was definitely him. He was wearing the clothes he died in, that awful shiny blue suit he always wore in France and that awful straw hat—you know, the one the English always think they need to put on in the Riviera.'

'Have you told anyone else about this?'

'God, no, of course not. They'd think—well, you know.' Gabriel had suffered a nervous breakdown soon after his second divorce.

'I think maybe it's delayed shock,' was all Mark could say. 'I imagine it's a common phenomenon.'

'I know. It just felt so weird, what with me driving his old car and everything. I looked in the rear view mirror and there he was. I looked again a moment later, and he'd vanished.' Gabriel had been left his brother's other car, another classic Mercedes, his favourite, a plum-coloured 1970 saloon with white leather seats and whitewall tyres. There were only fifteen of the left-hand drive models remaining in the world.

'I don't suppose there's been any word on what he was doing in Monaco that day?'

'I've asked around. Nobody has a clue. He told Catherine he'd be away for a few days. She was used to him going on his collecting trips.' As far as Mark could discern, Uncle Andrew visited private antique sales, but nobody knew if he ever bought anything. Apart from the few bits and pieces he'd left his family, he seemed to own no special collections. There was nothing but ordinary furniture in his country house.

They talked for a while, and Gabriel rang off, a little happier. But it wasn't the end of the matter.

The following morning, Gabriel Bayer said goodbye to his 19 year-old son Jake, who still lived at home with him, and headed into work earlier than usual. The flat straight roads that ran through the Norfolk Fens were obscured by patches of thick mist. Gabriel tuned to Radio Four and listened to a heated discussion about the future of the Anglican church. He had just passed Melton Constable when the radio fazed and faded. On either side of him, misted patches of marsh water glowed softly in the early morning light. He fiddled with the radio's tuner, trying to relocate his programme, when the dark man loomed at him.

The figure was standing stock-still in the centre of the road. Its arms were raised in warning. Gabriel swung the wheel just enough to avoid hitting him, and glimpsed his brother Andrew's alarmed face peering out from under his white straw hat as he passed. The vehicle's wheels had lost their purchase on the mist-slick road, and no matter how hard Gabriel tried to correct the drift of the car it slid further in the opposite direction.

A classic Mercedes has a solid tempered steel chassis. As the two front wheels spun free of the tarmac and slipped over the verge, they hung above the velvet green surface of the marsh for what felt like an age. Slowly, inexorably, the vehicle tilted and dropped into the dark still water of the fen. Gabriel fought to unclasp his belt, but found himself in the same situation as his brother. The blinding weed-green liquid began pushing at the seals of the windows. It sprayed in through the radio, the steering column, the radiators. Gabriel was hysterical now, unable to do anything except twist about in panic. He could have escaped if he had only retained his presence of mind, for the fen was not deep. But the water was muddy and impenetrable, the embodiment of icy death. As the Mercedes settled it rolled over and filled, and there was nothing Gabriel could do about it.

Nobody thought to check up on his whereabouts until darkness had already fallen. It took another day for the police to dredge the fen and locate his corpse in the weed-camouflaged car.

CHERYL BAYER

Mark was in his favourite Wardour Street café, an independent coffee shop with permanently steamed-up windows, when he bumped into Uncle Andrew's lawyer, Lycus Gerolstein. He had a pale oval face and thinning grey hair that added to his air of reticence. A stern but seemingly fair-minded man, he was greatly trusted by his loyal clients.

'May I?' he asked, joining Mark at his table. 'I thought I might find you here. There was something I wanted to talk to you about. You know you were always your uncle's favourite.'

'Yes,' said Mark, 'it's funny he decided not to show it. Not that I mind, I just don't understand what happened.'

'Well, that's what I wanted to explain. Your uncle made some big changes to his will in a series of handwritten codicils before his death.'

'What kind of changes?'

'Switching bequests from one side of the family to the other, that sort of thing. I tried to talk him out of them, because I felt the original will was fine as it stood. Hell, it had taken us many months to plan and refine it, to make sure that everyone in the family was treated with equanimity.'

'You don't think he was coerced into making the alterations, do you?'

'I wasn't there when he made them, but I can tell you the signatures on the codicils are definitely Andrew's, although they're pretty shaky. Lately I've had my suspicions.'

'When did he make these alterations?'

'Well, as you know, your uncle was in hospital quite a few times.'

'He was having blackouts. At first he just told me it was high blood pressure. But I spoke to the doctor and discovered he was due to have chemotherapy for lung cancer. After a while, he admitted the truth and his treatments began.'

'Obviously, I knew your uncle was unwell,' said Lycus. 'And when people become sick, families tend to gather in preparation for the worst. I checked with the hospital, and was told that several relatives visited him while he was there. I have a feeling the codicils appeared around then. As I say, I can't be sure until I've done some more checking. I just thought you should know.'

Lycus rose to go, but placed a hand on Mark's shoulder. 'At times like this, family members you know and love can behave strangely. This is just a friendly word of warning. I'd keep an eye on them if I were you.'

As Mark headed back to the office he rented, a dank attic with an alarmingly sloped floor in one of the last unrestored properties in Soho, he mentally drew up a list of suspects. Who might have manipulated the old man for his money? The idea revolted him. He looked around the office, at his obsolete computer, and the walls that were wet from the leaking ceiling. He was painfully short of cash. Projects had been hard to come by lately, and although he felt a little envious of his brother and his cousins, he could not bring

himself to ask them for a loan. It just didn't feel right. Surely his uncle would have left him money if he had wanted him to have it.

Pushing the thought to the back of his mind, he settled down to the morning's work.

Some time later on the other side of the city, Cheryl Bayer wrote out her name on a piece of paper and studied it with a critical eye. She had kept her former husband's name after the divorce but now, for the first time, the 46 year-old retail manager was thinking of ditching it. Andrew had left her his four-room flat in Stratton Street, Mayfair, choosing to bequeath his huge Buckinghamshire house to his younger second wife, Catherine. Why, she wondered, did the first wives always get the raw deals?

Okay, the flat was worth a small fortune, but it still didn't seem fair when you looked at what everyone else had got. Cheryl was trying to sell the place privately, and decided she would continue to live in it until she found a purchaser. The property had hardly been touched since the 1950s and prob-ably needed rewiring, but she resented the idea of paying out hard-earned money to fix it before the sale.

She studied the signature once more. That was it then. She would change back to her given name and finally put her marriage to Andrew behind her. She balled up the paper and tossed it into the bin.

Finishing her second bottle of red wine—she would have to watch the drinking if she was going to find another husband—she went to bed, and lay listening to the taxis sloshing along the wet street outside. She thought about Andrew, trying to remember how he had looked in their happier times, but already those memories were growing dim. What were the chances of contesting his will—could she even do it now that it had been implemented? The whole thing was so unfair. Why should the second wife get so much?

It was no use. She couldn't sleep. Getting back out of bed she walked through the half-emptied flat without turning on the lights. As she approached the kitchen mirror, she looked at her reflection and instinctively knew that something was wrong. Her shaded figure shimmered and buzzed apart as if it was made of flies, and reshaped itself into Andrew. He was leaning against the kitchen wall behind her, with his hands raised in a friendly gesture. He was smiling at her benignly. With a gasp, she span around, but

found nothing there. She hoped Andrew had not been able to read her unkind thoughts. When she looked back at the mirror he was gone, and she realised her sleep had overlapped into her drunken wakeful state, and he had never been there at all.

No more red wine. She decided to make some tea.

There was something wrong with the electric kettle. It was making a funny noise. Perhaps she had overfilled it. She honestly couldn't remember what she had done. She tentatively touched the side, but it didn't feel as if it was heating. She tapped the plug, tried the wall switch. The kitchen lights weren't working for some reason.

She wiggled the kettle plug more violently.

She saw the spark, and watched as it jumped with a sharp crack from the plug to the wall, vanishing under the wallpaper. It seemed to have actually gone behind the outlet. She could see it glowing red, burrowing through the paper. Suddenly it surfaced, burning upwards in a fierce crimson line. She knew she had drunk far too much, but she had never actually hallucinated before. She slapped her hands over the progressing spark, trying to stop it, but it continued to burn a path, searing and blistering the flesh of her palms. Now it was rising fast and branching into other patterns, burning channels across the kitchen wall, stopping once to flare and hiss, burning onwards again.

She stepped back and studied the wall, incredulous, trying to understand what was happening. Some kind of pattern was forming. It looked almost like handwriting. She wondered if she should try to call someone, or whether the fault would simply burn itself out. She knew she should have had the electrics checked.

The realisation of what she was looking at hit her. The burning ziggurat appeared to be her ex-husband's signature. God knows she had seen it enough times when he had signed money over to her. The thought was so silly she started to giggle. At precisely this moment the lines all flared, and the entire kitchen wall burst into a singe fierce sheet of flame.

———

JAKE BAYER

It seemed as if the rain would never let up. Mark Bayer had attended few funerals in his life, but in one month his presence had been required at three. He watched the gathered family guiltily smoking under the eaves of the crematorium like schoolchildren, and almost felt sorry for them. During the service, everyone had talked about how much Cheryl had doted on her husband, but Mark was beginning to wonder. After the divorce she had become an angry drunk. Nobody mentioned that.

Two of the relatives closest to Andrew were dead. It was almost as if his uncle had planned their fates from beyond the grave. But Mark couldn't bring himself to suspect that such a kind, conciliatory old man would want to bring harm to his family.

Cheryl had been burned bald and blackened, which had presumably saved the crematorium some time. Her flat had been gutted and rendered into an empty shell that brought vulgarity to the precious Mayfair Street. The coroner noted that the former Mrs Bayer had been drinking heavily and would not have been able to exercise clear judgement, and although he was puzzled by the striped burns on her hands, a verdict of death by misadventure was passed.

With no assignments to work on, Mark took the next morning off to go and visit Joan and Warren, his parents. Over lunch in their favourite restaurant, an monstrously overdecorated trattoria in Highgate, North London, he attempted to confront them about the codicils to Uncle Andrew's will, but they neatly deflected his questions. If they knew the truth, it seemed they were not about to tell him.

He was starting to suspect everyone. Even those closest to him were now behaving differently in the aftermath of his uncle's death. As Mark questioned his parents, he started to see how aggrieved they became when discussing Andrew's wealth, and how disappointed they were with what they had been left.

Everyone except Mark had been left amounts of money, but his mother had also inherited a somewhat peculiar emerald necklace, and his father had been presented with an art deco diamond skull cufflink and tiepin set.

However, it was obvious that his parents had been hoping for more; Andrew's spectacular Buckinghamshire house, perhaps. Surely they took precedence over his childlike second wife? Wasn't blood thicker than youthfulness?

Mark looked from Warren to Joan as they forked sweetbreads and *osso bucco* into their mouths, and saw them in a different, less flattering light.

Uncle Gabriel had a 19 year-old son studying at Cambridge. Jake Bayer had been left a brand-new Kawasaki motorcycle by his uncle, to replace the one he had had stolen the previous year. Gabriel had never approved of his son's love of motorbikes. Now that Jake was fatherless, he found that he was allowed to ride the glistening machine.

On impulse, Jake set off to visit his girlfriend in Manchester, and powered up the M1 hoping to catch her before she went out for the night. He, too, had become infected by the thought that the other side of the family was profiting more heavily from his uncle's death. He had lost his father (not that they had ever been close) and had been given the admittedly beautiful Kawasaki Ninja Performance Edition machine which his uncle had bought in readiness for his 21st birthday. But that was all he'd been bequeathed. His Aunt Joan and Uncle Warren had been left valuable jewels, and Andrew's second wife had inherited a huge mansion. It seemed unfair. Of course, his cousin Mark had been left nothing, but the guy was a loser, trying to build a tiny graphic design company in a recession, refusing help from anyone.

The lowering skies were brownish grey and the black road ahead was slick with rain, so he decelerated and concentrated on the traffic around him. With his father gone, Jake was the most senior male on his side of the family, and responsibility was expected of him.

A few hundred yards ahead, the articulated supermarket truck that had been pacing the Kawasaki for two junctions also decelerated sharply. According to the signs, one of the lanes was closed for the next mile. Most of the main truck haulage between London and Manchester was conducted on this route, and you had to remain watchful in wet weather.

Damn, the truck was coming close.

Jake loosened the throttle, watching the fast approach of the truck's backplate, and knew he would have to slow down fast. It was okay, though, because

there was nothing behind him. He checked the wing mirrors expecting to see a clear straight stretch of glistening blacktop. Instead, he saw his uncle's face. He was saying something, trying to warn him.

Shocked, Jake slammed on his brakes.

When he looked in the mirrors again, Uncle Andrew had been replaced by the steel grille of another truck, just feet from his rear fender and approaching at an insane speed.

The two great trucks slammed into each other, with Jake at their centre. The motorcycle flipped onto its side and was crushed as flat as a milk bottle top.

It proved impossible to fully separate Jake Bayer from the Kawasaki. His head was found under the wheel arch of the second truck. His left foot turned up two days later on the slip road of a Little Chef restaurant.

JOAN BAYER

As soon as Mark heard of his cousin's death, he became convinced that this string of accidents was no longer coincidental. But the main question which haunted him was this; even if Uncle Andrew had somehow planned for his family to be hurt, why would he want to harm his young stepson? It seemed as if the items specified by the will were somehow cursed to inflict damage on their inheritors. But how could that be possible? Uncle Andrew had loved his family.

Mark tried to discuss the matter with his brother Ben, who clearly thought he was crazy. He knew there was no point in going to the police. He tried talking to his parents again, but the deflection he had encountered before now turned to outright hostility. Everyone was bitter and confused by this inexplicable and disastrous turn of events. Mark sat in his gloomy office and tried to figure out an answer. His brother had been left money. Surely, if there really was a curse he would be spared—after all, how could a gift as universal and as abstract as cash ever hurt him?

Over the next few weeks, the aftershocks of death continued to ripple through the Bayer family. Jake's girlfriend was devastated by her loss, and

discreetly dropped out of school. Autumn crushed the life from London's trees and winter set in hard. It felt as if nothing could be healed.

Andrew's mother finally went to see the family lawyer about contesting the will. She felt that as Andrew's sister, she should have been left considerably more, so Lycus Gerolstein agreed to put her case to the rest of the family. However, they unanimously refused to grant her an extra tranche of cash from her brother's inheritance fund, and as a consequence, the divisions between them all grew deeper. Mark was at a loss to understand what was happening. He had always thought of his family as—well, typically English. They were scattered across countryside and city, eminently sensible, rather too respectable, slightly dull, slightly superior, but now they seemed vindictive, bitter, mean-spirited.

Mark's mother had changed more than anyone. Status and power had suddenly become ridiculously important to her. With his own salary running out and no new clients offering work, Mark had been forced to move back to his parents' house in Chiswick. That evening, he came home just as the first of the real winter storms was breaking, and found Joan preparing for her husband's annual office dinner. Shaking out his umbrella and leaving it against the banisters on the first floor hall, he knocked and entered his mother's dressing room.

He barely recognised Joan anymore. She had lost weight and Botoxed away her wrinkles. With her newly auburn hair swept up and the antique emerald necklace at her throat, she suddenly seemed like every other hungry social-climber who attended London's glitzy winter events. Now she spoke of little else than what had befallen the family, who had got what, and why they were not entitled to have it.

'Your uncle had always had his favourites,' she told him, trying on new lipstick and popping her mouth at the mirror. 'Catherine only married him for his money, everyone knows that. And she got exactly what she wanted. She's been left that house, which must be worth a couple of million. He even left her children the attached land, and they're not even his!'

Mark was miserable. He wanted his world to return to how it had been before the death of his uncle. He was sick of hearing about money. But their lives were broken and there was no going back.

'Well,' said Joan with a final snap of her handbag, 'I wouldn't be surprised if Andrew had kept a few other funds tucked away. He was always clever with his cash. Perhaps we should hire Lycus to look into the matter. He must know where everything is, he was as thick as thieves with your uncle.' She turned to her son, as if suddenly becoming aware that he was in the room. 'Are you sure you don't want to come with us tonight?'

'No, I'm trying to build a business plan,' he told her.

'It's so unfair. You were supposed to be his favourite nephew. I think it's disgraceful, the way he's treated you.'

'Where's Dad?'

'I'm meeting him there.' She rose and looked about her. 'Where did I put my jacket?'

'I think I saw it downstairs.'

Joan kissed him and went out into the corridor. Mark put on his headphones and went to work on his laptop.

His mother stood in front of the hall mirror and tried to work out what was wrong with her reflection. It was the necklace; it refused to hang straight. The emerald pendant at its centre was crooked, and the settings of the diamonds around it felt razor-sharp on her delicate skin. Annoyed, she unclipped the clasp at the back and attempted to realign the chain.

In the mirror, something was coagulating in the shadows behind her right shoulder, as if the very darkness was knitting itself into a shape. The penumbral figure was speaking to her. The flesh of Joan's neck prickled. She reached out a hand to the glass.

'Andrew?'

And then, just as quickly, it dissipated like smoke beneath her touch. Above her head an apocalyptic peal of thunder sounded, and the house trembled.

Mark's furled umbrella slipped from its position against the banisters and fell down into the hall. Its metal tip shot under the back of Joan's necklace, catching it, the handle yanking the chain down hard. Joan was wearing new high heels that slipped on the tiled floor and pulled her over. As she fell, the umbrella, now caught in the necklace, twisted as she landed on it, tightening the chain into a noose. The metal jewel settings sliced into her soft neck,

neatly severing her carotid artery. She frantically tried to pull herself upright, but the umbrella twisted like a garrotte and the jewels bit deeper. Her blood pooled in a scarlet mirror across the floor. For a brief moment she saw Andrew reflected, then she died.

OLIVIA BAYER

'Well, I continued working upstairs,' Mark told the sceptical policeman who was covertly checking his pupils to see if he'd been taking drugs.

'You mean to tell me that your mother was struggling to catch her breath just one floor below and you didn't hear a thing?'

'No, I had my headphones on. I didn't know anything about it until I went downstairs to get a drink.'

'And how much later was that?'

'I don't know, twenty minutes, half an hour.'

'And you didn't even get up close to check on her?'

'Why would I? There was blood everywhere. I could clearly see she was dead.' He knew that the image of his mother lying on the black and white tiles in a nimbus of her own blood would stay with him forever.

The officers who quizzed Mark after his mother's death were quick to rule him out of any involvement in what the forensics team termed a bizarre accident, because his computer log showed that he was at his terminal during the time of death, and it was clear that Joan Bayer had died alone. Mark's story perfectly matched the sequence of events, but the officers agreed that they had never heard of anyone dying in such a bizarre manner.

From this date on, Mark's father stopped speaking to his son. Mark moved out a few days after the funeral, and rented a tumbledown flatshare in Whitechapel. The strange story of the Bayer family deaths had been kept out of the press until now, but this latest addition to the role-call of the deceased received its first passing mention in the tabloids.

Mark had now begun to believe that some kind of embodiment of evil was hunting down his relatives, but although he tried to talk about it, none of the surviving family members were prepared to listen to him. Reading up about

wills on the internet, he was shocked to discover how many inheritance settlements caused the breakdown of family relationships. Eventually he was forced to reach the only logical conclusion—that this terrible chain of events was simply the kind of bad luck that followed the sudden loss of a family patriarch.

Mark was now seriously broke, and because he had lately been preoccupied, he lost the support of his only freelance client. He was on the verge of asking his brother Ben for a loan from the money he had been left, but at the last minute decided not to request any assistance. He could not explain why he decided on this. He simply couldn't help feeling that everything Andrew left to his family had been irrevocably tainted.

Olivia, Uncle Andrew's 21 year-old daughter from his first marriage, was a loner. She rarely spoke to any other members of the family. She loved the sea and lived in Brixham, Devon. As a consequence, her uncle had left her his 22-foot Fletcher speedboat. She took it out even on the coldest days, roaring along the blue coastline for an hour at first light if the tides were favourable.

One morning, Olivia inexplicably failed to pump the petrol fumes from the tanks and nearly turned the boat into a fireball that would have killed her instantly. She was been an experienced mariner. It seemed so unlike her to make such a mistake.

Shaken by her own neglectfulness, she pumped out the tank and set off at speed, forgetting to untie the aft rope from its mooring capstan. Twenty yards out, the Fletcher slammed to a jarring halt, catapulting her backwards into the freezing water, and the racing propeller blade bounced down, ploughing into her screaming face, mincing it into fish-chum. By the time the harbour rescue team pulled her out, there was nothing left above the ragged stump of her neck.

Olivia Bayer's father had also left her money, and this was now inherited by Catherine, Uncle Andrew's second wife. There were just four direct descendants of the Bayer family left alive; Mark and his brother Ben, their father Warren and Catherine.

———

WARREN BAYER

Mark had taken to meeting up regularly with Lycus Gerolstein, his uncle's lawyer, because they shared a morbid curiosity about the family's ill-fortune. As winter dragged on, they sat together in the little coffee shop on Wardour Street, trying to come to terms with each new twist of fate.

'I've done some more digging,' said Lycus one morning, opening his briefcase and pulling out a sheaf of papers. 'As you know, your uncle was admitted to the Harley Street Clinic on three separate occasions. Each time, he had been suffering from blackouts and memory loss. During the recovery periods he temporarily lost the power of speech. The dates on each of the codicils match these periods. It's my belief that your uncle was in no fit state to sign anything. He wouldn't have known what he was doing.'

'Then why were the revisions accepted?'

'We had no choice. His signature was on each of them, which made them legally binding documents. You understand, of course, that I am required to remain in a neutral position throughout this process.'

'Do you know who else was present when the codicils were signed?'

'His second wife Catherine was there on the first occasion. Gabriel, his brother, was certainly present two months later, when your uncle was admitted once more.' Lycus hesitated.

'And the third?' prompted Mark.

'Your father,' said Lycus with an air of apology. 'Warren went to the hospital with Andrew and stayed there overnight with him.'

Warren Bayer was late for the meeting at his head office in Clerkenwell. The tube platform at Angel was uncomfortably crowded, but he had not been able to find a taxi in the rain. As he watched the red dot-matrix board revise the train arrival times, he touched the diamond skull-head cufflinks Andrew had left him. Lately he had been burying himself in his work, trying to forget the tragedy that surrounded him. It was easier to place his grief at the death of his wife to one side than it was not to hate his own son for being in the house and doing nothing as she lay dying.

Just a few short months ago they had all lived in a state of distant equilibrium, but now the ruptures were tearing them all apart. Every action was

subject to examination, every phonecall a reason for suspicion. He hated the way he found himself behaving. It was just so damnably un-English.

Warren checked his watch. He was going to be late. The atmosphere on the platform seemed dense and stifling. A buffet of warm air announced the arrival of the train.

He studied the travel poster opposite, a fierce sienna photograph of a Middle Eastern desert. He looked hard at the centre of the poster. A blackish-green spot was appearing, as if mold was starting to come through from the wall behind. The black pattern grew, forming itself into the vague shape of a man. He looked around to see if anyone else was noticing the phenomenon forming on the poster, but the other passengers were going about their business as usual.

Fascinated, Warren failed to hear the announcement that the next train would not stop. He looked back at the expanding shape, and it seemed for a moment that Andrew was there, calling to him, trying to tell him something, if he could only get a little nearer . . .

The sound of the arriving train rose in his ears, and there was Andrew in his shiny midnight blue suit and white straw hat, stepping from the poster, desperately trying to communicate. In shock, Warren raised out his hands and stretched forward just as the hurtling underground train hit him, shattering both his wrists, splintering bone, tearing sinew and muscle.

He was spun around and cartwheeled in between the platform and the train, his severed hands with their cuffs and cufflinks still intact, sparkling in the shadows beneath the platform like forbidden treasures.

CATHERINE BAYER

Mark was seized by panic. Only three descendents were left alive. He tried to follow the chain of events that took place after the discovery of his uncle's illness, convinced that something had happened to ignite this contagion of damnation, but found nothing. At his father's service, he talked to his brother.

'Ben, you must promise me something,' he said as they left the crematorium, a pleasant London park filled with clipped English trees and a great

many bare rose beds neatly arranged like ledgers. 'You mustn't spend any of the money Uncle Andrew left you.'

'Don't start getting weird on me,' said Ben impatiently. 'It's not cursed, okay? Our parents died because they were messed up and distracted. I'm sure if either of them had been thinking clearly, they'd have survived. Shit like this happens to families all the time.'

'Yeah, right. Our mother was killed by her necklace. Dad's hands were severed. Christ, even you should be able to see that these weren't accidents!'

'I agree, it's kind of creepy, but any explanation you try to come up with would have to be a whole lot creepier.'

'How do you explain what happened to the rest of the family? You think they were all distracted? What if there really was an explanation for everything that has happened?'

'Like what? The old man secretly hated them all and cursed his belongings? If you believe that, you're as nuts as the rest of them.' Ben tried to pull away but Mark held him back.

'Think what you like. I'm just asking you not to spend the money for now. Not until I've figured this out.'

Mark walked away from his brother. He had always been close with Ben, but even they were being forced apart.

Catherine, Uncle Andrew's second wife, had chosen to stay away from this latest funeral. She was having problems of her own; she was becoming increasingly angry with her Russian builders. They worked hard, but they had a habit of leaving every door and window open. She had hired them to renovate the great neo-Georgian Buckinghamshire house Andrew had left her, and spent her days trying to keep out the wind and rain as the workmen walked mud through the hall. Now she could hear something slamming around upstairs, and knew they had left one of the windows wide again.

There was an icy draft coming from the main bedroom. She threw back the door and saw the problem; they had exited onto the scaffolding and left the place open to the elements. She went to the window and looked out, trying to see if she could see them. It was almost dark, and the scaffolds stretched off into tarpaulin-draped shadows.

The wind had risen. The tarpaulins banged and rattled like the billowing

sails of a ship. The weather forecast had warned of gales. Her workmen had clearly finished for the night. How could they be so thoughtless? She reached up to close the window and saw the figure standing outside on the planked terrace, peering in at her. Its fierce eyes glowed in the dark. He was shouting something, but the noise of the wind was snatching his words away.

Catherine was too startled to move.

She was still staring at her shadow-form of her dead husband when the gale lifted the tarps and rolled the scaffolding pole from where it had been carelessly left on the walkway. The steel tube swung down, flipped over and shot through the window, punching a hole through Catherine's chest, hurling her to the far side of the room in a spray of glass, wood and blood. She remained there, skewered through the heart, as the figure broke up and dissipated into the turbulent night air.

LYCUS GEROLSTEIN

'Something has been bothering me for days,' said Mark as they sat at their usual places in the little coffee shop. 'You were supposed to have lunch with my uncle on the day he died. What were you meeting about?'

'I told you,' said Lycus patiently, 'Andrew wasn't happy with his current investment portfolio and was thinking of changing his accountant. He wanted my advice.'

'You could have done that in London. Bit of an odd coincidence, wasn't it, you both being in Monaco?'

'Not really. I have a number of clients based there, and your uncle enjoyed driving along the Savaric cliffs. It crossed my mind that he might be keeping a mistress there.'

Mark thought for a minute. Something was scratching away at the back of his brain. 'Could I see the original will?' he asked.

'I don't see why not,' said Lycus. 'It's at my house. I thought I should keep it there, away from the rest of your family.'

'There's only two of us left alive now,' Mark reminded him. His heart was

beating hard in his chest. He did not want the lawyer to see how anxious he was.

'Tell you what, why don't you come down tomorrow evening?' Lycus suggested. 'I can show it to you then.'

The following afternoon, Mark made his way to London Bridge and caught a train to Sevenoaks. He found Lycus Gerolstein's house set back on a densely wooded hill near the station. The lawyer had never married and lived alone.

'Come in, it's a frightful night,' said Lycus, holding the door wide. 'It feels like these storms will never end. I thought you might cancel. Actually I'm very glad you could make it, because there's something I've been meaning to discuss with you.'

Mark settled himself in a deep sofa in the firelit lounge while Lycus poured some wine. 'You know, you're going to be a very rich young man soon,' said the lawyer.

'How would that be possible?' Mark suspected that his parents had left him money, but since his uncle's death the subject of inheritance had become objectionable to him.

'Catherine Bayer died intestate. Without a will, the house she had inherited from your uncle passes to you.'

'Surely it would go to the children from her previous marriage?'

'No. Andrew specified that in the event of his wife's death you should inherit their house.'

'I don't understand. Why would he do that? He deliberately kept me out of his original will.'

'Perhaps he had a change of heart.'

Mark sensed that the lawyer was lying. He felt sure that Lycus would have discussed the possibility with him earlier. 'Why are you only telling me this now?'

'I already explained that I'm not allowed to take sides. I'm afraid that meant restricting information to interested parties. Don't you see, if your family had known exactly what was in the codicils, they might have acted against each other?'

'You're talking about premeditated murder, Lycus. No, I can't allow myself to believe that. I want to see the original will.'

Lycus sighed and rose to his feet. 'Very well. Follow me.' He led the way upstairs, into a narrow extension that seemed older than the rest of the house. 'This is all that's left of an earlier building. 1720. Mind your head on the beams.'

Lycus led the way to a large room with a vaulted wooden ceiling. At one end a wood fire crackled in a large stone grate. 'This single room constitutes the whole of the original house,' he explained. 'This is where your uncle and I kept our collection. I've never shown this to anyone else.'

The lawyer's study was lined with beechwood museum cases. Mark approached one and peered inside. African, English and Spanish masks stared sightlessly back at him.

'They belonged to devil worshippers,' Lycus explained. 'No matter what each race believes in, one thing is constant to every creed. There's always a devil.'

'I suppose that's because we're all afraid of dying,' said Mark. 'We need to believe in someone who will allow us to strike a bargain.'

Lycus looked pleased. 'You're exactly right,' he said. 'It's human nature to seek an escape clause. The structure of every religion requires a mirror image. Every deity needs its opposite.'

Mark studied the carved fetish idols, their screaming faces and twisted wooden limbs. 'Quite a hobby.'

'Your uncle and I shared the same interests. We wondered if it was possible that the objects men made, the items they worshipped with, the things they owned, could become imbued with their spirits. Ever since priests first sold nails from Christ's cross, such items have had totemic value. They've always been in demand. Here we are.'

Lycus opened a glass-topped case and withdrew an envelope. 'Your uncle's will, and its codicils.'

He slid out the vellum within and spread the pages across the glass. Mark stared at his uncle's signature, as delicate as a spiderweb. Beneath it was a line that read; *Signature of Beneficiary.*

Above the signature of Andrew Bayer it said; *Signature of Notary Official.* In the space beside it, Lycus Gerolstein had written his name.

He checked all the documents, the first will and the three codicils. In each case, Lycus Gerolstein had signed his name.

'You were there,' said Mark, looking up. 'You were the officiating witness for all of these.'

'Well, I had to be, otherwise the document would not have held any legal power.'

'So you always knew who had tried to coerce my uncle into changing his will.'

'I told you before, Mark, it is a requirement of my profession to remain non-partisan. I knew that almost every member of your family had tried to persuade Andrew to change his mind. Each of them had patiently waited for him to become enfeebled before persuading him to sign. When your uncle recovered, he remembered little of what he had done. I had to tell him. By the time he was healing from his third attack, the bequests were in a hopeless mess once more. I wanted to spare you that knowledge.'

Lycus moved to a cabinet and withdrew a shallow walnut box, carrying it as if he was transporting an item of immense worth and fragility. Lifting the lid, he took out an ornately carved fountain pen and handed it to Mark. It was surprisingly heavy.

'What is this made of?' Mark asked, studying the chased silver overlaid on the cream casing. 'Is it ivory?'

'Something far more precious. '

'What did you do once you realised the original will had been messed up with codicils?'

'I drew up one final version that would sort everything out. It was this version Andrew signed in Monaco the day before he died. In order to receive your rightful inheritance, you need to countersign it. Just a formality.'

Lycus slipped out a thick grey sheet filled with tiny print and laid it down on his desk with great care. This page looked completely different to the others. He indicated the space at the bottom. 'Just on the line, if you will.' He casually waved a hand over the page.

Mark hesitated, looking at the pen again. 'First tell me,' he persisted, 'what is this?'

'It's a writing implement that was long thought lost. Your uncle used it for all his important documents. A superstition of his.'

Mark weighed the fountain pen in his hand once more. 'It's made of bone.

I went to art college, Lycus, I studied anatomy. It looks like it's carved from one of the metacarpals. The bones in the wrist that connect to the fingers.'

Lycus stepped closer. 'You're quite right, a rare antique, designed for necromantic purposes. Just a folk superstition,' he said impatiently. 'Sign.'

Mark laid the fountain pen down. 'No, I can't.'

'What are you talking about?'

'The bequests brought death to my family. If I inherit, the same thing will happen to me.' He recapped the pen and toyed with it, balancing it between his fingers.

'You have to sign, Mark,' Lycus warned, 'or you won't get a thing.'

'I don't want anything.'

'Don't be ridiculous. This will change your life. It will give you everything you ever wanted. You haven't got a penny to your name. You'll never have to worry about money again.'

'I don't want to receive an unearned gift. I'd rather give it away.'

'But that's absurd.'

'Is it? You remember when we met after my uncle died? I kept thinking— why would a lawyer seek me out in a coffee shop, just to tell me that he thought the will had been compromised? Men like you don't do such things without a reason, Lycus. You wanted me to become suspicious. Dissatisfied. You know what I think?'

A faint smile traced itself on Lycus's face. 'No, what?'

'I think everything you told me in those meetings was designed to get me here tonight.'

'And why would I want to do that?'

'You need me to accept my inheritance.'

Lycus shook his head in pity. 'How would that benefit me?'

Mark snatched up the pen. 'What's the secret?' he asked. 'Who did this belong to?'

'Give me that.' Lycus made a lunge for it, but Mark stepped back beyond his reach.

'It's not about who it belonged to, is it? It's who it was made from.' Mark turned the pen's barrel to the light and noted the inscription carved into the polished bone. *Gemacht von der hand unseres herrlichen Leiters.*

'I think I finally understand the nature of my uncle's will. I was his favourite nephew. He told me he was going to leave me the most precious gift of all. And he has.'

'What do you mean?' Lycus moved closer, playing for time.

'He gave me independence. By making sure that I was the only one who was excluded from the bequests, he protected me.'

'Interesting,' said Lycus carefully. 'I think perhaps it's time you knew the truth about your uncle Andrew. His cancer treatments were becoming progressively less successful. Each stay in hospital weakened him, although he hid it well. He didn't want to cause you any pain. When he discovered he was dying, Andrew feared that in his frail state the family would try to coerce him over the will—which of course they did—so he met with me and asked me if there was a way that I could help him.'

'And you had the answer. You were both collectors.'

'Andrew had long ago realised what his family was really like. He wanted to see them revealed in their true colours, but he didn't have long to live. I told him that by signing his will in the manner I proscribed, with the instrument we could purchase, his spirit could remain on earth long enough to confirm his suspicions. He would be able to see that justice was done. I told him that each family member who acted uncharitably would be destroyed by the item they were bequeathed.'

'Why would he have believed you?'

'I told you, he was a collector of the arcane. A will is the one document everyone needs to sign. What happens if such a document could truly decide your afterlife? Wouldn't you want to know? Especially if you had no other choice? Andrew believed me because it was I who found the pen.'

'That was why he went to France. The two of you bought it in Monte Carlo. The one thing I know about Monaco is that it's a tax haven, a place where private items are secretly traded.'

'Your uncle and I purchased the pen, and he used it to sign a final version of the will—a version only he and I ever witnessed. This one.' He tapped the grey page on the desk. 'Feel it. It's extraordinarily delicate to the touch. We rewrote the will on the flayed skin of a concentration camp victim, and signed it with the Fuhrer's own hand—or at least, a part of it. Imagine the power we

created! The very next day your uncle died, and became a creature of the shadow-world.'

'My uncle wasn't a vindictive man. He would never have wanted his entire family to suffer.'

'Perhaps not, but he was embittered by the thought of his impending death.

He could watch what happened after, but couldn't intervene.'

Mark thought for a moment. 'My uncle Gabriel phoned to tell me he'd seen Andrew, and then he died. What if Andrew was trying to warn him?'

'Perhaps you're right. Perhaps the real tragedy of Andrew's deal was that his bitterness left him as he expired, and he no longer wanted revenge. Instead he was forced to watch, powerless to intervene, while his relatives gave in to their base instincts, cruelly dying one after the other. He saw how all men can be brought down to animal behaviour.'

'It's you, isn't it? You want what everyone who collects this kind of stuff wants. Proof of the soul.'

'I merely carried out your uncle's wishes. Of course I wanted proof of the soul's immortality. The Fuhrer was an occultist, but that isn't what gives the pen its power. It holds his life essence. Just as all of the other items hold the souls of their owners.'

'You mean the jewellery.'

'I mean everything!' Lycus shouted. 'Everything your uncle left behind came from our collection. The steering wheel of Gabriel's car once belonged to Joseph Goebbels. Cheryl Bayer's flat had been the home of Alistair Crowley. The emerald necklace was made for Ilse Koch, the so-called Butcher of Buchenwald. The cufflinks had belonged to the serial killer Peter Kurten. The money, too, laundered from generations of Nazi looters through Swiss banks. Everything I persuaded your uncle to leave in his will had been purchased from collectors, often at a terrible cost. Even the rope on Olivia Bayer's boat had once been part of a hangman's noose.'

'What about Catherine Bayer's house?'

'That hadn't belonged to anyone notorious. But she had. Before she met your uncle, she had been the mistress of a notorious Washington warmonger.

Your family was right about her. She had an evil heart. I introduced them.' He sounded rather proud of the fact. 'You see, getting the pen and the parchment wasn't enough. The inheritances had to be filled with the same kind of dark energy. It was a brave experiment, to be sure, but one that paid off. A curious mind is a wonderful thing, Mark. Your uncle shared my fascination with the idea.'

Mark pretended to continue studying the will. His hands were trembling. 'Tell me something, Lycus. Did my uncle know he was going to die that morning on the cliffs?'

'Oh, he knew the cancer would catch up with him soon enough. But you know as well as I do, every gain must be met with a certain amount of sacrifice. Using the pen shaved a few weeks off his life, that's all. I think I really underestimated its power. It wasn't the only relic removed from the Fuhrer's bunker, but it's the only one that was used in necromantic ceremonies after the war. Now, I think it's time for you to countersign the will, if you would.'

Mark made a show of bending over the parchment. Lycus leaned closer, his lips slightly parted in anticipation. Mark prepared to place the nib against the sheet of flesh.

And, with the flick of his wrist, he sent the bone-pen curving behind him, toward the heat of the fireplace.

'No!' Lycus dived for it but Mark met him, punching him hard in the stomach. As they fought, the pen fell into the hottest part of the charcoal and began to burn. 'Get it out!' Lycus screamed, 'you don't understand!' But Mark slammed the lawyer onto his back and held his boot on Lycus's throat.

'If the will's agenda is not completely fulfilled, my soul will have to be surrendered in Andrew's place.'

'You shouldn't have let your passions get in the way of a deal.' He kept the terrified lawyer pinned down as the pen spat and cracked in the fire, which now glowed crimson. Lycus bucked sharply and threw him aside, diving into the fireplace, yelling as the flames attacked his hands. But no matter how hard he tried to grip the pen it kept slipping from his grasp, luring him deeper into the fire.

Wedged in the roaring fireplace, he turned back to Mark, the crimson inferno roiling over his arms, engulfing his head, tearing at his face, causing

his eyes to burst apart. The flames swirled around him in a fiery tornado, sucking the flesh from his charring bones. There was an immense explosion of blood-red flame and his body was lost inside the pulsing orange logs of the fire.

Mark threw the will in after Lycus, watching as the flesh smoked and burned with a strange green flame.

Then he put on his jacket and left the house.

The rain was easing up. He had almost reached the station at the bottom of the hill when his cellphone started to vibrate in his pocket. He checked the caller ID: *Ben Bayer.*

'I'm really sorry, Mark,' his brother began. 'I was broke. I just spent a tiny amount of the money.'

'How much?' Mark demanded to know.

'Just a hundred pounds. I was going to be thrown out of the flat if I didn't pay the rent.'

'Lock the doors, Ben. Don't move a muscle until I get there.' He closed the phone and set off with a renewed sense of purpose. The will had been destroyed. He prayed that he had acted in time.

Glancing up at the leaden storm clouds, Mark thought he saw his uncle's face, smiling down benignly.

THE CONSPIRATORS

At the next table of the hotel restaurant, three waiters took their places beside the diners, and with a synchronised flourish, raised the silver covers on their salvers. A fourth appeared, bearing a tray containing a quartet of tiny copper pots. Each waiter took a handle and proceeded to pour the sauces from the pots onto the salvers from a height of not less than eighteen inches. They might have been tipping jewels into coffers.

Court and Lassiter barely bothered to break off their conversation and look up at the display. They knew that these ostentatious rituals were the hotel's way of justifying the risible menu prices to tourists.

The waiters finished serving and tiptoed away, leaving the diners to warble and coo over their miniscule meals, some kind of cubed chicken in cream. The restaurant was steel, glass and black crystal, with the occasional tortured twist of green bamboo providing natural colour. It was as hushed as a funeral parlour. Everyone seemed to be whispering.

Sean Lassiter had ordered a steak, medium rare, the only item on the menu that looked like meat. He had eaten it as if he was in an American diner, using only a fork. The steaks were so tender you could do that here.

'When was the last time you knew exactly what you wanted?' he asked Court, raising his whisky tumbler and studying his former business partner through the diamond-cut lattice.

Oliver Court's palms were dry, but he still pressed them against his thighs. Lassiter had once been his mentor, and was the only man in the world who could make him uncomfortable with a simple question.

'Come on, Oliver, I saw the look in your eyes the first day I met you. Nowadays I can't read your eyes, because you're wearing coloured contacts. I remember, you were so hungry and envious I thought you might actually start taking notes during our meal. I see that look a lot, but it's not usually so obvious. When members of my staff get that anxious, it usually means they're frightened of failure and they're scared of being found out. Well, I can't blame anyone for wanting to make the best of themselves. But you were prepared to leave behind an awful lot in order to be a success.'

It was a gentle rebuke, but a rebuke nonetheless. Lassiter was old school; his compliments were backhanded and his criticisms were constructive. He knew the difference between perspicacity and merely being rude. For a businessman who had been on the road for the past forty years, he was immaculately groomed. His hair was sleek and white, his tan subtle, his suit quietly extravagant.

He's heard something about me, thought Court, shifting carefully on his chromium chair, which was too low. The central column of the table prevented him from stretching out his long legs.

'Have you got where you wanted to be?'

Court did not trust himself to tell the truth. From here he could see out through the curvilinear glass of the restaurant. In front of the hotel, trucks drove back and forth along the spot-lit spit of land that projected into the blackness of the Persian Gulf. The Indian workers went around the clock in shifts, building ever further out into the sea.

They had kept the conversation light while they ate. Families, schools, colleagues, holidays, topics suitable for food. The serious part required a clear table and strong drinks.

There was only one other drinker at the bar, a nylon-haired brunette with long legs, a tiny waist and perfectly circular breasts, like a character from a video game. The décolletage of her tight black dress was cut to the aureoles of her nipples. Lassiter assumed she kept herself more carefully covered beyond the confines of the hotel. They were in the Middle East, after all. Seamed stockings, high heels, a brassiere that must have presented an engineering challenge, she was about twenty three years old and blatantly selling herself. He wondered what the young Arabic barman thought of her.

Court caught him thoughtfully studying the call-girl's legs. 'How long have you known me, Sean?' he asked, buying time.

'Long enough to see where you're going.' Lassiter smiled. He'd had his teeth bleached. They shone peppermint white in the black light from the bar, and made him look like a game show host. He noticed Court following his eyes to the girl. 'It's just a honest question.'

In truth, Lassiter had been disappointed by his apprentice. Court needed the approval of others, and as a consequence, his ambitions were displayed for all to see. He never took advice, so why was he here? Somewhere deep inside Lassiter an alarm bell rang.

Court knew he could not be completely honest, because there was too much at stake. 'I think I've been pretty successful,' he answered carefully. 'There's still a way to go. That's why I value your advice.'

Lassiter looked almost relieved. Perhaps he didn't want to have an argument with his former pupil. 'Your division is doing very nicely, Oliver. You're about to expand it, you wouldn't be human if you didn't feel a little nervous. From what I hear, my directors will back you, but in these uncertain times you'll need to detail your long-term plans. Just don't be too eager. The English don't trust people who are anxious to please. It puts them off. They want negotiations to be tricky enough for their colleagues to see how hard they work.'

'I can't remember a time when I didn't look up to you,' said Court, catching the waitress's eye and sewing the air with his right hand, the universal sign for *check, please.* 'You've always been my—'

'Don't say mentor, Oliver, it makes me feel positively ancient.'

'I was going to say friend. I feel I can tell you anything and I'll always get a straight answer.'

'So long as it works both ways.'

'You don't have to ask that. I was still just a property agent when you gave me a job. Now I run the whole of the US division. I'd appreciate it if you could cast an eye over my proposals, just to get your feedback.' Despite the difference in their ages, they were now almost evenly matched in terms of their careers within the company. Lassiter still gave the hotel chain class and respectability. Many considered Court to be an upstart, but he had made

North America profitable again by building flashy boutique hotels aimed at kids with money.

Lassiter smiled at his glass, twisting it. 'It would be my pleasure, you know that.' Court was offering to show him his plans ahead of the directors' meeting? He'd want something in return, but what, and how badly?

Lassiter looked around at the empty bar, the midnight blue carpet, the silver walls, the glittering star-points in the ceiling. He wondered if this was what Heaven looked like, without a bill at the end of the evening.

'Excuse me for a moment.' Court rose from his chair and went to say something to the girl. After the exchange, she followed him back to join the table. 'This is my friend Sean Lassiter,' he said, introducing her.

'Hi, I'm Vienna.' She tossed her hair back in a movement designed to help her avoid bothering with eye contact. She was American, he supposed, or had been taught English by one. 'Look at this place. The Jews and Arabs agree so completely on soft furnishings, you'd think they could work everything else out from that.' She had as much confidence as either of them, but Court knew that if they ignored her, she would drop out of the conversation. She was a professional. She had brought her own drink with her.

'Mr Lassiter here owns the hotel.'

That wiped the smile from her face. 'Is that true?' she asked, lowering her glass. Court could tell she was racking her brains to recall the name.

'Well, I'm the managing director of the consortium that owns it,' said Lassiter, managing to make the role sound unimportant.

'He's being modest,' said Court, 'he owns the entire chain.'

If Vienna was impressed, she was too smart to show it. Her deal was with the Maitre D. She only cared about her direct contacts. 'Is it owned by the Americans?'

'No, it's mainly Indian and Russian money.'

'They charge non-guests an entrance fee just to look around the lobby of this hotel,' she said, 'but I guess you know that.'

'I don't suppose that affects you.' It seemed that, having made the effort to talk to the girl, Lassiter was happier talking to Court. 'You're not staying at the Burj Al-Arab, Oliver?'

'Even I can't justify that kind of expense. Besides, loyalty dictates that I stay here. I suppose you've got a suite.'

'Penthouse sea-facing corner, but not the royal suite,' said Lassiter. 'That's reserved for heads of state.'

'I heard quite a few of the rooms are empty.' The Middle East was part of Lassiter's domain.

'It's not just here. There's been a lot of over-construction. Look out of the window along the coastline. Everyone's been affected by the bad publicity lately, those stories of raw sewage being pumped into the sea, but it doesn't stop them from building.'

'You're not worried enough to reduce the cost of a room yet,' Court added. 'So, do we get to see your view?'

He wants to bring the girl, Lassiter thought in some surprise, *how will this work out?* 'Sure, if you want.'

Court paid without checking the total and stood up, placing his hand in the valley of Vienna's back. This small gesture was enough to seal the deal. She showed no reaction as she rose and left with them, the light from the neon bar-sign casting a crimson stripe across her neck that appeared to sever it.

'At these prices I thought you'd have your own elevator,' Court needled gently.

'Only the royal apartment has that. For security purposes.' Lassiter stabbed at the illuminated gold lift button. 'We need to invent something better than first class. The whole concept of privilege has become debased.'

'I read somewhere that you need to earn six million per annum to live like a millionaire these days,' said Vienna.

Court watched his boss against the dark golden glass of the elevator. Lassiter had started to put on the kind of weight he would never be able to shift. His new suit was already becoming too tight. He was in his mid-sixties but showed no desire to stop working or even slow down. *Sharks drown if they stop swimming,* Court thought. *The only way he'll stop is if he dies. I'm surprised Elizabeth still puts up with it.*

He wondered if Lassiter went around telling people how he'd given Court a start in the hotel business. Mentors had a habit of doing that.

'Welcome to my world,' said Lassiter without an obvious hint of irony as he held open the door for Vienna. The suite displayed all the accoutrements of wealth without any of the concomitant taste. A curved bar was lined with gold-leaf piping that rose to enclose a range vintage whisky bottles presented on sheets of underlit crimson glass like items of baroque jewellery.

'Want to try the whisky?'

'I'm staying with vodka.'

Vienna watched until her own drink had been poured, then went to the bathroom.

'She's very beautiful,' Lassiter conceded.

'She doesn't have to be here if she doesn't want to,' said Court. 'She's with your hotel, which presumably means she has quality control.'

Lassiter walked to the glass wall and looked down to the beach. Spotlights picked out the tall wavering palms that had been transported fully grown and impatiently planted into the unfinished esplanade. The crystal blackness reflected every glittering pinpoint in the apartment, creating a second starscape above the sea. There was no natural sound in the suite, only the faint but steady hiss of cold ionised air pumped up through the ventilation system, and the settling chink of perfectly cubed ice on glass.

'Allow me,' said Court, pouring a heavy measure of Scotch. 'It's a nice view. Although I don't like to look at the sea. I'd prefer to be surrounded by build-ings. City boy at heart.'

Lassiter accepted the proffered drink and downed it in one. He had been drinking hard all evening. The New Business Model Seminar was so stulti-fying that everyone had been pushing their upper alcohol limits for the past three days, and there was still another day to go.

'Did you learn at all anything today?' Lassiter asked. 'Spare me all those speakers from the Far East with their strangled English and aching politeness. Did you actually get anything out of it?'

'No, but I didn't expect to.'

They studied the view. Lassiter pressed his chilled tumbler against his fore-head. 'Look at it. There's no-one out there and nothing to see. You could be in Monte Carlo, Geneva or Madrid. That's the beauty of our European hotels, Oliver. Whichever one you use, there you are, home and safe again. Some-times I wake up and have no idea where I am. And it doesn't matter.'

'How's the seminar working out for you?'

'I'll go home four days nearer to my death with a sun-reddened face and a portfolio full of brochures my PA will eventually tip into the bin.'

'It's not like you to be a cynic,' Court observed. 'I remember when you first saw potential in me, the things you taught me, all that practical advice and optimism for the future.'

'I'm afraid my hopes atrophied somewhat when our so-called first-world society decided to hand over the reins of financial responsibility to a bunch of cowboy bankers.' He drained his glass, the ice clinking against his white teeth. 'I'm old enough to remember when selling was a challenge. These days I feel like a nurse spoon-feeding paralysed patients. Christ, I want to start smoking again, but these rooms are alarmed. Pour me another, will you?'

Court headed back to the bar. He picked up a matchbook, crested and labelled 'Royal Persian Hotel, Dubai' and slipped it into his pocket. 'How come there are no cameras in the corridors?' he wondered aloud.

'The Arabs are like the Swiss when it comes to issues of privacy. The rich need to treat each other in an adult manner because there are so many dirty secrets to keep tucked away.'

Court was not familiar with this reflective side of Lassiter. The man who had elevated as many careers as he had destroyed was going soft. Men became vulnerable to strange fancies when they felt their sexual powers waning.

'The most powerful religious leaders emerge from desert states, have you noticed?' Lassiter mused. 'Whereas political leaders nurture their theories in cities. One thinks of Pol Pot's agrarian revolution being discussed in smoky Parisian cafes. In my darkest nightmares I imagine a new business model, one where morals and decent behaviour are considered detrimental, where only grabbing the next million in the next hour commands any respect at all. And at some point—I'm not sure when—my nightmare became real. This is what we do, Oliver, and we all collude in the process. The definition of a conspiracy is the combination of any number of people in a surreptitious agreement to commit a secret, unlawful, evil and wrongful act. Think about what we do and ask yourself if you really want to join the next level.'

He's lost it, thought Oliver. *The great Sean Lassiter is stepping out of the ring to watch sunsets and talk hippy-dippy shit. This is too good to be true.*

'You've made your money, Sean. If you feel like this, why don't you just sell up?'

Lassiter regarded him from beneath hooded eyelids. 'There's no-one I trust enough. You want to know if that includes you. I groomed you, I knew what would happen. Give someone the benefit of your experience for long enough, and it stands to reason they'll eventually try to buy the company out from under you. I never held your success against you, Oliver.'

'That's because your own success always remained greater. It's easy to be magnanimous when you're at the top. What if I really wanted to buy the company now?'

There it is, thought Lassiter, *the real purpose of dinner.* 'I wondered when you would finally ask.'

'You don't think I'd look after the staff.'

'My people? I replace them like batteries.' Lassiter looked toward the bathroom door. The girl seemed to be taking a long time.

'Then why not sell to me?' Court walked over to the balcony and unlocked the doors, rolling them silently back. The cool night air was a relief after the chemically conditioned atmosphere. 'Hey, we can smoke out here. Doors and windows you can open forty floors up, they'd never allow this at home.' He laughed, patting his pockets.

With one last glance back at the bathroom, Lassiter joined him on the balcony. He leaned over the edge and looked down. 'You're right, there's hardly a light on in the entire building. We should be renegotiating the prices of the suites. Europe holds too many festivals and seminars at this time of the year. Half the salesmen in America leave home in March and don't get back until their houseplants are dead.'

'Your profits are down, and I've heard the next quarter will be even worse.'

'Maybe we did expand Europe too quickly. When a wolf is sick, the others decide what to do; whether you live or die depends on how important you are to the pack. You think we're going lame, one of the pack lagging behind?' He sighed wearily. 'Are you going to bite me on the leg and drag me into the bushes? Why not, it's what I would have done.'

The only sign of life came from the headlights of the gravel trucks swerving past each other in the distance, like tin toys on a track. Their thin bright

beams shone into total blackness. Back along the coastline, a line of steel towers glowed through the sea-mist like a phantom stockade.

Court realised that to get an answer he would have to give one. 'You asked me. What do I want?' he repeated. 'I want to reach the top of my profession.'

'That's not a desire, it's an instinct, like releasing air from a diving tank.' Given the amount he had drunk, he surprised himself with the analogy. It was true; his career was as lonely and claustrophobic as being under the sea.

'All right. Then I desire respect.'

Lassiter turned to study him. 'Surely you have that already. Don't you?' From the way he said it, Lassiter made it clear that Court had yet to earn it from his teacher.

'I suppose so. In that case, I don't know. That's the answer to your question; I really don't know.'

'Fair enough. I suppose that's more honest than saying you want our hotels to be the finest in the world. You're still only in your thirties—'

'Thirty four.'

'You have time on your side. Now I suppose you want an answer to your question.' Lassiter lit the proffered cigar and drew hard on it. 'I can't sell you the company, Oliver.'

'Why not?'

'It would be too obvious.'

'What do you mean?'

'It's what you want. I can always tell what you're going to do next. You're positively metronomic in your habits. I can see inside your head, which means that from a business point of view I can always out-think you. And if I can, others will. That's not good.'

'It's because I learned everything from you. You'll always be the one person who knows exactly what I think. You'll always outguess me.'

The ocean air should have started sobering him up, but it was having the opposite effect. Lassiter struggled to understand what Court was saying to him. The air was completely still, and there was no sound. Even the distant trucks moved past each other in silence. If his wife was here he knew she would appreciate the beauty of the night, but she was asleep in London. It

was late and he was still wearing his business suit, and polished black shoes that pinched.

'You know the story of the Caliph of Jaipur?' asked Court, draining his glass and setting it down on the balcony table. 'He hired the finest painter in the land to create a fresco of heavenly angels for the walls of his harem. When it was finished, he asked the artisan if it really was the best fresco in all the kingdom. The painter told him that there was no finer artwork to be found beneath the horizons, nor would there ever be again until someone else could afford his services. So the Sultan had him beheaded.'

Lassiter looked at him blearily. Only the whites of Court's eyes showed in the jet night, and then they were gone. A streak of silver sparkled in the ocean like a flash of static electricity, the signature of the moon. He felt tired and looked for a place to sit, but Court was crouching beside him. When he rose, he was holding Lassiter's right ankle. Court stood taller and taller, rising higher and higher, until Lassiter realised he could no longer remain upright. 'You're not drunk,' he said absurdly.

'I don't drink whisky.' Court raised his old friend's ankle higher, until pain shot through Lassiter's thigh muscles.

'Vodka—'

'Because it looks like water. Sure you don't want to sell?'

'Over my dead body.'

Court shrugged his shoulders. 'That was the general idea.' With both his hands clasped beneath Lassiter's foot Court leaned suddenly back, like a Scotsman tossing a caber, raising his arms smartly so that Lassiter lost his battle with gravity and found himself cleanly lifted into the air, over the wall of the balcony. His mouth opened in shock, but only the smallest sound emerged. His fingers grasped at the air beyond the low rail, too late, and he tumbled silently down, past the empty dark floors. The first part of the fall seemed to last forever, as if he was wheeling through the night in slow motion, like a firework that had failed to ignite, or a spaceman with a cut cord.

But then he hit his head on the concrete lip of the thirtieth balcony, and this sent him spinning madly out of orbit. His head turned from white to black, leaving a matching stain on the building wall. His leg hit

another ledge, his arm another, his head again, his arm, his leg, until there was hardly a bone in his body left unbroken—and that was long before he hit the ground.

Court stepped back into the room. 'You might want to come out now,' he called. 'We're alone.' He heard running water stop.

The bathroom door was padded crimson with gold studs. It opened cautiously. Vienna emerged with her makeup refreshed, like a meticulously restored painting. She took in the suite, three glasses, one occupant less, an open balcony door, and decided to say nothing. Had she an inkling of what had just happened? Her face was a mask. Court's decision to act had been spontaneous. He knew she could not have seen anything, and Lassiter had made no noise. He doubted that she cared anyway. It was not her job to care. She worked in a service industry.

'My colleague had to leave. Thanks for coming up,' said Court, feeling inside his jacket. He unclipped her handbag and dropped in a roll of banknotes. 'Maybe we'll see each other again.'

'I'd like that.' Vienna's smile was unreadable. She turned and walked to the door, seemingly aware of exactly how many steps it would take. 'You know where to find me.'

And she was gone.

Court closed the window and rinsed the glasses, placing them back on the bar shelf. He had left no other mark in the suite. Letting himself out, he padded along the corridor and caught the elevator to his own room. He had paid the girl too much, but would not have been able to get Lassiter back to his suite without her. Everyone knew that even though the old man loved his wife, he still needed to prove himself with the ladies.

He would heed mentor's advice and not suggest the buyout immediately; that would be crass. There were plenty of other preparations he could be making while the company came to terms with Lassiter's death. It would be interesting to see how long they could keep it out of the news.

Before the last day of the conference began, he took a stroll outside. The sky was a painful deep blue, sharper than knives. The pavements had been hosed down, and were already nearly dry. He circled the hotel but found no sign of any disturbance. Shielding his eyes, he squinted up at the balconies,

trying to spot where Lassiter had hit the building, but realised that he was standing beneath the ledges, and would not be able to see anything.

The day dragged past in parades of Powerpoint bar charts, each more candy-coloured than the last, as if their radiance could make up for their dullness. At lunchtime he saw two men who looked like plain clothes police. They were standing motionless in the reception area, in mirror shades and shiny blue suits. By the time afternoon tea was served, even Lassiter's reservation had disappeared from the records. Clearly, the hotel's reputation was more important than its founder's demise. *The things we create outgrow us,* thought Court, shutting down his laptop. *One day you own the company, the next even your PA can't remember you. I thought there would be repercussions. I guess Sean was right. It's all part of the new business model.*

Two weeks later, Court found himself at Domodedovo Airport in Moscow. He always seemed to be holding meetings in departure lounges. In the business class bar he had bumped into an old English friend, a nervy, sticklike redhead called Amanda, and had invited her to join him. Watching snow fall on airfields from behind picture windows always had a calming effect on him. Amanda was a seasoned executive with half a dozen personal communication devices in her briefcase and no hint of a private life. She told him she was going to try internet dating when she finally settled in one city long enough to do so.

'I was wondering what you thought about Sean Lassiter,' she said, slowly emptying another miniature bottle of Tanqueray into her glass. 'There's a rumour going around that Elizabeth was about to leave him.'

Court had no idea. Suddenly the lack of publicity surrounding his death made sense. 'I heard something to that effect,' he said.

'They hadn't been sleeping together for years,' she told him knowledgably. 'I was reading an article in the Economist about the similarities between successful businessmen and serial killers. They share the same lack of compassion, the same selfishness and determination to succeed. They exploit the flaws of their opponents, and lose their ability to judge on moral grounds.'

For a crazy moment he wondered if she had heard another, darker rumour,

but decided it was impossible. The buyout had only been discussed with a handful of board members. It would not be made public until after it was successful.

'I guess you're going on to St Petersberg,' she said. 'Where are you staying?'

'The Grand Sovetskaya. How about you?'

'Oh, nothing so fancy. That was one of Sean's personal favourites, wasn't it?'

'Well, it's part of the chain.'

'I slept with him, you know. Our flights were cancelled and we were stuck at the Espacio Rojo Hotel in Barcelona. I was really sorry to hear he died. Or was it the Severine in Paris? They have this fabulous spa treatment where they wrap you in oil-soaked gauze and place hot stones down your spine.'

He listened without hearing. The image of the old man pumping away on top of poor bony Amanda while whispering sales figures in her ears was best left behind in the departure lounge.

The Grand Sovetskaya was an unashamedly old-world hotel in the French style, with green copper gables and crouching gargoyles. In the domed reception area hung a crystal chandelier the size of a skip. The rooms were filled with dark wooden dressers, sideboards and wardrobes, and were locked with huge brass keys. There were twenty one floors of corridors that smelled of furniture polish and boiled cabbage, all identical and gently curved, like those of an ocean liner. Thick floral carpets and heavily lined drapes deadened all sound.

Best of all was the bar, a paradise for the serious drinker. The shelves were stacked with dozens of flavoured vodkas and an immense range of mysterious liquors, vaguely medicinal in appearance. Court suspected that the elderly hatchet-faced bar staff had arrived with the first guests. Heavy marble ashtrays lined the counter. This was clearly no place for lightweights.

Court was there to conclude the discreet negotiations with Lassiter's board, but if anyone asked, he was attending a forum staged by the Opportunities In New Business Development Commission. Discretion was second nature to him. He spent most of his life in hotels as quiet as libraries where the patrons were defined by the depth of their expense accounts. Lighting a cigar, he thought about Lassiter turning over and over in the warm night air,

a tiny flailing puppet whose existence had been erased almost before he hit the concrete. How many Indian workers had been employed to scrub the blood from the stones before another harsh dawn flooded the hotel with sunlight? Had the manager posted Lassiter's luggage back to his grieving wife? Had Elizabeth pored over the spreadsheets, graphs and overlays, hopelessly looking for answers?

He felt no guilt. Lassiter's downward spiral had begun before Dubai. Court had saved him the incremental degradation a man feels when he realises the company he has founded no longer needs or desires his advice. He waved aside the blue haze of cigar smoke and studied Vienna. She was seated in a red leather horseshoe between two short bald oligarchs. When she saw him looking, she momentarily forgot what she was saying. Her eyes lingered a moment too long.

Clearly, she was good at her job if she was travelling to international clients. For a second it crossed his mind that they might make an interesting team, but he knew that the best call-girls stayed at the peak of their trade by giving nothing of themselves to others. Even so . . . .

It would have been unprofessional to send her any kind of message while she was working, so he smoked and waited, and treated himself to a golden *Comte de Lauvia* 1982 Armanac. The Russians here were loud and unsophisticated, but Vienna never appeared bored. After an hour they were clearly drunk. Court had no idea what she said to them, but they suddenly fell into a sombre mood and rose together, bidding her goodnight.

She came to him with her shoes in one hand, and he realised how much they added to her height. 'However long your evening has been,' she told him, taking a sip of his brandy, 'I promise you mine was longer.' She licked her lips appreciatively and allowed her head to fall back against the red leather seat. 'Mm. Can I get one of those?'

The waiter appeared without asking, delivered and departed. She seemed content to drink and drift without making small talk. She wore another low-cut black dress, and a single strand of pearls. Her perfume had faded enough to allow a natural womanly odour, faint but arousing, to rise from her peach-coloured skin.

He relit his cigar and watched her, wondering how much she remembered

of their last meeting. The bar was almost empty. It was a quarter past two in the morning. 'How long are you staying here?' he asked.

'Two nights. I'm entertaining those guys.'

'They must be important.'

'To someone. Not to me. It's a job.'

'They left without you.'

'I sent them away.' She took the cigar from his fingers and smoked it for a minute.

'I'm here for—'

'I don't want to know why you're here.' She studied the glowing tip of the cigar. 'I'm sure you get tired of talking shop. I do.'

'So, Vienna, what would you rather do?'

She turned her eyes to his. Her pupils were violet, the lashes long and black. 'Shall I tell you what I would really like to do?'

He gave no response, but waited with a small catch in his breath.

'I would like to fall asleep in a great big soft bed with my head on your chest.'

'We can do that.' Then he remembered. 'Wait, they screwed up my reservation. I have two singles. We can push them together.'

'Thanks, but no thanks.'

'Well, where are you staying?'

She held up the key. It was the first time he had seen a genuine smile on her lips. 'I have the royal suite.'

Now he was impressed. 'How did you get that?'

'How do you think?'

They made their way to the twenty-first floor. As they followed the curve of the passage, Vienna entwined her fingers in his. *I don't have to tell this woman anything*, he thought, *she and I are the same kind*.

When she unlocked the door at the end of the corridor and turned on the lights, he was disappointed to see that except for an extra pair of curtains covering the end wall, the room was almost identical to his. It was unbearably hot. He removed his suit jacket, threw it on the couch and loosened his tie.

'Make me a drink,' she told him, 'I'll be back.' She headed for the bathroom. Something made him uncomfortable. He heard the bathroom door

shut, then silence. He poured two whiskies at the wet bar and thought for a moment. It was exactly what she had done in Dubai.

No, it wasn't.

She had waited until she had seen her own drink poured. Call girls always did that, just to be careful.

She wasn't going to drink anything. Then why had she asked him to make her a drink?

'Vienna?' He knocked on the bathroom door, but there was silence beyond. He placed his ear against the wood and listened. Nothing.

The room was spectacularly hot. Vienna was obviously missing Dubai. There didn't seem to be a thermostat anywhere. Then he remembered; his was in the bathroom. 'Vienna,' he called, 'turn the heat down, will you?'

The floor tipped, just a little, but enough for him to realise what had happened. He headed back to the bar and examined his drained whisky tumbler. There was some kind of white residue in the bottom of it. Sweat was starting to pour between his shoulder blades. The front of his shirt was darkening around his armpits and in the middle of his chest.

The carpet seemed to be pulling away beneath his feet. He needed cold air, fast. He reached the end window and pulled back the curtains, but there was just more wall behind them.

The big French windows were in the same place as the ones in his room. He lurched across to them and tried the right handle. It turned easily. He pulled the glass door toward him and a blast of subzero air filled the room. It was snowing hard. Almost instantly he began to sober up. He tried to think.

Stepping onto the balcony, he breathed in the stinging winter air, filling his lungs with ice. Fat white flakes settled on his eyelids, in his ears. His head was clearing fast but his reactions were still slow.

Too slow to stop the door from being shut behind him. Vienna was standing beyond the glass. She studied him blankly, as if watching an animal at the zoo. Her right arm was raised, her hand against the wall. She was pressing something. She wiggled the fingers of her left hand slightly, waving goodbye.

The steel shutter that fitted tightly over the windows was swiftly closing. He tried to seize its edge with his fingers, to push it back up, but it was so

cold that the flesh of his fingertips, still wet from his whisky glass, stuck to the metal, pulling him down.

And then it was shut. He tore his fingers free, leaving behind four small scarlet patches of skin. The sweat on his back was already turning to ice. He hammered on the steel shutter, but was shocked by its thickness. It barely rattled. Old French-style hotels always sported European shutters. He moved around the edges of the metre-wide balcony. A sheer drop down, no lights on anywhere. The rooms on either side had bricked-up windows.

The bitter wind had risen to a howl. He was in his shirtsleeves, and knew he had but a short time to live. He had been drinking all evening; his blood was thin. He fell to the floor of the balcony and pushed himself into the wall, but the ice and snow still blew through the balustrade, settling over him.

His first instinct was to assume he had been subjected to a woman's revenge. Then he remembered she was merely an employee.

He tried to laugh when he understood what had happened, but the saliva was freezing in his mouth. Even his eyes were becoming hard to move. He fancied he could hear the ice forming beneath his skin. Tiny crackles like rustling cellophane filled his ears.

Looking out into the night beyond the balcony, the darkness was sprinkled with swirling white flakes that looked like stars. He could have been anywhere in the world.

They'll leave the shutters down for twenty four hours, he thought, *just to be absolutely sure. Vienna will be back on a Dubai beach by then.*

His mind was growing numb. He remembered something from a history book he had once read. When the Persian matriarchs wanted to rid themselves of the most treacherous family members, they locked them away in sumptuous apartments and left them to die. From a business point of view, it made perfect sense to do so. He should have put forward the idea as part of his new business model, but, just as Lassiter had warned, someone else had thought of it first.

He found himself laughing as the freezing snow-laden winds whirled about him, and then he could no longer close his mouth.

THE BOY THUG ████████████████████████████

GIDDENS HAD BEEN RIDING WITH THE TWO GRAIN MERCHANTS FOR FOUR DAYS BEFORE he cut their throats. It never took less time than this. The pair had come out of Bismarck with fat saddlebags, but Giddens could not be sure what was in them. The tall one, name of Sweeney, had arranged to visit a bank before they set off, that much was certain, and his horse was heavier when he left. There was a story that the merchants were quietly moving gold across the state, travelling without protection so as not to draw attention to themselves. They weren't too smart; Giddens liked that.

His method was a tried and tested one.

At first he rode silently behind them, waiting for an opportunity to be useful. He did not have long to wait. The track was bad, and Sweeney's pot-bellied horse soon threw a shoe. Giddens palmed a thick briar thorn and appeared to extract it from the nag's hoof. The merchants were grateful, but wary of strangers. He rode beside them for three hours, jawing about the weather, the troublesome tribes further South, anything he thought might interest them, but they gave nothing away.

Soon he left, knowing they would get suspicious if he befriended them too quickly. Same thing next day; three hours of riding, then gone. Finally it got so they were expecting him, and then he knew he had won their trust. That was when they were as good as dead.

The rest of the gang had been running a parallel trail, and now moved in so swiftly that they were able to take the merchants' guns before they so much as looked up. Giddens took care of the killing. He buried the merchants side by

side in the creek at the end of the red clay ravine, then emptied out their saddlebags.

He found a brick of bills thick enough to keep them all warm through the winter. He allowed his best men to send small amounts of money home. There was also a cloth filled with gemstones, blood-red crystals the size of coat buttons, but they had no way of fencing such rarities, so Parson emptied fist after glittering fist into the river.

That was four years ago, when things were still good. A lot had changed since then.

The gang led by Parson and Giddens was made up of men who had lived with them in the Dakota Territories, and loyalties ran strong. They were uncles, cousins, brothers, and they had joined because they needed money, or needed to stay on the move, and preferred the nomadic life to breaking their backs on the hardscrabble dirt of their homelands.

Some of them had been soldiers who had left the military in bad circumstances. Others would not be drawn to their reasons for joining; they had stolen, or killed, or abandoned their families. Anything was better than slowly starving to death in townships that had failed to take root.

As the frontier moved westward the military followed it in, so the gang was forced to live between two shifting barriers of settlers and lawmen. There were too many people around now. The garrisons served as troop bases, from where attacks could be launched on Indians, and once they were in place it was time to get out. The settlers caused almost as much trouble. They kept a cold eye on strangers, and winning them over took a great deal of effort and patience.

In 1873, there were three memorable events that were to have repercussions for the gang. The territorial officials decided to harvest Black Hills timber and float it downriver to Missouri for new settlements. The first Colt Peacemakers got sold out of Connecticut by mail order for $17 apiece. And Sam Henry Ezekiel Franks joined the gang at the age of 8, making him its youngest-ever member.

The gang never took women or children as a rule. A few years earlier at the end of a bad winter, they had stopped a party of five men, four women and two little girls, tracking them through an overgrown route to the Cheyenne

River. It had taken Heck Giddens six days to convince the party of his good nature and honest intentions, but at last he had persuaded them to let him travel with them as a scout. Parson was waiting with the others down near the shoreline, and when the first two travellers appeared on the path he shot them both dead. The third he blinded, but the other two got back in time to warn their families. It turned into an unholy mess; Giddens cut the throats of the two little girls and stuck the most beautiful of the women with his knife because she kept screaming, although she took a long time to die and made a hell of a fuss.

It took another two days and nights to round up the remaining survivors. The men were rabbity little things and gave in easily when cornered, but their wives were hard, and had thin brittle bodies like boys. Parson and Giddens built them a shack in the woods, and kept them there for sexual purposes— the women could not leave because they had no horses or supplies—but the arrangement was to no-one's satisfaction, and at the end of the summer they were killed and buried in the woods.

As a consequence, the ban on women and children stayed in force as the gang went about its business. It was a strange time to be surviving as they did. It was hard to tell who to trust anymore; the prospectors, the railroad officials and the land developers were all arriving to stake their claims. The Sioux were being pushed into reservations, the remaining buffalo hunting grounds were under threat, tribes and militiamen were fighting among themselves, and nobody except a few men in the East knew what the government was planning to do next.

The gang—it had no name—had been working in a loose figure-eight for several years, cutting down from the grey shale below the treeline to hit the old expedition routes and settlers' paths. The winter of '72 had been harsh, and the numbers of travelling parties were down. The longest it had ever taken to win the trust of a party was almost three weeks. Each time it grew a little harder.

They were careful in their choice of victims. The risk was always weighed against the prize. They paid off their members in installments, usually when they were far from any town, to prevent them from heading for the nearest bar and whorehouse, where they might talk to the wrong people. It was,

Parson said, like a family, although here he was only guessing at the idea because his folks had thrown him into the forest at the age of two, and he had been raised by a fat little Yapa Comanche who had lost his own parents.

'We got to get a good haul in before spring ends,' said Parson one night, as the gang settled back into their old camp at Twelvetree Point. Only Giddens and his sidekick, a young halfbreed that Arikara named Blue Star, were still awake.

'There's talk of a party coming down from Fort Gray end of the month,' said Giddens. 'You know what that means.'

Parson did not need to be reminded. The fort held military gold reserves, and in the past had sent out interest payments with settling parties in the form of reshaped bullion. According to the prison warden, a gurning halfwit the Arikara had befriended, the bars were melted and pressed into leaves that were stitched into the floors of the ladies' saratogas, but nobody knew for certain if this was true.

'Gives us three weeks to prepare,' said Giddens, 'should be enough.' He was eight years younger than Parson, and took care of the planning. Over the past decade, he had perfected the art of inveigling himself into companies of suspicious strangers, but it never got any easier. The uncertainty of the times meant that men who were by inclination friendly now studied new companions with cold distance in their eyes.

'Get your Indian back up to that fort,' said Parson, 'and get that stupid old drunk jailer talking. We need to know how many they gone be.'

Parson told him little he did not already know. He and Blue Star had already made plans of their own. A schoolteacher and his wife, they'd heard, an old man, probably his father, two outriders with a cart, not a riding carriage but something to haul a weighty object—what were they carrying, and why would they be making the journey? There was no settlement this side of the river, and no way across for a cart. He went to the ridge and looked down into the blue night, thinking. It was logical to assume they were headed for one of the new Wyoming settlements, but the schoolteacher was supposed to be travelling with two escorts, and that smelled bad. No-one could afford to waste men on accompanying a civilian couple unless they were carrying something special with them.

Giddens kicked over the fire and lay awake for the next hour, feeling the earth cool beneath him. The mystery of the schoolteacher had dug into him now, and would not easily be released.

The weather turned foul in the last week of the month. Sun and moon both vanished, and rains turned the old settler's route into a mudslide. The gang resolved to set camp at Twelvetrees until Giddens brought in the party. None of them was deterred by thoughts of jail or hanging. They worked from necessity, knowing that each party they robbed might be their last, because each was smarter than the one before, and would not be gulled by a pleasant stranger with a helpful smile. Giddens knew it would come to an end some day, but not quite yet—there was talk of uprisings and a coming war with the red men, so minds were preoccupied and treasure parties grew reckless, risking plunder. Until the train arrived there would be no easy way through this route, and at least the gang killed quickly when they could, which was more than could be said for the half-starved bastards to their North.

Blue Star returned from Fort Gray to tell them he had seen the party setting off for a settlement downriver. The teacher was 'birdsmall', the wife was 'driedleaves', the old man a 'gravewalker'. Their carriage was little more than a wood platform on cartwheels and there was only one outrider. To anyone else this would have come as bad news, but Giddens still felt confident that they were delivering something important. To be given a scout at all was a luxury. The group would pass close to Twelvetrees Ridge in two days' time. Their outrider would arrive three or four hours ahead of them. The ridge formed a bottleneck through the tail of the forest, where the land opened out into flat brown earth. It was exposed but tightly contained. Even so, there was danger in an ambush. Better to befriend the teacher and win him over. Giddens was a man of some learning, and could exert considerable charm. It was his chief advantage over Parson, who was roughly born and branded through with it like a birthmark. He was bandy from riding and lack of greens, and had once received a knife in the eye, which had left it glazed. He did not look naturally trustworthy.

The others, who this year numbered about fifteen in total, were no better. None could read or write, and few spoke above a cuss. They were hungry and dirty and stank, and got sick from wiping their shit-stained hands on their

breeches before eating with their fingers, and when they fucked their women they often left them dead. Mostly they were like mean children, even Shug, who was the oldest and reckoned he was probably about fifty, although he could not rightly be sure—he'd seen too much to stay in kindly disposed spirits.

So Giddens rode out to greet them. He had an advantage; the path had washed out some half-mile South and he knew better than any guide how they could circumnavigate it. He sighted the party moving from the seagreen shadows of the pines, and drew in alongside. Within seconds the outrider, a soft-chinned, bug-eyed young man who looked like he'd never seen sunlight, had drawn close and was resting his hand on the rifle in his saddle.

'I hope your boy here knows the safest passage through these woods, sir,' he said, doffing his hat. 'Hector Giddens, at your service.'

The schoolteacher was indeed small, a bundle of female bones reshaped into a bookish man. He observed Giddens with a still eye. 'He knows the way well enough.'

He's been warned, thought Giddens. *I've seen that look before.*

'You know him well, then.' He indicated the outrider without glancing at him.

'We were introduced by Captain Mallory at the fort,' called the old man at the back of the party.

His father is the weakness. He's already given too much away. 'I should perhaps warn you, sir, that the path ahead will unseat your horses. We've had bad rains, and the road has been washed out in a number of places.'

'Thank you. I shall be wary of that.' There was a movement under the tarp on the cart. The teacher called back sharply, 'Stay down, Sam.' So there was another riding with them.

'Then I wish you well enough,' said Giddens. 'You need have no fear in these parts, although it never pays to drop your guard. "Covert enmity under the smile of safety wounds the world."'

'You know your Shakespeare, sir.' The schoolteacher tried not to look impressed. He held out a cautious hand. The outrider flinched. 'Lemuel Franks, and this is my wife, Mayla.' He indicated a stony-faced woman with centre-parted dark hair. She was dressed in a stiff, high-collar and grey silk

skirts unsuited for the terrain. 'Back there is my father, Abel, and my boy. Come out, son.'

Samuel Franks emerged from beneath the tarp, maybe 8 years old, small for his age. He looked feverish.

'He has not been well,' said the teacher's wife. 'His stomach.'

'Well I'm sorry to hear that. See the big green leaves at the base of the pine brush? Tear them up and boil them to broth, they'll improve his bowels. Pleased to meet your family, Mrs Franks. I feel I am in good Christian company.' Giddens knew she would appreciate the formality. He ignored the outrider, but kept a carefully respectful distance. He deliberately avoided looking at the cart behind them.

The first and most important thing was to give Franks a reason for trusting him, and to do that he needed to produce a reason for riding with them. To offer an immediate explanation would sound wrong, so he let Franks fish for answers. Giddens explained that he'd been living out here alone since his dear wife died of pneumonia. That he was lonely, a former marshal turned trapper waiting to be relieved of his post by Captain Mallory's men. These days he made a living scouting out forests for the logging companies. Sometimes he was glad of educated company—not too many of the fellows he ran into had any learning to speak of. It made a man hungry for good conversation. He allowed droplets of information to fall from him like thawing branches.

Blue Star's knowledge of the group's departure stood him in good stead. He was able to display his knowledge of the fort, its men and even its jail. They joked lightly together about mutual acquaintances.

Franks, in his turn, explained that he and his wife were to set up a school for the militia to teach them map-reading, for he was a geography teacher. As Giddens suspected, his wife was a bible-wringer and had been placed in charge of the new chapel. The outrider's name was Billy; he was Captain Mallory's grandson. That night, Giddens took his leave and promised to return early the next morning. Only Billy was displeased, because his authority had been usurped.

This charade carried on for five days and nights. Giddens was beginning to despair, because the party was moving further and further away from camp. He promised to ride with them one more day, but knew he was running out

of time. If Franks was really the guardian of a treasure, it had to be in the trunk they kept under the tarpaulin, but there was no way to it.

The boy's health and spirits improved. He asked to ride with Giddens, but Mayla Franks would not let him out of her sight. Lemuel knew about the land's geography, but had little experience of it. He rode badly, and more than once risked overturning the carriage when the path proved too steep. The outrider remained wary—hell, that was his job—and Giddens plotted a way to get rid of him.

He prearranged a meet-point with Parson and three others. If he failed to show, they would ride on ahead and stake the outrider's figure-eight, hoping to waylay him. Billy rode out early each morning, returning before noon to report. On the sixth morning, he did not return. Giddens went to see what had happened, and returned with bad news.

'I'm afraid your rider is dead,' he told them. 'He's in a glade about three miles west of here. Looks like his horse lamed itself and threw him. His neck broke when he landed, I don't suppose he felt any pain.' That much was true, although Parson had tortured him a while, trying to find out what the school-teacher was delivering. When he went too far and Billy left them for another sphere, Parson realized the outrider had died without giving them a clue.

Giddens offered his services, and they were readily accepted. A fine blue mist was settling into the valley ahead; the pines were laced together by a sheen of dew-filled spiderwebs, and even the birds had fallen silent. They rode without talking, but Giddens felt a tension building in his gut. Parson and his men arrived without sound. They fell in around the convoy and calmly, quietly strangled Abel Franks with a rope. Giddens cut Lemuel's throat from behind with a straight razor. Mrs Franks was too ugly even for them, so they twisted her neck and pulled her from her horse without so much as a pudgy hand raised in protest. These acts were not undertaken out of malice but from a sense of practicality; no-one could be left to report back. Lately the militia had been behaving in an excessively violent manner, and none of the gang would have reached trial after capture, so it was better this way. One of the horses grew frightened at the sight of blood and bolted. The others accepted their new owners.

Parson and Shug would have killed the boy but Giddens stayed their hand.

It was agreed that Sam was young enough to be trained for a different future, and two of the men took him back to camp. Giddens and Parson uncovered the tarp and broke open the chest on the cart. Inside were damp-riddled schoolbooks and clothes, nothing more. It made no sense until Giddens set to wondering if the treasure Lemuel Franks had been carrying was not gold but information. And what if it was the boy who held such knowledge? It would explain why they had kept him hidden under the tarp.

Giddens buried the boy's parents below the cottonwoods in the river bed and brought the old trunk along. When they reached camp he emptied the schoolbooks and bibles into Sam Frank's space, a hide they had stretched across the bushes for him. Giddens burned the clothes because they were evidence. Inside Myla Franks' Sunday dress he found around thirty dollars, two small gold coins and a small stash of jewelry, obviously paste and easily identifiable. The necklaces went into the river. More and more, he became convinced that the boy must know something of greater importance. So he waited.

In the same way that Giddens showed a stoical, infuriating patience with his victims, he now resolved to do the same with the child. He could see from studying the boy's still brown eyes that threats would provoke little response. He was his father's son, except for his jet hair and the tougher fibre within him. The only way was to win his trust. He was careful right from the outset, making sure that Samuel did not actually witness his father's bloody death, or his mother's strangulation. Sure, the boy would realize they had gone and that he had been adopted by a very different family, but in time Giddens hoped that he would become reconciled to his fate. The young were pliable. Giddens had seen it before; angry twin brothers had joined the gang on their eleventh birthday. He had never asked why they had run away from what seemed like a pleasant settlement, but had accepted them, fed them, taught them how to kill. They were gone now, in tragic circumstances, and he missed them.

Sam rode with them and did not look back. He never asked questions and he never complained. He took to riding with his arms around Giddens's waist, and rarely spoke about the past. One older man in the gang began to show a lively interest in the boy when he was washing himself in the creek, so Giddens stayed by his side at night, sleeping at the edge of the hide.

It was only a matter of time before Captain Marshall sent some men after them. Word had reached him that the Franks family had never arrived, but this news upset him less than discovering that his grandson Billy had gone missing. Giddens heard troops from the fort combing the forest on four separate occasions, but by now the trail had grown over, and besides, they never thought of searching the riverbed. Eventually the loss was written off, in that curious way the old West had of dealing with unforeseen tragedies.

One night the gang camped out in a wide Southern plain of rock and stubble where no fire could be kindled without being seen for miles, but it was warm enough for them to stay without. The stars had come down to brush the earth. Giddens hunched himself into his jacket and looked over at the boy, who was watching for comets.

'Did your father ever say why he was moving the family?' he asked.

The boy remained motionless, his large head tilted up at the spilled-out sky. 'We had relatives in Wyoming,' he said finally. 'We were going to meet them halfway and set up a mission. It was my Ma's idea.'

'But your old man was gone teach geography.'

'Only 'cause they was nothing else he could do.'

Giddens knew that a man like that was useless out here.

'And your grandpappy came.'

'Couldn't leave him behind.'

'Captain Marshall sent a rider along with you.'

'We heard about the scalping party.' There had been reprisals for an attack on a reservation, but that had been some three years ago.

'That the only reason?'

'My pappy didn't know the way.' He pointed at a silver streak in the heavens. 'There's one.'

Jesus, thought Giddens, *what the hell is wrong with the folk in this country? They deserve to be taken advantage of.* 'You want to ride with us the next time we go out?' he asked.

'Sure. My hands are cold.' He put his right fist into Giddens' jacket and they stayed in place, side by side, watching the stars drop from their orbits.

The next day they went looking for a party that was headed west, taking mail and supplies to a settlement known as Cricktown. The boy proved useful

in gaining the trust of the waggoner. Giddens introduced him as his son, and found that smiles soon appeared. The boy was damned cute, and knew how to sell it. He won the women over first. Suspicions quickly lessened, so that they were able to surprise the party and take it in half the usual time. He remembered the look of shocked betrayal on a ranch-hand's face as he cut his throat and thought *Hell, we haven't had a reaction like that in years.*

Sam got better. Soon he was clinging to Giddens and hitting their victims with so much bull about travelling with his daddy that there was hardly any more work to be done. He learned the trade real fast. It was difficult not to feel proud of a boy who figured things out like that. The rest of the gang adopted Sam as a mascot, sending him to check the trail ahead of them because he could get through low brush without making a sound. Only Blue Star kept away from him, because he had lost his standing in the gang.

But life was still hard. The winter of '74 was meaner than the last, and two of their men died of the cold. One was rock-solid and dead on his horse, which meant that Parson had been talking to a corpse for a morning without realizing it.

The pickings were mixed at best. One party headed for Yankton was carrying banknotes intended as a kickback for the mayor, which meant that the loss couldn't be reported, but too many setters travelled with just their bedrolls and the clothes on their backs. Old Shug was heard to complain that they'd have made more money as pirates. Then Parson got sick to his stomach and died of something wrongly cooked. They shoveled aside pine needles and dug him a pit, covering it with brush. 'Ain't nobody going to say a few words for him?' Giddens asked, and Sam stepped forward with a short speech he had written, which cheered everyone.

But losing the gang's first partner lowered their spirits. Nothing was quite the same for the next two years. New settlements were springing up in the sheltered valleys, where the worst of the weather passed overhead and there was plenty of game to be caught, and they regarded all strangers as enemies. Giddens knew that the days when he could charm the women out of their britches was coming to a close.

One day, watching the halfbreed slowly dismounting from his horse, he realized that even Blue Star was getting old. The gang got by on stragglers

and fools who had taken routes they had no right to be on, but it was a poor way to make a living. The only advantage they had was the boy; there was an innocence about Sam that could pull the wool so far over folks' eyes that they didn't feel the blade going in. Giddens would not let him take part in the kills. He needed to keep the boy fresh. In turn, Sam kept the gang on its toes, so that they learned from one another.

Giddens always knew when Sam was about to come up with some new idea. His brown pupils dilated and he would gaze into the distance, his lips pressed tight together. Then he would say 'How about if . . .' or 'What would you think . . .' and suddenly he would run off at the mouth with some scheme that got less crazy the more you worked it out.

On one of their increasingly rare trips into town he persuaded Giddens to purchase a great iron pot, which they dragged back to their new camp at the ravine and filled with water, keeping it boiling through the dark winter months, adding meat and bitter root vegetables that could cook for weeks and still taste good. They built several small bases deep in the hills and kept a cow for milk, so that they could stay healthy. As the boy grew, there was just one bone of contention between them. He didn't like what they did with the women. He didn't understand it exactly, he just knew it was wrong, and wanted them to stop it. Giddens said he would see what he could do, but could not promise that the men would easily change their ways.

The composition of the gang altered from time to time. Men went back to their wives or decided to chance their luck in another state, but around twelve of them stayed, a sufficient number to attack a band of travelers without mishap. During one miserable summer the gang was forced to steal clothes and kitchen utensils from a settlement as it moved upstream. When it seemed they could no longer scrape a living from their trade, more members drifted away, under oath never to mention what they had seen or participated in, upon pain of death. They had no romantic notion of being outlaws. They were of a criminal class far below the admired rebels of the time, and no townsfolk would ever welcome their arrival. Sometimes Giddens looked at the boy and was shamed by the way he made his living. He had grown up in the East, and been educated to appreciate the value of the classics. Now he hankered for the erudition to express himself, to somehow pass on what he had learned about

the world to Sam. A hole had opened up inside him like the gnawing of a rat, but it was too late to find a way of changing for the better.

Without realizing it, Giddens started to call the boy his son, and the sentiment had been quietly reciprocated. Newcomers to the gang assumed he was Sam's father, and neither of them did anything to challenge the notion. But there was something unspoken standing between them. Sooner or later it would be time for Sam to earn his keep by killing, and Giddens did not know if the boy would be up to it. He knew the subject needed to be discussed, but in the long and easy stretches of silence that passed between them on the forest slopes, he realized that he was afraid of losing his boy. Everyone treated Sam as the gang's natural heir, and even Blue Star had fallen into a kind of truce with him.

One evening the boy returned from hunting with the Arikara, and saw his adopted father dashing out a man's brains at the base of a tree. Giddens' face was badly slashed. The broken body yielded just a handful of coins, and was buried beneath the scrub. Nothing Sam saw affected him, for he had retained the blankness of his childhood. The gang's business made no difference to him; they might have been selling rabbit skins instead of fencing stolen goods.

Giddens had been keeping a mark on the boy's birthday, and understood with something of a shock that he was to be fourteen the coming week. The men had gone across the ravine to Fort Redcliffe, where they had a nice little trade going in dead men's weapons, and were not expected back until the next day. He tried to think of something special he could do for the lad, but as always the suggestion came from Sam.

'We could go to the buffalo plain,' he said.

'You won't see any, son,' said Giddens. 'They've all been driven out. The railroad has staked the land as far as you can see. Soon, when the fencing starts, the travelling parties will have to travel the long way around to go South, and they won't come past here no more.'

'Then we should hunt,' said Sam, who enjoyed the thrill of stalking an animal and killing it. 'Tonight we should stew venison, which is deer meat.'

He was always surprised when Sam sprang new words on him, and marveled at his memory. He realized now that he loved the boy more than he had ever loved anyone; no woman had come this close. They found a small

doe grazing in the bracken and clipped it, but it was the boy who brought it down. He was lithe, fleet and silent, and could get close without a creature suspecting a thing. They skinned the carcass and set the hide aside to be seasoned and dried, then carved the bony young animal into joints, although it would easily have fitted whole inside the pot. They added beans and roots and pilotbread.

Giddens had been saving the bottle for over three years now, and decided the time was right to uncork it. He poured brandy for the both of them. The boy coughed and punched his chest when he drank. A sooty cloud of bats rose in the red dusk light.

'You never hear wolves out here,' he said, listening intently.

'Not for years,' Giddens replied. 'They moved back to the deep timber.'

It was nearly dark now. The pot popped and boiled. A butterfly flickered about the boy, as white as phosphorus, and settled on his knee. He stared hard at it. 'I'm fourteen,' he said. 'Leastwise, in a few days. I'm ready.'

Giddens knew what he meant, but needed to disguise it for a moment more. 'What you mean, son?'

'I'm ready to do what you do.'

'I didn't want to speak of it before it was your time,' said Giddens softly.

'I just wanted you to know.'

Nothing else needed to be said. They sat by the pot and drank. Some while later, they heard a trap snap closed. An animal released a high cry of pain. 'You got something,' said Giddens, 'sounds like a hare.'

He turned to find the boy holding a Colt Peacemaker to his temple. 'I had to wait for the trap to shut,' said Sam blankly. 'You'd have heard me cock the gun.' He fired at close range, blowing out the rear left quadrant of Giddens' skull. The forced threw Giddens onto his back. The boy climbed to his feet and disappeared for a moment, returning with a Bowie knife and a logging saw.

He cut off Giddens' legs at the knees first, then severed his arms at the elbows and shoulders. It was hard work and he was soon sweating violently. Surprisingly, Giddens was not dead. He tried to speak, but after a while he just stared up at the sky and squeezed out tears, which the boy was careful to catch in a tin cup.

In an act of mercy, he cut off Giddens' head. Then he slowly added the old cowboy to the pot, piece by bloody piece.

When the gang arrived back next day they were starving hungry, and he was able to feed them all. He sat with them and drank his adopted father's tears from the tin cup. Then, once the gang had eaten their fill and had fallen into drunken stupors on their bedrolls, he quietly rose and returned to his hide. Digging beneath his blankets, he sorted through the old books Giddens had dumped from Lemuel's trunk. He gently removed and rewrapped the Shakespeare first folio. Then he slipped it into his saddlebag, mounted Giddens' horse and rode out of the camp, into the waiting night.

THE VELOCITY OF BLAME

'The best way to get rid of a really big Cambodian cockroach is to wrap it in tissue paper, drop it in the toilet and pour Coco de Mer Body Butter over it so it can't climb the walls of the bowl, because the buggers have clawed feet and can really shift. Even then, they sometimes manage to shuck off the paper and use it to climb back up out of the toilet into your bathroom.' That's what the man who sold Dorothy her guide book said. She was always reading me passages from the damned thing. It had a bunch of tips for dealing with the kind of problems you encounter over there. When they didn't work, she added her own twists. It was one of those manuals obsessed with hygiene and the strength of the dollar, and its contributors were so paranoid about being ripped off that you lost faith in human nature the longer you kept reading it. I made her throw it away when we decided to stay on.

I'll admit, it took us a while to get used to the bugs in South East Asia, but I thought they'd turn out to be the least of our problems. There would be other issues to deal with. The food, the people, the heat, the past, the politics. I should have added another problem to that list; lack of communication.

We came to Siem Reap to do the tourist thing, hire bikes and see the temples of Angor Wat at sunset, climbing over the temples of Ta Keo and Ta Prohm, where great tree roots entwine the carvings until it's impossible to tell what is hand carved and what is natural. We wanted to ride elephants, hang out in bars where you could still smoke beneath slow-turning fans, drive along the endless arrow-straight roads to the floodplains of the Tonle Sap Lake, eat fat shrimps in villages which had survived through the horrors of the Kmer Rouge, but no-one had told us about the people, how kind, placid

and forgiving they were. No other country in the world could have survived so many horrors and still have found such power to forgive. It didn't make sense to me, but then I come from a land that specialises in Christian vengeance.

It was our first visit to South East Asia, and we immediately fell in love with the place.

Siem Reap was little more than a dusty crossroads crowded with ringing bicycles, lined with cafes and little places where you could get a foot and shoulder massage. There were covered markets at each end of the town selling intricate wooden carvings, pirated books and gaudy silks, and barns where farmers sat on the floor noisily trading their produce, with their kids running everywhere, laughing and fooling around, the closest definition I'd ever seen of real community. That's a word we're fond of using at home, but there it means something entirely less friendly.

After watching Chinese dealers testing precious stones that had been dug out of the mountains, running little blowtorches over gems to prove their integrity, I bought Dorothy a ruby for thirty dollars.

'I'm not going to have this made into anything,' she said happily, 'I just want to keep it somewhere in a box so I can look at it and remember.'

Instead of frying ourselves by the hotel pool we wandered around the streets, where every merchant was calling out, trying to lure us into their store with special offers. Not so pushy that they were annoying, just doing business and quickly leaving us alone as soon as they realised we didn't want to buy. Now that Cambodia was finally stable, the Russians and the French were competing to build along the town's main road, and ugly concrete blocks were going up behind the 1930s colonnades. No plumbing, no drainage but plenty of internet access; welcome to the new frontier, where you could use an ATM machine but still had to step over duelling scorpions to do so. A national museum had opened, absurdly high-tech, half the interactive exhibits not functioning, as though some rich outsider had insisted that this was what the town needed to draw tourists. Less than a decade of peace and the nation was embracing its future with a kind of friendly ferocity, but you feared for the transition process, knowing that everything could still be lost overnight.

And I was finally vacationing with my wife. Gail and Redmond had

married and left home and were now living in Oakley, Virginia, which left me and Dorothy rattling around the house in Washington with too many bedrooms and memories. I'd been promising Dorothy that we'd eventually travel, but it proved harder to get away from work than I'd expected. After thirty seven years of marriage, during which time we'd hardly ever left the country, I decided enough was enough and applied for two months' leave, although I eventually had to take it unpaid. Of course, whatever time you pick to go away is never the right time, and this proved to be the case; there was an election pending and everyone was expected to help, but Dorothy put her foot down and told me she'd go by herself if I didn't step away this time and make good on my promise to her. She said; 'Politicians are like policemen, the work never stops and they never make much of a difference, so take a vacation.'

So I booked the tickets and off we went.

When I first saw the officials at Siem Reap airport emptying their collected visa-cash into leather suitcases right in front of the tourists who paid them, I'll admit I thought the worst, that the corrupting influence of past dictators lived on—and maybe it does in other ways—but after that day I saw nothing else like it and we had a wonderful time.

On one of our last trips out beyond the river we found ourselves in a town almost completely surrounded by dense jungle. The Tonle Sap Lake is tidal. For most of the year it's barely three feet deep, but during the monsoon season it connects with the Mekon River and reverses its flow, flooding the surrounding plains and forests, filling a vast area with breeding fish. The Vietnamese families living in the floating villages at the lake's edge aren't much liked by the Cambodians, but on the whole everyone rubs along. The effluvial soil is rich and the landscape is lush with vegetation. On that day we stopped in a village so small that no-one living in it could decide what it was called, and that was when we saw the house.

It was just a white brick box in a small square of cleared grass, but the surrounding forest canopy glowed emerald even at noon, and it looked like the happiest place on earth. What's more, the little house was available to rent. I mentioned it to Dorothy, who dismissed the idea at once, but I could see she was excited. A light had come into her eyes that I had not seen in

years. Dorothy never went out without makeup and jewellery. She cared about appearances, and what people thought of her. She was concerned about making a good impression. It's a Washington habit. But I could tell she relished the thought of not having to bother, even if it was just for a month.

'Well, I guess it wouldn't hurt to take a look,' she said finally, so we visited the owner, a tiny little old lady called Madame Nghor, and she showed us around. It was just about as basic as you can get. There was really just one room with a single small window, because the kitchen and toilet were kind of outside. They stood on a half-covered deck with a wood rail that overlooked the fields and the forest. There was also a plank terrace at the front facing the road. Life was lived mainly out of doors.

The monsoon had recently ended, leaving the jungle green but fetid. On its far side, palms had been cleared to build a factory, but the breeze-block building had never been finished. The village was so perfect that it could even keep progress at bay. Madame Nghor agreed to rent us the property for one month. The price seemed absurdly low, but maybe it was extortionate to her. We didn't really care.

We checked out of the Borei Angkor, the fancy hotel where we had only met other Americans, and moved right in to the tiny house. When we got in the taxi to leave, the driver automatically assumed we were heading to the airport and very nearly dropped us there. He was real surprised when we redirected him into the countryside.

Our tickets home were open so there was nothing else to do but tell our family that we had decided to stay on awhile. Gail thought we were behaving kind of weirdly but Redmond congratulated us when we told him.

'I won't be making many more calls,' I warned him. 'The charger we brought with us doesn't work out here. But we have our health and our money, and the change is doing Dorothy a world of good.'

'Just don't go native on us, Dad,' Redmond laughed.

Obviously, staying in the house was very different to being in the hotel. There were no fresh towels or little gifts on the pillow, and there was no room service or air-conditioning, but we loved it all the same. Madame Nghor offered to prepare food for us, and we took up her kind offer. On our second day, she called around with the other villagers to formally welcome us. The

women peeped shyly around the door and wouldn't come in. The men sat in a circle outside and offered us a strong, sour yellow drink they'd made themselves. I didn't like it much but it wouldn't have been right to refuse it.

We were sad to see so many of their children missing an arm or a leg. They danced about dextrously with just a stick or two to lean on, and Dorothy and I felt compelled to give them a few coins even though we knew we shouldn't. There was this kid called Pran, a skinny little runt about seven years old, who had lost both his legs and one arm. There were still thousands of landmines buried in the countryside around the village, and we were warned about straying from the marked paths when cycling to the next village for provisions. The damage of war always outlives the fighting, sometimes in ways we can never imagine.

The younger villagers spoke some English, and all were anxious to ensure that we would have a happy stay. Madame Nghor was especially thoughtful, and would bring us small gifts—a mosquito coil, candles, a hand fan—anything she could think of that might make our stay more comfortable. Her husband had died in tragic circumstances—I heard from one of the villagers that he had been murdered by a Kmer resistance unit about fifteen years earlier—and pain was etched deeply in her face, but now her life was simple and safe and she made the best of it; her story, we felt, was to have a happy ending. She and the villagers lived by the principles enshrined by their religion, peace and acceptance and harmony, and we found it a humbling contrast to the way we lived at home. You try to do the right thing but life in the West is complicated and hypocritical.

There were times when we felt like disoriented Westerners, not understanding what we were seeing. On a trip into Siem Reap we watched a fight explode out of nowhere between two men who were whisked away so quickly by police that I feared for their survival in the cells. Then, an hour later, we saw them in a café together laughing and drinking. Some of the food gave us fiery stomach cramps—we weren't used to eating such quantities of spiced vegetables without any dairy products—and the insects particularly plagued Dorothy, who would find herself bitten even though she tightly wrapped herself at sunset from head to foot. One night as I watched this ritual of protection, I found myself fearing for her. She seemed so much more fragile

here. Dorothy caught me looking, and told me not to fuss. She always had confidence in me.

The bugs were at their worst after a humid rainstorm broke across our new home one night. They flew into the shutters at such a lick I thought they might crack the wood. The next morning the warm, still pools under our decking were filled with giant centipedes and every type of crawling creature, some with pincers, some with horns and stingers, many as big as an adult fist. I shifted one multi-legged horror from the bedroom with a stick, and it caught me by surprise when its shiny black carapace split open and two vibrating iridescent green wings folded out. It lifted lazily into the air like a cargo plane, and I guided it toward an open window.

The following evening we opened a bottle of warm red wine and sat beside each other on the rickety wooden terrace, watching the sunset, Dorothy and I. Silence fell easily between us, but it was also a time for asking things we had avoided discussing all of our married life.

'Tell me,' she said after a long pause for thought. 'Do you ever regret working for the doctor?'

It was a question I had asked myself many times. 'I was young,' I replied. 'I was ambitious. We were denied information. We didn't know many of the things we know now.'

'But if you had known, would you still have worked for him?'

'Why do you need to know?'

'Because there were others who stood their ground.' There was no reproach in her voice.

'They knew more than I ever did. He kept us in the dark.'

'You knew about the carpet bombing. Everyone in Washington knew.'

'We didn't know what it would lead to. How could we? But to answer your question? No, I wouldn't have worked for Kissinger.'

As we were dressing, Madame Nghor brought us a ceramic pot and shyly set it on the low dining table. She looked uncomfortable about bringing it. 'This for protection—for—'and here she rolled one forefinger over the other in an explanation I could not understand. I looked into the pot and found it contained an oily red butter that smelled like copper and petrol.

'How do I use this? I asked.

'Not for you,' she told me gently, 'for your wife.'

I figured that explained her awkwardness. For the last day or so Dorothy had been suffering from cramps. Madame Nghor held her hand out over the edge of the floor and made a soothing flat-palmed gesture.

'Put it at night. You rub it like this to stop them from coming,' and again she did the finger-rolling thing that I took to be an indication of cramps. 'You have no trouble from them after, they stop and die. You must keep lid on pot tight. You want me to show?' I thought she looked mighty uncomfortable with what she regarded to be a personal subject, and by this time her embarrassment had spread to me, so I hastily thanked her and showed her out.

We were planning our first trip into the jungle, but Dorothy had not slept well, and was still in some pain. 'We'll postpone it to another time,' I told her. 'Besides, it's been raining and now it's hot again, so God knows what kind of insects will be out and about.'

'No, we'll go. I feel a lot better now, really. I'm not going to be a killjoy on this trip.' I explained to her about rubbing on Madame Nghor's home-made potion but it seemed too oily and liable to stain, so she decided it would be better to use when we got back. After tucking our shirts and socks tightly into our trousers and boots so that no insect could find a way in, we set off into the woodlands, clambering over great tree roots, stopping to listen to the calling of birds in the jungle canopy. The going was a lot tougher than we had expected, and after an hour we decided to turn back.

We had been hoping to stumble across one of the many overgrown temples that lay almost entirely buried by the returning jungle, and in one patch of cleared ground I rubbed away a layer of thick green moss to find the scarred stone face of an Apsara dancer staring up at me through the soft soil. With her raised eyes appearing above the leaves, it looked like she had been swimming through the grass and had just broken through the surface. As if she had been waiting for someone to come along and awaken her.

'You've let the sunlight fall on her face again,' said Dorothy.

'We could uncover the rest of her,' I suggested.

'You don't understand. The moss was protecting her from damage.'

We walked on. Dorothy was particularly exhausted by the journey, so we stopped by a stream and listened to the sounds of the forest.

'We should have done this years ago,' I said, taking her hand. Dorothy's hair had greyed a little and she had tied it back into a ponytail, but in the yellow light that fell through the branches she looked blonde again.

'The time was never right before, you know that,' she replied. 'At least we got to do it now.'

She looked down at her boots, lost in thought. There was a leathery scuffle of wings, and a bird screamed high above us, then it was silent once more. The stream was so clear that you could count the pebbles on the bottom. Dorothy looked down at her white tube sock and began to rub it. 'Damn.'

'What's the matter?'

'Nothing, maybe a scratch.' I looked and saw a small crimson stain the size of a penny. 'I don't think anything could have got in, these socks are really thick. I'd have felt it.'

'Better let me have a look.' I rolled down her sock. It was full of blood. 'I think you got a leech in there,' I told her. 'It won't hurt, but we'd better get you back.' I knew that leeches produced an anaesthetic in their bite so they could continue to suck their host's blood without being felt. They also have an anticoagulant in their saliva, so they can carry on feeding until they're fully gorged. Then they drop from the body to seek water, through which they can travel to find a new host.

'It could have carried on and on without me knowing it was there,' said Dorothy.

'No,' I told her. 'In the natural world parasites don't kill their hosts, because they'd ultimately kill themselves.'

'You mean it's only humans who do that.'

Soon the cover thinned out and the jungle opened onto a road that led back to the village. As soon as we reached the house we took off our socks and shoes. I found one leech attached to my ankle, and Dorothy had two. They were small and black, as soft as slugs but far more elastic and lively. They left splattery trails of blood as they twisted about on the bathroom floor. I stamped on their bloated bodies, sacs of blood that burst messily over the cracked white tiles. I had a sudden suspicion that there might be more of them on us.

'Turn around,' I told Dorothy. 'Take off your shirt.' As she peeled off

the wet cotton, I saw two more on her back, between her pale shoulder-blades.

When she saw the thin streaks of unclotted blood in the mirror, Dorothy yelped. I picked off one of the creatures and examined it. As I did, it stretched and swung around, trying to bite me. I was surprised at the speed with which it moved. I could see two sets of tiny hooks like pin-points, set on either end of its body. When I dropped it on to the sink it flipped over, end to end, like a slinky. It climbed the sheer sides of the bowl in seconds and disappeared into a wet corner.

'Let me light a cigarette,' I told Dorothy, 'I think you're supposed to burn them off.'

'No,' she said, trying to sound unpanicked, 'they bite deeper if you do that and tear the skin when you pull them. I think you're meant to flick them off with a fingernail.' She had read about them in her travel guide, and was right. A nail under the leech's body was enough to make it come away. My back was clear—I think they found Dorothy's blood sweeter. The harder part was catching them once they fell. You expect anything that looks like a slug to move slowly. I placed my finger above one and watched as it stretched and waved about like an antenna, desperate to reach me. There was something grotesque about its obviousness, as if I was automatically expected to forgive its uncontrollable hunger.

The sun was setting and the sky had turned a spectacular shade of crimson. Out on the balcony, the warm moist air was thick with flying insects. I felt as if our environment had subtly turned against us, as if it was saying *We've nearly had enough of you tourists now, time to go home. You've pretended to be like us but you really don't belong here.*

Dorothy was tired and in unusually low spirits. She hardly ate anything from the tray of pork and noodles Madame Nghor had left for us. She was still suffering from muscle cramps, and opened the pot of oily rust-coloured ointment, patiently rubbing it into the tops of her legs and over her belly until the room stank.

My calves and thigh muscles were sore from the expedition. We were not so young now, I thought, and would have to make adjustments to the way we behaved. It had been foolish of us to just take off into the jungle

like that without telling anyone where we were going—what if we had gotten lost, what would we have done? Just how quickly could things go wrong here?

I turned out the lights and we went to bed. The blackness was complete, but soon I saw lightning crackle above the tree-line. It looked like an electric trolley was running through the forest. The temperature started to climb, and within minutes it was unbearable. Dorothy was twisting and turning in her narrow bed. I was sweating heavily, and could not get comfortable. I went for a smoke on the terrace and stood at the rail, listening to the noises of the night.

Dorothy's questions about my life had bothered me. There were no easy answers. Had Kissinger's illegal bombing of this astonishing country opened the way for everything that followed? We went into other countries and created a vacuum that had to be filled by something. Every day took us further away from being the innocents we had so long pretended to be.

I reached the end of the Marlboro packet. I left the terrace door wide to let some air in and came back inside. It seemed more stifling than ever. I lay down on top of the bed once more.

An hour later, rain broke and fell hard, pounding on the roof of the little house. The temperature began to fall. It rained and rained until the sky wore itself out. Calm returned, and I must have dozed.

Dorothy cried out suddenly, making me start. I tried to find a light, but it seemed the electricity was out, and the candles were somewhere in the other room. I knew at once that something was amiss.

Dorothy was struggling to sit up. She called for me and I grabbed at her wrist, only to find her skin slick with sweat. 'What's the matter?' I kept asking. I probably frightened her with my shouting. I found my lighter, flicked it and tore back the thin sheet. Her nightdress was stained scarlet, and the material was shifting as if alive. I could smell something bad, like an infected open wound. She and I scrabbled to tear off the wet material.

As it ripped, I saw what was wrong; the area from her navel to the tops of her thighs was a black squirming mass of tiny bodies, slick and shiny with her blood. Leeches, it seemed that there were hundreds of them, sucking her life away from her.

I thrust my hand into them and instantly they began to flip onto my wrist and arm, attaching themselves, finding veins and biting hard. Dorothy screamed as I grabbed at them, trying to squeeze whole handfuls at a time, but they slipped through my blood-slick fingers. As fast as I flicked them away they came back, driven by their hunger for blood.

I needed something else. Finding the lighter, I struck it and thrust the flame into the wriggling slimy nest. Too late, I remembered that the ointment contained petrol. There was a soft pop of ignition and she was enveloped in thin blue flames. I grabbed my shirt and threw it over her stomach.

In the moment before the flickering flames were extinguished, I saw the horrific mess on her body, blood and burned leeches writhing everywhere, Dorothy shaking in pain and terror, and I . . .

It shames me to think back to that moment. All I could think about when I saw her was the roaring anger of the blame, someone to blame. Madame Nghor had given us the oil, she had somehow discovered who I was, who I had worked for in Washington, and had made up this concoction to draw the leeches to us. She was taking revenge for the loss of her husband, for the destruction of her country, for me being an American. That was my first reaction, the seeking of blame.

The screams brought Madame Nghor—and half the village—to our door. She put on the light, and I realised that in my panic I had simply failed to find the switch. I thought she had come to gloat and take pleasure in this bizarre revenge, and I must have rushed at her. I remember grabbing her thin shoulders and shaking her very hard. Two men who turned out to be her sons ran forward and pulled me away from her.

'What did you do to my wife?' I yelled in her face, 'What did you do?' I said some other things that it pains me now to remember. When she saw the pulsing mass of leeches that still quivered and crawled on Dorothy, Madame Nghor ran back down the steps and returned with something that looked like a can of lighter fluid, squeezing it wildly all around until every last one of the leeches had fallen away and shrivelled up.

Chaos. In the exposing glare of the overhead bulb, my wife lay sobbing, bloody and naked, on the bed before the shocked villagers. I stayed frozen in one place until Madame Nghor had pulled a sheet over her.

'You stupid man,' she scolded, wagging a cartoonish finger at me. 'This all your fault, not mine! This! This!' She picked up the pot she had given us. 'You put it on—'and when she made the smoothing gesture again I realised she meant I should put the oil on the floor, along the edges of the room, to keep the leeches out after the storm. It was not meant to be put on the skin. And the rolling fingers, she was simply showing us how the leeches moved and why it must be applied. I had misinterpreted so blindly, so badly. One of her sons dipped his finger in the mixture to show me. The thick red oil had cattle blood in it. The coppery smell attracted them, and they got stuck.

In shame and shock I started to laugh. I couldn't stop myself. Was this really how things went wrong in the world? Were mistakes always this fundamentally stupid? How could I have thought this tiny village woman might know I once worked for a political oppressor? It was absurd. Guilt, like some barely-visible fish resting in deep water, could surface without warning.

We took Dorothy to the hospital, but the burns themselves were superficial and there was no real damage. However, a ragged black patch of discoloured skin was left behind from the burned edges of the unhealed wounds, and her blood could not coagulate over the scratches my fingernails had left as I tried to dig the leeches from her. The doctor told her she would be left with scars.

Dorothy hardly spoke to me that day. We returned to Washington as soon as we could get a flight, slinking out of the village like criminals. The villagers watched us go in silence and embarrassment.

Seven months later my wife became ill and died. To this day I do not believe what the doctor said, and have convinced myself that her death was the result of some kind of blood poisoning, a delayed reaction to what happened that night.

Just before the year ended, I took early retirement. A new phalanx of eager young recruits was entering politics for the first time, and the thought just made me tired. I know at heart that I am a good man. I have made mistakes in my life, but the worst that night was the speed with which I sought to blame.

ARKANGEL ▆▆▆▆▆▆▆▆▆▆▆▆▆▆▆▆▆▆▆

THE RIVETS WERE WHITE GOLD, FADING TO CRIMSON AND BLOOD BROWN BEFORE THEY had been fully hammered into place. Iron plate and tempered steel, rods and bolts glimpsed through fire and steam in the cuprous stench of annealing metal. The world of the engines was ever like this.

The result was a magnificent piece of craftsmanship, but perhaps they were punished for showing too much pride. One of the workers brought in from Wolsztyn Depot had the four fingers of his right hand sheared off in the engine's coupling joint just hours before the dedication ceremony, and the cheap Russian grease they used on the plates infected the wound so badly that by the time the ambulance reached the hospital, his arm was a livid poison sac. Amputation should have caught the contagion, but no; they buried him beside the track less than twenty four hours after the Arkangel rolled out of its shed. No-one pretended the work was easy, but jobs were hard to come by back then and the line brought hope, even if the means of achieving such prosperity also carried lasting shame.

He caught every third word, then realised he was falling asleep. Josh Beckmann wasn't much of a reader. He threw the guide book aside and wiped the condensation from the car window, complaining about how long it was taking to reach the town. It was getting too dark to read anyway, and the journey was taking longer than he'd expected. Fields, grey woodlands and factories at low light levels, every Eastern European nation was like this. There was nothing out there to give a clue of what the country was really like.

Nick looked over at his old friend and wondered again what they were doing here. There was no real reason why he and Josh should still be friends; they had nothing much in common. At art college they had been as close as knives in a drawer. As an adult Josh was a collection of passions and skills to which he could barely relate. A degree in graphic design. A career in real estate. Hobbies that included calligraphy and rebuilding an old Camaro. Josh never kept his girlfriends longer than nine months. He was a reliable man to call in an emergency. He never forgot birthdays. He always spent Passover with his family. He had a temper. He had fallen in love with a girl he'd only met twice. That didn't explain why Nick should agree to accompany him on a pair of cheap, appalling Ryanair flights to a country he knew nothing about. Perhaps he was just curious.

And who am I? he thought idly. *I have a job I hate. I have a scrubby beard I stubbornly refuse to shave off. I have few opinions of my own, no faith and no loyalties to speak of. I am unformed and unfinished. And I have no idea—literally or figuratively—where I might be heading.*

The backfiring Mercedes powered past a sulphurous smelting plant, a low modern brick factory that glowed in the country night like the site of a nuclear accident, its rotten-egg reek forcing the driver to close the last inch of his window. A housing estate had been constructed next to the sinister block, its dark gardens bristling with frozen washing and plastic children's toys.

'Does it often smell as bad as that?' Nick asked the driver.

'All the time.'

'How can people live so close?'

'The houses were cheap,' the driver answered with a shrug. 'They can keep their doors shut.'

The dank green forest of spruce closed in about them. By the side of the road, an incredibly drunk old man was being helped home by his friend. The going must have been slow, because neither of them had much use left in their rubbery legs. The Mercedes had passed quite a few drunks on the way. One had toppled from his bicycle right in front of them. The driver had swerved around him, acting as if it was the most normal thing in the world to do. October in rural North-Eastern Poland; Nick figured there wasn't a whole

lot else for them to do except get smashed during the lengthening autumn nights.

They reached Chelmsk at nine, and saw even fewer people on the streets than they'd passed in the countryside. Beyond the smeared taxi windscreen were the high, featureless outer walls of the town, punctuated by nine immense dark churches. There had been fifteen before the war, according to the driver.

The town was stripped of features, silent, dead. No advertising hoardings, no pedestrians, no lit windows. Bare wide streets without cars of any description, a few shuttered shops, a windswept concrete town square with a green metal barn used for a vegetable market and yet another church at its centre, this one even more vast and forbidding. A plasticky orange pizza parlour was tucked into the ground floor of what looked like the only building to be built in the last sixty years. It was shut.

'Where is everyone?' asked Josh, pulling his holdall together as the driver pulled over. 'Jesus, it's Saturday night. Danuta is going to owe me for getting her out of here.'

The hotel was a surprise, a gabled coaching inn with a cobbled courtyard like the ones in Hammer horror films, empty white stables and a well that was too perfect to be real. The whole place was so freshly painted, planted and preserved that it might have been built a week ago. Johann, the boy running the inn, was younger than either of them. He could not take credit cards, so Nick and Josh gave him half of the cash up-front, for two nights. Johann took them up to their rooms, leading the way to a corridor that cut through the middle of the first floor. He eagerly insisted on carrying the bags by himself, smiling with a hopeful innocence that would not survive his youth.

Danuta was waiting for them in the bar, unaccountably nervous and fidgety.

Nick had forgotten how stunning she was, large black eyes set in a heart-shaped face, framed with glossy bobbed hair as black as obsidian. She wore plenty of makeup—her arms were paler than her cheeks—but the look suited her perfectly. A tiny waist and long legs accentuated by her black dress, silver buckled shoes, and the clincher—black-framed glasses that had the odd effect

of making her appear demure and dangerous. There was a sense of purpose about her. She constructed her English sentences with a determination that conveyed meaning by emphasis. It gave her an attractive way of stressing certain words. Unlike most of the girls Josh picked up in clubs, she listened and responded in a way that showed she thought carefully about everything he said. She knocked the rest of them out of the field, and Nick couldn't for the life of him see what she admired in his friend, unless she really was planning to use Josh as a means of escape. Nobody could have called him attractive. He was stout and dark, with thinning corkscrew hair, but could be smart and quick-witted, even charming when he made the effort, and she responded enthusiastically to that.

He had met her in one of those Soho clubs that were doomed to disappear after three months, and was a lucky dog for having done so. She had been standing at the bar in the same black dress and silver heels she was wearing tonight. He had singled her out among the bony suburban stalkers, recognising a timeless appeal in her that eluded the other girls in the room, who were dressed like Victoria Beckham and were out of date in the latest outfits. Danuta was visiting London with her sister, and had managed to slip away for a few precious, thrilling hours. She had come to enjoy the atmosphere of a London bar, and wasn't interested in meeting anyone. Her lack of desperation separated her from the crowd. The three of them had danced together, and ended up back at Josh's flat.

Danuta stayed around the next day, although there were urgent whispered arguments with her sister on the phone. Tousled and hungover, she peered out from Josh's white towelling robe with the sleeves rolled up, the dark flame of a votive candle. There was an indefinable sadness beneath her surface that flickered in moments of lost concentration.

Nick cooked them all breakfast. Danuta read the papers, commenting on stories. Josh sat at the kitchen table, smoking and looking anxious. The situation felt unusual.

Josh's suggestion—to come to Poland and bring her back to London—caught them all by surprise. Two months had passed since they met, and in that time he had not mentioned her once.

Danuta accepted a bottle of oak-flavoured vodka from the barman, and set

it down before them. As they drank, she picked at the silver label with an ebony nail and confided in Josh, outlining her reservations about the elopement. The couple had an intensity that left Nick feeling aware of his status as the single friend dragged along for support.

Looking around the bar, he studied the carved wooden rabbits and chickens on the counters and side tables. They covered virtually every surface, inane but curiously touching. Yellow gingham curtains, pickled fruits in great glass jars, bouquets of dried flowers, plaited loaves of bread suspended on the walls; it was like being in some kind of fairytale woodcutter's cottage. The place was cosy and comfortable, and the vodka dropped a warming root through his chest. There were only four other people in the place, all old men. It felt like four in the morning.

He heard Josh ask Danuta where everyone was, and she told them that people stayed home most of the time.

'It's not a typical Polish town,' she explained. 'They don't like strangers here and barely even talk to each other, except in church or the shops.'

'Why is that?' Nick asked.

Danuta shook the fingers of her right hand, a universal gesture of dismissal. 'Oh, you know, bad things. Old history. They don't like to forget, even though they should let go of the past.'

'That's why you have to leave this place,' said Josh. 'Did you tell your parents about your plans?'

'I wanted to, but I could find no way of explaining.' Josh had suggested that she should post them a letter before she left, then come to London and get waitress work until something better came along.

'So you didn't tell anyone at all?' Josh asked.

'Well.' She thought for a moment, framing her words. 'I told some of my closest friends—but not my family. It is difficult for them to know how I feel. My father is old. He would not understand.'

And there the matter was left.

Grandpapa should have been proud to be selected for such an important position, but a sense of foreboding crept through his bones every time he hauled himself up

onto the footplate of the Arkangel. Men had died building the train, and what
was this grand machine to be used for? Ferrying the directors and a lucky handful
of the town's best families on pleasure trips to the seaside!

Food had been scarce in the town of late. Even the price of turnips had
soared so much that people no longer fed shavings to the pigs. But no expense was
to be spared on the train. The priests said it would bring new prosperity to the
town, but lately they had been proven wrong every time they opened their
mouths.

Sighing, grandpapa adjusted his cap and signalled to the driver. With an
angry blast of steam, the shining behemoth rolled forward out of the station.

Nick had the impression that Danuta thought Josh would get serious with
her when they returned to London, and then she could tell her sister and her
father. But to anyone who knew him, settling down was clearly the last thing
on Josh's mind.

The distance between their future dreams made Nick uncomfortable,
because he saw the situation from both sides. He wanted to encourage Josh
to be honest, but did not know how best to broach the subject.

While they ate platefuls of *perogi* and drank more vodka, Nick figured out
what to do. Knowing that Danuta would have to go home to her parents'
house tonight, he decided to take Josh to a bar in town, where he could sit
him down in a quiet corner.

Except that nothing went according to plan. When he suggested going for
a late drink Danuta announced that she was coming with them, and they
could hardly turn her down. The trio left the inn and headed toward the only
open bar in Chelmsk.

The great dark churches dominated the town, forbidding and somehow
unwholesome, their decaying walls patched and repaired where wartime
bullets had taken their toll. It was so quiet that the click of their shoes echoed
against the peeling buildings. A series of tin lamps, suspended across the
empty cobbled street, formed sharp cones of yellow light. They passed a peculiar poster for gypsum cement that featured three bald plasterers, a gate
topped with a statue of a bear in striped trousers, and a shop with a giant

carrot in the window. On every street there was at least one building with a disproportionately tall gothic tower. There was no graffiti anywhere.

'I've never been anywhere as weird as this,' Josh said. 'It's like everyone's gone away.'

'They just remain asleep,' Danuta replied, somewhat mysteriously. 'The people here are very private. Too many years of trouble. Twice before in the last century nearly everyone in this town suffered badly. First during the war, then under the communists. Many were taken away. Many died. The ones who survived do not like to forget.'

'Are you sure this bar will be open?' Josh was shivering. He hadn't brought a sweater with him, and a chill wind was pushing down the temperature.

'It is owned by an old friend of mine,' she assured them. 'He knows I am going away. He will be open for us tonight.'

A small blue neon sign, *Artyk Bar*, hung behind railings in the basement of a tall grey building with scabby cement walls, as if ashamed to announce that it was open at all. Danuta held the gate back for them. Inside was another cosy, wintry room filled with the smell of spiced roast pig, but the spit had been cleaned and there was no indication that the place had ever experienced custom. The CD player was spinning something Nick took to be Polish pop, or possibly an album of Eurovision Song Contest winners.

The man behind the counter was wearing a richly patterned sweater of the kind you could only find in rural Europe. There were red and yellow elks dancing around his neck. He shook their hands with an old-world solemnity that belied his youth, introducing himself as Idzi, short for something unpronounceable. He was pleased to see Danuta, less thrilled to meet her new male friends. After a few vodkas he warmed and became talkative, but it was obvious that he used to go out with her and wished they had not broken up. He asked about London, the music, the clubs, the cost of clothes. He had come here from Gdansk when he was fourteen. Gdansk was cool, there was a lot to do at night, this town was too quiet for him. They answered his questions and drank. You could smoke in the bar—Idzi was surprised when they asked permission.

A couple of young guys in grey hoods and leather jackets came in, regular customers. They looked bored and vaguely angry. As they ordered beers at

the bar they kept looking across at Danuta, and were clearly talking about her.

'Do you have a history with these guys?' asked Josh.

'No,' said Danuta vehemently. 'They go to the same church as my parents.'

The boys kept looking. When Idzi was called over to share their drinks, a rift formed in the company. Small towns were the same the world over; everyone knew each other, outsiders were to be pitied or envied in equal measure.

Idzi asked Danuta to come over and join his pals. He was polite enough, seeking his guests' permission to take her away, but as she rose, Nick felt something bad. 'She's Catholic,' he reminded Josh. 'She's clearly torn up about the idea of leaving her home and family behind. Would you do that for her? Just don't screw around with her when we get back to London.'

'What do you mean?'

Josh was excited about having such a breathtaking girl hanging around with him, but he wasn't going to stay faithful for long. He liked Nick, he was someone whose advice you'd listen to. He was earnest and corruptible.

'She wants to get out of here, Nick.'

'She seems conflicted.'

'I'm not dragging her away. She's old enough to look after herself.'

'You're not just going to dump her on the street if you break up with her.'

'Let's drop it.'

They drank too much. Another bottle of vodka was opened, and that was soon reduced to empty glasses and a few sticky rings on the table. Idzi and Danuta came back to join them with a fresh bottle, a local brand without a label, possibly homemade. That was when the trouble kicked off.

Idzi and Danuta had been arguing in their own language, and it was obvious that the barman thought his former girlfriend was making a big mistake.

'Hey, she can make up her own mind,' Josh interrupted.

'I know what I am doing,' Danuta agreed. 'I am not a child.'

'You went to London and he seduced you,' accused Idzi. 'You broke your vows.'

'Oh Idzi, don't be such a child—'They lost the rest of her reply as she switched into Polish.

Idzi started to shout. The change in him was sudden and frightening. Danuta was too good for them, they were fucking English pigs who should stay away from good Catholic girls, they should forget they ever met her and go back to their own country, where everyone knew the girls were all whores.

Josh pushed back from the table as Nick and Danuta attempted to keep him down. Idzi's pals looked as if they'd been waiting for this moment, and came over to join in. When Josh threw his shot-glass on the floor and tried to land a punch on Idzi he found himself pinned down by the others, who slammed him back against the food counter. He kicked out at them, but one of Idzi's friends picked up the grill's steel carving fork and swung it over Josh's face like a pendulum.

The Europop disc jammed on a particularly inane phrase. It took Nick a moment to work out what was happening. He suddenly imagined Josh stuck like a moth on a pin, pierced through the cheek as one of the fork's tines held him in place on the counter's oak carving board. The boys were feinting at each other, jabbing and dancing back to a safe distance, but somehow the fork connected and raised a single crimson tear just below Josh's eye.

As Josh threw himself at the others, Nick pushed Idzi out of the way and snatched the fork back before any more damage could be done. Danuta screamed 'Stój!', and Nick was finally able to pull Josh aside.

The trio followed them, tumbling out of the club, with Nick and Danuta pulling at Josh. The wound on his face was mean but not serious. Idzi was throwing out a good line in nationalistic slurs, but the worst seemed to be over. At least the police hadn't been called.

Idzi must have landed one insult too many, because suddenly Josh slipped from their hands and ran back, kneeing the barman in the groin, kicking at his head as he went down. Nick forced Danuta to stay where she was, but by the time he got there things were serious. Josh kicked hard at Idzi's face, the alcohol instantly drawing blood to his flesh. Nick tried to haul him back, but could not stop the blows from hammering down. He heard the sound of Idzi's head repeatedly cracking against the foot of the railings, and it made him feel sick because he knew that the boy was being killed.

When Josh stopped, it was as if he suddenly realised what he was doing. Swaying from side to side, he seemed barely able to stand. He stared down

blankly at the writhing body on the pavement. Nick examined Idzi's face. Under the blue neon his blood was black as spilled oil. He was still conscious, moaning softly. Nick realised there was a good chance that his skull had been damaged.

Danuta pulled at the pair of them, repeating 'You have to go,' over and over again. Idzi's pals had run off, but she felt sure they would soon return with others.

The hotel was silent and asleep. They had not unpacked their bags, so it was easy to leave. Idzi knew where the visitors were staying—there wasn't anywhere else in town. His friends would quickly figure it out. As soon as Danuta said she would settle up with the manager, Nick knew that she wasn't planning to come back with them.

'It's the only way,' she said. ''They'll see that I'm still here and will realise they beat you. That's all they want.'

Danuta kissed Nick and gave Josh the briefest of hugs; she could not bring herself to do more. She watched them go, but Josh did not look back. There was no chance of finding a taxi—they had picked up the incoming one at the airport—but the train station was less than a mile away, so they set off on foot.

Heading along streets that sloped away to open parkland, they passed the biggest cemetery they had ever seen, hundreds of identical bone-white headstones stretching away to the treeline. They tried to keep moving along the shifting edge of the shadows, but the moon was bright enough to reveal them. Nick was convinced that they were going to be jumped and dragged back into the dark reaches of the undergrowth.

They were making a run for it across the clear green space of the park when the others came back, six or seven of them pounding at the ground with planks and iron rods, yelling and wheeling from beneath the trees. Nick could see that the only chance they had of outrunning the gang was to ditch their cumbersome travel bags. It meant losing his new iPod, but that was a small price to pay for not being kicked to death. He shouted at Josh and they threw their cases onto the grass, hoping their pursuers would stop to gather the spoils. Pelting toward the shuttered cafeteria that stood on the far side of the park, they ran into the alley behind and found that it connected through the

backs of houses on the main street. By keeping to the pathway they were able to stay shielded in darkness. Nick could hear Josh gasping raggedly beside him. His chest burned with the effort of drawing breath, but he kept up the pace until he could be sure that they had not been followed.

The squat, featureless whitewashed station stood at the end of a straight lane of pollarded trees, and was entirely in darkness. It was around 3:00am, and according to the noticeboard the first train out was not due for six hours. They could only hope Idzi's pals would not bother heading for the station once they realised that Danuta had elected to stay behind.

Nick and Josh walked the length of the platform and saw that the waiting room was open. It was dry and clean, and smelled of coal dust. There were wooden benches to sleep on. The authorities were clearly more trusting in Poland—in London, Josh said, the room would have been filled with rough-sleepers and junkies.

They were stone-sharp and sober now. 'Keep near the door,' Nick told him. 'We have to be able to get out fast if they turn up.'

Josh's face was still weeping blood. His right eye was sore and darkly crusted. Nick had a fierce headache, but he had left the aspirins behind in his overnight bag. He knew they could probably pay to jump an earlier flight, but they still had to reach the airport in one piece. After a few minutes their breathing returned to normal and they settled down on the benches, sinking low beneath the waiting room window, out of sight.

Nick pulled his coat tight. The sky was as glossy as black leather, studded with stars to the tops of the trees. There were no friendly lights to be found in the landscape. Nothing but the barren ice-chill of a country night.

A few minutes later he was disturbed by a faint noise. Twisting his neck, he looked up at the window. The planets above had all but vanished. Clouds were blotting them out.

He heard the noise again, an uneven tinging sound like ice splitting under a frozen lake. As he listened it evolved and grew, a steady clink like keys swinging from a chain, a rattle backed by the hiss of compressed air. His muscles had frozen on the hard bench, but he swung down his legs and forced himself outside.

The wind was rising, blasting bitter gusts along the platform. He saw two

things; at one end of the canopy, the zigzag of electric torches backed by dark
human shapes, moving quickly toward them. At the other end, the distant
black bulk of an engine riding the silvered track. Jets of vapour appeared
above it.

'Get up,' he hissed at Josh, 'I think there's a train.'

'It's not due for hours.'

'You'd better hope there is one, 'cause I think they've found us.'

Josh stumbled out onto the platform and looked along the line. 'It has to
be a goods train, it won't stop, otherwise it would have been on the timetable.'

Nick could clearly discern the outlines of several men now. They were
silently running across the coal-black shale between the tracks, heading for
the station stairs. He looked back at the train, a wavering shape that
announced its arrival through the singing steel below the platform. Squares
of yellow light bounced over the scrubland beside the line. 'It's a passenger
train,' he confirmed.

*The maiden voyage of the Arkangel set the pattern for trips to come. The directors
occupied the front carriage. Their respected guests spread through the second and
third. As the train chuntered amiably through Wolsztyn, the parents pointed it
out to their children; this was where the carriages had been so expertly crafted.
Sandwiches were consumed as the train plunged on through dense forest. Conversation became more sporadic. The fathers fell quiet while their wives tended to
the children. It was only when the conductor passed through the car with two
officers at his back that the mood changed to uncertainty.*

The rhythm of the wheels beat further apart. The train was slowing. As the
engine passed trailing clouds of steam, Nick registered the elaborate brass
plate fixed below the driver's door: *Arkangel*. He looked over his shoulder
and saw that the men were already on the platform. He could hear them
shouting. They would attack long before the train could be boarded.

As the two events converged, one overtook the other. The men were less
than thirty metres away. The train was not slowing fast enough. Its brakes

squealed, but the windows continued to flash past. Nick watched in helpless panic.

Suddenly the group stopped running. They came no closer.

The end-of-carriage door appeared beside Josh. It had an old-fashioned brass handle, not the electric kind controlled by the driver, and they were able to haul themselves inside. Idzi's gang stood motionless, staring at them in bewilderment.

The *Arkangel* had barely come to a halt before it began to draw out of the station once more. Beyond the far end of the platform was a level crossing. Perhaps it had merely slowed down as a safety precaution.

They made their way along the corridor. The windows threw harsh light on the startled faces of their enemies. They showed neither anger nor disappointment at the escape. As the train cleared the platform, Nick lowered the nearest window and watched the station recede into blackness. The men had clicked off their torches and were already starting to disperse. It made no sense. Nothing about the night was making any sense.

Nick took in their surroundings. The locomotive was an old steam engine, attached to a tender. It rode the rails sounding as if it had a beating metal heart. He had seen such machines in movies, but had never been aboard one. The carriages were old and shabbily luxurious, compartmented salons finished in green and cream paintwork, with inlaid wood panels and opaque glass light mantels.

Letting themselves into one of the single compartments, they settled on green baize seats. The heating was off, but at least they were getting away. Nick smelled mothballs and damp wood, coal, tobacco and cracked old leather.

The train had picked up speed and was now racing through dark woodlands.

'I had a map,' he announced. 'It was in my travel bag. I think there's only one railway line running out of Chelmsk. We have to reach the coast eventually.'

Josh wiped a bloody smear across his cheek and closed his eyes. There was nothing to do but settle back and wait for the ticket inspector to reach them. They still had their wallets, passports and credit cards.

'Have you looked at this train?' Nick asked him. 'The sconces have brass birds on them.'

'*Sconces?*' repeated Josh, opening one eye, incredulous. 'What the hell are you on about?'

'The fittings, the light fittings. They're carved like birds of prey. The same design is etched on the mirrors.'

Josh squinted up. 'Are they wearing crowns?'

'Yeah.'

'They're eagles,' he said, yawning. 'Polish eagles. It's an old train, what do you expect.'

The weather was turning. The clouds that had buried the stars were now lowering over the treetops. Rain began to patter against the windows. The train laboured up an incline. Blasts of steam were rhythmically expelled from the engine's lungs. The carriage rocked back and forth like a crib, but Nick was too wired to sleep. The rain beat audibly on the roof.

He felt the carriage pass over a set of points. Rising, he swayed out into the corridor, pushed down the window once more and looked over. The train had passed onto a branch line that consisted of single track. The forest was so close now that the branches of trees were brushing the sides of the carriage.

'I'm going to see if there's anyone else on board,' he called back to Josh. 'I think we just left the main line.'

'Do what you want.' Josh rolled his head against the seat's antimacassar, summoning sleep.

Nick tacked along the rocking corridor. The crowned brass eagles were on the walls here, too, their wings outstretched. Josh was right; it was the Polish eagle. But these were different. Their talons were knotted together by a coiled, scaly snake. Brass door handles were anchored with spiked, feathery wings. There were more snakes, cut into the moiré patterns of the woodwork, stitched into the green linen blinds, etched in the glass panels of the compartment windows.

There were only three carriages. In the third he found an elderly conductor, avuncular and dusty, with a luxuriant grey moustache. Seated on a tiny fold-down banjo stool, he had managed to fall asleep, which was a skill in itself.

His uniform was not standard Polrail issue. A badge sewn onto his cap depicted the eagle tethered by the serpent. Nick shook him gently. The conductor seemed surprised to see him, and asked him something in Polish.

'I'm sorry, I don't understand.'

'I am asking where did you get on?'

'At Chelmsk.'

'We do not often stop there anymore.' He sounded as if he might fall back to sleep at any moment.

'Well, you slowed down long enough to climb aboard.' Nick tugged his wallet free of his jeans pocket. 'Can I buy two tickets?'

'You do not need tickets.'

'Surely I have to—ah—'

'You have made a mistake by boarding this train.'

'You don't go to the coast?'

'No, we don't.'

'Well, is there a station where we can get a connection?'

'There is, and we must stop there, but it is not for you.' He checked his watch and rose on old bones, grimacing. 'If you knew about us you would not be here at all.'

'It slowed down, so we got on.'

'Well, you would not have done so.' The conductor was turning to go, moving with difficulty, as if he was walking on artificial legs. Nick noticed that the knees of his trousers had been ripped and badly restitched by hand.

'Hey, it was an innocent mistake.' Nick had no idea why he was apologizing.

'No-one is innocent on board the *Arkangel*.' He passed through the connecting passage into darkness.

Nick made his way back along the carriages, passing the length of the train, but there was no-one else in any of the compartments. He returned to the sleeping Josh and sat opposite with his forehead against the cold glass, watching the streaking rain. A sudden compression of air in the carriage told him they were rushing through a station. A sign flashed before his eyes, defying him to comprehend it; *Wolsztyn*. Then it was gone and they were back out in open countryside.

The wheels beat against the rail joints with a comforting *dickety-dack*. You never heard that sound on British trains anymore. The carriage rocked back and forth. The window shades rattled. A white flash illuminated the horizon, throwing the forest into relief. Seven, eight seconds, then thunder. The next gap was smaller. They were rolling into the storm.

Josh twisted in his sleep. In the mists of his mind he could discern the faint outlines of menacing grey faces with dark eyes and open mouths. He was backing away from them along an endless raised platform, but was moving too slowly to stay beyond their reach. The poor yearning creatures were ragged and thin, barely corporeal, more like charcoal drawings than flesh and blood. They extended their arms desperately in his direction, moving nearer, yet even as he felt the brush of their cold fingers he thought they would not harm him. They merely sought human warmth. Their unwashed stench rose in his throat as they swarmed on every side, pressing their filthy hands into his mouth, pushing down against his ears and eyes, pulling him away from the world of the living . . .

He awoke with a jolt and fled into the corridor, just as the storm broke overhead. Shaking, he made his way to the end of the carriage.

It was impossible to tell how long Nick had been asleep when the change of rhythm began to dispel his dreams. The train was slowing, emerging from a forest of silver birches. He opened his eyes and found the seat opposite empty. Stretching, he wiped a fan of condensation from the window and peered out.

A station, even colder and darker than the one they had left.

Hearing a carriage door bang open, he jumped up and left the compartment. Josh was ahead of him, already on the station platform. The train was bright and silent, the only source of light.

'Josh, what are you doing? Wait for me.' Nick ran after him, grabbing his arm. 'What's the matter?'

Josh looked back wildly. A moment later, his eyes dulled. 'I had a dream.' He looked around. 'Where the hell are we?'

There was a green metal sign on a pole. It read *Ordzandzin Depot*. There was no-one on the platform. The station looked as if it hadn't been used in years. The waiting train was silent, waiting, its bright empty compartments

far more appealing than the derelict station. They saw the silhouette of the conductor pausing to look at them as he passed along the carriage.

Josh walked along the platform to the stationmaster's office. He tried the door but it was locked. On the elaborate wooden arch above the lintel, picked out in red and gold, was the same carved symbol of the Polish eagle, its feet tethered by a coiling, fanged serpent.

'What do you think that means?'

'I don't know,' Josh shrugged. 'Eastern European shit. Look around. This place is shut. Why would they even stop here?' Beyond the station canopy rain continued to fall in a thick grey mist, removing all visual cues, deadening all sound.

Against the wall stood a row of rusting trolleys. Each one contained an empty leather sack with an unknotted drawstring at its mouth.

A square of yellowed paper blew along the platform, sticking itself against Nick's shoe. He reached down and picked it up. A flyer of some kind, dense Polish handwriting, a crude drawing of the train with the smoke from its stack transformed into a pointing hand. Exclamation marks, incomprehensible bullet-pointed commands of some kind. He screwed it up and let it fall.

The papers handed out to the passengers had a strange request printed upon them. For the sake of safety, it was desired that all valuables were to be handed to the officers for safekeeping before the train's arrival at Ordzandzin Depot. This included all wrist and pocket watches, wallets, fountain pens, rings, brooches, necklaces, tie-clips, bracelets, earrings, cufflinks, money clips and loose change. Furthermore, any important documents, including all identity papers, deeds of covenant and documents pertaining to property or wills should be handed in at the same time. In certain cases, the gentlemen would be required to write a short note of explanation to their nearest relatives in Chelmsk.

The uncertainty turned to fear now, especially when one of the children saw his family's belongings being unceremoniously tipped into a leather station bag and carted away on a trolley.

———

'What do you think we should do?'

'Man, anywhere has got to be better than here.'

Nick cocked his head. 'What is that noise?'

'I don't hear anything.'

'You can't hear that?' He loped along the platform of the derelict depot, listening to the sounds beneath the falling rain. Distant voices, a great many of them, but low and keening, now rising together in sorrow, crossing from harmonious melancholy to grotesque discord with such ease that he might have been listening to the wind in the trees. He tried to see beyond the canopy, but a sheet of rainwater was falling from the broken gutter on the roof, obscuring his view. There were darker patches just past the platform edge that looked like forlorn human figures standing in the rain, defined by raindrops.

There were hundreds of them, watching expectantly.

'We have to get out of here,' he called back, but received no answer. Turning, he found Josh holding a brown sack against him. The sack had a head of glossy black hair.

'Danuta?'

She was shaking with cold. 'I couldn't stay,' she explained, letting the burlap fall to the floor.

'How did you get here?'

'I borrowed Johann's car. I went to the station but saw the others arrive on the platform. I couldn't go in. Then I saw the train come through.'

'How did you manage to beat it here?'

'The road is new, it is much faster.'

'You knew the train would stop at this station?'

'It has to. The Ordzandzin Depot is a supply stop.'

Josh looked back at the idling train. 'But it isn't picking anything up.'

'No, the station is here to receive supplies, not provide them. You cannot get out here. There is nowhere to go.'

'What do you mean? Where does the train stop next?'

'There is one further destination beyond this. The Lubicza Terminus. That is the only reason why the *Arkangel* exists. Then the train heads back along the same line, but on the way back it does not call at Ordzandzin Depot. For now we are safer on board the train. But we will have to find a way to escape.'

'You're not making any sense,' said Josh, exasperated. The rain-battered shapes beyond the platform were shifting back and forth, becoming more agitated by the second. Their voices were rising above the wind and rain.

Behind them, the train's whistle blew. Moments later, the carriages started to move along the platform.

Danuta pulled at their sleeves. 'We must go.' They paced alongside the departing train and hauled themselves back on board just as it began to pick up speed. Nick watched the retreating figures of the naked dead standing beside the station in the downpour, his face pressed against the cold glass.

'What is going on here?' he asked Danuta. 'Why would a train like this run when it has no passengers?'

'It does have passengers.' She stared at him anxiously, willing him to understand. 'It has us.'

'Come in here.' Nick pushed her into the compartment. 'Why won't you tell us the truth? You saw those people back at the depot, didn't you?'

'They would not have let you leave. I told you, no-one like you can survive for long at the Ordzandzin Depot.'

'Then how did they let you get through onto the platform?'

'I am from Chelmsk. I am one of them.'

'You're not making any sense, Danuta,' he shouted at her.

'It is our fault that the train is here.' She took his hand. 'We don't have long before we reach the terminus. Listen to me carefully.'

The mood on board was very different now. Even the children had begun to sense that something was wrong. A couple of them cried that they wanted to go home, but were sternly admonished by their parents. No-one could truly believe their worst fears. It was a modern world. An explanation would be proffered, belongings would be returned with profuse apologies, the day would end well enough. Calculations were made about how long it would take to reach the coast. The fathers attempted to jolly their wives and children into happier moods.

Then, as the Arkangel slowed across the windswept plain toward its final stop, they saw the great dark bulk of the Lubicz Terminus approaching and began to fear for their children's lives.

Danuta looked anxiously at the darkening fields. 'My town—you ask why there are so many churches—three hundred years ago there were many more. All the priests in this part of our homeland came from our small town. It was one of the most pious and holy places in the country. But priests are supposed to be celibate, and even if our men of God were not, the children they sired were drowned in secret. In time our population declined. The farms began to die. The shops closed. The town elders met to decide what must be done. To increase the population they needed people who were not Catholic. They brought in Jews.' She glanced nervously from the window. The train was racing at great speed through forests of rain-lashed larches. 'The town grew again. By 1935 it was more prosperous than it had ever been—too prosperous. We were far from the German border, but not so far that we could ever forget what might happen, either. We were one of the first towns to suffer, but few knew of our plight. The piety of Chelmsk went against us; over the centuries, its ancient fortifications had been repaired and strengthened. Walls that had once been designed to keep invaders out now kept the residents in. Still, my grandparents thought they were safe. No-one saw that the churches which sheltered us would eventually be used to imprison our own families until the train could arrive. Who knew such things then?'

Nick could feel the train starting to slow down. Danuta rose in alarm, but he pushed her back into her seat. 'Keep talking,' he warned.

'We did not know that members of the *Sicherheitsdienst* were living among us. One day the newly appointed security officers announced that the town was to be closed for reasons of racial impurity. For too long there had been much mixing of blood. It was our great strength, and it was to become our curse. A work camp had been opened at Lubicza, and although we did not know then, our people were to fill it.

'My town had many blacksmiths and factory workers, men used to tempering metal. In 1940 we were instructed to build a train, a special express under the sole command of the *Sicherheitsdienst* commandants. It was to be a great honour for our town. They asked our families to choose the most well-loved man on the council to become the conductor in charge of the train. He would be privileged to oversee every level of its daily operation. That man was my grandfather.'

'The *Arkangel* was used to deliver your townsfolk to the work camp,' said Nick. Suddenly he understood the meaning of the symbol; the crowned Polish eagle restrained by a mighty serpent, the symbol of a new German empire being tested out here for the first time, a dry run for the entire world.

'Each time the train left Chelmsk, a few of the town's finest families were taken along with the commandants. There was no panic, only deception. They were told there was a spa resort, that they would return in a few days. When the train reached Ordzandzin, they were ordered to surrender all their valuables, their personal property. Money, watches, even the deeds to their houses, everything they had been advised to bring on the journey. It was collected and thrown out into the leather bags at the Depot. Sometimes people made a run for it when the train stopped. They would push their children out on the platform, only to see them shot dead before their eyes.'

'How long was it before the townspeople realised what was happening?'

'The commandants insisted that those families who left had elected to stay on the coast in places of greater safety. Sometimes they returned keepsakes that had been collected at the Ordzandzin Depot as proof of their wellbeing. When people ask how could the Nazis do this under the very noses of the people, this is how; by keeping any whisper of truth carefully hidden. People can be very naïve when they want to believe. My grandfather knew, because he stayed on the train until it had been emptied at Lubicza. But he could not live with the terrible burden of his work. One night, he called a secret meeting at the town council, and told them about the true purpose of the *Arkangel*. But among the people he told was a junior member of the *Sicherheitsdienst*. They took him to the siding where the train waited, and slowly drove it over his legs. They wanted the names of those he told. He took three days to die.' She looked to the window, but might have been seeing the world from a million miles away. 'Before the war there were nearly three and a half million Jews living in Poland. By the time it ended, less than 300,000 were still alive.'

'What are you saying, that this is a ghost train?'

'No, I said you would never understand. There is no secret to this story. I told you, people remember the past. They know what happened. It's said that after the war, the train was left in the sheds at Chelmsk. The engine was broken up for spare parts, and finally the carriages were sold to Polrail for use

on the passenger line. But there were stories, things seen and heard that could not be possible. So the *Arkangel* really did become a ghost train—in the sense that it was shunned by the living.'

The train was leaving the larch forest, heading out into the open plain that stood before the terminus. 'Believe what you like. The train is real. It runs when it has to. It cannot take me back to Chelmsk. I must alight at the Terminus.'

'You must tell me everything, Danuta. What will happen to us?'

She was trying not to cry. 'After the war the town was almost deserted. Those with any so-called impurity had been removed. Every remaining resident became precious to us. The town could not lose any more of its inhabitants. This is why the train exists. To keep the families of those who survived from leaving, and to remove those who are tainted, or who would lead them away. This is all my fault. I never saw the *Arkangel* before it appeared tonight.' She pressed the back of the hand against the cold metal door. It felt as solid and real as any national Polrail train she had ever caught. 'I am so sorry.'

The *Arkangel*'s brakes screeched and they were thrown forward. Out in the corridor, they could see the dark mass of the Lubicza Terminus thrown into relief against the night sky.

The convex roof of the train shed was backed by a large brick building topped with a square tower at either end. In a stroke of architectural arrogance, the crematorium chimneys had been built into the very fabric of the terminus. The building's crenellated gables reminded Nick of those on London's own railway cathedral, St Pancras Station. Between the chimneys, beneath the mocking spiked spires that rose along the edge of the steep roof, the eagle symbol was repeated in iron—but here it had changed form. The eagle had been crushed entirely by the triumphant snake that entwined its body.

There was only one railway track into the terminus. The platform extended on either side of the train. Here, grey linen sacks stood in metal frames, ready to receive the clothes of the passengers. They would panic now, of course, sensing their fate just as cattle led to the slaughterhouse would fear the smell of death. But everything about the station was designed to do one thing, and

one thing only; to herd the passengers forward toward the building's interior, through its great iron gates.

When the officers demanded that they strip their children and then themselves, a raw terror set in. From the windows they could see the passengers in the carriage ahead of them stumbling onto the platform. Their bare white nudity was profoundly shocking. The children were screaming and sobbing now, their naked mothers pawed and prodded by the guards, the men sometimes punched in the low spine with the butts of rifles if they questioned what was happening. Some of the older ones fell, and were trampled underfoot. An old woman with bloody dentures hanging from her mouth lay screaming and clutching at the passing legs until one of the officers of the Sicherheitsdiens stuck a bayonet into her soft lower belly and dragged it upward, eviscerating her. After that, it was decided that no-one should ever be killed on the concourse; the terrified crowd became too difficult to control. Lessons were quickly learned in the management of the damned.

'Where is Josh?' Danuta asked, looking around. 'He must not get off the train.' She looked into Nick's uncomprehending eyes. 'He's a Jew who seduced a daughter of the town.'

'He didn't seduce you, Danuta, you know what happened, it was a crazy night, we were all drunk and fooling around, we got carried away—'

'I'm pregnant, Nick. And I don't know whose child I'm carrying, whether it's Josh's or yours. What does that make me in the eyes of the dead? At best I am a whore. At worst, I'm carrying the child of a Jew who is also a murderer. Idzi is dead. He died on the street while you were reaching the station. Josh will be taken and so will I. None of us is innocent. We're not like those who died before.'

'Last stop,' called the conductor from somewhere further along the carriage. 'All those for Lubicza Terminus alight here.'

'Have you told Josh about the baby?'

'No, I thought if I hid the truth from him he would be able to leave, and

perhaps there was even a chance for me. I should have known there was no way out.'

'Your grandfather, can't he do something?'

'He is as much a prisoner here as everyone else.'

'There.' Nick pointed along the corridor at the figure framed in the doorway. 'Josh, stay on the train!'

Josh was stepping out onto the platform. Behind him, the conductor, Danuta's grandfather, stood impassive and unable to prevent any change in the fate of his passengers.

'God, look at this,' Josh called, looking up at the span of the roof as he walked further onto the concourse. Behind him a wall of sound was rising, a cry of terror so dense and discordant that it seemed like one great voice. It broke over them in waves, splintering into individual human voices, pleading, panicked, fearful, the voices of those who would do anything at all in order to draw one more breath.

Nick had no choice but to go after him. Josh was walking away. There was no time to explain. He grabbed Josh's wrist and tried to pull him back. 'We have to stay on board,' he warned, tugging hard.

'What, and go all the way back again, are you crazy? Listen to that, what the hell is that?' The wave was growing, towering above them, ready to crash.

'Josh, stay with me.' The distance between them and the *Arkangel* was lengthening. Nick knew that the further he moved from the train, the less chance he would ever have of getting back.

Danuta stepped down and joined them on the platform, but just as she did so they were hit by the breaking force of passing bodies. It was like being caught in a sudden rush-hour; as though everyone who had ever passed through the terminus had reappeared at the exact same instant, a living wall of flesh and bone that broke them apart with great force and swept them aside.

Josh's fingers rose and pawed the air to grasp at Danuta's hand. For a moment the connection was made and held, but then Danuta was torn from him, dragged down by those even more desperate. Nick launched himself forward and scrambled toward the pair of them, climbing on the backs and shoulders of the dispersing dead.

He could see the others clearly, but they were moving out of reach in the great churning sea of flesh. He was surrounded by the fearful faces of those about to die, each held in impression rather than detail. Their tormentors—men merely recruited to perform a duty, after all, replaceable faceless servants—were corporeally unrepresented in this seething nightmare. Goaded and panicked, the naked howling mass rushed forward toward the gates. High above them, crimson sparks danced in the ash-laden smoke that belched from the glowing chimney furnaces. The entrance to the crematorium was packed with rushing bodies; everyone who had passed this way, all at once. No fires of hell had ever born witness to such eager damnation.

Nick fought to stay afloat in the eddying mass, shouting after Josh as he was borne away toward the gates. Danuta resurfaced near him, and his fist connected with her raised wrist. He pulled hard. He would return her to the carriage and force her to ride the train back to Chelmsk. He would persuade her to surrender her unborn child, a trade that meant saving her own life. She had known the consequences of boarding the *Arkangel*. He owed her a debt of honour. More, he knew he loved her. He yelled at her to hold on, but the sound of his voice was lost beneath a million others.

He felt himself being carried backwards toward the open door of the train carriage, turning and tipping until he had lost all sense of balance or direction. When he managed to upright himself he saw the *Arkangel*'s pistons starting to pump, saw the conductor haul himself up into the train on shattered legs. Before the carriage door was slammed shut he glimpsed Danuta one last time. She had found Josh close beside her, and although they could not touch she seemed to draw comfort in his proximity. She looked around for Nick, saw him climbing to his feet in the doorway of the train, and placidly studied his face. Her eyes told him something else, that the child in her belly was his. As if she was freed by imparting this knowledge, she no longer resisted the movement of the crowd but complied with her fate, twisting toward the gates and brick chambers beyond like an exhausted swimmer drifting through an ocean of souls.

When he looked back at the scene through a caul of tears, he found that she and Josh were already lost from view.

The whistle shrieked and the train began to shunt once more. Through

blasts of steam and acrid coal-smoke Nick saw the station roll back and fade like a scene fragmented by migraine.

When he was finally able to raise his head once more and look from the window, all that remained was the empty plain, the ancient meadowlands, and the approaching forest of silver birches.

THE MISTAKE AT THE MONSOON PALACE ███████████

'ISKA KYADAAM HAL?'

'How much does this cost?'

Marion Wilson gave up trying to memorise the phrases. She looked up from her guidebook, switching her attention to the driver. 'Sorry, what did you say?'

'I said my cousin owns the best pashmina shop in Jaipur,' Shere told her. 'He will be honoured to make you a special deal because you are my valued client.'

Sure, she thought, *this guy is your cousin, your brother, your uncle, anyone other than some creep you cut deals with to rob rich, gullible Americans.* She impatiently tapped the guidebook with her forefinger, recalling the page about touts and conmen.

'I assure you, you will not find finer materials in all of India.'

'Forget it, Shere, it's not going to happen,' she told him. 'Trust me, I bought enough stuff yesterday to fill an extra suitcase.' In the three days that Shere had been appointed as her driver, they had visited jewelry stores selling silver bracelets that broke in half the first time you wore them, 'hand-woven' scarves produced by children in a Mumbai sweatshop and wooden statues of Ganesh that looked like they'd been speed-carved in the dark. 'Let's get on, it's already ten.'

'But Madam, this shop is of highest quality, government approved, everyone goes there, Richard Gere, everyone.' The driver was wobbling his head amiably. 'We stop for five minutes, no longer, and you do not have to buy if you do not wish.'

'Well, I do *not* wish.' She pulled a small plastic bottle of antiseptic wash from her trousers and poured a little of the blue liquid into her hands. She had been touching rupees so soft and brown that they looked as if they'd been used for—she dreaded to think what. She silently repeated the hygiene rule; right hand for taking money and greeting, because here the left hand was used as a substitute for toilet paper. Not that she was as pernickety as some. Iris, her companion from Ohio, had arrived in Delhi with an entire suitcase full of bottled water, which was taking things a little too far.

The little white taxi nosed its way back out of the crowded market square toward the main road, a dusty two-lane highway filled with overladen trucks, hay carts and sleeping cows. It was the end of the first week in July, and the monsoon season had yet to start, but the sky was dark with sinister cumulus. The ever-present pink mists that softened the views in every town they had visited had gone now, to be replaced by hot clear stillness. Marion wanted to open the window, to breathe something other than filtered freezing air, but could see black clouds of mosquitoes rising from ditches of dead water as the car passed.

Her attention drifted back to the guide book, which had fallen open on a list of Indian gods. The text was accompanied by tiny pastel drawings which made them all look the same. Bhairav. Ganesha. Hanuman. Rama. Shiva. Surya. Vishnu. Arrayed in lilac and yellow, blue and pink they rode birds, bore swords, cups, fire, tridents and bows, a vast network of deities who still seemed to hold some kind of power over the lives of ordinary people . . . she felt her eyes closing as the car swayed, and saw for a moment a bejeweled god lit by a curved prism of rubies and sapphires, spangling and spinning from his head. Feeling faint, she blinked the colours away.

She glanced up to the scenes rolling beyond the glass. Azure, crimson and sunflower bolts of cloth were stacked on the dirty pavement like a disassembled rainbow. The traffic was detouring around a buffalo that stood in the middle of the road, patiently chewing a plastic bag. It wore a gold-trimmed dress, its horns painted blue, its pierced ears laced with bells.

An ancient, bony man in a pink turban was squatting on the hard shoulder, cooking a chicken over an upright burning tyre.

A motorized rickshaw overtook them with two children and a piebald goat wedged inside it.

An elephant driver was asleep in a faded red *houdah*, waiting for tourist coaches that would not arrive—the latest wave of terrorist bombings had seen to that. A wedding band in yellow and silver uniforms was wearily donning the jackets they had dried on a row of thorn bushes.

A quartet of girls in identical yellow saris walked by, all listening to the same song on their mobile phones.

What do they think when they see me? Marion thought. *Do they even see me? Am I as invisible to them as they are in my country?*

What she first thought was a sparkling blue lake turned out to be a great ditch filled with empty plastic bottles.

'Where you want to go now?' the driver asked. Marion looked down at the guidebook in her lap and squinted at endless pages of forts and markets. Despite the low temperature in the vehicle, she felt overheated and fractious. She was still angry with Iris for deserting her five days into the trip. A few bouts of diarrhoea and she was calling her husband, making arrangements to return home. The secret was to keep tackling the spicy food until your stomach adjusted, Marion had been told. *You've an iron constitution,* her father had always said, *you're made of stronger stuff than your mother. You just have too much imagination.*

The driver had pulled the car over to the side of the road, and was talking to two young men with old faces, nondescript Indians of the type you saw everywhere, skinny and serious to the point of appearing mournful, with side partings and brown sweaters and baggy suit trousers hiding thin legs. Most of the men seemed to do nothing but sit around drinking *chai* while the women wielded pick-axes in rubble-filled vacant lots.

She tried to listen in on the conversation but realized they were speaking Hindi. 'Who are these people?' she asked, leaning forward between the head-rests.

'My brothers. They would like to get a lift. It is not far to their town.'

'I met your brothers three days ago, Shere, and these are not the same guys. You think everyone looks the same to foreigners? They don't, not anymore. Those days are over. These guys are not your brothers and cannot come in the car, it's out of the question. Besides, I thought we had to get to Jodhpur?'

'That is tomorrow. Today you may choose where you would like to go.'

To be honest, she was not entirely sure where they were going next. Everything on the itinerary sounded the same. She had picked it from four others on her travel agent's website. According to the schedule, she was staying in an old Maharajah's palace, a vast amber fortress that looked like a child's sandcastle in the photograph, now converted into a luxury hotel. She was tired of eating in ornate, deserted dining rooms. The only other tourists she had seen on the entire trip were a pair of elderly British ladies who seemed to be duplicating her trip town by town. Their reasons for coming to India mystified her, because she often overheard them sharply asking the waiters for poached eggs or sausages and toast, anything but Indian food.

She studied the arguing men from the window. Perhaps they were really his brothers. Everything here was designed to confuse, and everyone, it seemed had the same first impressions; the colours, the mess, the filth, the lost grandeur, the blurred light, the beautiful children . . . part of her wanted to explore the narrow backstreets alone, but the touts and beggars were simply too exhausting, and Shere insisted on remained by her side wherever she went. It was clearly considered too dangerous to let tourists explore for themselves. It seemed that they had to be brought in and unloaded, like boats being towed to docks.

But oh, the children. Tiny boys with withered feet or hands, dragging themselves along the central reservation of the road on little carts, kohl-eyed girls balancing crying babies on their hips, boys twirling coloured strings on their caps to attract attention or tapping with endless patience on the windows of idling cars, selling copies of Vogue, a grotesquely ironic choice of periodical to assign to a beggar. The country was a smashed mirror with some pieces reflecting the past, others the future. Between the tower blocks and tin-roofed slums a Dickensian tapestry was being endlessly unpicked and rewoven, a world where nothing could be achieved without carbon papers and rubber stamps, where ten did the work of one and one the work of ten.

Shere crunched the gears and pulled away from the men in some anger, swinging into the traffic without looking, so that trucks and rickshaws had to swerve from his path. 'So where do you want to go?' he asked, glancing at her in the mirror.

'I hadn't really—'

My relationship with this man has changed over the past week, she thought, holding onto the door strap. *He's so bored that he barely sees me. I thought I was in control, but now I wouldn't be able to do anything without him, and the further we get away from tourist spots, the more I am forced to rely on his services. The drivers run everything here.*

'Could you turn the air conditioning down for a while?' She flapped the guidebook at her breast.

He looked horrified by the idea, but did as she requested. She tried to study the book as they bounced through a convoy of trucks painted the shades of children's toys. Phrases swam up at her. 'Once known as the Land of Death'. 'Funeral pyres at dusk'. 'Nausea, cramps and exhaustion.' The pictures of the forts and palaces all looked the same; crenellated battlements, archways, turrets and domes. She turned the page. *Singh Pohl Monsoon Palace.* An ochre pavilion, perfectly proportioned, overgrown, surrounded by sandstone walkways and set on a perfectly square lake, the green water so still that it mirrored the building, doubling its size. She raised the book and pointed. 'I think I'd like to go here.'

He looked over his shoulder and studied the directions impassively. 'Forty five kilometers, maybe more. It is not on our route.'

She read from the guidebook. *Vishnu, the most human of all gods, still haunts the forests around the Singh Pohl Palace. A flute, a peacock feather and the colour blue announce his presence. An earlier temple to the god Parjanya exists upon this site.*

'Yeah, that's where I want to go.' A decision had been made. She could sleep for a while. Ted never came with her on vacations. He said he wanted to travel, but the truth was that he hated leaving the US, and complained so much when he did that he destroyed any pleasure in the trip. Ted was never around these days.

Her mouth was dry. Shere had provided iced water and hand-towels for her, but she wanted something else. She had bought a bag of *pedas* and fruit candies studded with cardamom seeds in the market. They had the kind of sharply spiced flavours you would never find at home.

They passed a partially constructed motorway on which just two men were working, slowing raking gravel in a manner that spread it across each other's

paths, each undoing the other's work. *How does anything run at all?* She wondered. *Over a billion people here, half of them shopkeepers selling nothing.*

Without the air conditioning she began to sweat. Her watch was gripping her wrist in a hot band, so she undid the clasp and dropped it in the bag at her feet. Pressing her head back into the rest, she studied the half-finished buildings of a small town slide by. Did no-one ever think to finish one house before starting another, or to plan the roads and pavements in such a way that prevented people from considering them interchangeable?

She liked the markets, the running and fetching, the tumble and bustle and sheer connectedness of everything. No-one seemed to be entirely alone, no matter how poor they were. Everyone had some kind of support system. At home she and Ted barricaded themselves in their gated community unlocked with an electronic key fob, and only saw the neighbours departing or arriving at holiday seasons. *If I needed help and couldn't get to the phone, I'd have to lie there until Ted got home,* she thought, *even assuming he was in town.*

The car screeched to a stop. In the road ahead, two half-starved dogs were fighting. One had buried its teeth in the other's left haunch. Loops of blood and spittle flecked the sidewalk as they rolled over each other. She opened the window an inch and the oppressive heat leaked in. Shere could not understand why his passenger was refusing the comfort of refrigerated air. *This place disgusts and frightens me,* she thought, *and yet I am drawn in. It makes me dream again.*

She was touring with three large pieces of Louis Vitton luggage. The driver did not seem to think this unusual. He was probably used to the strange habits of westerners, who toured as though they were moving house. Shere knew a place where they could stop for something to eat. A wall of oven-heat touched her as she stepped stiffly from the car. Ahead was a low white block in a bare, dusty yard. The straight road passed it, but there was nothing to see in either direction.

An ancient fiddle player witnessed her arrival, stood up and began to play a painful dirge until she had passed. The restaurant looked shut, but Shere waved her ahead.

'You don't want to come eat with me?' she asked.

'I have my own lunch.' Shere smiled and wobbled his head in apology. As

she approached the restaurant doors she saw the lights flicker on in the dark interior. Waiters were scurrying to don their white coats. She ate Butter Chicken and Pashwari Nan alone beside a window with cracked panes of plastic that had been stuffed with toilet paper to keep out the dust. The food was sensational, the bathroom after, horrific. She sat in the car with a gurgling stomach as the roads grew dustier, browner, emptier. On the horizon, a line of wooded hills appeared. Finally, the road curved and climbed. It grew hotter and closer, until she felt as if she was suffocating.

'The rains are coming,' he said, reading her thoughts, 'maybe tonight.'

'How much further?' she asked, but received no reply. *I shouldn't have picked this place,* she admonished herself, *too far away, and even the driver doesn't seem to be sure of its whereabouts.*

They reached a string of small villages where everything glistened with marble dust. Outside every house and shop stood large carved statues of Hindu gods. Men sat cross-legged on their forecourts, chipping away at great white blocks from which the gods were slowly breaking free. She could differentiate some now; Ganesha, Hanuman, Brahma, Shakti and Shiva, but the rest still looked the same. A guide had told her that there were over 330,000 to choose from. Who on earth bought these huge statues? They stood in rows like sentries on guard duty, ignored by children who probably found them as familiar as relatives.

A low brick wall—half finished, of course—ran around the edge of the town. She caught a glimpse of a sandstone building between the trees. 'I think the palace is over there,' said Shere. 'My friend tells me the World Heritage people, they came to look, and were going to make it a site of special significance. Good for tourism. But they decided not to.'

'Why?'

'Politics. I don't know.'

'Any tourists here now?'

'No, none. Not since the bombings. This is a ghost palace. Nobody comes here at night. Only the spirits live here now. You will want to walk in the palace?'

'Yes, I think so.'

'There is no guide for you.'

Good, she thought, *I've had enough of standing in the heat listening to earnest men reeling off building statistics.* 'Do you have any more cold water I can take with me?'

'We can stop.' He pulled up beside a small shop and purchased a bottle of water for her. While she waited in the car, a handful of children ran to the window and started tapping on the glass with distracted insistence. When she'd first arrived in the country, she had given all her small change to these hollow-eyed creatures, but the driver had stopped her, explaining that they were forced to pay their earnings back to gang-runners in the slums. After a few days she realized that her generosity could change nothing and would do nobody good in the long run.

Shere returned and they drove toward the palace. He swung the car off the main highway onto a back road, between tall dusty trees whose branches bent into arches from the weight of their own high leaves. A flock of green parrots blasted screeching into the air above them. Then there was only heat and silence.

She looked for a sign or a ticket booth, but there was nothing to mark the entrance to the palace. A single kitchen chair stood by a gap in the wall, where a guard usually sat. Drawn by the sound of the car, a few tiny children appeared, scampering toward her as they drew to a stop. Shere turned off the engine, then took a call on his mobile.

One small boy remained against the wall, holding back from the group. He watched Marion with the kind of sad resignation one usually only saw in disappointed old men. When the boy realized that he had gained her attention, he pushed away from the wall and bunched his fingertips, gesturing to his mouth. Ignoring the others, she beckoned him over.

Her belongings were grouped around her on the back seat. She found the brown paper bag of candies and waited. His shyness surprised her. He seemed to be waiting for some kind of a sign. She realized she was frowning, and smiled instead.

He came a little nearer, then stopped. She held the sweets up against the window, remaining motionless. The other children saw that she was not looking at them, and gradually dispersed. *I choose you,* she thought, *because you are trying hard not to look as if you care.*

Shere finished his phonecall and turned to see what was happening.

The boy remained with his hands by his sides, studying her, as if trying to see a friendly spirit within. He cautiously approached, but two little girls remained at the window with their hands outstretched, blocking his way.

Marion handed them each a silver-wrapped sweet, then passed the bag through the window to the boy. Clutching it to his chest, his serious eyes briefly locked with hers, and he ran away. She watched him go with a vague sense of dissatisfaction. *What did you expect, that he would show gratitude?*

'You are ready to visit?'

'I'm ready,' she sighed, feeling suddenly empty. 'You don't have to come with me, I can find it.'

'I can come with you.' He didn't sound keen.

'It's fine, I have this. It's all I need.' She held up the guide and tapped the cover, then slipped out of the car.

'I'll be here.' Shere got out, opened her door, then took the opportunity to light a cigarette.

'I know you will. I won't be long.'

Slipping the guide into her back pocket, she followed the overgrown path into the complex. Ahead, a family of white-haired monkeys with triangular black faces scattered at her approach. *Everyone's a part of something here,* she thought, *even the monkeys. I'd like to be part of something. Would Ted even notice if I didn't come back?* The incline to the palace was low but steady, and the heat was dense, tangible. Sweat formed on her face, in the small of her back. *Something must break soon,* she thought, *this is unbearable.*

The first building she reached was a pillared pavilion containing a bull shrine. The carved black bull was life-sized and kneeling, garlanded with artificial jasmine flowers, so perhaps the villagers were still worshipping here. Beyond this, though, came disappointment. The lake had dried out, and appeared as a shallow rubble-strewn cavity in the ground, littered with plastic bottles. *Due to global warming,* she had read, *the shrinking monsoon season means that lakes and rivers all over India are drying up, many to vanish forever.*

The shattered remains of a pair of marble lions guarded the arched entrance to a platformed complex, and a tall Mughal swing had been placed

by rooms that she knew would have once have housed a harem. But the swing itself had fallen into disrepair, and the semi-precious gems that should have been inset in the arch had long ago been prised out by robbers. The main pavilion was complete, but in a sorry state. Instead of the smooth amber and ochre walls in the photographs, she found herself looking at colours that had faded and died to streaked greys and dirty browns. The inset mirrors and plaster carvings of the interior walls were ruined, and the ornate *jaali* screens were nowhere to be seen. Nothing was as it appeared in the guide-book. *Next time buy a recent edition,* she reminded herself. *Like there'll be a next time. Ted wouldn't allow it again.*

Set at right-angles to the pavilion was a structure raised on four great fluted plinths, each beset by a pair of squat lotus urns, but the building did not look safe enough to enter. In the quadrangle formed by the buildings, bathing tanks and a complex network of stone gullies must once have been filled with water, but were now dried out and dead. She cupped her hands to shield out the sunlight, and looked to the roof, which was lined with terracotta pitchers. Somewhere in the woods beyond, a bird thrashed and screamed.

There were other buildings to explore, a small mosque with dried-out marigold garlands on its steps, a partially ruined tomb, but she did not have the energy to investigate them all. Outside the royal apartments, peacocks pecked at the sunbleached ground. Clearly the villagers had been here, for the birds' tail-feathers had been plucked, presumably to sell at the market.

In the shadows of the tomb's canopy she saw a small seated figure, and immediately recognized the boy. *He's different to the others,* she thought, *quiet and more thoughtful.* Through the trees she could make out the far edge of the village. After studying the scene for a few more moments, she turned to make her way back. *If I had seen this ten days ago I'd have been more impressed, but I've walked through too many of them now. They're all the same. They lack life.*

She tore open a moist tissue and wiped her forehead. She found Shere leaning beside the car, smoking. Surprised by her fast return, he went to grind out the cigarette. 'It's okay,' she told him, 'take your time.'

She opened the passenger door and slid onto the back seat. The sun was still high. They had stopped early for lunch. Surely it could only be about two

o'clock. She fished on the floor for the sweet bag containing her watch, then remembered that she had given the bag to the boy.

How could she have been so stupid? What had she been thinking? The watch had been a gift from Ted, solemnly presented in order to make amends for his behaviour. The damned thing was encrusted with diamonds and worth around fourteen thousand dollars, even now. She had never really liked it, but that was less to do with its appearance and more because it represented an expensive apology. Over the years she had grown so blasé about wearing it that she had become careless.

The boy had been sitting in one of the temples in the palace. She had to go back and find him.

Shere caught her alarm. 'Where are you going?'

'My watch. The boy.' It was not an explanation, but all that she could manage right now. The monkeys scattered as she strode back up the path thinking *Insurance, sales receipt, Ted, how will he ever be persuaded to give it back—*

As she approached the palace's large central pavilion, she became aware of the change in light all around her. The gardens had lost the little colour they possessed, darkening to olive, the walls deepening to camelskin.

She crossed a cracked courtyard and climbed the palace platforms, peering through the stone latticework in search of the child. She had her purse; she would offer him rupees and have him return the watch. After all, what would he want with such a thing?

She became aware of a presence behind her, a tall figure bisected by shadows. She turned, startled, and found herself facing a huge stone statue of a god wearing a strange cloud-crown. He was holding an eight-petalled plant in each hand. On the floor was a wooden plaque written in English. It read;

'PARJANYA is the Old God of the Heavens. He rules lightning, thunder and rain. He controls the procreation of plants and animals, but can also punish sinners. His powers are a mighty wonder to behold.'

She studied his wind-damaged face. A faint but defiant smile played on his lips, as if he wished to play a game, or be challenged. As if he was waiting to show his strength. She shivered. A wind had risen. Dry leaves scuttled across

the terrazzo floor. In the last few minutes a wall of rolling cloud had appeared on the horizon and was sliding across the sky like a steel shutter.

Stepping back from the statue, which seemed to be smiling at her in the half-light, she headed from one building to the next until she reached the sunken groves of the *charbargh*, the walled paradise garden divided in four quarters to represent the four parts of life, but the boy was nowhere to be found.

The only thing she could do now was persuade Shere to take her to the village and ask the shopkeepers if they had seen him, but already she sensed that they would unite behind the child and her mission would fail.

The first fat drop stained the dust at her feet like ink falling from a pen nib. It made an audible *ploc* as it landed. A second, *tac*, hit the steps. Looking up, she saw that the clouds entirely covered the sky. Moments later the droplets multiplied by tens, hundreds, thousands, millions, from a shower to a roaring downpour, to a thunderous cascade, to a sound like the end of the world. Visibility dropped to zero and she stumbled up the steps into the open-sided pavilion, watching in wonder as rain unlike any she had ever seen deluged the palace.

At his car, Shere swore and threw down his cigarette as the first drops fell. He heard raised voices; a massive cheer of excitement filtered through the trees from the village. His client would already be soaked unless she had managed to take shelter. If she complained to the tour company, they would dock his pay or worse, place him on a circuit where he could make no money from the shops and restaurants he recommended.

There was no point in looking for her; the uphill path was already turning into a mudslide. She would have to wait for a break and return as best she could.

A change was sweeping over the monsoon palace. The dried out walls had blossomed into bright ambers, ochres and fiery reds. Tiles were washed of their dust to reveal fierce blue glaze beneath. Mosaic panels covered with geometric lapis motifs sprouted and bloomed like orchids, glistening ornamental patterns emerging on the *chhatris* of the pavilions. Grey walls revealed hidden blues, yellows and greens. Earth was washed from the courtyard to reveal a polished marble floor inlaid with designs; floral bouquets, fruit trees

and wine decanters. The gutters filled with rivulets that became gurgling streams, then pounding torrents, water shooting out of stonework spouts as the fountains sputtered into life. Marion grabbed the wet pages of the guide-book and searched for the pictures of the palace.

'*But it is the magic of the monsoon that restores the Palace*', she read, '*for this forgotten complex of sandstone buildings and gardens was created to activate special effects during the rainy season that would delight the Bharatpur kings. The palace's reservoirs are designed to fill instantly, fed by water-steps which pump streams through pipes to the peacock fountains.*'

Following the guide's floor plan, she looked straight ahead and saw that what she had mistaken for piles of pale stones were in fact great marble peacocks. Rain was rushing down the steep gullies to be forced into the narrow stone pipes surrounding the birds. Water gushed from behind their long necks in shimmering rainbow fans, perfectly replicating the bird's plumage. Marion was stunned. All about her, pipes and pillars were spouting water shapes, birds, animals, flowers. The pavilion's overhanging balconies and kiosks channeled rain into intricate patterns that held formation for a moment before breaking apart and falling to earth.

The palace had been built to provide royal delight during the monsoon. It needed heavy rain to come alive. Water swelled and saturated the parched earth and the arched halls around her, filling them with colour and vigour. She walked, then ran through the white cascades between the inundated pools and reservoirs.

A long low belch of thunder sounded from somewhere between the ground and the clouds. Looking to the roof of the opposite pavilion, she saw a series of heavy stone balls forced by sprays and jets of water to roll slowly across the concave roof, then back from the far side, artificially producing the sounds of a storm. The ditches around her were filling fast. Shielded from the downpour, they formed graceful mirror geometries that reflected the falling rain. She looked to where she had last seen the boy sitting. The curiously curved roof of the tomb now made sense; its upturned reflection was that of a boat, ferrying its precious cargo to safety.

She was crying uncontrollably now, tears pouring down her cheeks in an unstoppable flow. Her white shirt was stuck to her shoulders, her breasts. She

fought the urge to tear the transparent material from her body and wade into the lake. A sense of understanding flooded through her, filling her with compassion. She no longer cared about her watch, her luggage, her husband, her home. The trappings of her life had vanished in the revelation of the tempest. Unashamed of crying or calling to the gods, her voice joined the thousands of others who celebrated the coming of the monsoon.

The boy splashed through the streets with the paper bag clutched in his fist, and found his uncle closing because of the rains. Uncle Javed's decision to delay the repairs to his roof would cost him dearly. Later on this very night, part of the shop's ceiling would fall in and ruin his new stock of winter jackets and saris.

The boy showed his uncle the watch, and received a clip across the ear for his trouble. 'Oh Karan, you will cause your mother to die of despair,' he scolded, 'for producing another little thief like your brother. Hasn't the poor woman had enough trouble in her miserable life? Why do you want to see her suffer further?'

'I didn't steal it,' Karan insisted. 'A rich American lady opened the window of her car and handed it to me.'

'Such a little liar!' Uncle Javed cried, trying to seize the boy's thin neck. 'What kind of monster have we raised that he should steal from the very people who come here in trust? Was she very rich?'

'You steal from them all the time,' said Karan, stepping back from his uncle's grabbing hands, 'every time you sell them a shawl and tell them it was sewn by a lady who took twenty months to make it all by hand.'

'That is the art of business, you rude child. Every woman wants to be told the story behind her purchase, in order to make it more of a bargain.'

'But your stories aren't true.'

'They are exactly what people wish to believe. Price has nothing to do with value. And this—' he held the glittering watch aloft, '—must go back to the tourist you stole it from.'

'But I'm sure she has gone.'

'Did you look for her?'

'No.'

'Well, that is a blessing. My heart aches to think of the trouble you would

have caused by making her think you were a thief. Come on, we have to visit old Mister Chauhan. He will be able to tell us how much the watch is worth. We must know how big a thief you have become, in order to find the right penance for your sin.'

Karan reluctantly agreed to go along, but first he made sure that Uncle Javed returned the bag to him.

The boys in the village said that Mister Chauhan was about five hundred years old, and had once been introduced to Queen Victoria in Old Bombay. His skin was so wrinkled, it looked to Karan as if someone had magically transferred his features to a brown paper bag, then screwed the bag up and flattened it out imperfectly. Mister Chauhan owned a brass-rimmed magnifying glass the size of a hotel dinner plate. He raised it by a pair of horn handles and held it over the watch on his cluttered desk. For several minutes there was complete silence in the cramped antique shop. Finally he set down the glass and turned to the boy.

'There are thirty six diamonds of extremely high quality inside this watch-casing, but there is also something missing.'

'Missing?' Uncle Javed looked at his nephew in puzzlement.

'No serial number,' said Mister Chauhan. 'On Cartier watches of this type there are two types of authentication. On the downward stroke of the Roman numeral seven one can see, with the aid of a strong magnifier, the word 'Cartier' written in script. That is one sign. The other is the serial number on the back of the casing, but there is none.'

'So typical that my thieving nephew should choose to steal a worthless fake, ' Uncle Javed complained, giving the boy another clip around the ear.

'I did not say it was a fake,' Mister Chauhan continued. 'This watch is very genuine indeed. It is extremely rare, so rare that someone has erased the number to prevent it from being traced. Every Cartier can be traced by its number.'

'Why would somebody remove it?' asked Uncle Javed.

Uncle Chauhan sucked his teeth and thought for a moment. "I can think of two very good reasons. Either the person who bought it did not wish it to be found, because he made the purchase with bad money.'

'He avoids his taxes. He is a crook.'

'Something like that.'

'What is the other reason?'

'A man might make such a purchase for his mistress, whose name he does not wish to be recorded on papers as the watch's owner.'

'The lady was not a mistress,' said Karan, 'she was a wife.'

'Then perhaps her husband repents and gives the watch he buys his mistress to his wife, after first taking the precautionary measure of removing the serial number.'

Uncle Javed looked as if he had just seen a fortune fly out of the window.

'Mister Chauhan, you make a fine storyteller,' laughed Karan. 'If I did not know you better, I might be tempted to think that you were inventing such a marvelous story so that I might agree to sell it for a small amount.'

'The watch cannot be repaired or serviced by Cartier,' Mister Chauhan explained. 'And this is the very thing that any prospective buyer would want.'

But even as he looked into the boy's unblinking brown eyes, Mister Chauhan knew he had lost. For this was India, where the past was not important, and anything could be repaired. He sighed and ordered the *chai* to be brewed, knowing that it would be a long evening. The bargaining began in earnest. Karan had seen the greedy fire in Mister Chauhan's eyes, and knew that the process of negotiation would be lengthy and arduous.

In fact, the formalities took three days and involved one boy and five men from two villages. Part of the problem was that the arrangement had to be kept away from the knowledge of the local police constabulary in order to avoid an unacceptable level of commission being deducted from the sale. At the conclusion of the deal much money was assembled, assurances were written out, whisky and *masala* tea was poured, everyone involved was sworn to silence, and Karan rode the train to Bangalore, to begin a new life.

Shere Banjara, the driver for Jacaranda Tours, fifty two years old and married with five children, was severely reprimanded and fined for the loss of his charge. The paperwork involved took over a year to sort out. Finally he was moved from his base in Delhi to Kolkotta, where he quickly learned that the new circuit could reap him unexpected rewards from a fresh generation of middle-class businessmen looking to buy carpets and tapestries for their second homes.

As the years passed, the dry and rainy seasons replaced each other like cards falling upon a gaming table. The monsoon palace was denied world heritage status due to a dispute over the ownership of its land, and remained over-grown and forgotten by all except the monkeys, doves and peacocks, who lived within its evening shadows. Parjanya sat in the dusty shadows and bided his time.

Then, one overheated day, just before the arrival of the monsoon, when the air was so scorched that it felt like you might carve a hole in it to breathe, some workers angrily threw their pickaxes and shovels down onto the hard dry soil and started shouting at one another.

'What the bloody hell is going on here?' asked the project foreman, striding over. Work had fallen behind, and it was starting to look as if they would not be finished before the rains came, which would be disastrous because the road had not yet been sealed and they needed to take the shack down now.

'The villagers tell us we cannot remove Maran or we will bring bad luck to the area,' said one of the workmen. 'We need to dismantle any obstacle today.'

'Wait, you are talking about this? *This?*' The foreman pointed to the chaotic arrangement of tin huts that stood in their path and began to laugh. 'Bulldoze it flat. Pass me a pickaxe and I'll do it myself.' He spat *paan* on the ground dismissively.

'You don't understand. A promise was made that Maran would never be moved.'

'Who was this promise made to?'

'An old man called Javed who lived in the village.'

'Javed? That scoundrel? He has been dead for over five years! The past is the past. Knock it down.'

The workmen reluctantly moved toward their tools, but before they could continue their work, a horn sounded and they were forced to move to the sides of the road to allow for the arrival of a white Mercedes. Everyone agreed that the man who emerged from the rear seat looked like a younger version of Shahrukh Kahn, the Bollywood superstar. He walked over to the tin huts, examined them and beckoned the foreman.

'How far over the boundary line?'

The foreman looked at the ground and thought. 'Twenty feet, at least.'

'You know how long Maran has lived here?'

'The men tell me fifteen years.'

'Sixteen. You know why?'

'Something to do with guarding the palace and keeping it in good repair, but there's no paperwork—'

'You don't need paperwork for everything. Let me deal with this.' As he approached the huts, a pair of green parrots screamed and rocked the ornate wire cage that hung from the lintel above the front door. He tapped respectfully and stepped back, waiting.

The grey-haired woman who appeared in the doorway studied her visitor and smiled. 'Come inside,' she instructed. 'I wasn't sure if you would get here in time. The *chai* is almost ready. I've learned to like it sweet. I never took sugar at home. Have that chair in the corner, but be careful, the leg is broken.'

The interior of the hut was crowded with decorative ornaments that had been presented to her by the villagers over the years, mostly Hindu gods. 'Let me look at you.'

Karan adjusted his collar and slicked back his hair, ready for inspection. 'I did not believe you would stay, Maran.'

'Marion,' she corrected. 'Oh, I come from a long line of very determined women. Besides, if I deserted my palace, who else would do the job? You people are losing respect for your past, all this rushing toward the future.'

'And "you people" have not done the same?' asked Karan. 'This is not your palace. It is not a cause you can simply adopt, like a child.'

In the soft light Marion looked younger than her years, the way she had been when he first saw her. 'You're right, of course. I can't explain what I feel. But I know you can't take his land.' She touched her bare tanned neck, remembering. 'I wanted to look nice for you but the damned monkey took my necklace. He's probably buried it out by the *jharna*.'

'The gardens of the monsoon palace have never been accurately measured, you know. We could go beyond their walls right now, trim a hundred yards off and no-one would ever know.'

'Shame on you, to even think of such a thing. He will know. Parjanya will know.'

'I have no other choice. But you, do you really want to stay on here?'

'I have no other choice either. I burned my bridges long ago.'

'Where is your husband?'

'Maybe he stayed with his mistress,' she said carelessly. 'I wrote him some letters. I don't know if he got them.'

'I'm sorry.'

'Don't be, I'm not. I'll become like the old British ladies who still live on in Delhi, complaining about their landlords and going slowly crazy. Something about this place encourages the irrational . . .'

'I could move you back into the village. Javed's children have offered you a home.'

'No,' she said firmly, 'I need to be within sight of the pavilion. I've seen the designs for your little housing project, Karan. A gated community? I stayed here to get away from such things. Don't tell me it's progress, because it's nothing of the kind.'

'It's what people want.' Karan smiled. 'Didn't you know, we're all middle class now, even if our castes can never change.'

'Well, it seems to me that we have to strike a deal, but I have no cards to play. Are you hungry? I could make you some *paneer*.'

'No, I had a pizza.'

'You could have me thrown off the site tonight, if that's what you want.'

'I could, but you know I would never do it.' He sipped his *masala*. 'You make this better than my mother used to. So, this is what we'll do. You stay here. I'll shift the boundary back, everyone's happy.'

'Everyone except Parjanya.'

'It is the only solution I can offer.'

'It sounds like you already had that in mind. You can't do it without changing the planning application, can you?'

'I can change the application with a few handfuls of rupees. We need to reduce the size of the estate because the surveyors are arriving from Delhi next week.'

'It's a shame. I thought the monsoon palace would eventually be accepted as a world heritage site. Now, more than ever, Parjanya needs a guardian here.' Marion laughed softly to herself.

'What is funny?' Karan asked.

'I was foolish enough to think that such an ancient, magnificent monument might be saved by a bag of sweets,' she replied.

'The palace will be protected, but the condition is the partial surrender of its grounds,' said Karan.

'He will not let you take his land,' she said simply.

'Listen, Marion, I have respect for you, but you cannot change what must be done.' Enough. She exasperated him. Karan rose and took his leave. Outside, as he spoke to his foreman, she imagined the dessicated ground receiving fat drops of quenching rain.

The men moved in. The yellow bulldozers and earthmovers backed away from the hut, but surged toward the low dry-stone walls and pushed straight through them, gouging channels in the soft red earth. The workmen marched forward behind the vehicles, an advancing army clad in bright protective jackets.

Marion stood in the doorway and watched, smiling to herself.

They cannot steal the land you have protected for me, Parjanya hissed in her ear. *They are arrogant enough to think that their machines will make a difference, but they forget I control the Heavens.*

Parjanya made the rains come. She looked up into the sky and saw it cloud over within a few seconds. The first bolt of lightning split the air and hit the cabin of the lead earthmover. A scream came from within. Men swarmed around the stalled vehicle as smoke billowed from its electrics.

It was the heaviest monsoon squall she had ever witnessed. The rain increased until nothing could be discerned from the door of the hut. She heard the ominous rumble of wet earth as a torrent of mud poured over the broken walls, punching the workmen's legs from under them, swallowing them in thick brown effluvium. The men were all choked and drowned, or were crushed and buried. Their machines were overturned on top of them, hammering them flat, bursting their soft shells into the bubbling cauldron of mud. The monkeys stared out from the shelter of the palace, hooting in triumph. Soon the mud would dry again and it would be as if the workmen were never here.

A beatific smile crept over Marion's face as she returned to make fresh tea.

Karan unknotted his tie and fanned himself in the blast-furnace heat. He watched Marion slowly retreat into the shadows, lost inside her visions. One of the workmen jammed his shovel into the hard dry earth, leaned back and caught his eye, grinning knowingly. *Pāgala aurata.* Crazy lady.

Karan wondered what was going through Marion's head. It was a funny thing about those who came to stay; the ones who didn't believe often ended up believing a little too much.

Let her keep her dreams, he thought. *I'll only take eighty yards from the garden. No-one will notice. If they ask, I'll tell them it was a mistake.*

Somewhere in the dense treetops behind him, the first cool breezes rose.

BEAUTIFUL MEN

THE COAST

Out in the bay, the last jet-skiers are looping past each other in the setting sun. Nearby, on Cap Ferrat, the summer parties are coming to an end. The Mistrale is rising, whipping petals and pine needles into the air, stippling the surfaces of sapphire swimming pools. This year the Russians have moved in, filling the hotels vacated by Americans. Everyone wants to know where the Americans have gone. They are fondly remembered; in past times they were generous and jovial, but now they have completely vanished. Restaurant owners blame politics, but only in the vaguest terms. The Riviera towns are safe havens, far from the threat of fundamentalist attack. Nobody here feels like the end of the world would affect them.

The hot winds are still bringing firestorms to the hills. Yellow Canadair seaplanes blast the flames with seawater, but already there are fewer people to witness the drama. Houses are being locked up for the coming winter. Entire areas are falling asleep, even though the temperature has barely dropped from the height of summer. Many slumber beneath the cliffs of the Massif Central, the great fold of rock that creates a microclimate so warm it is nicknamed 'Little Africa', perfect for growing figs and clementines, perfect for hiding from the world.

The light hurts Ryan's corneas. The low sun on the sea fractures and pierces, but he will not don his glasses, for he must see everything now. Speedboats burn the last of their precious petrol cutting geometric patterns through the azure waves. A fierce golden light bathes the pink breast-shaped cone of the Negresco, and turns the slow curve of the Promenade Des Anglais

into a shimmering ribbon, studded with the rubies of homegoing brake lights.

Ryan checks his Rolex and begins the countdown in his head. Already the first neon striplights are outlining the hotels of Nice. The last ferry of the evening is arriving from Corsica. The pizza restaurants in the port are preparing themselves for the extra business it will bring. The buildings have drawn in the brightness of the day and will feed it back as night energy. Everything is interlocked, as unstoppable as time, and will remain so until the very last moment.

Ryan leans against the warm stone of the seat and turns up the music in his headphones. He smiles at those who pass and waits for the vermilion dusk, patiently watching as the city goes about its business, tethered to routine, absorbing upset, heedless of harm, happy to exist at all.

And he thinks to himself, what a wonderful world.

THE GIRLS

On June 13th exactly four months earlier, he is seated in much the same pose but further around the bay, in a pulsing basement nightclub with sweating red walls, like a chamber of the heart. He watches as three glistening girls with thick St Petersburg accents squeeze together for their web-cam interviewer, pushing for screen space.

They are being questioned about what they look for in a man. The interview is being projected on high-res screens all around the room, greedily repeating their behavioural tics in fierce scarlets and cyans, like coursework for anthropology students. The girls shriek that their guys need broad shoulders and firm definition and a sense of humour, but above all property, nice cars and lots of money. He studies them from the bar and thinks it odd that those who see the most beauty in the world are the least equipped to handle it. And those who see nothing at all are the best survivors, at least while their looks hold out.

Ryan examines these Russian dolls with a dispassionate eye, and tries to see what they want him to see. All he can find is what's on display; bleach-

cuts and cleavages and flicking hair, posing bodies, thrusting hips, tossed heads, sparkling jewellery, forced laughter revealing weirdly whitened teeth. He makes himself listen, because all he can really hear is a sort of hysterical high-pitched squeaking in the background while their sexual postures talk over them. Men only hear bodies in nightclubs.

Unravelling their logomania, he tries to form an opinion about what they're saying, even though the effort nearly kills him. He thinks *that's what you tell everyone you want, but I know you; you'll settle for less, much less because eventually you'll have to. Because girls like you are ten a penny here and beautiful men with lots of money might want you but only for a night, then they'll throw you out without breakfast and drive away to someone else. Why? Because they can and you can't without looking like hookers.*

That's not sexist, he thinks, *that's practical.*

The girls of the Cote D'Azur ask for a lot but have to settle for very little. They'll date a man who disappears for days at a time, who lies to them constantly, who'll never hold down a job or have any money, who's as fat and bald and ugly as a pig, who'll let them down every single time. They pretend they want perfection, but their expectations are gradually reduced to such a low level that their men can get away with anything.

Ryan blames the Single Switch, a mutant autogenesis hardwired inside girls' brains that trips one day, and suddenly a light shines behind their eyes telling them to find a man fast and have a child. This is the moment when their ideals carbonise and they behave like someone blindfolded for a party game, rushing about to grab the first shiny male who comes within range, no matter how venal, bitter and hate-filled they are. Because many men really hate women, hate them so much that they can barely prevent themselves from lashing out. But the Riviera girls have to pair off before they spend too much time alone and turn strange, devoting themselves to horoscopes, crystals and cat sanctuaries, and filling their homes with false memories.

That's not unfair, he thinks, *that's realistic.*

———

THE ONE

Ryan knows this to be the case because he is the kind of man the desperate girls chase. He always goes after the silly, pretty ones because he ticks all their boxes. Youth? He'll say he's twenty-six when he's actually twenty-nine. Job? He's employed in broadband sales and marketing at Cap 3000, the vast shopping mall to the west of Nice. Looks? His hair is thinning, his gut stretching, but he has an olive tan and height is a big advantage. Sixty percent of all CEOs are over six feet tall, he reminds himself, and nearly all are men. Personality? He can make a girl laugh and feel that they have the measure of him. Brains? He graduated languages and new technologies, and is unusually well-read. Money? He's on a good salary, has just been promoted, gets new cars and annual bonuses. Eligibility? He's single! There are no ugly surprises and no hidden children.

Willingness to commit?

Ryan is dating an awful lot of women in this, the year before his thirtieth birthday, two or three at any one time. But in the nightclub that night, on May 13th, he meets Lainey Gray, a tall, thin-shouldered American who teaches at a language school in Villefranche. She talks to him on the cancer deck, a rubbish-strewn stairwell at the rear of the building where the patrons once took drugs instead of sneaking smokes, and catches him before his psychic armour goes on. None of Ryan's usual nonsense works on her. She studies him with detached amusement, a half-smile playing on crimson frosted lips, and he knows she can see right through him. But she sticks around, because she is waiting for him to exhaust his bag of tricks, and wants to see what's left behind.

Smart girl.

Maybe too smart. There's Ryan thinking he's laying traps to catch her, and she's already caught him. Over the next month they meet six times before she even lets him touch her. You can love a girl like that.

Their first six dates:

An unwatchable dubbed rom-com with Sarah Jessica Parker at the Nice Etoile. They reach a mutual decision to leave before the end and go for pasta in the Old Town. A Warhol exhibition at the Museum of Modern Art,

followed by a brasserie meal in Place Messena. She goes to his flat but only stays for coffee. His best friend Sean's birthday party at the K Club. Ryan drops a couple of pills but doesn't tell her. He genuinely believes she hasn't noticed, until she stares hard at him and suddenly goes home on her scooter without saying a word. A crowded lunch in the Cours Salaya where they have to shout and mime across the table to each other. The afternoon is spent pushing through crowds of tourists on the Promenade Des Anglais. He goes to her flat in Mont Boron, but she coolly kicks him out after an hour, explaining that she has to get up early next morning. 'Mesrine' Parts 1 & 2 followed by icy steel platters of fruits de mer at the Café De Turin. He eats a bad oyster. A party for one of her work colleagues, Marisia, at the Chinatown Dim Sum restaurant. Ryan leaves her there with the intention of calling another girl, but something prevents him.

Then, a few days after that, the walls come down between them.

From date seven onwards they're at each other like dogs on a hot Spanish street. Lainey can't keep her hands off Ryan. Ryan doesn't have time to look at anyone else, and isn't interested anyway. A couple of his former girlfriends leave sulky messages but he puts them off, then deletes them from his mobile.

Over the next three months, Ryan and Lainey continue to grow closer. They have their first argument, then fuck like lunatics. Devastated by the thought of someone else's happiness, many of their single friends stop bothering to call. Ryan meets Lainey's parents on their first overseas visit. They're sweet and totally confused by Europe. Ryan realises that he has been caught, but enjoys this strange sensation without understanding why. One day the pair find themselves in Habitat and think *Oh shit, we're choosing furniture together. She must be The One.*

THE CHASM

Ryan knows what's coming next, but finds the idea of a mapped and stable future depressing beyond all endurance. He has always assumed there would be more to life than just finding a mate and slowly turning into his father, but the odds are against him. He becomes depressed, and has no idea what it will

take to excite and revitalise him, so he simply allows events to take their natural course. Like the girls being interviewed in the club, he sees little real point to life, which makes him well equipped to survive it. But surviving isn't living.

Lainey does not share his pessimism, but senses an emerging pattern of hairline fractures between them. The gaps quickly expand until they join to form a chasm. Ryan knows that his girlfriend has a passionate, wayward spirit, but fears for the emptiness in himself. He has nothing to offer her. He never bares his soul because he not sure he has one.

And Nice has a raffish charm that takes away any sense of urgency, a sense of elegant disgrace that encourages bad behaviour. The town gave the world a healthy salad and the word 'tourism', but not much else. The rest of its pleasures have to be patiently uncovered. The English built its extraordinary coast road, where hookers in *Barbarella* outfits now cruise beside grannies, rollerbladers and *petanque* players.

Whether he ends up staying with Lainey or not, Ryan thinks he'll stay on. He feels more settled here than in England. This is the city he dreams of most; slightly disturbing, slightly surreal, filled with the sensual luxuries of wasted time. Watching the sunset liners returning from the South, he is so filled with the desire for tropical deceptions that it's possible to not to see the new poor; the MacDonalds outlets, the lost Algerian children, the tramps asleep in doorways. Like California, this part of Europe has become the place to head when you're too rich, too recognizable, too stupid, too burned out to live anywhere else. It's expensive and selfish, and no-one here cares whether you clean pools or once opened for Oasis.

Ryan marks time and watches the world, his compass spinning.

For all he knows, he might love Lainey. But he doesn't love her enough.

THE BEAUTIFUL MEN

Then, something inexplicable happens that ends his former life.

Lainey has a loud friend called Lex, an Easyjet steward based at Gatwick who flirts and theatrically emphasises his words, punctuating his conversa-

tions with expansive hand gestures, and Ryan wants to argue with him every time they meet, so he finds excuses not to meet up with Lainey whenever she makes arrangements for them.

But one night the trio end up having a good time, mainly because Lex stops trying so hard to be liked. Three days later Ryan meets the pair of them at a new bar in the port, and that is where he first notices them, standing right in the centre of the room.

The beautiful men.

Ryan assumes they're gay; anyone would. He figures that the new acceptance of gay men gives them permission to be as ordinary as everyone else, and now most of them are. The flamboyant clothes and outrageous behaviour of the past has been relegated to old photographs, the former ghettos have been decimated by rent hikes and invading coffee shops. The bars which were once the exclusive province of Riviera queens are now as blended as the wines served in them. But, just as one would occasionally spot a small flock of stunning, unattainable girls, as attenuated and exotic as African flamingos, Ryan starts to notice the beautiful men, half a dozen of them, each so ridiculously perfect that he can't imagine what they ever looked like as children. He wonders if they have been conjured into existence by a coalescence of pure atoms, or perhaps they are man-made and spend their nights floating in amniotic fluids being recharged.

Each night they drift into Lex's favourite bar, *Le Six,* and order cocktails, standing apart from everyone else, not even looking around, just quietly talking to each other, so unreal that you want to pinch their flesh for reassurance.

Lainey notices them, and Lex definitely notices them, and everyone assumes they're models because their expensive clothes are casually immaculate and their hair and skin looks retouched. They are all in their early twenties, tall, dark, thick-armed and slender-waisted, with an other-worldly presence that rises above traditional notions of beauty. *Nicois* men are naturally dark and beautiful, so it takes a lot to stand out.

It is strange that Ryan should even notice them at all, but the simple truth is that they disturb him. They are the wind in the tops of the pines, the tremble of the seismometer needle before a quake. They ruffle still waters and

scatter seagulls, they part crowds and make cats cower. They appear shallow to the point of absurdity yet are somehow the opposite, as if they are magnetically connected to life, as if they are the essence of life itself.

THE SEVENTH

As soon as Ryan sees them, he starts seeing them everywhere he goes, throughout the bars and restaurants and art galleries of Nice, on empty night streets and at busy midday intersections, the same six beautiful men, all in dark glasses, all standing a little apart from one another, never touching anyone else, moving aside so that they don't come into contact with mere mortals, as though something cataclysmic would happen if they did.

And then one day, they are joined by a seventh, the most perfect one of all.

Ryan cannot describe him without sounding infatuated. The object of his obsession is ell over two metres tall, with tousled black hair and clear dark skin, a wide jaw and the strangest blue eyes Ryan has ever seen on a real human being. He never wears shades. He is muscled and long in the thighs, wears a steel and leather bracelet on his right arm, skinny jeans and shiny black boots, a jet shirt open at the neck. And when he has occasion to smile, something astonishing happens. He draws down the stars. The air fills with errant electricity, and seems in danger of igniting.

'They started turning up about six weeks ago,' says Lex one night when the three of them are at the bar. He eyes them with a combination of lust and fury. 'They always hang around together. Never talk to anyone else. Probably nobody's good enough for them.'

'And you're staring at the tall one,' Lainey tell Ryan.

'No, I'm not,' he lies indignantly.

'Yes you are. You may not realise it but you can't take your eyes off him.'

'He's wearing a great shirt. And you've got to admit he's hot, for a guy. I'm comfortable with my sexuality. It doesn't make me gay to say that.'

'No, I guess not,' Lainey sighs. 'You're not being judgmental, which is a good thing.'

'Do you know how much effort it takes to look that hot?' asks Lex. 'I bet

he gets up at five in the morning to start his workout and conduct some kind of intense moisturizing program. They all have eight-packs now, it's the new musculature. He's probably a model or a professional whore, which amounts to the same thing.'

Here's the odd thing, thinks Ryan. *When you experience extreme beauty, you tend to think of it as other-worldly, but I see the opposite in this man. I'm drawn because he's completely at ease in his world, entirely connected with it. He is no angel; he smokes and drinks and has a dirty laugh, but there's something so unknowable and expansive about him that you can't help but be fascinated.*

THE PURSUIT

Something very strange is happening to Ryan, and he knows it. It feels like love but can't be, surely. He fights against the word 'obsessed', but the more he sees, the more he wants to see, and when the beautiful men aren't there he feels a little more lost, and little less alive.

'Charisma' means 'bearing the gift of divine grace', and that is what they have, the beautiful men, a calescence that begins to escalate when they enter a room, perhaps not a physical heat but something Ryan perceives to be uncomfortably hot. He begins finding excuses to hang out in their neighbourhood—the bars and restaurants to the east of Avenue Jean Medecin. He starts lying to Lainey about where he is going, but Lex sees him around and clearly decides to keep his counsel.

Ryan continues to change each time he sees them. He feels a disgust at the way he's behaved with girls in the past, as if just being in proximity to these demigods somehow has the potential to make him a better person.

But it is a drug. Each time he sees their leader he wants something more. In the crowded bars of dying summer he can stand quite close, but it still isn't enough. He tries to hear what the beautiful men are saying to each other, but can never catch the words. Then one night when Lainey has a cold and is staying home, the two men find themselves pressed close together in a scruffy pub behind the flower market. It is the first time Ryan sees him without his friends. He raises his eyes to find his searching gaze returned.

The effect is one of electrocution.

Ryan went to a Catholic school and emerged with a tangle of doubts and suspicions he has never bothered to work through, but this man presses against his heart and catches his breath between parted lips, inhaling and returning it to the universe in an act so perversely religious that he almost faints. He shakes his head as if to clear the clouds from it, but the sensation only grows. The man is still staring at him. It's as if he does not entirely occupy the space in which he stands. The weight of him is slightly blurred, shimmering with dark matter.

Holding his stare, the man steps back towards the door, and Ryan can only follow.

Outside a light rain sparkles in yellow squares of light. They walk in silence through the streaming alleyways of the Old Town. Ryan follows, knowing that he would pass through fire to remain this close. He sees how others move out of their way, as if the sight disturbs them in some fundamental manner. They reach the square of Sainte Reparate and slip inside the church. Within the cool grey space, Ryan instantly loses the sights and sounds of the city. Beneath the church's old wooden roof the man he is following stops in the deserted nave and slowly turns. He watches as Ryan draws closer, and closer still.

THE ADMISSION

Ryan is suddenly filled with terror. He cannot comprehend what he is doing here. It makes no sense at all, and feels as dangerous as tapping Death on the shoulder. The man he has followed is watching him with a mystifying, silent blankness. Their faces are little by the guttering penance candles that line the pews.

Ryan takes a step closer, so that they are but a forearm's length apart.

'My name is Phosphoros,' says the man in clear but oddly weighted English. 'You must not touch me. But you can answer this for me.'

Ryan stops and waits while Phosphoros, the light bearer, the morning star, taps out a battered cigarette and lights it, the flame streaking his wet face with gold. 'Why are you here?'

'I don't know.'

'Think about your answer very carefully. I must ask again. Why are you here?'

'Because I love you.' Ryan cannot believe he has said this, and tries to bite back the words.

'You don't know me.'

'I don't have to. I just know what I feel.'

'It is very dangerous for you.'

'I don't care.'

'You understand what I am.'

'I think so.'

And you are not afraid.'

'No.'

It might be Ryan's imagination, but the beautiful man's mouth appears to be moving out of synch with his voice, like a poorly dubbed film. The words of Phosphoros resound in Ryan's head, disorienting him.

'Why are *you* here?' Ryan throws the question back.

Phosphoros sighs. 'We are the rebels. We believe that people should be told. We will probably be punished when we return.'

'What should we be told?'

'That you cannot be saved.'

Ryan touches his forefinger to his chest and looks around. 'You think that's what I want? To be saved?'

'I do not mean you. I mean the world. You will dissipate to atoms very soon now. All humans will. Do you think it will help to know what is going to happen?'

Ryan cannot think of an answer. He had not been expecting to trigger some kind of metaphysical debate in a French church. It briefly crosses his mind that the man with whom he has become obsessed is mad or drugged, just another beautiful burnout who's had too many late nights. But Ryan needs to believe. He wants answers. It is human nature to seek solutions.

'You're saying the world is going to end? No, it wouldn't help me to know how. But it would change me.'

'And you want to change.'

'Yes.'

'Why?'

'Because I don't like myself. I'm lost. I think most of us are.'

'Then come to me.' Phosphoros holds out his arms in welcome.

THE VISION

The pose bothers Ryan, reminding him of a hyperreal life-sized statue of Jesus in the chapel at his old school. Yet he steps into his angel's embrace without hesitation, and feels his warm arms close like wings about his shoulders.

Phosphoros flicks aside his cigarette, exhales and kisses Ryan fully and deeply. It should feel like a sacrilegious act, but is the reverse.

There is a sensation of molten rain in Ryan's mouth that floods down his throat and into his chest, setting his soul aflame.

The grey walls of the church fall away and he sees. Truly, he sees.

It will begin exactly six weeks after this night. The future unfolds in flashes of brilliance that damage his eyes.

A huge bomb detonates in a Siberian oilfield.

The Russians blast the most important Sunni temple in the Middle East.

Saudi Arabia collapses into a state of civil war.

The oil pipelines are cut. The troops are unable to hold back the crowds.

The loss of oil stops electricity, and the loss of electricity stops water. America attempts to form alliances, but is rebuffed. China no longer needs its help. Elderly men shout across vast tables. The crowds mill like panicked animals. The buildings fall. The west is left unprotected, and like a card house it collapses.

The end comes with indecent speed, but the suffering lingers on for years. After-images of cataclysm roll past in a blur of pixels, endlessly looped on the world's dying television screens. The future screams, then starves, then whimpers, then fades to a nagging soundless pain that reduces everyone to animals, then insects, then microbes.

THE DECISION

Ryan breaks free, severing the circuit. The walls of the church close back in. He blinks and tries to focus. 'This is why you're here,' he says, forming the words with difficulty, as if drunk. 'You know what's about to happen. You're testing us, to see if we should know as well.'

'We're here to help. You need to tell me. The decision is yours.'

'How many others have you asked?'

'We have only asked the ones who have seen us for what we are. The ones who are drawn to us against their natures. We need to know how you wish to survive, with or without this terrible knowledge.'

'If everything will be gone in just a few passes of the sun,' Ryan replies, 'I want to be awake, not asleep. If I can't survive, I want to live. Please, don't take the memory away. Leave it inside me.'

'As you wish.' The angel Phosphoros seizes him by the hair and kisses him with a vicious force, and this time it feels as if some part of his soul is being restored, forcing the fire of life into him, so that even though he is shivering and frozen in the darkened church, every nerve in his body is alive with energy.

Phosphoros releases him and studies his face to remember it. 'I should tell you that all the humans we approached reached this consensus,' he says. 'You are the last one to be asked. The seven of us were right to come here, right to question. Upon our return we will throw ourselves upon the mercy of our elders, and present the evidence of your strength. If we are successful in our entreaties, we will end the world a few seconds before you yourselves can destroy it, in a vast and sudden conflagration, so loud that it is silent, so bright that it is blackness, and there will be no anguish, no suffering, nothing left at all. I hope this is of consolation to you.'

'I don't need to be consoled,' Ryan tells the angel. 'I feel—' He struggles to find the right word—'completed.'

Phosphorus releases him and steps back, to be joined by his six friends, who slowly emerge from the shadows. Ryan follows them outside and watches as they rise up in the rain and become streams of luminescence that burst and glow within the night clouds over the sea, before finally vanishing from sight.

Ryan finds that he is quite alone. His sense of loss is like a bruise upon his heart. He thinks of Phosphorus soaring away, of the risk he took to prove the strength of man, but the sensation of love is quickly replaced by confusion. He cannot understand what he is doing here. His chest is sore. He feels as if he is recovering from a great sickness. Digging his mobile from his jacket pocket, he is about to call Lainey but changes his mind. All he knows now is that he needs to be by himself. The knowledge he has been given carries an enormous weight, and he must rediscover of his spirit.

In the time that's left his journey takes him back to his family in London, and then to the shoreline of Nice once more, where he feels most at rest. By the time he returns, America has recalled its citizens and Lainey has gone. Nobody knows where she is. Ryan knows he will never see her again.

THE END

And now, with just minutes to go before the end of the world, he leans back against the warm stone of the seat, and turns up the music in his headphones. He smiles at the passing pedestrians and looks down at the bay, waiting for the angelic interception, the soundless flare of vermilion light that will tell him they succeeded. He watches as the city goes about its business, tethered to routine, heedless of harm, happy to exist at all.

Once he was lost and miserable. But now the precise details of the world's conclusion are burned into his cortex. He understands the fall of angels, the hopes of men, the nature of love. Ryan smiles to himself, truly content for the first and only time in his life.

He knows that there are others out there who were touched, who are now watching and waiting for the final hour to arrive. He thanks the beautiful men. He knows that joy has the breadth of an atom, and is quickly gone. But while it is here it must be treasured, for there is nothing else that we can do.

Here it comes.

BRYANT & MAY'S MYSTERY TOUR ▪▪▪▪▪▪▪▪▪▪

Early on Christmas Eve the Home Office called Arthur Bryant of London's Peculiar Crimes Unit with an urgent request to attend the scene of a crime in King's Cross. Bryant did so, then called his partner John May with instructions to meet him at 10:15am beside a bus stop in Marble Arch, but with no explanation as to why. It was muggy, grey and wet, not at all appropriate to the festive season, and May resented being dragged away from the PCU's offices.

'Ah, you got my message, good.' The elderly detective hailed his partner with a wild whip of his walking stick, and nearly pruned a passing tourist. Bryant resembled a beady-eyed tramp more than an officer of the law. He had misbuttoned his shapeless brown cardigan and dragged a moth-eaten Harris tweed coat over the top of it. A sprig of holly protruded from his battered trilby, looking less like seasonal decoration than a sign that he had lately been trapped in a bush. 'I got here ahead of time and had a potter through the German Christmas market in Hyde Park. Four pounds fifty for a knockwurst. They're getting their own back for the war.'

'You had your mobile with you?' asked May, surprised. Arthur was three years his senior but several decades behind the rest of the world when it came to technology.

'I did have, yes,' Bryant admitted, tugging his trilby further onto his head. 'Here's our bus.' He indicated the old open-topped Routemaster that was pulling up beside them.

May was suspicious. 'Then where is it now?'

'I think I dropped it in the Princess Diana Memorial Drain. Don't worry,

it'll just keep going around. I'll get it when I come back. Well—' He threw out a hand so that May could haul him on board, 'you're probably wondering what this is all about.'

'And why we need to meet on a sightseeing bus, yes,' said May, leading his partner inside the idling vehicle. The portly driver looked back over his shoulder, watching them through the glass. 'I've seen the Regent Street lights already.'

'It won't do you any harm to see them again. I think Christmas gets better as you get older,' Bryant remarked somewhat unexpectedly.

'Do you?'

'Oh yes. You have to buy fewer presents because most of your friends are dead. Let's go inside, I can't face the stairs. Let me fill you in. There was a rather sad little murder in King's Cross during the night. A 54 year-old cleaning lady named Joan McKay was strangled to death in her third floor flat in Hastings Street. The HO felt the case warranted our involvement.'

'But this bus doesn't go anywhere near King's Cross.' May checked the route on the wall and saw that it tacked through central London on a loop.

'Oh, we're not going to the murder site. I've already been there.' Bryant seated himself on the arrow-patterned seat at the front of the bus, next to a gingery young man who was standing in the aisle with a microphone. His badge read: *Hi! I'm Martin!* 'I wanted you here so that you could help me apprehend the murderer.'

The Routemaster pulled away from the stop at Speaker's Corner, heading into Oxford Street. Shoppers were out early, but many had already left the city to spend Christmas with their families. 'My Uncle Jack used to get up on his soapbox over there, just after the war,' said Bryant, tapping the rain-spattered window. 'He was used telling people what they shouldn't do, like that man who used to wander the length of Oxford Street with the board that said 'Less Passion Through Less Protein'. He'd pick a different subject every week, 'Ban licentious theatre, hang Sir Anthony Eden, shoot the Welsh, he'd rant about anything so long as it involved getting rid of something or someone. Not a terribly positive attitude, I suppose, but at least Speaker's Corner still gives us some semblance of free speech.'

'Now, does anyone know the name of the great b-i-i-i-g department store

on our right?' Martin the tour guide was as proud and patronising as a first-time father. There were no takers. 'Anyone?'

Bryant listlessly raised his hand. 'Selfridges, opened in 1909 by Harry Gordon Selfridge. He coined the phrase 'The customer is always right', and was the first salesman to put products out on display where they could be touched.'

'Well, I don't know about that,' said Martin.

'No, but luckily I do,' Bryant countered.

'We're catching a murderer on a bus?' whispered May in disbelief.

'We are now heading toward Oxford Circus, which was once described by Noel Coward as the Hub of the Universe,' announced the guide.

'This boy's a dunderhead.' Bryant jerked a wrinkled thumb at Martin, who overheard him. 'It was John Wyndham, and he was describing Piccadilly Circus.'

Bryant occasionally worked as a tour guide in his spare time, but his revolutionary methods of involving the general public in his talks tended to frighten off casual tourists. He forgot most things, but never the facts he had painstakingly gathered about his city.

'I don't understand,' May persisted. 'It sounds very straightforward. Why did we get the case?' The PCU only handled investigations the Home Office found detrimental to government policy. A death of the kind his partner had described would usually fall under the local jurisdiction of the Metropolitan Police.

'There are three oddities.' Bryant ticked them off on his fingers. 'One, after strangling Mrs McKay the murderer ordered two pizzas and calmly ate both of them. B, he slept overnight in the apartment. And three, his victim was killed after he left.'

May considered the matter as the bus turned into Regent Street. 'I'm sorry, Arthur, you've utterly lost me.'

'Do try to pay attention. The murderer left the flat at 7:15 this morning, not realising that his victim was still alive. Mrs McKay struggled to the window to raise the alarm, but the effort of opening it was too much for her. She lost consciousness while sitting on the sill and fell out into the street, landing on a gentleman called Sir Ian Lowry—'

'The MOD bigwig?'

'The very same. Sir Ian was leaving a call-girl's flat on the ground floor, where he had apparently stayed the night. Mrs McKay broke her neck and his leg. And that's why the HO called us in. Obviously, it's a serious security breach because Sir Ian is privy to all kinds of military secrets. It doesn't help that he was putting the call-girl's services down on his expenses. Private secretary, if you please. The girl has already been brought in, the coroner has certified that Mrs McKay bore the bruises of strangulation around her neck, and all that's left is the apprehension of her killer.'

'So I'm here to help you identify him,' said May, still a little confused.

'Oh, I know who the murderer is.' Bryant cheerily flashed his oversized false teeth. 'You were complaining about getting old the other day, so I thought this would be a chance for you to test your fading faculties.'

The old-fashioned Routemaster bus stopped outside Hamley's toy store and the driver stared impassively ahead as a single Japanese tourist came on board. May looked around. There were now eight passengers seated downstairs. The rain was falling too heavily for anyone to remain on the upper open deck. Bryant checked his ancient Timex. It was 10:44am.

'You already know the murderer's identity?' asked May.

'Better than that,' replied Bryant smugly, 'I can tell you the precise time he'll be arrested. At 11:26am.'

'Are you saying we're looking for somebody on board this bus?'

The tour guide was attempting to deliver a potted history of the Haymarket, and was not happy about being distracted by these chatting elderly men. 'There are seats further back,' he pointed out.

'We're quite happy here,' insisted Bryant. He withdrew his pipe from his top pocket and absently struck a match to it. A hefty woman in an LA Dodgers baseball cap, an oversized sweatshirt and huge baggy shorts reacted with horror behind him. 'Oh-my-Gahd, that's disgusting,' she complained. 'Hey, it's illegal to smoke that thing.'

'Yet it's apparently not illegal to dress like a gigantic toddler, Madam, which I find most curious.'

'Listen buddy, if you'd take my advice—'

'I'm not your buddy, and if I took your advice I'd be enormous.' Bryant

turned back to his partner. 'So take a look around and tell me who you suspect. Give me the benefit of your observational skills.'

The ancient bus was now chuntering toward the rainswept plain of Trafalgar Square. 'On your left, Nelson's Column, finished in 1843, with four bronze panels at the base depicting his naval victories,' said Martin the guide.

'His left arm was struck by lightning in the 1880s and he only just got it X-rayed a couple of years ago,' said Bryant. 'That's the NHS for you.'

'So you know exactly where the murderer will get on this bus, how long he'll stay on and where he'll get off?' asked May.

'Indeed I do.' Bryant could be supremely annoying when he was the only one holding privileged information.

At 11:02am, the bus stopped near the corner of Craig's Court. 'Pall Mall derives its name from a 17th-century mallet and ball game played here by, er, members of royalty,' Martin the tour guide stated with a hint of uncertainty.

'Everyone knows that,' said Bryant, fidgeting in his seat. 'Tell them something new. Alleys of shops are called malls because they're shaped like the game's playing sites. Did you know that Pall Mall is only worth £140 on the Monopoly board?'

'I don't think he cares too much for your interruptions, accurate though they may be,' whispered May. 'You're unsettling him.'

'Some people deserve to be unsettled,' Bryant replied. 'When a man is tired of London he should clear off. Oh dear, he's wearing a clip-on tie.' Coming from a man as sartorially challenged as Bryant, this was a bit rich.

When the bus stopped halfway along Whitehall, May surveyed the new arrivals. One of them was a murderer, but which one? There were now eleven passengers on the lower deck; two Americans, two Italians, two Chinese, one Japanese boy in a mad hat and two couples of indeterminate origins. He decided that the murderer had yet to put in an appearance.

'Was this woman McKay in her own apartment?' he asked.

'Correct.'

May thought of the call-girl living on the ground floor. 'Did she look after the other girls? Was her killer a client?'

'No, she had nothing to do with them.' Bryant sat back, trying not to listen to the tour guide's incorrect description of the Cabinet War Rooms.

'But the killer left behind a clue to his identity.'

'No, it was something he took away with him that gave me the lead.'

'Well, I don't see how you could possibly know what he took.'

The bus continued along Whitehall, picking up three more passengers, and lumbered toward Parliament Square through thickening traffic. May eyed the newcomers with suspicion. A German couple—he overheard their conversation—were taking pictures behind a fiftyish man with unmistakably Russian features and anxious, flitting eyes. May studied the Russian's loud Italian jacket, his unshaven chin. A sad little murder, Bryant had said. This man had dressed in a hurry, without stopping to shave, and looked around every time the bus came to a halt. But if he was the killer, why would he make his escape aboard a slow-moving tour bus, on a trip that ended back where it began?

'Who can tell me the name of this building?' asked Martin the tour guide.

'Houses of Parliament,' the assembly muttered faintly, as if being asked to recite a prayer in church.

'Now, many people think Big Ben is the name of the tower . . .'

'Dear God no,' Bryant sighed loudly. 'Can't he come up with anything more original than that?'

Martin shot him a filthy look. 'But it is actually the name of the single bell housed inside . . .'

'Absolute rubbish.' Bryant thumped the guide on the arm with his walking stick. 'There are five bells in St Stephen's Tower, young man. The other four play the Westminster Quarters, variations of 'I know that my redeemer liveth' from Handel's Messiah.'

'Your information is not correct?' the German husband asked the guide, puzzled.

'Look, who's giving this bloody tour?' Martin's cheeks were turning as red as his hair.

'It could be him,' said May, pointing to the Russian. 'He's got a shifty look about him. Oh—that doesn't sound very scientific, does it?'

'I'll take over if you like,' Bryant snapped back at the guide. 'These people aren't getting their money's worth.'

'But Arthur, how do you know when he was due on the bus? That just leaves . . .'

'Listen mate, I don't have to put up with this. My shift ends here, anyway.'

As the bus stopped in the corner of the square, Martin threw down his microphone and tapped on the glass, signalling to the driver.

As he made his way along the aisle, May said, 'The guide, it's the guide. And he's getting away!'

Bryant did not move a muscle as a moon-faced young woman with scraped-back hair and a ponytail rose and took over from the departing Martin.

'Hello, my name is Debbie, and I'm your guide on the last part of this tour,' she told them. The bus pulled into the traffic and made its way around the square.

'Why didn't you stop him?' asked May with growing incredulity. The ginger-headed tour guide was walking quickly away along the crowded pavement with his hands in his pockets.

Bryant pulled back his sleeve and held up his watch so that his partner could read it: 11:19am. There were still another seven minutes to go.

'Who can tell me the name of this building?' asked Debbie, pointing to Westminster Abbey and cupping her hand around her ear.

'Is there some special nursery school where they're trained to speak in this fashion, I wonder?' said Bryant. The bus headed back onto Victoria Embankment.

'Where does the tour go from here?' asked May, keeping an eye on the Russian, who seemed to be sweating.

'Around Covent Garden, where the lovely Debbie will probably regale us with selections from 'My Fair Lady', then back toward Oxford Street,' said Bryant.

'You said it was something he took with him that gave you a clue,' May repeated, checking out the Japanese boy's strange headgear.

Bryant rested his chin on his knuckle and regarded the stippled thread of the Thames that could be glimpsed between buildings. 'The lovely Debbie will ask them to name the river next,' he muttered.

'He was so unfazed by the thought of murdering Mrs McKay that he stayed all night . . . ' mused May.

'I wonder if anyone knows where the lion on Westminster Bridge comes from?' asked Debbie.

'Because he was used to her . . . ' May followed the thought.

'Good Lord, an intelligent question,' Bryant beamed delightedly at the new guide.

'It stood on the parapet of the Lion Brewery until 1966, near Hungerford Bridge . . . ' said Debbie.

' . . . because he was married to her,' said May.

'Yet we have come to regard it as a symbol of London . . . '

'And he stuck to his routine, ordering pizza for them both, sleeping beside her and getting up the next morning . . . '

' . . . so when we photograph the lion standing proudly beside Big Ben, we recreate the traditional link between members of parliament—and alcohol.' Debbie flourished a smile.

'Oh, bravo!' exclaimed Bryant, 'I like her!'

' . . . and he came to work just as he always did, because he couldn't think of what else to do. He had to stick to the schedule. Not the tour guide at all, but the bus driver,' said May as the truth dawned.

'Correct. His timetable was still on the kitchen counter, but his jacket, cap and badge were all missing from the flat.' Bryant rose unsteadily to his feet and pressed the stop bell. 'That took you long enough,' he sniffed. 'I'm sorry, Debbie. I'm afraid the tour will have to terminate here.'

May looked out of the window. The bus stop faced New Scotland Yard. It was exactly 11:26am.

'He won't run off,' said Bryant. 'He wants to be taken in for the murder of his wife. He loved her. But the neighbours said she never stopped nagging him about his weight.'

The Japanese tourist and the Russian took some very nice photographs of the two detectives leading the devastated driver down from his cabin. 'Arrest ye merry gentlemen,' said Bryant with a grin as the flashes went off.

'You've got holly in your hat,' May pointed out.

'Yes,' said Bryant, 'I like the smell.'

'Holly hasn't got a smell.'

'It does, actually. The bright, spiky appearance is all bravado. If you gently break the stem, you'll smell it—there's a bitter tang inside,' he explained. 'Like so many people.'